Failure to Thrive

Katharine M Sweet

Sweet Tales With Spice

Contents

Book One: Failure to Thrive

Book Two: Faking it For Now (coming soon...)

Content to Note

While Failure to Thrive is a cozy romcom focused on two characters finding their way to each other some elements of their pasts may be upsetting to some readers. Please take care of your mental health and be aware of the content that may be touched upon in this book. There are minor spoilers in the warnings.

- Medical trauma
    - Treatment post car accident - minor injuries
    - Characters having difficulty breathing
    - Mentions of blood and injuries
    - Child born premature and being treated - memory
- Child abuse
    - Grooming of a teenage minor - memory
    - Emotional and mental abuse of a child - past
- Domestic Violence
    - Emotional and mental abuse of a woman
    - Physical abuse of a woman
- PTSD
    - Post-imprisonment
    - Post-escape from domestic violence
    - Panic attack
- Violence
    - Physical fighting both mentioned and on the page

As with all of my books, this one is special to me, so much so that I borrowed my grandmother's name for it (Love you Grandma).

But this book is dedicated to my brother, David.

You convinced me to watch the live action One Piece and when the found-family dynamic inspired me to write this book we spent the next seven weeks drafting it together. I talked through scenes and you gave me nods to anime/manga to hide in it. Without you this book would not have the personality and heart that it has. I bet no one can find them all, some of them are so niche, but we'll know.

I am blessed to have a sibling, who is also one of my closest friends. You listen to me ramble for hours about whatever is on my mind - sometimes not so willingly, but I'm the oldest, so you don't have a choice. P.S. Sorry about all of the ER trivia you know now.

As kids we pretended to be X-men in the backyard and as adults have some of the most honest conversations: this book is for you. Specifically, chapter 28 and the last scene of chapter 36 - you'll know the line when you read it.

CHAPTER I

Summer 2004

"Say it again," Jerry's perpetually annoyed voice rattled in Russ's ear through his cellphone.

Russ sighed, a hand over his eyes to block the noon sun. The muggy heat made the collar of his uniform shirt cling to his neck. "I will stick with this job. I will not make your job as my parole officer any worse than it already is. I will stop fucking up my own life."

"You've been out five months and this is job number three. You only did five years and you are damn lucky to be out already, all things considered. So be grateful and reintegrate into society." Jerry was an old man who seemed so annoyed with life that Russ wondered if he'd ever experienced joy.

"'Cause washing dishes in a hospital cafeteria is so vital to society." Russ rolled his eyes.

A thunk caught his attention and Russ begrudgingly looked through his windshield, vision blurry as his eyes adjusted. A petite woman leaned against the trunk of her car, nearly doubled over from a coughing fit.

"Imagine that, sick people at a hospital," he muttered under his breath, reaching for his pack of cigarettes before deciding against it.

A boy with identical blonde hair to the woman was attempting to keep her on her feet. The kid couldn't have been older than eight—scrawny looking too.

"Are you listening?"

"Yeah, be on time, don't punch anyone, and be home before my monitor goes off." His eyes stayed on the kid and the woman he assumed was the kid's mom as he pulled his keys out of the ignition of his car.

"I didn't say any of that. Just stay out of trouble and don't make me regret recommending you or *you* will be the one to regret...."

Russ snapped his phone closed, ending the call. He climbed out of the car and slammed the door, hearing it echo in this nearly empty section of the parking lot.

The kid turned towards the sound and Russ. His blue eyes narrowed, and if the kid had fur, it would have bristled as he tried to make himself look bigger. Russ opened his mouth to announce himself, but was cut off.

"Stay away from my mom!" *Okay. She was definitely the kid's mom.*

"Easy kid, I was just seeing if you guys were alright." He held his hands up to show he was harmless. At least he didn't have any tattoos on his palms, unlike his knuckles. Hand tattoos made some people nervous, and the kid was already worked up.

"We don't need help from some creep who was sleeping in his car!" The kid shifted his feet the gravel crunching under his shoes.

"Excuse me?" Russ arched his eyebrow; now he was offended. He wasn't gonna pick a fight with a child, but he wasn't going to be slandered either. He got closer to them, trying to assess the woman a little better and so the kid would stop shouting at him. "I was *not* sleeping in my car, and I'm not a creep."

"Are so. Get away."

"Liam..." The woman did her best to straighten herself, but she was still leaning her hip against the car, clearly struggling. "Don't yell at the man. You shouldn't be rude. Look at his shirt, he works here and he was probably taking a break. Apologize pl—"

Another round of coughs wracked through her frame, and this time she lost her footing. Russ caught her elbows and bent his knees to accommodate her height and kept her from falling. *Christ on a stick!* She couldn't weigh more than a buck-twenty, she was skin and bones.

Why'd she park them so far out? He glanced at the car and noticed that it took up three spots, and the front bumper was crunched against the light pole.

"Mom! Mom? Are you okay?" Keys rattled in one of the kid's hands and the other clutched a worn-out handbag.

Russ grunted and swept the woman up into his arms.

"Hey! What are you doing? MOM!"

"I'm helping get your mom inside. Come on and stick close; the ambulances come in that way," he said, gesturing with his head and Liam followed, needing three steps to equal each one of his strides.

"I'm sorry..." She gripped his shirt, her voice wavering. "You can put...."

"It's not a problem. You should have parked in the front, someone woulda parked your car and helped ya inside." Russ stepped up onto the sidewalk, noticing her eyes were fluttering. "Hey, stay awake now. Pretty sure the pup can't tell them your medical history."

"I have notes! I can *so* tell them," Liam huffed. "And I'm not a puppy!"

The woman coughed again, struggling to speak, "Liam...."

"What's your name?" Russ questioned, trying to keep her conscious.

"Aster Reign."

What other things should he ask her? What questions did they ask on medical shows when they were trying to figure out if someone was in their right mind? "Do you know what day it is?"

"It's Tuesday if you want the day of the week, and June 1, 2004, if you want the date." Her face was pale, eyes still closed, but her cheeks were flushed red. Despite this, she still seemed to have a sense of humor.

Russ smirked down at her. "Well Aster, you did a shitty job parking your car. Pretty sure your front bumper is toast."

"Pity, that was my favorite part of my car." Aster shivered in his arms, but she still had a slight bit of sass in her voice.

The heat outside was punishing, but they were almost to the entrance. He glanced back, realizing that the kid had stopped. "Hey, let's...."

"I hurt the favorite part of your car?" Liam's voice cracked, his lip quivering.

Oh Russ did not have time for this. He was gonna be late at this rate and have hell to pay for it. "Pup, if you got her here in one piece you did a good job, come on now."

The automatic doors opened, and the rush of air conditioning made him sigh in relief.

"Sir, is your wife conscious?" The nurse behind the desk was already on her feet rushing toward him, and someone else was yelling about code something. He'd need to learn what those codes meant if he stuck around.

"She's not...."

A gurney was rushed in front of him. "Set her down here. Ma'am, can you hear me? Do you know where you are?"

Russ set her down gently as the new nurse shined a penlight in Aster's eyes. She flinched but responded, answering the nurse's questions before coughing again, doubling back over. Blood stained the palm of her hand.

The nurse in navy scrubs pressed a stethoscope against her chest. "Try and take a deep breath for me." Aster kept coughing and Liam made a distressed sound. The nurse's brown eyes met Russ's. "Sir, how long has your wife been sick?"

Liam piped up, "She's been—"

"Sweetie, your father needs to answer. Sir, how long has your wife been sick like this?"

"She's not my—"

"This guy isn't my dad!" Liam glared over at Russ. "My dad is an asshole. This guy's just a creep from the parking lot."

Russ glared back at the kid, then clarified to the growing crowd in scrubs. "I was in the parking lot before my shift. She collapsed and I carried her in. That's all." He turned to leave, "I need to get down to…"

"You aren't going anywhere," the nurse barked, grabbing his wrist while ordering someone else in scrubs to take Aster back for tests. The staff moved her gurney down a long hallway and Russ was left with the nurse. "I've got questions, so you and your son are staying right here."

The term 'your son' was apparently a step too far for Liam. Maybe it was hearing the term son twice in a row, or the stress of his mom being sick, but that was the end of Liam's patience. The kid screamed bloody murder, yelling about how he wasn't 'the creepy guy's son' and insisting that he wanted his mom.

Russ was torn between running out the door and looking for the nearest stairwell with roof access. He was not cut out for this amount of drama.

"It's okay, sweetie, it's okay. My name's Julie and we're going to help your mom, but she needs a few tests to figure out why she's sick." Julie knelt down to Liam's level, touching his arm, "What's your name, huh?"

Liam clutched his mother's handbag like a life preserver. He was doing his damndest not to cry, despite the tears dripping down his cheeks. "Liam."

"Heather, can you grab someone to sit with Liam?" Julie requested.

The nurse from the front desk, Heather, walked up to them. But Russ wasn't having anymore of this drama. This was *not* his mess. He spoke before Heather had a chance to. "Look, I'm supposed to start in the cafeteria today," he said as he looked at his watch, "as of ten minutes ago. Is there any way you can call down there and tell them why I'm late? Like a note or something?"

Heather arched her eyebrow. "You waited until your shift had almost started to bring her in and now you want a note? No. You need to stay up here and go over what you saw in the parking lot."

"Aster is awake, she can talk to you. Or the kid…." He looked down, but Liam was gone.

Julie motioned her hand towards the bathroom. "He's in the restroom and when he's done—"

Sirens screamed up to the doors and an ambulance team crashed through the open doors. The paramedics were working on the patient, calling out vitals to both nurses who had immediately shifted their focus and stepped in to triage this new patient. With their attention averted, Russ booked it to the stairs and made his escape. If they needed him, they could find him down there. He was not going to fuck up his parole over being late.

Chapter 2

Deep breath in. One. Two. Three. Hold it. One. Two. Three. Deep breath out. One. Two. Three. Repeat.

Russ took one more long set of calming breaths before exiting the stairwell in the basement where the cafeteria was. Well, he hoped it was there at least. He looked at the map on the wall across from the elevator door to the right of the stairs. *Yup.* He needed to follow this hall all the way down to the right and he should walk right into it.

"Fifteen damn minutes late when I pulled in fifteen minutes early. I should have bailed already. Bad omens left and right," he muttered to himself, shoving his hands into the starchy pockets of his new uniform. It was the first day of the six days he'd be working in a row—that's what he gets for waiting until Tuesday to start work to not have a Monday. The HR lady thought the joke had been funny at least. Jerry had clapped the back of his shoulder hard enough that he'd lurched forward, so he'd managed a laugh to save his skin. Paula, the hospital's HR woman, was Jerry's cousin, and she was the reason Russ was being given a shot here despite his ankle-monitor and very strict schedule.

The seating area in the cafeteria was only partially lit, and the corner to Russ's left was eerily dark. Shouldn't all the lights be on? Hospitals didn't close, so this place would be open all the time too, wouldn't it? There weren't many people seated or standing, but Russ scanned the room until he noticed the 'Employees Only' double doors. *Bingo.*

Between him and the double doors were the cafeteria serving lines, complete with sneeze guards. The industrial refrigerator system showcasing a display of cold foods hummed next to the pop dispenser. Part of the prep area was in view of the tables, probably to accommodate special requests. Pretty standard set up for a large capacity serving kitchen.

Going through the double doors, he was met with the smell of hot dish water and the sound of easy-listening music. No one seemed to notice him for the moment; one guy washing dishing at the back, another checking on pots on the stove, and a woman ducked into the walk-in freezer. The easy-to-sanitize metal surfaces complete with commercial grade food storage and cooking appliances and an efficient open concept layout was, more or less, what Russ had expected. Simple enough to get the job done day-in and day-out.

He steeled himself for the onset of yelling and negativity, but was instead met by a smiling, heavier-set man as the others in the kitchen continued their tasks.

"Hey Russell. I'm Ian Peters, nice to meet ya." Ian extended his hand and Russ shook it back, wondering how Ian knew him at first, but then he remembered his badge had his name and picture on it. But again, why wouldn't Ian remember the name and face of the parolee who was going to be working for him?

"I know I'm late..." Russ started to explain.

"Oh no, don't sweat it. Tricky was upstairs fetching a food cart when you brought your wife in, so he told me all about it. Hell of a way to start your first day." Ian thumped his back, nearly knocking him off his feet. "Listen, if you need to start tomorrow so you can get things arranged for your family, don't sweat it. We've all been there a time or two."

Russ's head was spinning. Too much new information, entirely too fast. He needed to put an end to some of this nonsense immediately. "Look I'm not sure who Tricky is...."

"Oh," Ian laughed and hollered over the radio and water din, "Tricky, you were right, it was Russell you saw. Wave, would ya?"

A dark-haired, lanky younger man who looked like he hadn't slept in a week flashed his palm up to them and then went back to dishes without a word.

"Don't let him bother you, kid's got a lot on his plate. His name tag says his real name, but he don't answer to anything but Tricky, not a clue where that nickname came from. On that note, you got a preferred name Russell?" Ian scratched a note on his clipboard. "I can't guarantee these knuckleheads ain't gonna ignore it and call you whatever they want, but we can put the effort in. Jerry stopped by with Paula and said that you work hard but gotta stick to a strict schedule. I'll make sure all my shift leaders know so there aren't any problems."

Russ blinked. "Um...Russell or Russ is fine. But the lady I came in with isn't my wife or girlfriend or anything like that. She collapsed in the parking lot. I just carried her in so she could get help."

"Oh so we've got Captain America working with us now?" A woman he gauged to be roughly his age smirked at him as she played with her cross necklace. She turned her head to the opposite side of the kitchen and yelled in Spanish to one of the cooks, who flipped her off as a reply.

"Russell, this is Yesenia. She's the lead for the cashiers, and she'll teach you to use the registers in a couple of days in case we need to use you in a pinch."

Ian was still talking while Russ shook Yesenia's hand. Her bright pink and purple nails were long, which surprised him. He remembered from working fast food out of high school that the girls were always fussing about having to keep their nails short.

"I don't do food, I can keep my nails." She withdrew her hand. "Anyone ever tell you you've got pretty eyes?"

Russ's face grew hot, and he looked away from Yesenia, not sure how to respond.

Ian barked out a loud laugh. "Russell, you've been hit on by another member of the staff. Consider yourself initiated. Come on, I'll give you the grand tour. We'll need to get you a net for your facial hair until you shave."

Russ sighed. "Am I required to be clean-shaven?"

"No, but you'll need to wear the hairnet every shift otherwise." His boss scratched his head. "And most folks don't like 'em."

"If it's a choice between my goatee and the hairnet. I'll suffer with the hairnet." Russ felt out of sorts enough already without feeling naked from a bare face.

"Alright, we'll get you some for your locker." Ian patted Russ on the shoulder again. "Welcome to Creekside hospital, Russ."

Russ had worked in the restaurant industry three times, if the concession stands when he was in high school counted, and twice if it didn't. The cafeteria was nothing like any of those experiences. The pace was steady and ordered, with only small spikes of busy times. Nothing like a lull followed by the insanity of a dinner rush or a bus full of highschool football players coming back from an away game that he'd experienced when working at the latest closing fast-food joint in town.

He'd lived in this town his whole life, doing a whole lot of nothing. There was a point in time when he thought he was getting out, but that chance went up in flames. He was a fixed point in this forgotten half-rural, half-urban, mid-sized town where far too many people knew him. Well, on the other side of town, people knew whose grandson he was and shook their heads. Whereas on this side of town, in the shadow of the closed manufacturing plants, with bail bondsmen every other block, plenty of pawn shops, and where the water often stained clothes yellow, he could be more anonymous. Not everything about this town was bad, but it was bad enough.

He shifted his leg under the table and his monitor knocked against the metal chair leg. He cursed and rubbed his calf, despite the monitor not weighing a lot, it made his leg hurt. *Maybe it was psychological?* He'd ask the shrink about it at his next court mandated session. Therapy was a requirement for his parole, so he might as well get some use out of it.

"Without the pin, run it without the pin. It works without the pin."

A familiar voice caught his attention and Russ lulled his head to the right towards the cashier stand. Sure enough, there was Liam facing off against Jose, whose English wasn't the best.

The kid shoved the card at Jose again, "It works without the pin. I *know* it does."

Russ glanced at his watch, they'd been here almost six hours. Surely the kid must have eaten before now. The only thing he was trying to buy was an apple, the cup of water the kid was holding wouldn't cost anything. Forcing himself to stand, Russ snagged a sandwich and chips before getting in line behind Liam.

"I got it, Jose," Russ handed his coworker a ten dollar bill. "I'm gonna grab a coffee too."

"Coffee's no good here," Jose countered, shaking his head.

He rolled his eyes. "Coffee's coffee."

"I don't need you to pay for my apple." Liam huffed and stomped his foot.

Russ leaned down to his level, informing him, "well too bad, I already did." He grabbed the apple and gave the kid a nudge towards one of the empty tables. "Sit."

Surprisingly, the kid did as he was told and sat down. Russ grabbed himself a cup of coffee and took an experimental sip, coughing at the acidic taste.

Jose laughed, "Told *you* so."

Rough English, and he's still got jokes—*great.*

Russ sat across from Liam and kept the food he'd bought closer to himself. "Have you eaten today?"

Liam's eyes focused solely on the sandwich. "I had most of a Pop Tart for breakfast."

He braved another sip of coffee, "Most of one Pop Tart? Why only that?"

"It's all that was left in the backseat. I didn't want to get into the trunk." Liam inched his fingers towards the sandwich, eyes narrowing as Russ rested his hand on it to keep it where it was.

Much as he needed to know the answer to this question, Russ didn't know if he particularly wanted to know. If the answer was the bad one, what was he going to do? He certainly didn't know how to help. "I'll give you the sandwich, if you tell me the truth. I know you might not want to, but...."

"Only weak people lie." Liam folded his arms over his chest.

"Jesus, Pup," he yelped, "do you have any kind of filter?"

Liam traced his finger over the table, not making eye-contact as he clarified, "Is that the question I have to answer to get the sandwich?"

"It isn't. Are you guys living in your car?" Russ held his breath, waiting for the kid to freak out or make a run for the door.

"No. We're only moving. It's a couple of days between beds. Can I have the sandwich now?"

That answer was practiced, rehearsed like a line he'd heard over and over. Those two were definitely living out of her car. How long had they been getting by like that?

"Yeah," Russ moved all the food closer to Liam. "Does your mom have anyone to watch you?"

Liam took a giant bite of sandwich, chewing while he talked. "I don't need to be watched."

"I don't think the hospital would be okay with you not being watched while your mom's a patient," Russ pointed out, but he wasn't even sure of that himself. What happened when there wasn't anyone else to watch a kid while their parent was being treated? Liam's dad clearly wasn't around, and from the sounds of it, that wasn't a bad thing. Eight-year-old's didn't call their fathers assholes out of the blue.

"They have to notice I'm not being watched." Liam took a drink from his cup. "I hide in the closet when the nurses come in for tests and stuff. Or I tell them that my grandma's in the bathroom, and it takes her a while."

"So, your mom's been sick for a while, huh?" If the kid knew this many work-arounds, he'd had practice.

"No, she was in a car accident before. I learned then." Liam struggled opening the chip bag and Russ held his hand out for it. The kid hesitated, but handed it over.

Russ opened the bag, his watch beeping to warn about his break being over in a minute, and let Liam have it back. "If you figured that out in one trip, you must be pretty smart."

"I'm not." Liam shifted his body away, leaning his shoulder against the back of the chair.

"Russ, break's up!" Tricky hollered from the employee doorway. "Got a load of dishes to finish before you can split."

That was the most words Russ had heard from Tricky all shift. Ian must be a stickler for clocking in on time, that was gonna suck. He ruffled the kid's hair on his way by, "Stay out of trouble, Pup."

The kid curled away more from the contact as he promised, "I'll pay you back for the sandwich."

"Don't sweat it."

"I will." Liam seemed determined to get the last word in, so Russ let him have it.

Russ handed Jose the last five he had in his pocket and subtly pointed to the top of Liam's head. "If *he* needs anything else, use this."

"Sure, sure," Jose flashed him a smile, and Russ got the impression that while Jose might struggle speaking English, he understood it fine.

CHAPTER 3

It was quarter-to-ten when the lights flickered and Russ looked up, concerned, before he noticed Marc leaning by the switch on the wall.

"Aye new guy, boss said you were out by ten, no if, ands, or buts," Marc barked like a drill sergeant, but the tattoos against his dark skin didn't indicate he hadn't been in the military. Russ thought he recognized a couple of them from his state-enforced vacation, but he didn't want to make assumptions. Marc was a powerfully built man.

Russ also hadn't heard a single cuss or inappropriate word out of Marc since he started his shift at eight that night. Marc had kept a close eye on him without starting any kind of conversation. But judging by the way the taller man was hoovering by the time clock, they were about to have their first chat. Russ wasn't a small guy, so potentially being cornered by someone taller and obviously stronger than him made him nervous. Prison hadn't been a picnic, and bigger guys unsettled him now. At least there were cameras here, but getting sucker punched by Marc would still hurt like a bitch.

Russ got to the time clock with his badge and craned his neck until he made eye-contact with Marc. "So, I take it we're talking before I leave?"

"I am married with four kids and I haven't gotten in any trouble since I was twenty-two. I did time from sixteen to twenty-one. Now I do prison ministry with my church. I visit the prison you got out of and I probably know your PO, but before I go that route," Marc pointed to the back of the kitchen, "Let's chat in the walk-in."

Russ blinked. That was entirely more information than he was expecting out of this man. Why the life story before the invite? What was happening?

Fighting every survival instinct in his body, Russ followed Marc into the walk-in, noticing that everyone else kept doing their jobs and averted their eyes. *Oh fuck.* There weren't any cameras in here. *Was* he about to get jumped?

His stomach dropped as Marc stood between him and the door, leaning against it as he looked down with crossed arms. No way out but through this mountain of a man.

"Look, I don't know what Ian told you, but..." Russ trailed off as Marc grabbed the metal rod Tricky showed him that he'd need to use to chip ice away from the blower in the late summer.

Marc tapped Russ's ankle monitor with the pole. "Who's your PO?"

"Jerry Gristol. Marc, look..." Sweat gathered at the nape of Russell's neck.

"I know him well enough, and I'll ask him if I think you're lying, but I hope you'll be honest with me."

What the hell did Marc think he was gonna lie about? As far as he knew, Ian had told all of the shift leaders everything important about him. He was a parolee, which eliminated a lot of his rights, like his right to privacy. The look on Marc's face made Russ think he might soon be losing the right to walk without a limp. Dude looked ready to beat the brakes off him and not look back.

"Why'd you go in? Anything to do with kids?" Marc tightened his grip on the pole, the muscles in his forearms flexing. "My wife visits me with my kids, and I like seeing my kids. Do I have to tell her to keep my kids away from here *because* of *you*? Are you going to be a problem?"

"Wait! What the hell? NO! I beat up a cop." In a near blind panic, Russ put his hands up and stumbled backward. Was this a good idea? Should he have told Marc that? It seemed better to admit what he'd done versus what Marc was thinking, but Russ wasn't entirely sure.

Marc took a decisive step toward him.

"That's all it was, I swear. It was a bar fight that got out of hand. I beat up the wrong guy and ended up doing five years." His blood pounded in his ears as he tried to assess any advantage he could get in this space. "Nothing to do with kids, I..." There was nowhere to go and Russ lost his balance. "Fuck!"

Instead of Russ hitting the floor, the metal pole clattered to the ground. Marc caught Russ's arms and jerked him forward, putting him firmly on his feet. There was a silent moment as Russ considered trying to sidestep Marc and book it to the door, but Marc still had a grip on his forearms. No way to escape.

First came a firm warning. "Don't be swearing in my kitchen. Not that word at least." The larger man thumped one large hand on Russ's shoulder and shook his hand with the other as he started to laugh. "Beating up a cop, huh? Let me know when you can go out for a beer. First one'll be on me. You got any kids? Wife at home?" Marc held the door open for them.

Russ was confused, but answered reflexively, "No, just me, myself, and the mice in my trailer."

"Let's get you outta here, Russell."

"Okay?"

This was certainly the craziest first day that Russ ever had at a job.

The trailer door always stuck. Russ had to put his shoulder into it whenever he came in from the outside. The sound was way too loud and it echoed in the sparse trailer park. He only had five minutes to spare when he crossed the threshold, well in range of the box that wirelessly connected to his ankle monitor. Home at 10:45PM, a new record. The kitchen crew had been hoovering by the walk-in when he and Marc came out, Marc laughing and Russ pretending the hazing was funny to him too and hadn't made his heart stop. But even with the scare being funny to his coworkers, they didn't seem that bad, yet.

The monitor beeped for the third time and turned green to signal he was in range at the appropriate time. Technically it would have worked if he was within 150 feet of the monitor, but Russ didn't like cutting it close. Jerry kept a close eye on his parolees, but the old man was just trying to get the pension he was four years away from. Jerry had no desire for trouble and Russ wasn't trouble for him, with the exception of gainful employment. The rules for the monitor were laminated and taped to the wall in the kitchen by the monitor, with Jerry's number highlighted in case Russ needed to call him if something went wrong. He'd need to plug the monitor in to charge while he was cooking so he could relax later without being connected to the wall.

Russ flopped on the couch and one of the boards creaked ominously. "Not tonight. If you're going to break, please not tonight."

The couch held up its end of the bargain for living in the trailer and not being left to rot on the side of the road by not collapsing. He'd cleaned this thing so many times, but he still kept a blanket over it, not daring to touch the fabric itself. His stomach growled loudly. Nothing in the fifty-foot trailer was very far away, but it felt like so much effort to make something to eat. *Did he still have a pack of ramen left?* Much as he didn't want to get back up, cooking would help him relax.

The range didn't want to start; like everything in this trailer, it was second hand at best. The gas clicked a few times, before Russ gave up and started it with a lighter from the junk-drawer. It was hot immediately, and he snagged his pot and pan from inside the oven. The pipes whistled as he filled the pot with water before setting it to boil on the burner.

He needed more storage in this place. Stretching his arm up, he tapped the ceiling. Maybe he could add some hooks from the ceiling near the wall to hang his one pan and one pot so they didn't have to live in the oven when he wasn't using them? He plugged the cord of his monitor in so it could charge. Jerry was looking for a different unit for him, one with a replaceable battery so he could charge one while the other was in use. Russ had all his fingers and toes crossed, that Jerry found one soon, he nearly killed himself every time he did this.

A snap and a clatter made Russ jump and look towards the half-useless bathroom off the living room, and he sighed. He'd go clean the trap out after he ate. Thankfully there'd been fewer mice each week, so maybe he'd finally gotten them all. Not that they couldn't find ways in, so it was going to be a never-ending battle. He threw the noodles into the boiling water and opened his fridge, glaring at the three cartons of eggs staring back at him. At least he had some spring onions and carrots to add to the mix, but he was almost out of butter. Hopefully he could grab some at the gas station near work, because otherwise he was shit outta luck until Saturday.

Butter sizzled in the pan, and his perfect one hand egg crack had two eggs frying on low heat. *Chop. Chop. Chop.* The small but sharp knife made quick work of the vegetables. The sound of popping grease and smell of sizzling onions filled the air, reminding him of better days when he lived with his grandparents. He'd always been decent at cooking, never good at it, but he'd never gotten any complaints. Maybe if he'd focused on cooking, he'd be working at a restaurant instead of tethered to this trailer and scrambling to come up with recipes from what he could buy off his neighbors. *Fucking eggs.*

Russ rocked the eggs in the pan, making sure the bottoms were cooked through before flipping them with his spatula. Boring as eggs were getting, they were good protein and he could do a lot with them. Tonight they were just going on top of his cheap noodles. He took one step toward the far cabinet and barely kept himself upright as his tethered leg stopped short.

He cursed loudly and rubbed his leg. At least he hadn't yanked it out and fucked up the plug again. Jerry had not been impressed, and in his words, "I'm too old and too fat to chase you. You mess with that monitor, I've got a taser and a revolver, that's how I chase at my age."

Russ would eat, watch the end of the ballgame that should be on, then go to sleep. He wouldn't fall asleep on the couch and wake up panicked to the beeping of his uncharged babysitter.

CHAPTER 4

Beep. Beep. Beep. Beep.

A cold hand closed around her wrist and Aster gasped, attempting to move away as pain raced through her.

"Oop, sorry about that," a calm female voice reassured her, almost familiar. "It's okay. Take a slow breath."

Aster blinked, her eyelids felt heavy as she tried to make sense of her surroundings and the woman holding her wrist.

"I'm Penny. Do you remember me from last night?" Penny's brown hair was tied back in a ponytail, and a stethoscope was around her neck.

Aster shook her head, then nodded. She vaguely remembered talking to someone before they took her for tests. She reached for her pearls and scratched at her neck, not finding them. A sharp intake of breath caused her to yelp in pain.

"Aster?"

"I'm—" She started coughing and was handed a cup of water.

"Take a slow sip when you catch your breath. Not a gulp, in case you start coughing again. I'm gonna listen to your lungs, okay?"

Aster clutched the cup and did as she was told.

"Take as deep of a breath as you can for me." Penny's stethoscope was cold on her back.

Drawing in air was difficult, her lungs felt heavy.

"Can you try one more for me?"

Aster started coughing again, struggling with what felt like a mass in her throat.

"Cough it out if you can," The nurse encouraged, rubbing her back.

Spots danced in front of Aster's eyes as she tensed her body, trying to force out whatever was stuck. Finally, a chunk of red splashed into the cup and Aster managed to get the air she needed.

"Easy now. You're okay," The nurse's hand was on Aster's back as she spoke, "for the next couple of days, you're gonna get those from time to time. Cough up as much as you can and don't swallow it."

Penny seemed nice. Aster wished she could remember her better, but the whole of yesterday was a blur. She'd started to load the car with Liam and....

"My son..." Her eyes filled with tears; dear God, where was Liam?

Penny pointed to the chair by the window to her sleeping child. "He's right there. I'm not sure if it was your mother-in-law or your mother, but someone came to get him late last night and dropped him off first thing this morning." She wrapped the blood pressure cuff around Aster's bicep as she continued, "Normally we wouldn't let him stay here without an adult, but he said his grandma would be back soon. And he's convincing with those puppy-dog eyes."

Aster nodded, touching her temple; she had a headache.

"And he's so detailed. Writing down everything we said in his little notebook. Stubborn too, making sure he spelled it correctly," Penny scribbled on the chart. "Liam said you hit your head when you were getting in the car. He was worried about you. Told us all about the accident you were in last month. Was Liam hurt at all? He wouldn't talk about himself."

Liam turned over in the chair away from them and muttered something before sighing loudly. He was faking being asleep.

Aster wanted more water, but couldn't bring herself to ask. Penny was a nurse, not a waitress. "A truck hit us, but it hit my door and the front of the car. Liam was in the backseat on the other side so he wasn't hurt. I don't understand why I started coughing up blood now. The accident was almost a month ago. We were still in Ohio."

"Let's get you a fresh cup of water."

Penny took the cup with the blood in it away and brought her clean water, which Aster drank hastily. Her throat ached and she rubbed her fingers against her collarbone; she felt exposed.

"I'll get the doctor. She'll go over your test results now that you're up and about. Breakfast is about an hour from now. Do you want a snack? I can call down to the cafeteria for you," Penny offered, one hand on her hip, but her expression friendly.

"I got you an apple, Mom. I put it in your bag." Liam appeared next to her bed, rubbing his eyes. "I bought it yesterday, but you slept all night."

Penny's eyes moved to Liam, but she said nothing.

"I think the apple will be fine for now. Thank you, Penny, I appreciate the offer."

The nurse nodded. "Hit the call button if you need anything."

Aster's hand went back to her neck. "Liam, do you know where my things are?"

"They put them in the bag and it's in your closet," Liam answered quickly before racing to the closet, nearly hitting himself in the head with the door as he opened it.

"Careful," Aster admonished as Liam carried the plastic hospital bag to her.

He set it on the bed by her hip before running to close the door. There was no one else in the room with them. He scrambled up on the bed on her other side, snuggling against her and nearly tangling himself in the IV line. "I was really scared."

Aster ignored the pain and gingerly curled her arm around her son. "I'm so sorry, Liam. I'll be okay."

"You promise?" His voice was muffled by her shoulder, but he was crying. She'd failed him. Her poor baby.

She kissed the top of his head. "I promise, my sweet little prince. I'll be okay," Aster reassured him, squeezing him tighter. She could take the pain, he deserved to be held. "Where did you sleep last night?"

"Closet." His little hand patted the plastic bag, "your shirt was big enough to stay warm in."

"I'm glad. Did you eat?"

"Mhmmm." Liam's breathing was already deepening. He was going to fall asleep.

Aster managed to get the blanket over him and keep her arm with the IV free on top so it was accessible. Using her other hand, she awkwardly fumbled through the bag's contents until she found her necklace. She'd done it enough times one-handed when Liam was little that she was able to unclasp her necklace, turn her head, pinch the strand with her chin and re-do the clasp so her pearls were around her neck again. She hoped they'd let her keep them on; she couldn't remember ever taking them off for more than an hour or two in the almost ten years she'd had them. It was stupid to keep them. They felt tight, but it was a familiar pressure. *Pressure made perfect.*

She felt herself dozing again. At least this time, Liam was safe in her arms.

"Aster, you're falling asleep on your feet. You need to be in bed. You're recovering."

Her body swayed to the right as a pair of hands caught her elbows. She couldn't muster any words, her soul was in that plastic cage with wires and tubes coming in and out of him. His tiny body was a fraction of the size it should be.

"How'd she get down here?"

The voices were so far away.

"That's the third time she's been down here without someone."

The tips of her fingers were getting numb.

"She's probably ripped her stitches."

"Aster, can you hear me?"

That was Edith. Aster remembered Edith. Edith promised she'd watch over her baby. Adam Liam Reign was safe in her care.

"He's so small," she croaked out, her fingers touching the plastic case.

"He'll be fine, hun. You need to rest so you can hold him when he's ready for it." Edith was trying to get her to sit in a wheelchair.

Aster tried to stay on her feet, she couldn't see her boy if she sat down. He wouldn't be able to see her.

"Sergeant Reign. Can you convince your wife to rest? She's putting her body through too much."

Allen's palms were heavy on her hips, forcing her to sit in the wheelchair. He tucked her hair behind her ears, his blue eyes piercing hers, "Aster, love, you need to rest. Come on now." His hand cupped her chin. "Trust me, everything will be fine."

She wanted to cry out that she couldn't leave Adam. He needed her. She'd failed him at his birth, she couldn't abandon him now that he was out in the world. Allen started to wheel her out of the room and she bit her lip to keep from crying out, tears dripping down her cheeks.

"What did you say about my son?" Allen's voice was angry, but Aster didn't hear the response or what had upset him.

One of Allen's hands was still on the wheelchair, but the other was on her shoulder, pushing her pearls into her skin. "They don't know what the hell they're talking about. He's my son, and he's perfect despite everything."

Aster noticed Edith was staring at them and she stopped crying, smiling at the nurse. Everything would be perfect. She just had to be better. Everything would be perfect from now on. She would make sure of it.

She wouldn't fail anymore.

"Why can't I stay with her?" Liam's voice woke her up, and she struggled to open her eyes. She was so tired. "I'll be out of the way, I promise."

"It's the rules. Safety first."

Aster blinked, the male nurse talking to her son was out of focus.

Liam huffed. "I'll be safe *with* my mom."

"It's not safe for her for you to be climbing up on her." He pointed over towards the window, "You can sit in the chair, buddy, but not on her bed."

"I'm not your buddy." Liam glared at the nurse. "I don't know you."

"Liam..." Aster patted Liam's back as he was still nestled between her and the bed rail, "don't be rude."

"Good afternoon, Aster. You've been sleeping since breakfast, but lunch will be up soon. I'm Nathan, your nurse for the afternoon." He pointed to the chair, "I need your son to sit in the chair so I can work, please."

Liam huffed, "I don't...."

"Do what he asks. For me, please?" Aster ruffled Liam's hair and gave him a big smile.

"Okay...." Liam scrambled down and folded his arms over his chest keeping an eye on Nathan.

"Quite the guard dog you've got there," Nathan checked her blood pressure. "He said his grandmother is coming up to get him later. Do you know when that's going to be?"

Aster looked down at her lap. "I'm not sure. I'll try and call her later." Panic was rising. She had no idea what she was going to do. If they called child protective services... if they called Allen....

"Your blood pressure's higher now than it was this morning. Are you in more pain?" Nathan questioned.

"No. I'm just nervous in the hospital. I don't like them."

"I failed to thrive. We lived in the hospital for too long when I was born." Liam had started coloring in one of his books as he parroted the phrase he'd heard far too many times.

Aster winced, Nathan was staring at her. She might have attempted to ramble an excuse, but someone called out that lunch was here.

"Why is the creep from the parking lot bringing you lunch?" Liam demanded, already on his feet again.

"Kid, I'm not a creep."

Aster turned, recognizing the low, warm voice and kind face. The man from the parking lot yesterday.... She hadn't caught his name, but she remembered the strength of his arms as he swept her up and carried her with ease into the hospital.

His blue eyes softened as they met hers, as he smoothed down his goatee, "I swear I work here."

Aster couldn't help herself and started laughing.

CHAPTER 5

Aster took a bite of her pasta, but kept her eyes on Russell as he set an additional dish on her tray.

"They told us you didn't eat much of your breakfast, so figured you'd want extra lunch." He inclined his head towards Liam, who was drinking the orange juice that had been included with her morning meal.

Aster felt ashamed and grateful at the same time. He was making sure Liam got something to eat. "Thank you."

"No trouble."

"How'd you know what room she was in?" Liam questioned.

Russell sighed, "Because Reign isn't a common name. Everything in this hospital is noted in case someone has an allergy." He turned the dish to the side, showing: Reign, L. in permanent marker. "I must have misheard you yesterday. I thought you said your name was Aster."

Her hand went to the pearls around her neck, tugging them tight against her skin. "My legal name is Lillian. I was named after my grandmother, but she died when I was five. Everyone started calling me Aster after that, it's my middle name."

"It's pretty. Well, both of your names are pretty, I mean." Russel cleaned up the breakfast dishes. "Huh. Looks like someone ate this."

Liam folded his arms over his chest. "She said I could."

"Pup, I'm not gonna call the cops. Chill out."

"Don't need to call them." Liam pulled his arms closer to his body. "I can wash dishes or something."

Russell glanced back at her, but Aster wasn't sure what his expression meant. His eyes were hard to read. He fixed his attention back on her son, his voice softer than before. "It's fine, nothing to sweat over. When's your grandma coming for you? Your mother needs to rest."

"I can take care of my mom. Grandmother will come when she can." Liam fidgeted as he lied. He pulled his knees up to his chest and fixed his gaze out the window.

"It's 9 to dial out." The watch on Russ' wrist clanged against the metal rail.

Aster jumped and coughed, barely catching the bloody phlegm in a napkin. She folded it over, embarrassed at how jumpy she was.

"Sorry, didn't mean to scare you." Russell had gotten closer, but hadn't touched her. His hand was near the call button for the nurse. His fingers were tattooed with "R.U.N.6" across them, but she had no clue what that could mean.

"It's okay." She sipped from her straw hoping the water would soothe her throat.

"Like I said, you dial 9, then you can call out of the hospital system." He pointed with his other hand, there was a skull and crossbones flag tattooed on the back of his hand. A pirate flag. "I can get you a phone book if you need one."

Aster shook her head. "I'll be okay. I have numbers in my notebook."

"Alright." He turned to leave. "I'm Russ by the way. The nurse, Nathan, called me Russell, but everyone calls me Russ. I hope you feel better, Aster."

"Thank you, Russ." She smiled. Despite the tattoos, he seemed kind.

Liam scrambled back into bed with her, and she let him have the second dish of pasta. "He's weird."

Aster chuckled and took a bite from her own plate. "He was kind and he brought you a plate. You'll need to write him a thank you note."

"I guess." He ate another big bite and she slowed down with hers so she could give him some extra. Liam still had pasta in his mouth as he asked, "How are you gonna call a grandmother? I don't really have one. Do you?"

"I don't." She pushed the rest of the pasta from her plate onto Liam's. "We'll figure something out."

"Or we'll run." Liam's little voice was serious as if he already had a plan started in his head.

"That's gonna be plan D at least." She kissed the top of his head. "I'll think of something."

She had no idea what to do and she couldn't risk Allen finding out about any of this. If she'd only gone straight to Margie when she first left, maybe this wouldn't have happened. But she'd wanted to at least let Liam finish up the school year. She hated all the things he was being put through because of her bad decisions. Her little boy deserved to be happy.

"No matter the age. You treat all ladies the way you'd want your mother treated. Got it."

Aster was going to request they give her less pain medication going forward. She kept falling asleep without meaning to and waking up feeling out of sorts. She turned her head to the door, but her eyelids felt so heavy. Liam was in the doorway but she couldn't make out who was talking to him. It was a male voice. Russ maybe? She struggled to sit up, and started coughing. God it hurt so much to cough.

"MOM!" Liam was at her bedside in a flash. "Mom, are you okay?"

She attempted to reassure him, but she kept coughing and it was hard to catch her breath. The door opened as her fit subsided and Aster took the water cup that Liam had been trying to give her. "I'm alright."

"Oh that sounded like quite a rough one." The older woman in the doorway had kind hazel eyes and her permed dark gray hair was coiled against her head. She was wearing a neon colored jacket and she waved as she entered. "How are you, Aster? And you must be, Liam, what a handsome young man you are."

"Thank you." and "I'm alright." came out in sync from Liam and Aster.

She leaned down to Liam and patted his head. "I'm Grandma Marilyn. Since your grandmother isn't available, you're stuck with me." She chuckled at herself, "I'm here to look after you while mom's busy."

Aster blinked in disbelief and Liam looked at her confused.

"Now young man, I'm in desperate need of a Vernors. Can you go buy me one from the vending machine at the end of the hall, please?" Marilyn handed him two one-dollar bills. "My legs aren't what they used to be."

Liam took the money, "Mom?"

"Go ahead. Be back quick." Aster was nervous about letting him out of her sight, but she also needed to know just who this person was and how she knew about her.

The moment Liam dashed out of the room, Marilyn squeezed her hand. "My Rusty called me, said you were in a bit of a pickle. Now you tell me all about it and let's figure out the best way to help you two angels."

Tears dripped down Aster's face—she tried to stop herself from breaking down—but it was no use. She was an utter failure. She'd put Liam in danger. They'd been sleeping in the car for almost two weeks while they were getting up here from Ohio. She barely had enough money to pay Margie, if the trailer was even still available. Allen had turned off her phone after she left, and she kept messing up the minute cards for the phone she bought from the gas station. Margie had probably sold the trailer by now and even if she hadn't. Aster didn't have a job or any way to make money. She certainly didn't have any skills that would help her get on her feet.

She pulled her arms closer to her chest, but felt a pair of arms encircle her. Marilyn smelled like warm vanilla and wintergreen, and reminded her of the pink mints she used to get from the ladies at church. The hug was strong and made her safe like she was back in her prior life, working at her mother's daycare. Before Allen married her, before she was step-mother to Allison, before she was a mother to Liam, and long-before she left her husband and her home in disgrace. Marilyn patted her back and Aster tried to stop crying as she pulled back from the embrace.

"You poor thing, there, there. Everything will be alright." Marilyn had rings on two fingers of both hands and she cupped Aster's chin in her palm. She wiped Aster tears away with a tissue she'd pulled from her pocket. "How long have you been in town, dear?"

Aster swallowed and took the tissue to blow her nose. "We got in two days ago, I think? I started to get sick and time gets a little fuzzy."

"Are you visiting or moving in?"

"I was trying to move here. A friend of my late grandmother owns a trailer park here…" Aster picked at her nails. "She was going to sell me a trailer. I don't know if it's even still available. I haven't talked to her in months."

"Which park? Do you know the name?" Marilyn smiled, "I know this town like the back of my hand. There's only two parks in the town proper and one just outside, it backs up to state parkland. That's Everygreens."

"Yes. That's the one. I thought it was called Evergreen though."

The older woman laughed, "Well, that's Margie's park. Technically it's Evergreen Park, but everyone calls it Everygreens."

"You know Margie?" Hope was beginning to nip at Aster's heels. She had to believe that somehow this would all work out.

"I've known Margie and Bridgette for years. Rose and I played euchre with those two for more than twenty years. Bless Rose's soul, she went to heaven at the beginning of this year." Marilyn rested her hand over her heart. "I miss her something terrible. It's her trailer that Margie was going to sell to you."

"Is it still available?" Aster questioned quickly, then flinched, "I'm sorry that was rude. Do you know if it is I mean?"

"I can check for you for sure." Marilyn smiled like she had some secret she was holding back.

"I have your soda." Liam came in with the can Marilyn asked for, clutching it for dear life. "The Russ guy said I had to be careful with it or it'd get too fizzy."

"Thank you so much young man." She patted his head again and Liam smiled up at her. "Rusty's a bit too serious for his own good sometimes."

Nathan appeared in the doorway and Liam ducked behind Marilyn. "I see your grandma got here, Buddy. Think I can borrow your mom for some tests?"

Liam leaned around his 'grandma,' his eyes narrowing at the sandy-haired man. "Still not your buddy."

"Tough crowd." Nathan chuckled, then addressed the older woman. "Marilyn, I didn't realize you had any grandkids other than Russell."

"Aster is one of Rose's grandkids. I'm just filling in. Now Aster, if you're alright with it, I'm gonna take Liam with me to run out some of his energy at the park right across the way."

Aster bit her lip. It would look so odd for her to argue, but she barely knew Marilyn. She whispered a prayer under her breath and nodded. "But you'll bring him back before too long, right?"

"Oh of course, deary. I'll have him back around dinner time."

"Liam." She motioned for her son to come close and squeezed his hands. "You be very good for Grandma Marilyn. Do what she says. I'll see you later today, okay?"

Liam looked nervous but agreed. "Yes, mom."

"I love you so much." She kissed his knuckles.

"Love you too." Liam muttered quietly.

"Come on young man." Marilyn held out her hand and Liam took it. The two disappeared out into the hallway.

Nathan checked Aster's blood pressure and noted it on her chart.

She cleared her throat, "How do you know Marilyn?"

"She was here for all of Rose's cancer treatments." Nathan drew in a deep breath and tapped his pen on the chart. "She was the *only* one here for Rose at the end."

Tears pricked at Aster's eyes for poor Rose. It wasn't hard for her to have empathy despite never meeting her. But what was an acceptable answer for her absence with this ruse Russ and Marilyn had begun?

"Aster?" The nurse flipped one of the pages on the chart over. "I didn't need you for tests. I needed to talk to you without your son in the room. I didn't think you'd be honest with him here."

Oh god. He knew. The hospital knew. She was going to lose Liam. They were going to take him away, it had all been a ruse.

The beeping on her heart monitor increased and her breathing quickened.

"It's alright. You have no reason to panic." Nathan caught her hand. "Aster, were you safe where you were before you got here?"

Aster could barely make out his eyes through fresh tears. "I wasn't." Despite the pain, she doubled over trying to hide. "I wasn't ever safe after..." She couldn't say the words. She couldn't say everything had been fine, until Liam. Her son was the best thing that ever happened to her, but according to her husband, Liam was the worst mistake they'd ever made.

"Aster, I promise you're safe here. You're going to be alright."

Chapter 6

"Mom! We got pizza!" Liam raced into Aster's room, looking more lively and joyful than Aster had seen him in months.

"And I got to swing on these cool swings, go down this huge slide, and there was a spinning thing, but I felt really dizzy so I only did that once. And then..." Liam took in a big gulp of air. "Mom, Grandma Marilyn, is the coolest. She's got wood beads on her car seats."

Aster blinked as she tried to process the onslaught of information.

"Slow down, Liam. You left me in the dust." Marilyn appeared in the doorway. "Aren't those bags heavy? You're so strong."

"I'm supposed to carry things for you, you're a lady. I'd want someone else to carry my mom's things." Liam set down two plastic grocery bags in the chair by the window.

She laughed out loud. "I see Rusty is still handing out his grandpa's wisdom. My Titus was a stickler for treating ladies like ladies. He was old fashioned and a bit of an angry cuss, but I loved him."

Liam cocked his head to the side, "Where is he? When do I get to meet him?"

Aster winced as Liam asked questions she was worried she knew the answers to. "Liam...."

"Well, I'm pretty sure he made it to heaven after a stint in purgatory." She smiled at Aster and set a smaller black bag on her tray where her dinner had been. "There's some toiletries in there for you."

"Thank you so much." Aster opened her arms as Liam climbed up onto the bed with her. He smelled clean. "Did you take a bath?" A tiny spark of fear crept in, where had he gotten cleaned up? Who had been around when that happened?

He snuggled against her chest. "It was so cool. Grandma Marilyn took me to a huge pool and kicked all the old guys out of the shower room then blocked the door. I got to shower in this giant room all by myself."

"No one really argues with an old lady." She winked at Aster. "Now I know he's not supposed to sleep here. But he's being very stubborn on that point. There's a pillow in one of the bags for him and a blanket will show up later. I just have this feeling."

Aster eyes were teary even as she smiled. "How can I ever repay you?"

"Well, there's a couple of packets for you to go over to get some help for you and Liam. Start with that and I'm working on the trailer situation." Marilyn yawned. "Now, it's time for me to go home so I can catch Wheel of Fortune before I fall asleep. Do you need anything before I scoot for the night?"

"I think we'll be alright." Aster kissed the top of Liam's head. "I'm getting discharged tomorrow afternoon. They don't want to keep me longer than they have to." She was glad they weren't insisting on her staying without insurance, she was going to be paying this bill until she was old enough to be a grandmother herself.

"You're okay now?" Liam asked.

She brushed his hair away from his face, "I will be. I just need to rest, take medicine, and come back for some tests."

"I'll help with everything, Mom. Leave it to me."

"Well, I'm sure I'll be seeing you two soon. Get some rest."

"Wait!" Liam bailed off Aster's bed and hugged Marilyn's legs. "Thank you for everything, Grandma Marilyn."

"You're so welcome, Liam. Keep an eye on your mom."

"I will." He grinned up at her and they both waved goodbye. He scooted back up to her, "I'm gonna pee and brush my teeth, then I'll hide in the closet so the other nurse doesn't see me. I really like Grandma Marilyn. She got me a new book and a light to use. Can she be my grandma for real?"

"Maybe." Aster sat up more fully. "Liam, I'm proud of you for being so brave."

"Mom, we're both brave. We're brave together."

Paperwork never was something she struggled with. Aster had always been a me-thodical reader and her parents had put her to work with the daycare's paperwork even as a young teenager. She knew how to take her time and check the boxes and often understood the odd governmental language with a little effort. After filling out so many forms over the years, it made it easier when she started doing taxes for herself and Allen after they got married. The forms for getting state insurance and food assistance weren't that complicated, but there was so much repetition.

She shook out her hand and took a long drink of water. There was still light coming out from under the closet but she hadn't heard a page turn or any noise in over an hour. Liam was almost certainly already asleep. The clock read 9:45 PM, no wonder she was tired herself.

The only stack of paperwork she hadn't touched was the domestic violence information. She had left Allen, signed the divorce papers, he'd given up custody of Liam for now, even agreed she could move them out of state. Surely getting a state away from him was enough. She didn't need to drag his name through the mud. He'd never hit her. It wasn't really abuse, but it could have gotten there if she hadn't left.

Maybe if she hadn't been so bad at being a mother for Liam—if she hadn't gotten everything wrong with his pregnancy—then maybe it wouldn't have all fallen apart. She tried her best at every turn, but it wasn't good enough. Her hands moved unconsciously to the scar on her stomach. Liam hadn't even had a real birth, he'd been cut out of her. She hadn't been able to feed him. Allen had been so patient with her through all of the struggles with Liam's first year. Had she been able to handle things on her own and stay focused on Allison, then things would have been alright. But she hadn't been able to keep her household running like she should have.

But nothing seemed to go right after Liam was born. Allen had gotten hurt on the job when Liam was three and Allison was struggling in middle school. Aster had been so overwhelmed that Allen's mother had moved in with them for six months. Joyce was demanding, and it was all Aster could do to keep up with housework under her mother-in-law's watchful eye. Allen had gotten more critical after that. The meals Aster cooked were okay instead of good, her outfits too showy instead of feminine, and her parenting of Allison was unacceptable at all times. Joyce remarked about how small Liam was constantly, about how he was behind where Allison had been at that age. How Carla had been effortlessly good at being a mother and wife. How Aster would measure up eventually.

Aster's fingers gripped the pearls around her neck, tugging them tight. Crying to herself was pointless. She didn't need to be so emotional. Her hands went to her cheek, oh God, she was crying.

The light coming in from the hallway increased, someone had opened the door up more. Penny was the nurse on for the night, and she'd ask so many questions after reading the notes Nathan no doubt left. Aster hurriedly wiped off her cheeks and blew her nose. Attempting to paint a more neutral expression on her face.

"Are you alright?"

Not nurse Penny. A male voice. She gasped on reflex and groaned at how much it hurt her side.

"Sorry, I didn't mean to scare you." Russ stepped into her room, a crocheted blanket in his arms. "You were crying. For a minute there, and I almost left, but my grandmother will kick me in the ass if I didn't bring the blanket to the kid."

"Sorry." Aster didn't know why she was apologizing, but she felt like she should.

He didn't respond, but looked around the room. "Where's the pup?"

Aster pointed to the closet. "I think he's asleep already."

"Good. Too tired to tussle with him." Russ opened the closet door slightly and knelt down for a moment before returning with the blanket.

"Wait...."

"There's two of them. Won't have to sneak one out in the morning if there's two that look the same." He laid the blanket over her legs, the blues hues formed a zig-zag pattern. "You can fold 'em up together when you get discharged."

"Did your grandmother make them?" She ran her hands over the downy yarn.

Russ sat down in the chair by the window. "Yeah, she got good at them last year. After Rose died, she needed something else to keep her busy."

"Did you know Rose well?" Aster hadn't ever felt yarn this soft and it was so pretty.

"She was grandma's fishing buddy my whole life. Margie and Bridgette were never much for going out to the lakes. They didn't like the worms or algae. But the four of them loved playing cards together. Taught me way too young how to gamble and table talk." Russ's eyes were fixed on the clock, but his voice was soft and reassuring, even chuckling at the end of his recollection.

"Marilyn said you knew Margie. I was moving up here to her trailer park." She wished she had her notebook. She had notes about the arrangement. "But I haven't been able to talk to her for months, so I'm sure it fell through."

Aster didn't want to admit that she didn't know what to do, but she didn't.

Russ cleared his throat, "So did my grandmother tell you anything about me?"

"Not really. But she calls you Rusty."

"Yeah." His eyes moved back to the clock. "Please don't call me that. She's the only one who gets away with it now. I don't have long, so I'm gonna explain this quick."

He must have a family to get home to or another job perhaps?

"I got out of prison five months ago. I was there because I got in a bar fight and it got out of hand. But I didn't kill anyone, and I've never hurt a woman or a child." He breathed out, like the secret had been weighing him down. He scratched the back of his neck as he continued, "here's the thing, when I got out five months ago, Margie sold me a trailer for a grand. It was supposed to go to a friend of a friend who was moving up here, but she didn't end up coming. So, I'm pretty sure I'm living in the trailer she was going to sell you."

"Oh." Aster blinked. Well that was that. Nowhere to go. She didn't have enough money for a deposit on an apartment and outside of the people she'd met in the hospital, she didn't know anyone. Russ was rebuilding his life, she couldn't be angry with him for buying the trailer. She couldn't be mad at Margie for selling it, Aster hadn't been in contact with her. The whole situation was a shamble.

Russ stood up and walked up to her bed. "I'm on parole for two years. Moving is hard when you're on parole. It's a whole thing with your PO. There's paperwork which is long and frustrating. And Jerry's not about paperwork, so I'll end up doing all of it and not just my half. Plus there's so many rules about timing, and I'm pushing it right now to make sure I'm home on time. So anything to make this situation easier—"

"Um," she interrupted quietly, "if you're telling me that you can't move then I understand. I should have found a way to communicate with Margie about why I didn't come up right away. It's not anyone's fault but mine."

"Huh?" He looked confused as he ran his hands through his dark blonde hair. "Wait no, I'm not getting to the point right. Look, Aster, the trailer's got two bedrooms and I'm really sick of eating eggs. It'd be fine if you two crashed with me for a bit. One of us will find another place, and then we can go from there."

Aster had no idea what eggs had to do with the situation, but her brain had connected the rest of the dots. "Are you asking me to move in with you?"

Russ sighed. "Kinda, but not in a weird way. Just in a you need a place and I have room kinda way. I get it's not ideal."

"Was this your idea?"

He shook his head and rested his pirate flag hand on the railing, "No, it was my grandma's, and you don't argue with Grandma Marilyn."

"I don't know." She pulled at her pearls. She didn't know this man. She didn't have anywhere to go. *But was this the right path? Was this the right thing to do?*

"Hey," Russ's fingers brushed over hers. "I think you've got your necklace on too tight. You're imprinting your skin. Be careful not to hurt yourself. You need to take it easy."

His fingers were resting atop hers. There was no movement to increase or decrease her pulling, only the light touch of existence. Being present in that moment and connected. It was hard not to look at him, but she didn't want to see his pity.

"Too much pressure I think." His voice was so low, like he was trying to solve a puzzle in front of him.

She swallowed, mouth suddenly dry.

Russ's other hand moved to her chin cupping it gently despite his calloused fingers. Her pale eyes met his darker ones, even in the low light, she could see the darker ring around his irises. His voice was low and quiet, it was hard to hear him even this close. "That asshole did a number on you."

Aster flinched away and Russ stepped back. She clasped her hands together in her lap. She was fine. She was perfectly fine. Allen hadn't done anything to her, she'd gotten away before it had gotten bad. "I don't have much money. What would you want me to do if I said yes to this?"

"Do?" He cleared his throat awkwardly, "I don't want you to do anything. I just need some help around the house and someone to pick up groceries for me since it's next to impossible for me to do it myself." He snagged the pen from her chart and scribbled an address and phone number on the water cup. "My number and address. If you decide you want the room, call me, or just show up. I work the overnight shift tomorrow. Night, Aster."

She blinked trying to process what just happened.

Russ left her room, but he immediately came back in. "No, actually please call first. That's it. Goodbye for real this time."

The room was quiet and she strained to listen as his footsteps disappeared down the hall. Aster picked up the cup: *Russ 555-789-0226, Evergreen Park, Green Lane, Lot 1023*

"Until one of us finds another place."

CHAPTER 7

Jerry was relaxed by cop standards. He didn't take himself too seriously or act like he was god's gift to the world. Jerry was sixty with a full head of thick dark salt-and-pepper black hair and heavy set. He always wore suspenders under his suit jacket to keep his pants from falling down. For all the non-stereotypical cop things that Jerry was, he knocked like a cop. A cop on a mission to wake Russell up in the most inhumane way possible.

Bang. Bang. Bang. The walls of the trailer rattled as Russ forced himself off the couch, pacing to the door and opening it.

"It's eight in the morning," he grumbled.

Jerry spit off the side of the plastic steps and eyed Russ's appearance. "And I've been up since five. You ready to go?"

"Yeah." Russ put his shoes on and stepped outside, blinking at the already too bright sun. "Does my anger management have to be scheduled this early?"

"Since I have to drive you and it interrupts my normal Thursday, yes."

Russ made sure the trailer was locked and followed Jerry to the car. "You want me in the back?"

"Can you behave yourself, *Rusty*?" Jerry leaned on the open driver's door, the vehicle lowering on that side.

"Jerry, my behavior so far is why I'm still breathing. So yeah, I think I can manage." Russ narrowed his eyes.

The older man barked out a laugh, "Ha! You aren't wrong. Get in the front. But don't touch my coffee."

Russ buckled himself in and they left the park slowly to account for the kids playing nearby, between Margie's trailer and the makeshift meeting house. They were shooting each other with Nerf guns, and hollering back and forth. They noticed Jerry's car and started making siren noises at them.

"More kids this morning." He whooped the portable siren atop his sedan and the kids all scattered as if they were on the run. Jerry took a drink from his cup, but it didn't disguise his smile completely.

Russ pushed at the empty coffee-cups in front of the passenger seat with his boot. A clean car was not a priority for Jerry. "School let out last week."

The radio played Bad Company and Jerry turned it up as they stopped at the first light. Russ checked for his phone, but he must have left it on the counter. His pocket was empty except for some loose change and lint.

"So, what's on your mind?" Jerry questioned.

"Why do you think there's something on my mind?" Russ folded his arms over his chest, which was stupid. He had something, or rather *someone*, on his mind, and he needed to talk to Jerry about it.

"Well, the whole time I've known you, I've never known you not to sing that song when it comes on. Now is the thing on your mind going to be a problem for me?"

"I thought you said my existence in general was a problem for you."

Jerry took a gulp of his coffee. "It is. But you're a mild headache problem, and I want to keep it that way. I almost like ya."

"Jerry, that warms my heart. You have no idea." Russ cracked his knuckles.

"And that settles it. You're about to become a major headache to me." He took the right turn too fast and they both slid sideways on the vinyl seats. "You're buttering me up. Why?"

"It wasn't my idea." Russ figured he should start with his best defense before presenting his case.

"Whose idea was it? Marilyn's?" Jerry was too smart for both their sanity's sake.

"It was."

"Tell her I can't get you more time out in the world. It's a no-go."

It was fair that Jerry assumed that was Marilyn's goal. She seemed to think that 'house-arrest' meant any house, not confinement to only one location. It took Russ three dinners to explain how working parole functioned.

"No. It's about someone staying with me." Russ wished his window rolled down, he needed air. "She—"

"She? Dammit, Rusty!" Jerry yanked one of Russ's curls which were growing in and more pronounced with the humid weather.

Fuck he was gonna have to cut it. His last self-hair cut had not turned out well. Matter of fact, the last hair cut he'd attempted had Bridgette doubled over with laughter when she saw him.

"You've been there less than three days and you're trying to shack up with someone! What are you thinking?"

"It's not like that. She's got a kid and my grandma thought...."

Jerry slammed on the brakes. "Tell me you're kidding."

"I'm not."

"Forget headache. You're a damn gunshot wound."

The drives back from Russ's therapy sessions were usually quiet. Russ wasn't ever in the mood to talk after, and it was almost time for Jerry's morning snack. The schedule was: therapy, then the bakery for two cookies, both of which were Jerry's. If it was the first week of the month, they went to the drug testing center so Russ could piss in a cup, then wait at the police station for results, before finally Russ would be allowed to go home.

When, they skipped the bakery and pulled through a drive thru donut shop instead, Russ knew Jerry was actually annoyed as they drove straight to the station in silence. Russ sat in Jerry's cluttered office, filling out every piece of paperwork he was handed and struggling to spell everything correctly. They had a *delightful* 'come to Jesus' conversation about how if Aster was a felon, it was a no-go, and Jerry would have to speak with her within three days of her moving in.

"I know you didn't do anything with kids, but this does mean you have to submit for random alcohol and drug testing."

Russ shrugged. He hadn't ever been a drug guy, and he'd been sober since getting out. Not a moral thing, just cheaper—booze could get expensive. "That's fine. Will it affect my monthly fees?"

"No." Jerry handed him another form, this one blocks of text with open signature and date lines at the bottom. "If she fucks up, then it could come back on you. If she has drugs or a gun, or makes money with anything illegal, then it impacts you. You still want to go through this?"

"She needs somewhere to live." He skimmed the form. "And it's just a couple of weeks."

"Gonna be hot this summer. Miserable for three people in a small space. You have AC?"

"No. I'll see if I can find a window unit for the living room." Russ signed and dated the form before handing it back. "What's next?"

"I'd suggest a grill to cook outside." Jerry was always so proud when he made a good point. "As far as paperwork we've got another handful of forms."

He wordlessly accepted what he was handed started on the latest batch. This was just a statement about how he met Aster and Liam.

"You want a cup o' coffee?" Jerry was already half out the door.

"Sure, if you're offering." Russ resisted the urge to chew on the end of the pen as he attempted to spell sandwich for the third time. There really should be another 'h' in that word.

"Hulston. Where's Jerry?"

The fact the other cops recognized him was a testament to how often Jerry brought him in because he liked his temperature controlled office rather than the unpredictable outdoor weather.

Russ didn't look up from the forms, mostly to avoid knowing who was talking to him. "He went to get coffee."

A heavy hand landed on his shoulder. "You fail a drug test?"

"Nope." He kept filing in the blanks. Do not engage. *This guy was trying to get him to engage. His actions were his responsibility.* "Just doing what Jerry asked me to."

"He should keep you on a shorter leash." The grip intensified and Russ stopped writing. "With everything...."

"Yander. No one invited you into my office." Jerry interrupted, pushing by the other officer forcing Yander to remove his hand. Jerry set down the two coffees he held. "I know you aren't in here bothering my parolee when he's got nothing to do with you."

"He's a scumbag."

"He's not your problem." Jerry's voice was biting as he pointed out to the desks in the open bullpen behind Russ. "Now go handle your own work, unless you need my help to find your desk."

Russ followed an adage from his elementary school days and kept his eyes on his own paper. He did not want to be in the middle of a cop fight.

"Do you need a map, Yander? Is it that hard?" Jerry asked when the other officer didn't move, clicking his pen and scribbling something onto a piece of paper before holding it out. "Here ya go. Now get lost."

"This division is gonna be better without you." Yander snarled.

Jerry just chuckled. "Maybe so. But until then, you've got three more years to smile my way."

Yander cussed under his breath and stomped away.

Russ took a sip of the terrible coffee. "Thank you."

"Any day I get to annoy that city-boy prick is a good day." He gulped down a swig from his cup despite the heat. "You finished yet?"

"Yeah. I think so. Is that the last one?"

"Yup." Jerry took it back and leaned back in his chair to review it. "How do you not know how to spell sandwich?"

CHAPTER 8

Jerry dropped him off at the park at noon and Russ figured he'd be able to catch an hour nap at least. He picked up his cell phone and noted the four missed calls from his grandmother. That wasn't good. He plugged in his monitor as he returned her call on his home line. He had to have a home phone and internet for the monitor to work correctly. Lucky him another bill. This model happened to have an answering machine built into it which was convenient.

"Hello?" She answered in one ring.

"Everything okay?" He leaned against the wall tapping on the phone's base. The circle in the middle showing that he had one message and he was very aware of that one message.

"Oh yes. I got here and you weren't home. I'm at Margie and Bridgette's. I'll be down shortly."

His grandmother hung up without waiting for a reply and Russ sighed. So much for a nap. He was going to be miserable working all night with such little sleep. He'd been up all night cleaning. The blinking message was from Aster. *"I...I mean, we'd like to take you up on the room you offered. But just for the summer, so I can save up some money. If you've changed your mind please let me know. Thank you. Um...bye and uh...see you tomorrow, I guess."*

He snagged a bottle of water from the pack by the fridge and took a drink. He needed to eat something before he left and pack a lunch, but then again he could eat at work. Ian wasn't too picky about them having a bowl of soup or something while they were working, packaged items were really the only things strictly inventoried.

Russ raised his eyebrow at the too-loud for his grandmother knock. Had Jerry come back? It didn't sound like a cop knock, but it was too loud for his grandmother. He took a step forward and nearly bit it as the cord stopped him. "Son of a bitch." He yanked the connection apart and threw the door open.

Not Jerry. The screen door was between him and a man who looked familiar, but Russ didn't recognize him. The gray haired man was sporting a silvering beard which he smoothed down, eyeing Russ critically. He turned away and hollered past where Russ could see. "You weren't lying, Marilyn. He's Bailey's spitting image."

Bailey. Russ's mother. He didn't even remember her, save a few blurry memories filled in by his grandparents.

"Come on, we've got stuff to bring in." The man motioned for Russ to follow him out, so he unplugged himself and did so.

Grandma Marilyn had driven her car up to his trailer, trunk already open. "Rusty, you remember, Erving don't you?"

Russ offered his hand to the other man. "Afraid I don't. Nice to meet you again, I guess."

"You were only ten, or so when we met." Erving had a knuckle popping handshake. "I was friends with your grandpa Titus; drove trucks for the same company. He was always proud of you."

Erving might as well have punched him in the gut, all Russ could manage was a nod in response. It was just as well, Erving wasn't paying attention to him. "Amos! The trailer's in the other direction. Turn all the way around. See the trailer with the green roof? That's the one you need to look for."

Russ followed Erving's eye-line to a lanky kid walking towards the woods on Russ's side of the park. The trailer with the green roof Erving was pointing to was on the opposite side.

"That boy couldn't find his ass in an open paper bag." Erving rolled his eyes as he muttered under his breath. He hollered at Amos again. "AY! Where is your cousin?"

Amos shrugged and pointed in opposite directions.

"Those two are gonna be the death of me this summer."

"Grandpa, we're not trying to kill you." Another boy laughed, as he crawled out from under Russ's trailer. His black hair was messy, even under his tan and red ball cap, and his grin nearly split his face.

"What were ya doing under there?" Erving caught the kid by the collar and hauled him the rest of the way out and up on his feet.

"Looking fer worms." He laughed, it echoed in the quiet park. "Amos! There's no worms under this trailer but I saw a snake. Come 'ere!"

"Seagar." Erving lifted the kid off his feet so they could look eye to eye. "Calm down."

"But...It was so boring being in the truck for that whole time and we're going back on the road tomorrow morning." Seagar, clearly unfazed by the manhandling, turned to Russ. "Mister, you don't mind if I look for snakes under your trailer, do you?"

"You probably shouldn't. You could get bit," Russ countered.

"I don't think the snakes are poison here. They're poison in California. That's where I live, but Amos lives in Kansas. We picked him up on the way here for the summer. Didn't we, Grandpa? We're going to a water park tomorrow. But it's hours away!" Seagar finally took a breath.

Russ didn't think he'd ever sympathized for another person more in his life. Erving had this kid in the car with him since California and had another trip coming up? Russ would have lost his mind. Wait a minute. He had a kid moving in with him later today. He was regretting saying yes to his grandmother's plan.

Russ dared to ask, "How old are you Seagar?"

"I'm seven until August, then I'm eight. Amos is eight, but he won't be nine until Christmas." While Seagar continued explaining, Amos had wandered up to them. "His birthday is on Christmas so we have cake on Christmas and extra presents for him. Last year—"

"Stop." Erving covered Seagar's mouth in the most non-malicious-yet-utterly-done-with-the-child's-talking way possible. He set his grandson on the ground and grabbed Amos' hand, locking it with Seagar's. "Both of you go to the trailer and get a bath. Separately! So it don't end in a water fight." He handed Amos a key with an anchor keychain. "Don't lose this."

The boys nodded and Seagar took off running, dragging Amos behind him.

His grandmother was laughing, leaning against her car. "Lord, Erving. How are you gonna keep your sanity next week with them at the casino?"

"This is why I was trying to convince you to tag along." Erving marched back to his pick-up truck and pulled out a child sized mattress. "I'm happy to spend my summers with my grandchildren, but sometimes I'm tempted to put sleep medicine in their dinner. Where are we putting this?"

"Putting what?" Russ cocked his head to the side utterly confused. Did Erving mean his trailer?

"Rusty, that poor boy hasn't had a real bed in months. We're gonna fix up the little back room for him before he gets here with his mama," Marilyn explained. "Don't worry, I got a deal on it."

"Oh okay." Russ awkwardly opened the door for Erving, giving the other man directions. "It's just past the living room, the door's closed. It's empty."

Marilyn pulled a bag of blankets out of her trunk.

Russ's brain finally caught up with him. "Wait, how did you know Aster agreed to move in?"

"Rusty, when has anyone ever successfully won against me?" She smirked. "And besides, I confirmed it this morning, when I brought those two breakfast."

Well, he couldn't find the error in that statement. If there was one thing Russ learned growing up, it's that you don't argue with Grandma. He reached out to help her, "here I can...."

"No, no, get the frame for the mattress and set that up." She shooed him toward Erving's truck.

Russ pinched his fingers between two pieces of the frame and cursed out loud. "So how much did this put you back? I've got some cash I can give you."

"I already told you not to worry about it. Now let's hurry up." Marilyn wrestled with the blankets in her arms. "Aster said she was getting out around four."

"Okay, Grandma." He'd find a way to sneak money into her purse before she left.

"Oh and I called Nestor about fixing that second bathroom. He should be here soon." She passed by him and through the trailer door with Russ hot on her heels, arguing.

"Wait, wait, wait! Nestor charges an arm and a leg for everything. Why would you call him?"

"Because he always shows up when I call."

"Grandma, he charges interest when you can't pay up front and he knows no one keeps that kind of cash at home." Russ complained as he locked the frame together in the small empty room. "I'm gonna owe that man a kidney."

Marilyn patted his arm. "That's why I'm covering the mattress."

"Thanks, Grandma." Russ deadpanned as Erving dropped the box spring down.

"Not a lot of room for a little boy. He's gonna be scaling the walls in here." Erving looked out the window. "Guess he could play in the woods there, it's away from the road and in sight."

"It's such a shame I don't live in the house on Maple anymore. I bet Liam would have loved your old treehouse." Marilyn started putting sheets on the bed. "I hope blue is alright. I wanted it to match the blanket he has."

CHAPTER 9

It was only seven at night and Russ already regretted every life choice he'd ever made. He'd only been at work an hour, but with all the cleaning and such, he hadn't had a chance to charge his monitor so he was tethered to the sandwich station for at least another hour.

Aster's car hadn't started, so his grandmother went to get her, which meant they'd missed each other. Russ had to trust that his grandma wouldn't: A, lose the key in her bottomless purse and B, give Aster enough lay of the land that she'd be comfortable in the trailer overnight without him. Then again maybe it was better he wasn't there. It would give her a little time to herself. They hadn't discussed where she was going to be sleeping or how things were going to work with all three of them living under one roof. Too little thought went into this arrangement, and now he was unsettled by all the unknowns.

Stressed as he was, all he had do was fake being calm and get through his shift. There were so many unknowns. Situations like this one was what his shrink had talked to him about just this morning. Russ was too impulsive, then he got angry about the consequences. He didn't want to do the 'internal work' to figure out why he felt the need to jump to decisions so quickly.

"Hey, it's Russell, right?"

Russ looked up at the sandy-haired nurse he'd met briefly in Aster's room yesterday. Thankfully his badge was turned the right way so he could read it, because Russ hadn't remembered his name.

"Yeah, but everyone calls me Russ. You go by Nathan?"

Nathan nodded as he yawned and rubbed his hands over his face. Russ noticed the holes on Nathan's eyebrow and near his lip left behind by piercings that had been removed for his shift.

"I haven't been this hung-over since college." The younger nurse cracked his neck and looked at the food options in front of him. "I thought a sandwich would be better for my stomach, but I think I need grease."

"Carbs are better." He shrugged, then offered. "You eat meat?"

"Of all varieties." Nathan smirked, before thinking better of what he'd just said and cleared his throat. "If you've got an idea to help this, I'm down to try whatever."

Russ decided to ignore the innuendo. Ian had accidentally cut open a bag of cornmeal, so they'd gotten a little more creative with the menu tonight. Which included homemade potato chips, well they were on the thicker side, so maybe closer to fried potato slices. His co-workers had liked them enough to convince him to make another two batches.

Since he was limited with his range without unplugging himself and going through that song and dance, he'd work with what was in front of him. Thicker bread to start, a slice of cheddar cheese on each side, coleslaw, pulled pork on one side, fried potatoes on the other, then barbecue sauce to finish it off—that looked right. Russ set the creation on a plate and covered it with an empty bowl.

"Leave it for a minuet. The cheese'll melt." He offered the plate to Nathan, who looked confused but took it.

"Never had potatoes on a sandwich, but looks good. Thanks, Russ." The nurse offered him a smile and left the station.

"Russet!"

The sharp female voice using close enough to his name was enough to make Russ jump out of his skin. *Oh no.* Somehow Russ already had an enemy here and her name was Heather. She was the charge nurse from the ER. The one that he'd asked for a note because he was late his first day and she'd scoffed at him.

Heather's lips were in a thin line and she was looking at him expectantly.

"Um...How can I help you?" Russ asked. Then he realized she hadn't used his name. "Oh and Russ is fine, you don't have to use my full name."

Unspoken request: please don't use my full name.

"I didn't say Russell. I said, russet, like a potato." She checked her phone. "Why on earth would you put potatoes on a sandwich? Bread already has carbs."

He didn't want to rat Nathan out for being hung-over. Even if Heather wasn't his boss, the gossip would likely spread. "He said to make him something interesting. So that's what I came up with."

"Mhmmm." She put an apple on her plate. "I'll try some of the chips, but not on bread."

Russ used the tongs to put some chips on her plate. "Can I get you anything else?"

"You're out of yogurt in the front." Heather was beginning to strike Russ as *not* a people person.

"Sure." Russ turned back towards the kitchen, "Tricky, can you grab the yogurt crate and bring it up here to re-stock?"

No verbal response, but the walk-in opened and closed decisively.

"You can't be bothered to do it yourself?" Her eyebrow was arched.

He took a slow breath in and out. "I have to stay right here for a bit."

Thankfully Tricky appeared holding out the crate to Heather. "No raspberry. Everything else is there."

She took a plain yogurt without acknowledging the black-haired man. Instead still muttering about potatoes on sandwiches as she walked away.

"Did she call you russet?" Tricky questioned as he knelt to fill in the yogurt. "Like a potato?"

"Yeah. I think...?"

"What did Heather call him?" Marc came around the corner.

"Russet," Tricky supplied.

Yesenia let out a laugh. She and Marc had been adjusting the week's schedule so they were standing shoulder to elbow in the side hallway. "I think he kinda looks more like golden than a russet potato."

She patted his arm as she walked by explaining the joke to Jose in Spanish.

Russ groaned and forcibly unplugged his monitor so he could go scream in the walk-in.

"Wait, *Rusett*. Take the extra yogurt." Tricky handed him the crate then jogged back to the dish area.

Russ had never heard the kid talk so much, nor wished for his silence more. Now he had a damn nickname. Was that progress? Was that being a part of a team and part of the world? As the cold air hit his face, he wished he knew.

Marc was leaning against the wall as Russ exited cold storage.

"Sorry. I'll settle down." He sighed.

Marc waved him off. "You're fine. It's probably gonna stick though."

"Well, the last place I worked at just called me asshat, so Russet's an improvement." Despite himself he chuckled and Marc echoed it.

"You get everything you needed done today?"

Russ grunted as he lifted his leg to check the charge on his monitor. "Yeah. Therapy every Thursday mandated by the court. I appreciate you and Ian for working with my schedule."

"I guess working with you one night a week won't be so bad."

Russ looked up at the taller man sheepishly. "Can I ask you question?"

Marc nodded.

"Do you know how to build a treehouse? I've got a lady and her kid staying with me for at least the summer, and I think'd it be good for him to have space outside to play."

"No." Marc clicked his tongue. "None of my girls have asked for one of those."

"Okay. Don't worry about it then." Russ started back towards the sandwich station.

"Russet, ya potato." Marc gripped Russ' shoulder stopping his momentum. "I said I didn't know how, I didn't say I wouldn't help. You aren't working on Sunday and neither am I. Brother Thomas at my church knows how to build everything. We'll come out with some guys and help ya. Make a cookout out of it."

"Why would you do that? You barely know me," he said utterly dumbfounded. "Why do you want to help me?"

"Cause you need it." Marc pointed to the woman looking lost by sandwiches. "Now, get back to work."

Russ did as he was told, because he couldn't think of a way to argue.

Chapter 10

The drive was bumpy, the wooden bead seat cover on the passenger seat felt odd on Aster's back. It didn't help that she was still in a lot of pain, breathing hurt and coughing was agony. Despite all of it, she smiled as the sun broke through the clouds. Marilyn's window was rolled down letting the breeze and much needed fresh air in. Windmill Creek, tucked away in rural Michigan felt like a different planet from the stuffy Ohio suburb she fled.

Liam read the road signs aloud as they passed them, excited, as Marilyn told him about places in the town. Without glancing back, Aster knew he was jotting everything down in his notebook. This was good. Her car didn't work, very bad, but the fresh start was good.

They stopped to pick up groceries and a few supplies for the trailer. Aster kept the tally of the items running in her head with the tax and knew she had enough. When it came time to pay, Marilyn snatched two twenties from her hand and paid for the rest, not letting Aster argue. They stopped by a mechanic stop near the edge of town and James agreed to tow her car and let her know if it was worth fixing. Aster kept her fingers crossed. Her funds were limited, and she needed her car so she could find work.

"Is this place in the forest? Are we gonna be living in the forest? Like Sleeping Beauty or Robin Hood? That would be so cool!" Liam questioned, bouncing in his seat as they turned down a road flanked by impossibly tall evergreen trees.

"Everygreens is nearly in the woods. Backs right up to a state park. There's a giant oak tree right by Rusty's trailer." Marilyn coughed as if stopping herself from saying something.

Aster had only known kindness from this woman, but she couldn't help the concern itching at the back of her mind. She pulled at her pearls as they turned into the park. The large wooden sign with raised letters announced: Evergreen Park.

"The trailer is near the back. We've got to make a quick stop first." They stopped at a large baby-blue doublewide trailer framed by lilac bushes, windchimes singing from their metal hooks, and a bed of multi-colored flowers with a path of cement circles leading up to the door.

Liam scrambled to get out of the backseat first, opening her door for her. Aster rested her hand on top of his head. "Thank you."

He nodded and grabbed her hand, blue eyes full of concern. "You look tired, Mom."

She forced a full smile, she didn't want him to worry. "I'm alright. Just a little sleepy from the medicine. After we settle in, I'll get some rest."

Marilyn knocked on the door as Aster noticed the Office sign and rent drop off box. Her eyes moved to the flowers, it smelled so wonderful. Maybe she could plant some things by the trailer? June was just starting; hopefully she wasn't too late.

"Mom, look, a hummingbird." Liam whisper-yelled as he pointed to the jewel-toned bird sipping from a flower up the path.

"Very pretty." She watched the tiny creature flit about before zipping away when the office door opened.

A woman, who looked roughly Marilyn's age came out, a ball cap firmly on her head, with locks of pink and purple peeking out. "Hand to god, you could be Lillian's twin from our crazy days."

Margie. This was Margie. Aster had spoken to her on the phone. Her grandfather, Charles, was the only family member who'd been in her corner when she left Allen. He had told her about Grandma Lillian's friend up north. Margie had the same phone number for more than 40 years, and it had been a ray of hope for Aster.

Margie had a slight limp but confidently walked up to Aster, as Liam ducked behind her. Her dark brown eyes misted over as she cupped Aster's chin in her hands. "Just look at you. I'm so glad you got here. Welcome."

"Margie! Ask before you get in someone's space. Chrissakes she just got out the hospital." The new voice, laced with a New York accent, came from a woman in overalls decorated with iron-on patches.

"She frets. Sounds angry. Always fretting." Margie winked and stepped back, but caught Aster's free hand. "I'm Margie and that's my roommate Bridgette. If you need anything—and I mean *anything*—you let us know. If we have another trailer open up, it's all yours."

"If I can afford—" Aster started, but was promptly cut off.

"That's not what she said." Bridgette offered her hand. Colorful tattoos covered her arms, one particular one was the image of the virgin Mary with folded hands that was slightly faded. "Nice to meet you, Aster. And hello to you too, young man."

Liam leaned around, but kept a tight grip on Aster's hand. "Hello, nice to meet you both." He bobbed his head.

Marilyn cleared her throat. "It's almost six and we've got groceries in the car. Just wanted to stop and say hi. These two need to get settled."

"Fair enough. We'll swing by tomorrow and see if you need anything. Rusty's been slow repairing that trailer." Bridgette shook her head.

"Oh he's been doing just fine. Don't let her scare you. She's a Virgo and nothing's ever good enough." Margie shooed them back to Marilyn's car.

"Then why am I still with you?" Bridgette questioned.

"Because *I* am your perfect work in progress." Margie chuckled before thanking Bridgette for handing her a flower.

Marilyn drove slowly down the packed-down dirt roads that connected the park. Near the end of the path, overlooking the woods and the oak tree Marilyn had described was a tiny mint-green trailer with a man exiting it wiping off his hands. *He wasn't Russ. Who was this?*

Marilyn got out first.

"Stay in the car for a second, Liam." Aster climbed out before her son could argue.

"Working like new." The short red-haired man swung the door back and forth.

"I appreciate it. It looks like you added new wood to the frame there." Marilyn was looking over the work critically. "Did you need to?"

"You wound me, Marilyn. I wouldn't do extra work just to add to Russ's tab." He tightened the bandanna on his head. "You must be Aster. I'm Nestor."

She nodded, fingers moving to her necklace, thumb rubbing over the smoothness of the pearls.

"Everything should be good in that second bathroom now." He swung over the rail and handed her a ring with two keys on it. "One for you and one for your kid." He grinned and waved at Liam through the car window.

Marilyn opened the trunk. "Nestor, help me carry these bags in, please."

"Of course. I remember the rules: never argue with Grandma Marilyn."

Chapter II

Marilyn and Nestor had helped get her bags into the trailer, pointed out where things were and promptly exited to give her and Liam some space.

"Should we make something to eat first? Chicken nuggets and french fries maybe?" Aster hated to make a junk food meal, but she was exhausted.

Liam, who had been wandering around the limited space, stopped and itched his head. "I guess. Or maybe soup and grilled cheese? It smells like soup in here."

It did smell like soup. Aster checked the slow cooker on the counter and there was a note on the lid: **Tomato soup - Not fancy. Dinner if you want.**

What a thoughtful gesture and one of her favorite comfort foods. Russ couldn't have known. Aster smiled. "Marilyn said the room you can sleep in is just past the living room. Go put your backpack and blanket in there, and I'll see if I can find the pots and pans."

"Okay!" Liam nearly tripped himself with the blanket dragging on the ground. He folded it up better and raced down the hall. His heavy steps rattled the walls.

The thin walls were going to take getting used to. She'd need to be so careful not to be noisy and to walk softly. Get Liam trained on that too. They were guests. Her throat felt tight and she coughed before letting go of her pearls.

"MOM!"

Liam's scream sent her running down the hallway. Aster wasn't sure what he was upset about, but she wasn't taking any chances.

"Mom, look!" Liam wasn't scared or upset. He'd been yelling in excitement, his eyes shining. "Look. This is a room for me!"

The room was decorated simply: a bed, a desk with a chair, a bookshelf, a storage box, an open closet, and a little dartboard with plastic tipped darts. There were books on the shelf, clothes in the closet, sheets and a pillow on the bed with a stuffed shark. It wasn't a place for Liam to sleep, it was a room for him.

Tears filled Aster's eyes and she hurriedly wiped them away as Liam whirled around to face her.

"I'm too old for stuffed toys, but we shouldn't tell Grandma Marilyn. She must have done this." He climbed onto the bed, careful to keep his 'in the house' shoes off the bed. "There's a giant tree outside! I think I like it here."

"Russ must have helped with all of this," she muttered, more to herself.

"Naw. He wouldn't have. He's a creep."

Aster sat next to Liam on the bed. "You have to stop saying that. He's letting us stay with him. You need to be polite."

"But he was sleeping in his car and dad said that homeless...."

"No." Aster snapped, making Liam jump. She clasped and unclasped her hands. "I'm sorry. I shouldn't have raised my voice. But you know not everything your dad says is correct, right?"

"I do." Liam hugged the shark plushie, despite his insistence on being too old for it.

She sighed. "Russ works at the hospital, and obviously he's not homeless. We're in his home. He was probably taking his break. You need to be nice to him. Do you think you can try that for me?"

Liam dropped the toy and wrapped his arms around her. "I'll try, Mom, promise. It's gonna be good here. I know it."

Aster kissed the top of his head. "It will. Now let's make grilled cheese to go with the soup." She yawned. "And maybe go to sleep a bit early."

Dinner was simple, and as Aster moved throughout the space, she found notes everywhere. Russ's handwriting was scrawling and messy but legible. And the notes were incredibly helpful. A note on the microwave warned not to use it at the same time as the dryer. Notes on the washer and dryer that they couldn't be used at the same time either. Note on the mirror in the bathroom closer to Liam's room to turn the fan on if they used the shower since the steam would set off the smoke detector. There were three notes by the black box for his monitor to NOT touch under any circumstances.

Aster made sure Liam understood that he was never to run by that box, throw anything in the direction of that box, and basically to keep away from it at all costs.

She washed dishes while Liam took his bath and changed into the clean pajamas that had been bought and washed for him. There was also a note that the rest of those clothes still needed to be washed. Maybe she should start on that tonight? She leaned against the counter as she got through another coughing fit and decided that dishes were enough cleaning up for now.

"Are you okay, Mom?"

She nodded, gripping the counter as she caught her breath and spitting into the sink before rinsing the blood down the drain. "Ready for bed?"

"I guess." Liam shifted on his feet.

They'd been sleeping in the car for weeks, curled up in the backseat together, washing up in gas station bathrooms and eating snacks instead of real food. It must feel strange for him to have a bed again.

"Come on, my little prince. I'll read you a story, and I think I saw a light in there for you. Just because it's a new space."

There was a nightlight in the room, one of those atmospheric lights. When she turned it on, it painted the ceiling like an ocean with moving water and swimming fish on a loop. She only made it halfway through Robin Hood, when she noticed Liam was already sound asleep.

Aster brushed away the stubborn locks of blond hair that always seemed to cover his right eye and kissed his forehead. "Sleep tight. I love you."

She hesitated to close the door, but he would be fine. There wasn't far to go in the trailer. The only note that had been folded over had been taped to the refrigerator; it had her name on it.

Aster took her dose of medicine for the night and filled a glass of water before sitting on the couch. She didn't see any coasters, so she set the glass on the linoleum floor.

Aster.

Sorry we're missing each other. I know that makes it awkward as hell. I'm done with work about 6 and I'll be home no later than 7. I have to charge my monitor, so I'll be in the kitchen for at least two hours before I can go lay down to catch some sleep. You can sleep in the bed tonight, if you want. The sheets are clean.

If you want to sleep on the couch, there are extra blankets on the end of my bed. If you use the bathroom nearer to the main bedroom to clean up, let the water run for a minute before you get in. The second bathroom and kitchen are fine. I'll have Nestor come look at it when I can (he's a handyman of sorts). Help yourself to anything you want as far as food. Eggs especially. Hope Liam likes the room. If he wants to change anything, that's cool.

There's pajamas in the dryer for you. My grandmother handled those, not me. My cellphone and hospital number are by the phone on wall—call if you have questions. Just don't unplug the monitor (black box with all the neon notes on/by it). I'll explain how that all works tomorrow. I'll see you tomorrow and we'll figure the ins and outs out. Get some rest.

-Russ

P.S. There's peppermint tea in the cupboard by the stove. Supposed to help with getting junk out lungs. Hope that helps.

- The trailer creaks when the wind picks up, but it won't blow-over. You're safe.

Aster re-read the note until she couldn't make out the words. Tears dripped down her cheeks and stained her shirt. On shaking legs she retrieved the pajamas from the dryer and inhaled the clean scent of fabric softener. She held them to her chest as she dropped to her knees sobbing, that word echoing in her mind. *Safe. Safe. She was safe.*

CHAPTER 12

Aster expected a sleepless and restless night, so the sound of the trailer door opening nearly sent her off the couch in shock.

"Shit." Russ closed and locked the door behind him. "Sorry. I didn't think you'd be sleeping on the couch."

She covered her mouth as she coughed, shoulders shaking as it intensified. Russ's footsteps were definitive as they got closer to her, but he stopped short of touching her. He handed her the tissue box from the coffee table. She spit and sat up more fully, pulling the blanket to her chest.

"You good?" He knelt in front of her, still keeping his hands to himself.

Aster nodded, not trusting her own voice and she could hear a beeping now.

"I need to go plug my monitor in, but I'll be in the kitchen if you need me." He grabbed one of the dining table chairs and took it with him to the kitchen area.

The trailer was open so she had a clear line of sight and watched him connect the cord from the black box to the device around his ankle.

"You can go sleep in the bedroom if you want," Russ offered. He got himself a glass of water, seeming to have just enough tether to reach the sink.

Her pearls refastened around her neck, she blew her nose and took a drink from her own cup of water. "I don't think I'm comfortable with you being between me and my son."

She winced, expecting Russ to be offended. He'd been nothing but kind, and she was all but accusing him of trying to hurt Liam. How ungrateful could one person be? She needed to apologize.

"That's fair."

Aster uncurled her fingers from her necklace and stared at him mouth agape.

He wasn't looking in her direction, his back was to her as he looked through his own cupboards. He pulled out a packet of instant lemonade and shook a bit into his glass. Thunk, thunk, thunk the spoon hit against the inside of the cup. He finished mixing his drink and leaned against the counter, facing her again.

"You wanna talk things out, since you're awake? If not, I can read so you can go back to sleep."

She looked at the clock on the DVD player. It was 6:30. The sun was already pouring in through the windows. Maybe she could make some thicker curtains? Whichever of them was sleeping in the living room would appreciate it. It was so bright, it seemed brighter than it should be this early. Daylight savings time was in effect here. She'd had to change her watch when she was in the hospital.

"Liam will be awake soon." Aster got to her feet and took one of the chairs with her to the kitchen. "He's an early riser."

"Okay." Russ sat down on his chair and she on hers. They were about a foot apart, an invisible table between them. He looked down at her feet. "I see my grandma warned you about wearing shoes in the house."

She nodded. "Marilyn said that flip flops would probably be fine, but these were cheaper."

The off brand crocs were green and white adorned with the logo from the dollar store on the toe. She and Liam had matching pairs.

"It'll get muddy when it rains, so you don't wanna track the outside, inside. Then it's too cold to be barefoot in the winter and, as old as this unit is, I don't know if it's ever really clean enough." He shifted in his chair and took a long drink, his adam's apple bobbing as he swallowed. "You find everything you needed last night okay?"

The realization hit her like a brick. She hadn't said anything about the state of the trailer. "I did. The notes were helpful and I can't...." She rubbed her pearls with her thumb, trying to ground herself. "I can't thank you enough for Liam's room and the soup. It was too much and I don't know how to repay...."

"It's nothing." Russ touched her wrist, coaxing her hand down to her lap. "The soup was me, but the rest was my grandma's idea, and he'll need that stuff. We'll deal with you paying me back later, if we need to."

Aster let her hand fall as he directed it, the heat from his hand warming hers. He pulled his hand away and scratched at his collarbone, t-shirt moving enough for her to see a date tattooed under his collar.

"You aren't wearing your uniform," she blurted out, then clapped her hand over her mouth.

"Pastel green isn't my color. It's already muggy outside, I took it off when I got off shift." Russ arched his eyebrow. "Are we gonna have a dress code while you're staying here?"

Aster blushed and focused on her own hands. "No, no. I just realized you weren't wearing it because I saw your tattoo." She touched her collarbone. "Which is fine. Those are your tattoos and your body. I wouldn't want to make rules about your space. As in a dress code or really anything else. That's not fair to you. This is your home; we're guests."

"Hey, Aster—" Russ interrupted her. "You aren't a guest. If you're uncomfortable with something here, you say so. If you need anything changed around, you do so. This is *your* space too. You and Liam should be comfortable in your space."

He leaned forward, resting his elbows on his knees and his chin on his hands. "I don't need the details, but what made you run? Did Liam's dad hurt you guys?"

"No, it..." Aster could barely force the word out through her tightening throat. "It could have gotten there, but it didn't. We got out before it was bad. Our divorce was finalized earlier this year. I wanted to let Liam finish the school year before we moved. We stayed with friends, it was fine."

"Okay." Russ didn't look convinced.

Aster was used to no one believing her. Leaving her town and her step-daughter behind had painted her in a bad light. Even though Allison hadn't wanted anything to do with her by the end, she felt guilty about it. Aster had become Allison's stepmother when she was seven, but had been in the girl's life since she was a toddler. She thought of herself as a mother of two, but her husband... Allen had made it clear how he felt about her son before she left the house she'd called home with only a suitcase. Allison was *his* child and Liam was her son. She bit down on her lip.

"So this isn't the worst trailer in the world, but it'll get hot this summer and cold in the winter."

This was the second time he mentioned the cold. Aster made a mental note to check thrift stores for warm clothes and a coat for Liam.

"I'm gonna try and find a window AC unit for the living room. If it gets miserably hot, then we might all be camping in here for the sake of sanity." Russ explained then took a drink of water. "Any allergies for you or Liam?"

Aster shook her head.

"Okay. Anything you or the kid won't eat?"

"I can cook for us." She volunteered. "I don't want to be a problem."

"Not a problem. I'm used to cooking." He sighed and tapped the counter restlessly. "Cooking calms me down. I *like* to cook. Unless you have a burning desire to be in charge of the meals, I'm happy being the chef here in my kitchen as I get an actual say in the menu. Eggs, eggs and more eggs for every damn meal."

A giggle erupted from Aster. She had no idea why it struck her as funny, but she couldn't stop herself. Through her laughter she asked, "Why do you hate eggs so much?"

Russ blinked at her, head inclined to the side. Her laughter must have completely confused him. After another moment of her trying unsuccessfully to stop laughing, he nearly started laughing with her.

One corner of his mouth pulled up as he fought back his growing smile, revealing a dimple on his right cheek. It finally transformed into a lopsided grin as he explained. "Erica lives a trailer down and has chickens. In a pinch, I can always get eggs to eat without making my grandma go shop for me. It's hard to get groceries due to the whole house arrest thing. For the last five months, I've eaten more eggs than I have in the past five years."

"So groceries can be my job, and I can pay of course."

"Part. You can pay for part of it. I'm going to be eating too."

"But you're cooking." She countered, forcing herself to keep her hands in her lap. He couldn't give her money for the food and then do all the cooking.

"Yeah, but I get to be lazy and not do dishes." His half smile re-appeared. "Cause I think that'll be a perfect job for the pup."

"I told him that needs to be nicer to you." Aster truly felt bad for all the attitude Liam had given Russ. Her son had manners, but it was like the divorce and their subsequent move had changed him. He was still sweet to her, but he seemed to be distrustful of everyone else. Marilyn was the first person she'd seen him be open or receptive to in ages. He'd always been a gentle and kind boy. His recent temper confused her, but it wasn't his fault. He was scared. "I'm sorry he's been so aggressive."

Russ waved it off and stretched one of his legs out. "He's trying to protect you. He seems like a good kid. Custody gonna be a thing? I need to know if his dad's gonna show up here to pick him up."

"No." She glanced down the hall to Liam's door. "He didn't want to see Liam again after we left."

"Asshole." Russ stood up and pulled down the coffee pot. "You want coffee?"

"I thought you were going to bed after your monitor charged." She was confused. Russ told her that he was working until Saturday then had Sunday and Monday off. *Didn't he need to sleep?*

"Not making it for me. You said Liam's an early riser and it's after 7. What does he like for breakfast? Maybe I can start winning him over."

"I don't think making him waffles will win him over completely," Aster countered, smirking despite herself, "but it's not a bad way to start."

"Hmmm." Russ took the container of heavy cream out of the fridge and put it into the freezer. "We'll see about that when I make the whipped cream to go on top of them."

CHAPTER 13

Hot water poured down Russ's body as he scrubbed himself clean. Fridays were officially going to be his least favorite day. Anger management on Thursdays at 8 AM, hopefully a nap before the overnight shift, trying to sleep immediately after getting home, and needing to be back to work by 1 PM. He said a prayer for Jerry to find another monitor with a replacement battery. Not getting to bed until 9 AM and running on three hours of sleep was going to be the absolute death of him.

He turned off the water and ruffled the excess water out of his ever lengthening hair with his towel. Add a haircut to the list of things he needed in addition to sleep and a caffeine IV. Breakfast hadn't been a total disaster, but it could have gone smoother. The aftermath was still replaying in his mind.

Liam had eaten two full plates of waffles, but eyed Russ like he had horns whenever Aster wasn't paying attention. It probably didn't help that Aster and Liam had eaten at the table and he had been stuck on his chair in the kitchen. The trailer needed more electrical plugs or a long extension cord that he could drag throughout the house.

Aster had started on the dishes when Liam marched up to him and asked point blank if he'd killed someone. Aster had dropped the plate in her hands and it shattered when it hit the ground. Russ's fists clenched not from anger over the broken dish, but from the rush of apologies from Aster and the sheer terror on her face. Liam had flinched away, racing to help his mother clean up the mess.

Russ had unplugged his monitor and hauled Aster up from the floor, worried she was going to hurt herself. It had been the wrong move. She'd cried out and nearly fallen, trying to get away from his grasp. Thankfully he'd kept her on her feet, but they'd locked eyes for a moment and he knew that look. He'd terrified her and Liam got between them without a moment's hesitation. Barking that Russ better not hurt her and the accident was his fault for asking a bad question.

Russ couldn't leave the space because of the damn charger. He could have gone into the bedroom, but his brain was so frazzled from upsetting her that he blanked on the fact that he didn't have to be in *that* room. He apologized for scaring her and asked her if she and Liam could take his car to fill it with gas and pick up vegetables for dinner. He'd handed her sixty bucks and within twenty minutes the pair were dressed and out the door. Aster assured him they'd be back before noon before locking the door behind her.

He wiped steam from the mirror, staring at his reflection. Did he look thirty-five? He felt eighty-five. Tattoos decorated most of his body. Idiotic boredom or alcohol had been the cause of most of them, but not the date over his heart. The date over his heart was the day his grandparents had officially adopted him, and like his best mile time on his knuckles, it meant something to him.

Russ pulled on a pair of black shorts and flopped on his back on his bed. Thankfully he'd remembered to turn on the stupid overhead fan. Too hot. He was already too damn hot. When he got mad, he got hot sometimes.

Deep breath in. One. Two. Three. Hold it. One. Two. Three. Deep breath out. One. Two. Three. Repeat.

Calm. He needed to calm down. Then the memory of Aster's eyes. The fucking terror in her eyes. *What had her ex done to her?* Russ had a court ordered obligation to abstain from violence, but if he ever saw this asshole in person, it might be worth breaking that rule.

But then seeing the light in her eyes when Aster had giggled. There was something so crystal clear in her moment of joy that made it impossible to resist the urge to break down and laugh with her. Even if he controlled himself for the most part, he hadn't been able to keep from smiling.

Objectively Aster was a beautiful woman, but then there was Aster when she was happy. Happy Aster looked like a yellow flower turning its face towards the sun. Happy Aster sounded like a song that Russ had never heard, but knew he'd be singing along with it whenever it came on. People could be objectively beautiful on the outside, but ugly on the inside. Aster was the kind of pretty that came from the inside out. She shined in those little moments of joy he'd glimpsed. But the fear from this morning? Just as intense. It concerned Russ. While her ex might have stopped short of hitting her like she said, he'd hurt her in other ways.

Whatever he had done to Aster and Liam it was clear that getting away was the best thing for them. They could spend the summer here. With everyone that his grandmother knew, Aster could get a job. There was a school not too far from here. What grade were eight-year-old kids in, third or fourth? That sounded right.

There was also the nagging thought that Aster shouldn't be sleeping on the couch. But if she was comfortable there, then who was he to argue? His grandfather would kick his ass if he knew that he was letting a lady sleep on the couch. Those dinosaur-aged values were ingrained in him, but Russ couldn't force Aster to be where she didn't want to be. He had this sinking feeling that being manipulated was part of Aster's past.

Her constant pulling on those pearls worried him. He knew a coping mechanism when he saw one. There was a reason he liked to keep the wall at his back. Better to know no one was coming up behind him.

As much as he knew this living situation was going to be awkward, he'd be lying if he said he was unhappy with the company. Even if half of the company was a nervous, aggressive kid who apparently thought Russ was capable of murder.

The door closed as Aster and Liam returned. Russ rubbed his hands over his face. He was absolutely fucked. The faster he found a new place the better. This place could be their new home. They didn't need him.

CHAPTER 14

Sunday morning. The sun was already blindingly bright even with his eyes still closed. It was too early, too bright, too hot, and something was burning. *Something was burning!* Russ flipped off the couch, smashing his knees against the unforgiving floor.

"Shit." He growled, scrambling up to his feet. Black smoke rising from the pan with Liam holding a cup of something to dump on whatever was in the pan. "Wait!" Russ barked. The last thing they needed was a grease fire if the kid had tried to make bacon.

Liam dropped the cup, water going everywhere. "But it's smoking, that means fire!"

Russ snatched the pan from the stove, noting it looked like batter of some kind and, and ran it under the sink, more smoke rising. He left the pan in the sink, cold water still running, and opened the window to let out the smoke. Crisis averted, he turned his attention to the mess on his counters. Flour dust, egg shells, and cut-up strawberries littered the space by an oversized mixing bowl.

"I think your stove works different. I didn't want it to burn. I was trying to make breakfast then it got messy and I was trying to clean up and then smoke and then...and then..." Liam's voice cracked. "My mom's still sleeping. I did this on my own. She didn't ask me to do anything. I did it. Don't be mad at her. It's not her fault. Be mad at me."

"Liam. I'm not mad." He sighed. "Get the paper towels and clean up the water."

Karma was a joke. Russ had convinced Aster to sleep in the bed last night, and this was the thanks he got from the universe. A messy kitchen, his trailer nearly being lit on fire, and the kid freaking out.

He assessed the frying pan, finding a plastic ring melted to it. Was that the ring from his measuring cups? *Fantastic*. Now they needed a new pan. What the hell had he been trying to make?

The kid was on his hands and knees soaking up the water using one sheet at a time. Since Liam wasn't paying attention Russ swiped a spoon into the batter and tasted it. *Fuck!* He barely resisted gagging on whatever it was. It was somehow too sweet and intensely salty at the same time. If it wasn't so awful, Russ might have applauded Liam on his physics defying ingenuity.

"I'll clean it up. You won't even know I messed everything up when I'm done." Liam dried the front of the counters, his voice up an octave. "It'll be like I never did it."

"Hey." Russ nudged Liam's foot with his own. "You messed up. It's not the end of the world. What were you trying to make?"

"Muffins." He muttered not looking up from the floor. "But you don't have a tin sheet like we had at my old house. And I thought I remembered the recipe, but then it was bad and it kept getting worse."

Russ knelt down to get on Liam's level. "You're right, I don't have a muffin pan. But I can show you how to make strawberry biscuits. Would you like that? Were you trying to make them for your mom?"

"But I messed up." Liam narrowed his eyes at Russ. "Why would you help me after I ruined things?"

He sighed and pushed himself back upright. This kid. "Nobody's perfect."

"Allison is." He wadded up the soaked paper towels and put them in the trash. "She excels. Always in the top percentiles. She doesn't fail."

"Who's Allison?" That was a name that Russ hadn't heard before. A cousin maybe?

"My half-sister. She hates me. I took all the attention from my mom and stole her birthday."

Russ liked to think of himself as a guy who could put a mystery together, but Liam's answer left him stumped. He didn't want to push, as the kid looked a minute away from crying. Weird shit to say about his sister. Kids didn't come up with 'top percentiles' on their own, not at eight. He had to have heard the phrase tossed around by an adult. Probably by his dad, because Russ couldn't see Aster talking to Liam like that. But stolen her birthday? What did that even mean? Kids said wild shit.

"Well, she's not here and you are. Let's finish cleaning up, and I'll show you how to make the biscuits." He dumped the batter into the trashcan and pointed Liam towards the stove to finish wiping it down. "Did you use all the strawberries you and your mom picked yesterday?"

"No. There's still a green box in the fridge."

Russ pulled the strawberries, butter, and heavy cream out of the fridge. "Get the pan out from under the oven drawer then turn it on to 450. Can you reach?"

"Yeah on my tiptoes." Liam did as he was told.

The part of this fiasco Russ found the most shocking was Aster hadn't woken up during any of the crashing around. She must have been as tired as Russ was afraid she was. It was good she was still sleeping.

"There's a step-stool by the washer and dryer. Go grab it."

"Why?"

Ah there was the feisty pup in child form Russ was used to. The defiance was better than him being fearful.

"Cause you're too short to see what we're gonna do without it." Russ chuckled and despite a huff, Liam went and retrieved it.

He handed Liam a whisk and put the flour, sugar, and baking powder into the bowl. "Keep the whisk in the bowl and make little circles, not too fast or we'll have flour everywhere."

Liam bit his lip, repeating the instructions while performing them as Russ chopped up the butter.

"I'm gonna put the butter in a couple of pieces at a time and we're gonna mix it with our hands."

"We should wash our hands first."

"Good call." Russ nodded.

He had to help Liam work the butter into the dough, it wasn't the easiest task, but Liam certainly didn't give up. The kid was determined to learn and do it correctly. They added the rest of the ingredients and greased the pan before putting it into the oven to bake.

"Who taught you to zest lemons?" Russ questioned as he and Liam washed the dishes.

Liam dried the fork Russ handed him carefully. "The TV. Mom likes lemon things."

"Good to know."

Liam put the utensils away and pushed the drawer closed. "Thank you, Russ."

"No prob—"

"Something smells good." Aster came around the corner, skirt swishing around her ankles. Her pale pink t-shirt complimented the flowery bandanna covering her head. She looked less tired than yesterday, healthier even. It had been the right call to push the issue of her taking the bed.

"Mom! I made strawberry biscuits to share." Liam ran to his mother and hugged her legs tightly. "Russ helped a little, I guess."

She hugged her son, but her eyes met Russ's as she mouthed a 'thank you' with a blindingly bright smile. "That was nice of him. I'm sure they're amazing."

It stirred something in Russ. Seeing her smile made him feel out of sorts. Nope. This wasn't okay. Aster was staying here to get on her feet. He could not be looking at her like he was. Time to get his head back on straight. The last thing this poor woman needed was more drama in her life.

"No trouble. Gonna take a shower. Liam, keep your eye on the timer and be careful not to burn yourself."

Liam stomped his foot. "I know. You told me three times already!"

"Then I'm telling you a fourth time." Russ shut the bathroom door with more force than he intended. He situated the plastic bag over his monitor and started his ice-cold shower.

The trailer was dark when a creak broke the quiet, throwing Russ out of sleep, off the couch, and to his feet. "What the fuck?"

Aster jumped back from the board she stepped on, eyes huge, coughing from her prior gasp and attempting to apologize. "Sorry," another cough racked her frame and she put her hand on the back of the couch, "I didn't mean...I'm sorry...I—"

He rounded the couch and touched her elbow. "Easy. Sit down, I'll get you some water."

She sat down on the couch, but seemed to be catching her breath.

"You want your painkillers?" He paced to the kitchen, yawing and still feeling disorientated.

Aster shook her head and kept her arms pulled close to her chest. He handed her the glass of water and sat down on his chair, running his hands over his face.

She gulped down some of the water, before setting the cup on the coffee table. "I'm sorry. I didn't mean to startle you." She was wearing a t-shirt, sleep-pants and a bandanna covered her hair, but all of her exposed skin was covered a sheen of sweat.

Russ yawned again. "Too hot or are you hurting?"

"I'm still sore, but the only prescription the hospital gave me was for blood thinners." Her hands went to her neck, but her pearls weren't there. She fidgeted with the collar of her shirt tugging it up higher. "And I'm hot. We had air conditioning in the house before."

He nodded and forced himself back up. "I got a trick for that." He passed her the TV remote, requesting, "find something boring. We need to kill twenty minutes."

Her eyes were full of questions, but she didn't ask any of them, so he continued with his task. He went straight to the bedroom and yanked the top sheet off the bed taking it with him.

"What are you doing?" Aster wondered as he opened the freezer door.

"Helping." He stuffed the fabric inside and grabbed himself a bottle of water before returning to the living room. His eyes went to the screen. An infomercial about a cleaning product was playing.

"Why did you put the sheet in the freezer?" She persisted.

Russ closed his eyes. "I'll show you in twenty minutes. Are you alright?"

Aster gulped down more water. "I think so. Nightmares."

He made the mistake of glancing over at her and she had pulled her knees up to her chest. "You wanna talk about it?"

"Can't. I never remember my dreams, only the feelings they give me."

Russ arched his eyebrow. "You never remember your dream? Never, never?"

"Honestly, I couldn't tell you a single dream I've ever had." She shook her head. "Do you remember yours?"

Sometimes too well, especially since you've been in them lately. He leaned back against his chair, trying to crack his back. "Here and there. Sometimes, I think I've already gotten around and ready for work, then my alarm goes off. Those are the worst."

Aster's shoulders shook as she quietly laughed. "I can imagine." She lowered her eyes, "I'm so sorry I startled you awake. I feel—"

"Please don't feel bad or apologize. I'm jumpy." Russ sighed before continuing, "It isn't like you did it on purpose to mess with me. Did you?"

She shook her head, but seemed to understand that he was picking on her. "Of course not. I'm not used to the creaking."

"Your house didn't moan and groan?"

"No." She hugged her legs tighter. "It was built just before Allison was born so it was basically new when I moved in. Carla designed it."

That was a name that didn't sound familiar, but Russ had a theory. "Carla was your ex's wife before you?"

Aster nodded.

"Surprised your ex got to keep the house when they split." To his knowledge divorce meant splitting all the assets so the house should have been sold. Shouldn't it?

"They didn't split." She corrected quietly, "Carla died when Allison was four. I was the second wife."

"So, Allison is Liam's half-sister."

Aster nodded, and picked up the cup taking another long drink. Clearly this wasn't something she wanted to talk about.

His eyes went back to the TV and attempted to change the subject. "You think that pink foaming stuff would get the stains off the bathroom floor?"

She looked confused, then realized he was referring to the infomercial still playing. "I don't know. Why?"

"Dunno." He shrugged. "You ever order a dumb something from one of these?"

"No. Why would I? They always seem silly." She yawned and leaned against the arm of the couch. "Have you?"

"No, but my grandma did once. It was a dehydrator to make your own jerky and shit like that." Russ smirked at the memory. "Worked great until it caught on fire. Grandpa was pissed when he found out."

"He wasn't there when it happened?"

"He was, but he was in the garage. Grandma put out the fire, gathered me up, and we went to McDonalds." He chuckled. "Grandpa came there spitting mad and all she did was give him a hamburger and a coke."

Aster covered her mouth as she yawned. "He didn't yell at her?"

"He yelled plenty, but not at her." Russ ran his tongue over his teeth. "Grandma was not-so-secretly excited because she knew he'd wanna replace all the cabinets so they'd match. We spent the whole summer re-doing the kitchen."

"How old were you?"

"Ten, I think. I was still in elementary school." He scratched his goatee. "Hey, don't be falling asleep. You're going back to bed, so I can have my couch."

"I'd offer to sleep out here, but it's so hot in the bedroom, I think you'd be more miserable." Aster sat back up, eyes drooping closed.

"Should be fine with the window open." He was confused now.

"I couldn't get it open." She admitted sheepishly.

He sighed. "Then say something. It'll take me less then a minute to fix that, and I don't want *you* to be miserable. Hang on."

Russ paced back to the bedroom and gave the window two quick shoves before it opened with a whine. He'd grease it before he went to work, if he had any WD-40 and if he didn't, he'd risk the detour and grab it from the gas station.

He paused in the kitchen and took the sheet out of the freezer. "Up on your feet and come 'ere," he beckoned.

Aster walked on the balls of her feet to get to him and took the sheet when he offered it. "It's cold."

Russ smirked and tapped her nose. "Poor man's trick. Lay down with the cool sheet on top of you and should be able to fall asleep."

"Oh." She grinned up at him. "Thank you."

He motioned for her to go. "It doesn't last long. Go. Goodnight."

"Goodnight." Aster nodded and retreated into the bedroom.

Russ crashed back onto the couch with a heavy sigh. Every time he learned something about Aster's ex, it made him want to punch something. That fear in her eyes when she'd woken him up, he hated it.

Deep breath in. One. Two. Three. Hold it. One. Two. Three. Deep breath out. One. Two. Three. Repeat. Don't think angry thoughts while you're trying to sleep.

Aster's smile popped into Russ' mind and he cursed. *No, thinking about that would be even worse. Do not think about the pretty lady living in the trailer with you. Bad, bad idea.*

CHAPTER 15

"I think your friend is here." Aster peeked out the window of the trailer. "A green minivan just pulled up."

Russ nodded and stirred the garlic potatoes one last time. He unhooked the ankle monitor cord and made sure the burner was off.

He heard Aster telling Liam to mind his manners with Russ's friend and Liam agreeing, but the nervousness was clear in his voice.

"Marc's a nice guy. He's just...tall." Russ trailed off after his own awful description.

"Tall?" Aster questioned.

Russ held his hand a few inches over his head. "Tall."

The three filed out of the trailer as Marc and his family got out of their car.

Russ remembered Marc's wife's name was Sariyah, but he didn't know any of his kids' names. There were three little girls with various colored braids and a baby dressed in lavender in Marc's arms.

"Nice little place." Marc nodded and offered his free hand to Aster. "Pleasure to meet you, Aster." He looked down at Liam, who'd raced next to his mother. "And you're Liam? Excited about your treehouse?"

"Yes, sir." Liam nodded his head.

Russ was flabbergasted, feeling his blood pressure rise. *What the hell? This was some horse-shit!* He wasn't going to fight an actual child, but why did he get creep right off the bat and Marc got a sir and a nod? Rude.

"This is Joi." The baby grinned at her father as he used her name and his other daughters waved as he introduced them, "Imani, Noni, and Zuri. Liam, I think Noni's your age. Aren't you eight?"

"Yes, sir."

"I'm Sariyah, Marc's wife." Sariyah shook Aster's hand and nodded at Russ, before holding out her hands for her youngest. "Alright. Gimme Joi and start unloading the van, before everyone gets here." She inclined her head to her older daughters. "Girls, snap to it. We've got set-up to get done. Imani, help your sisters."

"Yes, ma'am." Imani was the tallest. She had light pink and black braids. Based on how she directed her younger sisters, she must be the oldest.

"Liam, why don't you help..." Aster trailed off and looked around her. "Liam? Where did you go?"

Russ could see the panic in her eyes. Not having Liam in her line of sight made her nervous. He glanced around and chuckled, pointing behind Aster to where Liam had gotten to. The kid held out flowers for the girls, handing a daisy to each one of them.

Noni batted her eyelashes at Liam as she smelled the white flower in her fingers.

"Oh. How cute!" Sariyah cooed to Aster. "You've got a little gentleman on your hands."

"Hmmm." Marc narrowed his eyes at the sight.

"You settle down." Sariyah patted Marc's broad chest. "He's being sweet."

Russ brushed by Aster, whispering low enough so their company wouldn't hear. "Um, he stole those from Erica's flower bed. Blame the chickens if she makes a fuss."

Aster clapped her hands over her mouth as his grandmother pulled up with two white vans behind her gold sedan.

It was officially a party now. Now if they could manage to build this thing without anyone noticing his ankle monitor, it would be a good day. Marc said his people were all from his church. Marc worked with their prison ministry, but there was a difference in working with convicts inside the prison versus associating with them in the wild.

His grandmother waved as she got out of her car. "Rusty!"

"Grandma Marilyn!" Liam rushed over and hugged the older woman.

"Rusty, huh?" Marc snickered.

Russ looked up at his boss. "I'd rather everyone keep calling me Russet if it's all the same to you."

"Like a potato?" Aster wondered aloud.

"Yes, because I am a potato."

Liam laughed loudly. "Creepy like a potato."

"Liam!" "Hey!" Aster and Russ responded to Liam in perfect sync.

Russ wasn't an idiot, and when his grandfather was alive, he'd helped out plenty. However he didn't recognize half of the tools that were hung up on the walls in Brother Thomas's van. The stacked up wood looked far too nice for their project. He figured they would use some old pallets or something. This was going to cost a fortune. He hoped he had enough to pay for all of this.

He glanced back to where Aster was sitting with Sariyah on a picnic blanket, rocking Joi in her arms. The sunlight reflected off the lighter locks of her short hair peeking out from the bandanna. Liam was playing hide and seek with the two girls closest to his age. Marc was setting up food on a white folding table with his grandmother. Russ also knew he wasn't imagining all the eyes in the park were definitely on their lot at the moment. The worst part of this, was he couldn't actually help with the actual building of the tree house. The oak tree they were building the tree house on was out of range for his monitor. He should have called Jerry. Surely the old man would have been willing to sit outside and watch for a plate of food and some company.

"You can take the lumber over to the saw horses and we'll start cutting after I measure a second time." Brother Thomas thumped Russ on the shoulder and pointed to the edge of his trailer's plot.

Russ didn't want to argue, but he also couldn't let all this work go into something he couldn't repay. "I appreciate all of this. But I figured we'd do something simpler. This looks like way too much and I'm not sure I have enough to cover...."

"With gusto." Thomas cut him off as he unhooked a triangle-shaped tool from the wall.

"Huh?" Arguably not his best response.

"Do it with gusto. Pride. Your will. Your all." The older man elaborated. "If it's worthy of doing, it's worthy of all the way, with everything you got. Everything I've built, from the Jackson building downtown to my kid's soapbox derby cars—I've built everything with my whole soul. If something I've built lives on, then I live on."

"That's an amazing way to live." Russ shoved his hands in his pockets. "I'm grateful for your help, Brother Thomas. But if I'm honest, I'm not sure how to pay you back for all this."

One of the girls squealed and laughed as Liam *tried* to tag her out, clearly letting the girl beat him to the designated safe zone.

Russ sighed. "I can't even help besides carrying things to a point. It's a lot of work that you and your friends are putting into this. You guys barely know me. Marc just met me, and I...."

Thomas laughed and shook his head. "Sometimes, you need to be okay with accepting help when you need it. We all need help now and then. Now, I'm too old to be lifting those boards. Get to it."

Russ acquiesced. "I can do that. Thank you."

"No trouble. Any friend of Marc's is a friend of mine."

CHAPTER 16

"Rusty, come help me with the tiller!" Marilyn called out and Russ jogged over to his grandmother's car, pulling out the gardening equipment. "It's only early June, we can still get peppers, tomatoes, and plenty of herbs planted in time."

A garden. Aster had always wanted a garden back home, but Allen had thought it was a waste of time. She patted baby Joi's back absent-mindedly as she watched Russ and Marilyn go back and forth on what part of the yard to dig up with the rototiller.

"I can take her if she's getting heavy. Lord knows it's hot to be holding a baby." Sariyah offered, taking a drink from her bottle of water.

"She's alright." Aster smiled down at the sleeping child. "I miss Liam being this small."

"He's such a little gentleman for being an only child." Sariyah inclined her head to where Liam was handing out water bottles.

Aster bit down on her lip. "He has a half-sister. Allison's seventeen. They were never very close."

"That's a pretty big age gap for sure." She adjusted her sunglasses. "Is she with your ex or with her mom?"

This was a hornet's nest waiting to be hit. Maybe it was better if she talked about it with someone? She'd been so alone with her feelings about Allison.

"Allison's with her father. Her mother passed away when she was four. I married Allen when she was seven."

"Instant family." Sariyah pursed her lips before asking. "How'd you meet him? Most single dads I know end up with single moms, cause they don't go out much. Church?"

Her fingers curled around her pearls. "Sort of. My parents owned a daycare that Allen's church recommended, and I worked there. Allison started attending when she was two."

"How old were you when you met him?"

Aster coughed, leaning her body away from Joi and Sariyah. "Sorry. I'll be right back." She handed Joi to her mother and scrambled up, rushing into the trailer. Her coughing fit continued and she doubled over as she wrapped an arm around herself.

It hurt, her throat hurt again. This was the first bad fit she'd had in a few days. It felt like someone had cut off her airway. She moved closer to the bathroom, worried she might throw-up. Her vision swam as she took unsteady steps, still choking.

The light in the bathroom was intense as she hit the switch, but it was her own reflection that made her stop. One of her hands was gripping her strand of pearls so tight to her neck it was constricting her breathing. She pulled her hand away from her neck and slid down to the floor.

Aster took long slow breaths, trying to make sense of herself.

Pressure makes perfect.

She took the necklace off and held it in her hands, her entire body shaking. Allen had given it to her right after they started dating. He'd bought her new clothes: dresses, skirts, slacks, and dressy tops to replace her t-shirt and jeans. More grown up. He'd wanted her to look like the adult she was instead of a highschooler. She had been nineteen when they'd gotten married, which was old enough to dress like a proper adult.

Pearls clutched in one hand, while the other touched the ends of her hair resting slightly below her jaw. Her hair....

"Aster?"

Russ's voice broke through her thoughts and she quickly refastened her necklace. She cleared her throat before answering. "I'm in here."

He poked his head in the bathroom. He was sweaty. The sun was merciless today. The trailer had an awning, which Russ had pulled out to make sure they had shade to sit under. His hair was longer than she thought it was.

"You alright? Sariyah said you rushed inside." His eyebrows were knitted together as he knelt down next to her leaving space between them.

Aster managed a nod. "Just a coughing fit. I didn't want to scare anyone."

"Running away tends to worry folks." Russ offered his lop-sided smile. "You're lucky it's just me checking in on ya."

She lowered her eyes, "Sorry, I...."

"Hey." Russ tapped the floor in front of her and she turned her attention back to him. "Don't apologize. You need a minute or you wanna come back out?"

"Can I have a minute?"

She requested it before she had time to stop herself. She really wanted a few moments of quiet to gather her thoughts and calm down. But Liam was out there, and they had guests, she needed to make sure everyone was taken care of. She was being a bad host. It was important to make a good impression. Marc was Russ's boss, and if she embarrassed him in front of his boss, that might affect his job. *What if—?*

"Take your time. Plenty of eyes on your pup. And he's being way nicer than I've ever seen him." Russ stood up, knees cracking as he straightened. "Should I be worried? Is he gonna spring another murder accusation at me? Cause I don't need more bad in my reputation."

She tried to stop it, but just like the other morning, he made her giggle. This time it erupted into full uncontrollable laughter. Despite the twinge of pain, it felt good to laugh.

Russ shook his head and held out his hand. "You want a hand up?"

Aster used his hand to balance herself as she got up off the floor, still giggling a bit. "Thank you." His hand was warm under hers, even keeping it flat the contact was like a small static shock. She blushed for sure, she could feel the heat in her cheeks.

He ran his hands through his hair to get it out of his eyes. "Come back out when you're ready."

She nodded, taking off her bandanna to fix it. Her hair was a disaster and she turned the water on to wash her hands.

"Oh, and Aster?" He leaned back in from the hall, but whatever he was going to say seemed to slip his mind. Russ was looking at her, seemingly seeing something that she was unaware of.

The water got warm over her hands.

"Yes?" she finally questioned, unable to guess what he wanted.

"Um. Did you..." He trailed off again then continued in a rush, "did you want to plant flowers? We can till up a patch for you while we're getting the garden done."

Aster grinned at him. "That would be amazing. If it's not too much trouble."

"No trouble. See ya out there in a bit"

Russ was gone from her sight and out the door before her hands reached the soap.

She washed her hands. Russ was a kind man. She and Liam were lucky to have met him. The sooner they could get out and on their own feet the better, it wasn't fair to impose on him. He deserved good things.

CHAPTER 17

Aster was sitting at the picnic table with Sariyah and Marilyn chewing her food slowly, forcing herself to relax. The men, sans Russ, were finishing up the treehouse, Russ was planting the garden and kids were playing in the space between their trailer and Erica's. She only knew who Erica was by name as Russ explained he got his eggs from her. Her chickens were ever present in their little fenced in area and, beyond, when they felt like it. Aster swore she heard Erica calling out to a man, but Russ said she lived alone.

"Liam, you need to get something to eat." She called him over receiving a dramatic groan in response.

"One more round, please!" he pleaded. "It's Noni's turn to be it."

Aster glanced at Sariyah before conceding. "One more hide and seek, then you need to eat and get some water."

"You girls too." Sariyah confirmed.

A chorus of "Yes, ma'am's" came from the little ones.

"You'll have to keep an eye out for frost, but you should be able to get plenty of tomatoes and peppers for sure." Marilyn took a drink from her disposable cup. "Potatoes too."

Sariyah switched Joi to her other shoulder. "Speaking of potatoes. Marilyn, did you make these garlic potatoes? They are amazing."

"Oh no, Rusty made those. He's always loved to cook." She laughed, before correcting herself. "Well maybe not always. He got lippy when he turned thirteen and said he didn't like my dinners, so I told him to cook for himself if he thought he could do better. Little turd cooked better than me after a week and half."

Aster covered her mouth as she laughed. Imagining a teenage Russ stubbornly adjusting a recipe until it was perfect, just to push his grandmother's buttons.

"Marilyn, could you hold Joi for a second? I'm gonna take some water over to those stubborn fools." Sariyah handed over her baby and Aster got up to help her hand out water.

After they distributed cups to everyone finishing up the treehouse, Aster got another cup for Russ. She walked over to where he was knelt in the dirt digging out a hole. "I have water for you." She held out the cup awkwardly.

Russ leaned back on his heels before accepting the cup and, after taking a drink, he poured the rest over his head. "Thanks. It's way hotter than I thought it would be today."

"No clouds," she said, pointing up. "What are the odds?"

"Only get ten sunny days a year, we must be some kind of lucky." He pointed to the flowers next to her feet. "Hand me one of the Marigolds?"

"Of course. Can I ask why plant flowers with the vegetables? Is it to attract bees?" She asked because she couldn't think of a reason to plant flowers here otherwise.

Russ pushed his hair back with a grunt. "Naw. They keep aphids off the tomatoes."

"You know a lot about gardening."

He chuckled as he planted the flower, patting the earth down around it. "Grandma always had a big garden. Grandpa was gone driving during the week, it was my responsibility to help."

A door slam made her jump. She needed to learn to relax. Every sound echoed in the park. Aster was nervous about Liam being too loud.

"Saul!" Erica's voice rang out from the other side of her trailer.

Russ was scrambling up from the ground.

"I thought you said she lived alone." Aster was confused as Russ rushed in the direction of his neighbor's trailer.

Liam screamed and Aster's heart stopped. He sounded terrified.

"No." A little girl's voice barked out as Aster rounded the corner on Russ' heels.

Noni stood shoulder to shoulder with Liam, her hand outstretched in a stop motion to the giant dog in front of them.

"Sit." Noni ordered and the dog complied.

"Well I'll be d..." Russ trailed off, as he got a hold of the dog's collar. "I'm surprised Saul listened to you."

Saul was as shaggy as he was tall. His fur was reddish and curly, but most dogs Aster had seen with fur like that were smaller. This dog was nearly as tall as the kids, his massive tail swished against the grass.

Noni shrugged her shoulders. "Dogs like me."

"You have campfire hair." Erica didn't appear as old as Marilyn, but her eyes had a far away look. She was staring at Noni.

"Thank you, Ma'am." She bobbed her head. "Is your dog friendly? May we pet him?"

Aster bit her lip. Liam was scared of dogs, he'd been bitten at a police outreach picnic.

"Saul's a Great Dane and a Spanish Water Dog all mixed up. He likes the chickens." Erica patted her dog's ginger head.

Russ tapped Erica on the shoulder. "She asked if they could pet him."

"Oh yeah. He's friendly." Erica grinned widely, showing off her missing front tooth.

"See, we can pet him." Noni extended her hand to Saul, petting his side with Liam following suit, despite his obvious nerves.

"Liam, show Noni where she can wash her hands, please. It's time to eat." Aster wasn't sure about a dog this big around the kids, but Russ's hand never left the dog's collar.

"Why don't you take him inside, Erica? Just 'cause of all the company."

"Oh surely. Lots of company to prepare for. You need eggs?" Erica started back to the trailer with Saul in tow.

"Not today. But thanks."

"Tomorrow then." Erica waved and disappeared.

Aster blinked. Why did it feel like Erica wasn't responding to the questions Russ was asking?

The trailer door banged open and closed. Aster needed to remind Liam not to slam the door. The door crashed open again.

"RUSS! The box is beeping and blinking red!" Liam yelled from the doorway.

Russ cursed under his breath and walked around his car.

"It stopped now!" Her son confirmed.

"Thanks, Pup."

Aster came up next to him. "I'm so sorry."

"It's fine." He shoved his hands in his pockets. "About Erica, she's fine. Just had a little too much fun in the sixties, so talk slow and take her in stride. Forgot about her dog, I'm so used to him lumbering around. Saul's harmless, he just slobbers and will steal food out of your hands."

"Thank you. I appreciate you being there." She pointed to the table. "You should get a plate. It looks like the tree house is done."

Liam raced up to them holding out his hands for Aster to inspect.

"I trust that you washed your hands." She pushed back his hair. "I think you need a haircut."

"No." Liam covered his head with his hands, then motioned for her to come closer.

Aster leaned down and Liam cupped his hands around her ear as he whispered his secret. "Noni, likes my hair. Don't cut it, Mom, please."

"I'll take your haircut. I need one." Russ chuckled and motioned to the treehouse. "You and your mom will have to paint it, but whaddya think of your treehouse?"

Liam rubbed his toe in the dirt of the driveway. "It's cool, but it's kinda high in the tree."

Noni raced up to Liam. "My momma says we can go up in your treehouse after we eat!" She grabbed his hand and dragged him to the table.

"Awesome. It'll be cool up there. I love climbing trees." Liam changed his tune with a bit of encouragement.

Aster smiled. Seeing Liam come out of his shell filled her with joy. The challenges were far from over, but he was happy here.

Russ brushed his grandmother's hands away from his shoulder as she picked on him about needing a haircut. Everyone at the table was sharing stories and laughing. She couldn't remember the last time a gathering felt this peaceful.

Sariyah waved her over. "Come sit."

CHAPTER 18

Aster and Liam had lived in her hot car for a couple of weeks, and they'd survived it, but they were spoiled by always having air conditioning in the house. The trailer had been miserably hot all day. Opening the windows helped, but she had to be careful about what appliances she used. Cooking in the slow-cooker and in the microwave was going to be the only way they made it through the summer. Russ had hung a rope line from the trailer to the Liam's treehouse to use instead of the dryer. Well, to be more accurate Russ affixed it to the trailer and she and Liam had attached the other end to the tree with Russ's direction. Aster was proud she was able to complete the task without messing it up and without falling out of the tree. Climbing up there made her heart skip a beat, but she'd done it. Aster made a note on the whiteboard hung next to the door to pick up clothes pins.

Liam had been outside all day in his new tree house. It had taken forever to get him to come inside both yesterday and today. She had spent the day going through wanted ads in the free paper, trying to find a job. There was a bus stop at the entrance to the park, so tomorrow they could go to the library. She could use the computers there to look for work. The mechanic had given her the good news that her car was repairable and the bad news was it would be expensive. He'd agreed to let her make payments, then he would fix it. Priority one was getting a job. She could work through any residual pain.

Russ wasn't home yet and it was almost eleven, which was odd. She knew he had to be home on time. Aster stirred the contents in the slow cooker making sure the stew was warm. She should have showered earlier. She'd wait until morning in case Russ wanted one, she didn't want to risk him not having hot water.

She finished washing her and Liam's dishes and set them in the drying rack as the door opened.

Russ kicked off his shoes and put his slippers on before dragging a chair over to sit on. He plugged in his monitor, sighed, and leaned back in the chair.

Aster took a bowl down and dished out a portion, adding a spoon, then offered it wordlessly to Russ.

"Um. Thanks. And hi." Russ took the bowl from her but looked confused. "I don't normally eat right away or forget my manners."

"I'm sorry." Her eyes went right to the patterned tile. "I thought you'd want something as soon as you came home. I shouldn't have assumed, I can leave you alone, if you want, no trouble."

"How was your day?" Russ cut her off. "Somethin' happen?"

"No." She could feel how wide her own eyes were as her fingers went to her pearls. "It was a good day. Nothing happened."

Russ arched his eyebrow, "Then why are you keyed up?" When she didn't reply, he set the bowl down on the counter. "Aster, We're roommates, you don't have to do things for me. But you certainly don't need to apologize when you do something kind."

"Bad habits." She couldn't think of how else to explain it. How could she put into words that a hot plate needed to be provided without words? Silence needed to pervade the house while her husband calmed down from work. How the smallest deviation from the normal routine would result in a lecture. Push back was met with belittlement. Everything was her fault whether something was done or not done.

"A new place is good space," he cleared his throat, "to break bad habits."

"You rhymed."

The corner of his mouth turned up and the dimple on his cheek appeared. "Yeah. The doc I see for my anger issues said something like that. Thought it was decent advice."

"I like it." She looked around the trailer, trying to decide what to say next. "Did you want some quiet? Time to yourself?"

"I like your company..." Russ pushed his hair away from his face, then checked his monitor. "If you're gonna be up that is. Don't let me keep you from going to bed."

"Would you like a haircut?" Aster offered.

"Huh?"

"I used to cut my husband's hair, and I've always cut Liam's." She explained, "plus yours seems to be getting in the way."

Russ stretched his arms over his head. "I mean, if you're offering, I accept. I'll go shower so it's wet."

"No, you should have the full experience," she countered, going to retrieve the supplies she needed before he could argue.

Bridgette had given her an old hairdryer along with some other styling products, tools, and even a little make-up, telling her it was easier to start over when you felt good about yourself. Aster was starting over regardless of her feelings, and while she couldn't fix herself, she could help Russ. She'd put the tools and products in the little tote they kept under sink in case it leaked and put a towel on top of it. A haircut was a simple thing, but getting one always put a spring in her step. Something about the renewal of it. Russ wouldn't likely care as much, but even still. It was a way to give back.

She carried the tote to the kitchen and set it on the counter Russ was resting his hip against.

He glanced at the tote before asking, "A haircut is an experience, huh?"

She nodded and shook out the towel. "It should be. You take care of your goatee instead of shaving it."

"Cause I look like I'm twelve without it." Russ ran his tongue over his teeth under his lip. "I can just..."

"Let me." Aster interrupted, touching his shoulder. "I want to do this. Let me, please."

His eyes met hers, there was more dark than light blue to them at the moment. The dimmer light must have caused them to dilate. He cleared his throat. "Sure."

"Do you have enough cord to sit in front of the sink?"

"Yeah." He snagged his chair and brought it to where she requested. After sitting back down, he looked up at her, questioning, "this good?"

"It is." Aster tested the water, making sure it was warm, before pulling out the sprayer. "Can you lean back a little? I need to make sure the water doesn't go everywhere."

Russ silently complied and Aster ran her fingers through his slightly curly hair, wetting it completely.

She massaged the shampoo in first, gently scratching her nails against his scalp, carefully but firmly. He let out a soft sound.

"Too hard?" she questioned.

"No." Russ's eyes were closed as she continued washing out his hair, rinsing it out before starting with the conditioner.

Aster took her time with the conditioner, saturating it completely and letting it rest. "You have very thick hair."

"It's the stupid curls." Russ kept his eyes closed. "It was a mess in high school. Used to shave it."

She started massaging his scalp a second time. "That's a waste. It's so pretty. I mean handsome. It's nice. You have nice hair." She corrected herself as she rinsed the conditioner out, checking the water temperature periodically.

"My ego isn't that fragile. You can call my hair pretty." His voice was low and relaxed. "This feels nice."

Aster smiled at him despite him not being able to see her. "I'm glad. Thank you for letting me do this."

"Shouldn't argue with a lady when she says please."

"Alright, sit up." She took the towel and ruffled the excess water out of his hair. "I think we should leave some length on the top, but buzz underneath. It'll help you keep cool." She moved in front of him as she finished up with the towel.

"I'm not picky, it's under a hairnet most of the day anyways." Russ opened his eyes and they stared at each other for a long moment before his lip quirked up in a small smile. "I trust ya."

She bit her lip and touched the top of his head. "Look right, please. Now left." She nodded. "Yes, longer on top, but shorter than it is now and buzzed underneath."

The plan was easier in her head than in practice, but she could do this. She cut Liam's, hair all the time. She was good at this. She turned on the clippers and buzzed it first. Turning his head this way and that as she worked. Russ stayed still but loose, eyes closed, following whatever requests she made. His scissors weren't as sharp as she would have liked, but she made do.

"How was your day?" she asked as she snipped his locks. She should have asked him earlier.

"It was fine. Cooked, cleaned, and repeat." He sighed as she ran her fingers through his hair. "You think about doing something like this for work?"

"I don't think I could afford to get licensed to cut hair, and I'd have to go to school besides that." Aster continued to trim as she answered him.

Russ lulled his head to the side as she moved it. "No, just head massages. I could fall asleep right now."

"You'd be awfully uncomfortable in the morning." She assessed her work, before making more cuts.

"Worth it." His shoulders lowered, as if she was draining the tension out of him.

She brushed some loose hairs away from his neck and he jumped. "Sorry, didn't mean to startle you."

He cleared his throat and shifted in his chair. "It's fine."

Aster swept up the hair on the floor into a pile to keep from making a mess. She plugged in the hairdryer and started to dry his hair. Russ had been relaxed, but now he seemed tense. Maybe it was the hairdryer? She used a comb to get the stray longer hairs gathered to level it. Alternating between drying his hair and finishing the cut. She was finally happy with it.

She used her fingers to finish styling it. He looked good. It wouldn't need much effort to look nice. "Here's the mirror. Tell me what you think."

Russ held up the mirror and blinked in the light as he opened his eyes. "Damn. I look better than I have in five years."

"Glad you approve." She gathered everything up and took it back to the bathroom. Hopefully he hadn't noticed her staring at him. He cleaned up nicely, but that should be the last thing on her mind. The haircut was a thank you for all he'd done for her and Liam, nothing more.

She was on her way back out to clean up the kitchen when she collided with Russ with a surprised yelp, nearly falling backward. His hands kept her steady and upright. Those blue eyes of his searched her face, looking for something. "You good?"

She nodded, not trusting her voice as he let go of one of her arms.

"Thank you for this," Russ ran his fingers through his shortened blonde hair. "The haircut, I mean. I, I appreciate it."

"You're welcome."

He was still holding her elbow, and neither of them moved. He smelled like spices and sweat. No doubt the hospital kitchen was hot.

She swallowed. "I should finish cleaning up the kitchen before I go to bed. I'll try and get up early."

Since Russ wouldn't take no for an answer about her sleeping in the bed, they'd come up with a compromise. She would sleep in the bed during the night, and when she got up in the morning, he would use the bed for a few hours before he had to go into work. Sleep was a struggle, and she felt awful when she woke up past nine, but her body wouldn't relax. Little sounds threw her into an alert panic, so sleep was a few hours, then awake for an hour, and then back to sleep for another hour or so. She was tired, but she could still complete the house duties.

"I don't mind, and you've been on your feet all day." Aster insisted.

Russ' hands fell away and she moved forward without meaning to, nearly touching him. The only thing keeping them from sharing breath was their height difference. "I'll clean up. Go to bed."

"I should...."

His fingers brushed under her chin, lifting her face up to look into her eyes. He started to lean down and her heart stopped. What was happening? A car backfired and they both jumped away from each other. Russ shifted his gaze behind her. "Just let me, please."

Aster managed to nod and Russ retreated to the hallway.

"Night, Aster."

"Good night."

He closed the door behind him and Aster rested her hand over her thumping heart.

CHAPTER 19

The best and worst part of summer were the long days. The trailer got blindly bright before Russ was ready to get up from the couch. However, today was Thursday. Which meant he needed to be up by seven, so he was ready before Jerry showed up.

He stretched out on the couch and rolled over to get up.

"Can you teach me to make breakfast burritos?" Liam's voice nearly sent Russ off the couch.

"Ack!"

Liam was surprisingly quiet if he woke up before Russ did. Aster's quiet didn't surprise him, but Liam was a little boy, and the fact that he could be damn near silent threw Russ for a loop. The boy was perched, cross-legged on Russ's oversized chair, staring at him. This eight-year-old was more serious than half of his work crew. When Liam wanted to learn something, he was going to learn it, and it was going to be perfect. A fine trait to be sure, but it didn't negate how unsettling it was to wake up being watched.

Russ grunted as he put his feet on the ground. "How long have you been watching me sleep?"

"I dunno." Liam shrugged. "Felt like a long time. Will you help me?"

He ran his hands over his face through his hair, which Aster had cut last Tuesday. It was nice to not have it constantly in his eyes. "Why do you want to make them? You've eaten peanut butter sandwiches every morning since we built the tree house."

"Cause Seagar likes 'em." Liam explained shifting side to side already full of energy. "He eats them back home. I want to make food for us to eat this morning."

Coffee. Russ needed coffee to survive this without snapping at the kid. Erving had come back with his grandsons in tow and the three boys had hit it off instantly; mostly. "You have to make one for Amos if you make 'em for you and Seagar. We don't let anyone go hungry."

He started the coffee pot and retrieved his two new frying pans.

"I *know*. Amos is okay. He just thinks he's cooler because he does martial arts back home. But he doesn't know anything about cooking, so I'm better at that." Liam followed him into the kitchen. "Cosmo is gonna play with us too, we met him yesterday. He's only here every other week 'cause his dad lives here."

Russ opened the fridge motioning for Liam. "We need the carton of eggs, tortillas, shredded cheese, butter, and since we don't have peppers, we'll use the salsa instead."

Liam leaped forward, but Russ grabbed his collar, asking with more growl than intended. "How many ingredients do we grab at a time?"

"One." Liam huffed.

"Why do we grab one at a time?"

Liam snatched one of the egg cartons. "Because I broke the pickles when I tried to carry too many things." He furrowed his eyebrows at Russ, before setting the eggs on the counter.

"Oi." Russ bopped the top of Liam's head. "Am I mad about the pickles?"

"No." Liam sighed with his whole body before retrieving the cheese.

"Why am I not mad?"

"Cause we all make mistakes."

Russ ruffled Liam's hair. "That's right. We need to be persistent; not perfect. We should make one for your mom and Jerry too. Should we use bacon or sausage?"

"Sausage." Liam answered definitively. "It mixes good with the eggs and bacon set off the smoke detector yesterday."

"Sausage it is. I'll brown that in a separate pan." He cut the plastic cover away from the meat, set it to cook in the pan, and put the knife in the sink. This would be simple enough. "Any questions?"

"Why do you get arrested on Thursdays?"

I meant about the dish. Russ took a deep breath and corrected him. "I'm going to therapy on Thursdays, I'm not being arrested."

"Why do the cops take you to therapy? Are you criminal insane?" Liam turned on the water before fetching his step stool.

Russ ground his teeth. "I am not insane. I made a mistake. I go to therapy so I don't get mad and make the same mistake again."

"Oh." He washed his hands as he wondered aloud, "Maybe I need therapy. I get mad a lot."

Russ cracked one of the eggs into the bowl. "Let's see how you feel at the end of the summer; then we can talk to your mom. I've learned not to act in anger; there's consequences when you do." He slid the bowl to Liam. "Use your words, take deep breaths, and think before you act."

"Okay." Liam rubbed his forearm over his eyes, then grabbed an egg. "Let's cook now."

"Sounds good, pup."

Russ dragged his chair up from the edge of the yard and set up by the trailer door. The smell of peppermint was already in the air. Aster said bees made her nervous, so he affixed planters to the trailer framing the door. They planted the mint plants in them and it smelled nice whenever he got near them.

Liam was already playing in the tree house with his friends.

"I'm gonna be a robot pirate!"

Russ didn't recognize the voice, so it must be Cosmo. Seagar sounded like he snorted sugar and Amos never yelled.

Liam countered just as loud. "You can't be a robot and a pirate! Robots can't swim."

"Maybe he's a waterproof robot!" Seagar offered as he leaned out the window and waved at Russ.

Russ waved back despite his fervent wish the kids had a volume button.

"Can robots be waterproof?" Amos questioned next to Russ, making him jump enough to spill his coffee.

"Kid, where did you come from?" Russ gasped out, he hadn't heard him at all.

"I went to my grandpa's trailer to pee, and now I'm back." Amos shrugged and started back towards the park.

Russ snapped his fingers and the boy stopped, his green eyes questioning the motion until Russ pointed at the tree house.

"I knew that." He yawned, before racing to the hanging ladder and climbing up.

Russ closed his eyes to enjoy the quiet for a moment. It was broken almost instantly.

"You can't drink soda with breakfast! Your teeth will fall out!" Liam was back on the warpath.

Seagar was laughing, still hanging out the window. "Mr. Rust, can we paint a pirate flag on the tree house?"

"Liam's call, not mine." He hollered back as Erica's trailer door opened.

Her chickens went crazy clucking to be fed, while Saul trotted up to Russ to see what he had to eat. He scratched behind the dog's ears and raised a hand to Erica. She filled Saul's bowl with water from the hose then watered her plastic plants.

"Russ. How are you this morning?" She meandered over and patted Saul's head. "You need eggs? I won't have any 'til tomorrow. My ginny hen's getting lazy, might be time to fry a chicken."

Russ winced at the thought of the last chicken she'd dressed. "Warn me before you go butchering it. I don't want Liam to see it."

"See what?" Erica cocked her head to the side, then looked up at the sky. "Yes, I think we're in for a hot summer."

He worried about Erica. Most days she was just a smidge off, but other days it seemed she had genuinely misplaced in her mind. "If you need help when it gets hot let me know, okay?"

"My daughter's coming to see me and her boyfriend's coming along." She sniffed the peppermint plants. "He's such a nice young man."

If it was the same guy Polly was dating back in February, no he wasn't. That guy was an asshole. "Polly find a new guy?"

"No, no, same one. He's better now." Erica leaned down and whispered to Russ, "He promised to be better, and Polly won't come see me without him. So no calling the cops if Kevin gets loud." She pressed her finger to her lips, "I promised not to make a fuss anymore."

Well that didn't sit well with him at all. "Alright, but you let me know if he causes you any trouble."

"Oh surely. Have a good day now." She walked back to her yard with Saul lumbering behind her and tied him up in the shade of the trailer by his water dish.

"Look, the great beast of the deep! It guards the treasure!" Seagar shouted, half out the window.

Amos, who was sitting in the other window nodded his head, "We need to come up with a plan to fight it!"

"No, befriend it. Best course of action is make it our ally," Cosmo countered, swinging on the rope. "What do you think, Liam?"

Liam poked his head into view next to Seagar. "We shouldn't hurt it."

If the morning hadn't been so quiet, Russ wouldn't have heard all of the nonsense. It was good the kid was making friends, he needed them.

The door behind him opened and he glanced back at Aster. "Morning," Russ greeted her.

"Good Morning." She smiled and sat on the trailer steps, coffee in hand. "Thank you for breakfast."

"Liam made most of it."

Aster looked up at the tree house as the boys hollered more nonsense at each other. "I'm so glad he made friends. You said they don't live here all year."

"Erving's their grandfather, he owns the trailer with the green roof. He brings them out here for the summers," Russ explained. "Hope it's not too rough on Liam when they leave."

She looked down at the ground. "He's had a lot of change. I wish I could shield him from some of it. I know he's hurting."

"Keep him talking about it." Russ finished off his coffee. "Therapist says talking things through is the most important part. Make sure he knows you hear him. You can let him know that you're hurting too."

"I don't want to scare him." Her fingers curled around her pearls. "He already feels like he needs to take care of me. I'm such a failure."

"Bullshit." He snarled. "He's fed, clothed, and you love him to death. The rest you can figure out." He hated how she talked about herself. Whatever she left hadn't been easy, but here she was standing on her own two feet.

He might have said more, but Jerry pulled into the driveway. He gripped the foil wrapped burrito and set his empty coffee cup on the chair. "My keys are on the hook, if you need to use my car."

Chapter 20

Three hours of fucking sleep on this fine Friday and Russ was at his wit's end, pulling in the driveway. He was too old for sleep deprivation, and his body was done. It was nearly eleven. He needed to get out of the car, thankfully they'd been slow tonight and he'd spent the last hour plugged in, so the need to charge his monitor wasn't imminent. All he wanted was to shower and crash. He was exhausted to the point that even eating seemed like far too much work.

His trailer's lights were on, but so were Erica's, and that wasn't normal. Russ glanced over to her driveway and he didn't recognize the Camero parked behind Erica's rusty van.

He opened his door and strained to hear anything out of the ordinary. Most folks had their windows open because of the heat, so there was a mix of television programs blending together. The Tiger's game was on in Erica's trailer and loud enough that Russ could sit outside and get the play by play.

The air felt unsettled. Something was wrong. He fished through his glove compartment and snagged his cigarettes and lighter. Before he went to prison he smoked a pack a week, but it was too expensive of a habit to keep up when he was inside. Now he kept a pack in his glove compartment for 'emergencies,' aka when he couldn't calm down and was in danger of losing his shit. This was only the third pack he'd bought in the almost six months he'd been out on parole. Maybe the anger therapy was working?

His chair was still next to the house, so he sat down and faced Erica's trailer. Lighting the single cigarette he'd brought with him, he took a drag, attempting to calm his nerves.

He glanced around as the bug zapper lit up at the edge of the property. Saul was tied up outside, it was warm enough for him to be out, but Erica always took him inside at night. Russ drummed his fingers on the arm of the chair.

"Get the fuck out of the way!" That was Kevin.

And yup, Kevin was still a douche bag.

Polly's voice was just as shrill. "I don't have to do anything! Fucking make me!"

Russ closed his fist on the arm of the chair, metal biting into his fingers. *Deep breath. One. Two. Three. Breath in. One. Two. Three. Hold it. One. Two. Three. Breath out.* Another drag on his cigarette. He could stay level-headed and calm. The last thing he needed was to get involved and get sent back to jail.

The side door opened and Erica motioned for Saul to come to her.

"Leave 'im outside, ya bat. He tried to bite me!" Kevin's voice was slightly slurred.

So he was drunk on top of being his *charming* self. *Fan-fucking-tastic.*

Russ couldn't make out what Erica said, but she took the dog inside with her. It was quiet. The game was still blaring and there were so many sounds in the park, but for him it was silent. All he focused on was Erica's trailer and how he didn't hear anymore yelling.

The door burst open again, this time banging against the trailer loud enough to echo. Kevin, cigarette hanging out of his mouth, was dragging Saul back outside.

Saul didn't bark. Russ had never heard that dog make any noise other than sloppy drinking and eating, but Saul growled at Kevin.

"You want me to give you something to growl at? Huh?" Kevin jerked Saul's collar and put his cigarette in his free hand.

"AY!" Russ was already on his feet. "Tie him up and let him be."

"Who the fuck do you think your talking to?" Kevin let go of Saul, who immediately raced back into the trailer.

Russ flicked his cigarette to the ground and stomped on it to put it out. "An asshole who thinks he's a tough guy."

Polly rushed out of the trailer and grabbed Kevin's arm. "Baby, he's been to prison. Let's go back inside. I'll take care of the dog."

It was slow motion to Russ, Kevin didn't say a word to Polly. Instead he backhanded her, sending her to the ground holding her face. Then everything moved far too fast.

"Get up. I didn't even hit you that hard."

"You fucking bastard!" Polly cried, still cradling her cheek.

Doors were opening all over the park, because live drama was live drama. However none of it mattered to Russ. Because if there was one thing that he learned from his grandfather it was you *never* hit a woman.

Kevin turned to Russ with his fists up. "You want some ya—?"

Russ didn't let him finish. He hooked Kevin's closer leg with his boot and sent him to the ground with a thud. He should have left it there. Kevin was on the ground, but Russ wasn't letting this go. He kicked Kevin in the ribs with enough force to roll him towards Erica's trailer.

Polly screamed for Russ to stop, but he didn't.

Instead he hauled Kevin up off the ground by the arms and slammed him against Erica's trailer. "You piece of fucking shit! You think hitting a woman makes you a big man, huh?"

Russ dropped him and stepped back, letting Kevin get steady on his feet. The drunk looked like he wanted to attack.

Good. He wanted Kevin to attack. He wanted the excuse to go another round with this waste of space.

Polly was pleading with Kevin to let it go, so the cops didn't come. This only made Kevin more amped to fight Russ. The rage clear in his bloodshot eyes.

"Do it." Russ snarled, rolling his shoulders. "You wanna hit somebody? Hit me! I *fucking* dare you."

Kevin swung wildly and caught Russ square in the face. He grinned no doubt at the sight of the blood dripping from Russ's nose. However that grin faded when Russ smiled, showing off his bloody mouth.

"That all you got? My grandma hits harder than you, ya pussy." Russ cackled, jabbing Kevin twice in the ribs doubling him over. Kevin cried out as Russ got a fistful of his hair and slapped him across the face like the bitch he was. "Come on! You were all big and bad before. Fucking do something!"

The blood was pounding in his ears, and he could all but see red. Kevin was kicking at Russ' legs in desperation, but it was pointless. Russ tossed him to the ground, spitting out blood. "Get up." He growled, kicking the dirt between them.

"Get on the ground and lace your fingers behind your head!"

Oh fuck! He had actually been seeing red. The cops were here. They must have been patrolling by the highway exit, looking for drunk drivers. He was going back to prison. Russ assumed the position, but glanced back at his trailer. Aster was in the doorway, with Liam clinging to her. The kid was bawling. *Fuck.* What the hell had he done?

"You too. Get on the ground!" The cop barked at Kevin.

Kevin groaned, but still managed to be mouthy. "Fuck you, pig. I haven't done shit. That asshole attacked *me*!"

"I'll get statements from both of you." He handcuffed Russ, warning him. "Do not get up from the ground."

Russ nodded, because quite frankly, he knew better than to run his mouth. If Kevin kept up his act, they might end up in the same cell tonight. Well, if he had terrorized poor Aster and Liam and was going back to prison, he might as well earn it. Kevin was a deserving punching bag.

The cop had a baby face. No more than twenty-five, and he looked jumpy as he attempted to keep a handle on the situation. "Folks, if you aren't directly involved, go back to your homes."

Doors slammed as the cop requested and Russ dared to look back at his own trailer door, which was closed. He sighed and let his body relax as much as it could.

Kevin was still arguing with the cop. "Naw. I was arguing with my girl and he rushed me like some sorta psycho."

"He didn't even mean to hit me," Polly supplied unprompted.

Russ rolled his eyes. She was high. Polly was gonna get them both arrested tonight. Good. They'd be away from Erica that way.

Kevin attempted to pull away from the cop's grip and a bag of white powder fell to the ground. There was a bit of scuffle, but in a matter of moments Kevin was handcuffed and Polly was zipped tied, begging to the cop that she didn't know.

The part of this that was making Russ nervous was the age of the cop. If he felt the situation was out of his control, he might panic and do something stupid. Something lethal. Russ hated the idea of going back to prison, but he hated the idea of being shot more.

His trailer door opened again and he made eye contact with Aster. She looked less scared than before. It might not be the best idea to talk, but he didn't want to leave her without a net. "There's money in a cigar box in the dresser. Talk to Margie, she'll go easy on you about the rent while you get on your feet. Just stay. You're still welcome to stay."

"Russ." Those blue eyes of hers, so damn pretty, but her lower lip was indented by her teeth. Scared and stressed over his bullshit.

"It's fine. I can handle going back." He offered her a smile, he knew didn't reach his eyes. "Take care of the place for me, okay?"

Another car pulled into the driveway behind him and Russ didn't even bother to look. It was more cops. Officially a party now. He closed his eyes.

"Boy, when you mess up, you really mess up." Jerry growled, gripping Russ's shoulder. "You're lucky I was up watching the game when your girl called."

Chapter 21

"So how do you feel about the actions you took last night?" Dr. Collins, the therapist Russ saw every Thursday asked, sitting with the bars between them.

The doctor seemed like a decent guy. Didn't bullshit too much, but made Russ think too hard. His head always ached after their sessions and all he wanted was to nap.

On the plus side, he had gotten almost a full night's sleep, which didn't speak very highly of his mental state. Normal people didn't sleep well after beating up another person.

Russ ran his hand over his goatee. "Well, I probably don't feel as guilty as I should."

"Why do you say that?"

"Because I was clearly stronger than that douchebag, and I shouldn't have kept going. Shoulda separated them and called the cops."

Dr. Collins made a note on his ever-present pad. "Do you think it would have helped? Separating them?"

He looked up at the gray ceiling. "No. Not really. But violence got me into prison, and it's what's gonna send me back." He sighed and dropped his head, the floor was just as gray. "It's my fault. Shoulda stopped."

"You are responsible for your actions. Your intentions might have been noble, but violence isn't acceptable in the eyes of the law."

"Don't I know it." The din at the jail was steady, but Russ couldn't focus on any of it. He was a monster. So much for learning to control his temper. "I just wished I hadn't scared them."

Dr. Collins adjusted his glasses. "Scared who? Polly and Erica?"

No, that wasn't who he had been thinking about at all, but he didn't want to drag Aster and Liam's names into it. So he lied. "There's a handful of kids at the park. None of them needed to see or hear all of that. Sure some of them did."

"Russ, I think you might be the worst liar I've encountered." The doctor laughed, before circling back to why they were here. "I can't help you if you won't let me. Now back to the incident. What were you thinking about when you struck the other man?"

"Generally when I lose my temper, I don't think." He cleared his throat. "I guess I was thinking about my grandfather and how he told me to never hit a woman."

"Was that before or after Kevin hit Polly?" The doctor looked through his notes.

"After."

He nodded. "Hmmm. Were you on edge before he struck her?"

"I guess. I thought he was going to burn Erica's dog with his cigarette."

"Have you wanted to hit Kevin before?" Dr. Collins pressed, as if he was trying to get Russ to remember something.

"Not really, but I've never liked him." Russ rolled his tongue over his teeth under his lip. "Look, Erica told me they might be visiting and I was worried. Kevin was an asshole last time. I didn't want him to hurt Erica."

"Reasonable." He scratched another note onto his pad. "Do you remember why you wanted to hurt him?"

"I didn't really want to hurt him for fuck's sake. I just reacted," Russ pushed his fist into his palm, the sting of the broken skin refocused him. "He hit Polly, and I went from zero to a hundred. I lost my temper in the stupidest way possible, and now here we are."

"I see." The doctor stood up, pocketing his pen.

He was confused and jumped up, calling to the doctor. "Wait, that's it? That's all you wanted to know?"

"Russ." Dr. Collins addressed him frankly. "You just said you didn't want to hurt Kevin. You reacted to violence happening in front of you the way you've learned to handle it. But you took responsibility and were honest with the police. The only thing you seem to be worried about is the effect on others. You haven't even asked me to help keep you out on parole."

Russ shrugged. "I figured why bother."

"For the record, you should bother for yourself." The doctor waved to the cop outside the cell block. "I'll give Jerry my recommendation. You better be grateful for him. Otherwise you'd likely be going back in regardless of my recommendation."

"Wait. I'm not going back?" Russ drew in a shaky breath. "How?"

"You've got a hell of a parole officer, that's how." Jerry grumbled and motioned for Dr. Collins. "*Rusty*, I'll be back for your sorry ass after I talk to the doc and get done with Aster's paperwork."

The bars slammed behind the two free men and Russ sank to the floor covering his face. He managed to control the sounds threatening to escape, but he wasn't able to stop the tears that ran down his face. He wasn't going back in. Russ wiped his cheeks off with this forearm. He was still free. Or free-ish at least.

Aster was waiting for him in Jerry's office. Her hair was completely covered by a scarf, and she tugged at the hem of the sweatshirt she was wearing over her sundress. He only knew it was a sundress, because she'd dried it on the line, and he recognized the giant blue flowers on it. Russ could only imagine how upset the whole situation last night had made her, and now she was here. Her nervousness wasn't a surprise. Police stations weren't a fun place to be. Picking up someone from intake was a step worse.

"You've got an hour to get home. You need to call HR and tell them if you're going to work or not." Jerry explained, handing over the forms for Russ to sign. "Then you call me with whichever way you decide to go. Don't lie to me."

"I won't." Russ scratched his name on the appropriate lines. Even if he was dumb enough to lie, he wouldn't. Paula, his HR person, was Jerry's cousin and it wasn't like Jerry wouldn't double check with her. "What time is it?"

"Just past nine." Aster supplied. His car keys were clutched in her hand, knuckles turning white.

"I'll probably work tonight. Better to be busy." He dated the last page and initialed it. Better to be out of the house and give Aster space. He also realized that his pint-sized critic wasn't there.

Jerry took the paperwork back and filed it. "Alright, good to go. Pleasure speaking with you, Aster."

She nodded her head. "You as well, Officer Gristol."

They walked towards the door, but Russ clearly heard Jerry's comment to Dr. Collins. "Hell of way to get revenge."

Revenge? Russ didn't have a long running rivalry with Kevin. He was just an asshole he'd gotten into a fight with, nothing more. But if Kevin had more drugs in his car, or if Polly admitted to more crimes, then perhaps Kevin was going upstate. Guess, that could be considered revenge. Did he have an enemy now?

The sun was intense when they stepped outside and it was muggy as hell. Work was going to be miserable. He'd consider staying home, but he was well rested and had time to get ready. He should go.

Aster held out his keys. "I hope you don't mind. I couldn't ask first."

"I told you, whenever you need the car, just use it. As long as you don't make me late for work, I don't care." He took them back, but didn't move towards his car. "Where's Liam?"

"Erving came to check on us last night after the police left." Her thumb rubbed at her pearl necklace. "He's keeping an eye on the boys this morning."

Russ drew in a deep breath of fresh air, and before he could stop himself, he pulled Aster into a hug. He shouldn't have gotten into her space, but his eyes were watering, and he didn't want her to see how shaken he was. Part of the reason he wasn't going back to prison was Aster's quick thinking to call Jerry. He was too grateful not to hug her.

The expected reaction was for her push back to get away from him and look uncomfortable, but she didn't. Aster hugged him back. Her arms slipped around his waist and she pressed her body to his.

"It's okay," she reassured him. "We can go home now."

Home? Christ, when was the last time he'd thought of anywhere as home? After moving out of his grandparent's place, he'd lived places, but never considered them a home. The apartments and trailers he'd occupied between then and now had been places to lay his head and not much else. *We can go home.* Not let's go back to *your* trailer or *the* trailer, but we can go home. *We* can go home. She considered the trailer her home and well, it was. The creaky, drafty single-wide up on cinder blocks was a home, because they had made it one. He hadn't realized how much she and Liam....

He tightened his grip on her shoulders and she didn't fight it. Instead her hand rubbed circles on his back and he leaned his face into her shoulder. On the sidewalk outside of the police station he was fighting the urge to break down, clinging to this tiny woman.

"I'm really sorry about everything. I shouldn't have...." Russ drew in an unsteady breath. "I shouldn't have lost my temper like that. It's not fair that you had to deal with...."

"It's alright." Aster patted his back. "I handled it. We're all okay."

She pulled away and he let her out of his arms, but kept his eyes on the ground. He couldn't bring himself to look her in the eye.

"We need to pick up freezer pops on the way back. I promised the boys." She tugged at Russ's sleeve. "Come on."

"Right." He sniffled and pulled himself together as he joked. "You got money for that?"

"I mean, you said there was money in that cigar box. I thought it was mine now." Aster smiled at him.

It wasn't the reserved smile that he'd become accustomed to. It was a cheeky smile, mischievous even. Where had this come from? He liked it, it made her glow.

Russ felt himself grin back at her. "You trying to rob me, Sunshine?" He winced the second he said it. *Oh hell no. Do not give the pretty lady living with you a pet name.* Not okay.

She giggled. "No, you told me where it was. Liam said we're all pirates this summer. So, I'm playing by those rules."

He threw his head back and laughed. "All right, let's go."

"Stay home tonight," she requested. "You've had a rough day, er, night. We can watch movies with boys, it's supposed to rain."

CHAPTER 22

Margie and Bridgette's trailer was air conditioned, and as nervous as Aster was about leaving Liam alone with his friends, it was nice to sit in the cool air. He would be fine; he was playing with his friends, and they weren't that far away. If something happened, one of them would come tell her. Russ was in the trailer as well; she had nothing to worry about and she was allowed to do non-mom things.

July was hotter than June, and it had been arid. She bought a sprinkler last weekend to keep the garden from dying.

"I'm worried they're gonna call off the fireworks this year. The ground's so dry." Marilyn was sitting to Aster's right, looking at her cards. "Pass."

Bridgette cursed under her breath across from Aster.

"No table talk." Margie reminded her roommate and touched Bridgette's wrist.

"Are you trying to look at my cards?" she questioned, her New York accent intensifying the longer the game went on.

Margie smirked. "I don't need to look at your cards to beat you."

"This is why we don't ever let them be a team when we play," Marilyn explained to Aster. "They fuss at each other the whole game. Pick the suit now, Aster, it's your call."

Aster was straining to remember the rules. Everyone had passed including Marilyn, who was the dealer. Whatever suit she picked became trump. Aster had three red suit cards that were all high, and the card in the middle was a spade, a black suit card. Bridgette had cursed when Marilyn passed, but that could be because Aster's last pick had lost them all but one trick. The player who played the highest card of the four on the table 'took the trick,' which meant their team won that round.

"Hun, it's just a game. Don't sweat it." Bridgette rolled her neck shoulder to shoulder. "This is why we don't let Erica play, we're here for thirty minutes while she picks a suit."

"Diamonds." Aster called the suit and bit her lip. "I'm worried about Erica. She was so upset the day after all that mess with Polly and Kevin, but then it was like it never happened."

Marilyn shuffled her cards. "She'll be alright. Her granddaughter, Holly, is starting college in the fall, and she's gonna be living with her. Holly is her son's daughter. Travis lives out west. Tried to get Erica to move in with him a dozen times."

Aster played her ten of hearts.

"Holly's a sweetie. Travis visited Erica last summer with her." Margie played the king of spades, which meant she didn't have any hearts.

The play could mean she and Bridgette might have a chance at winning this game.

"Shame about Polly. She was a good kid." Bridgette laid down the queen of hearts. "Travis took off to college, and she just struggled."

"It didn't help that Erica's husband died soon after. Polly was a daddy's girl. She's still got good in her." Marilyn played the Ace of hearts and took the trick. "Just needs a little help to see it." She set down the ten of diamonds to continue the game.

"How old was Polly when her father died?" Aster examined her cards and decided on the queen of diamonds. She hated the idea that losing a father figure had started Polly on the wrong path. *What could that mean for Liam?* She sipped on her iced tea.

"Thirteen, and Travis was twenty-one." Margie tapped her cards and laid down the ace of diamonds.

Bridgette played the jack of spades. "I forgot those two were so far apart in age. Polly's always been wild."

Margie took the trick, and that was two tricks for the defending team. Aster kept her eyes down, slightly nervous that she had put her and Bridgette's team at a disadvantage as Margie set down the jack of hearts.

Bridgette played the nine of spades and Marilyn played the jack of diamonds. Well, there went the two highest trump cards in one round.

Unfortunately, the only diamond card she had left was the king of diamonds. Aster furrowed her brow. She was not good at this game, and it didn't help that now all she could think about was how Polly was the younger child in an age gap situation of two children with no father figure and she'd turned to drugs. Liam would never, but she pulled at her pearls listlessly.

Marilyn took the trick. "Well, that may be the case, but everyone is different and one situation doesn't define another."

Aster tried in vain to keep her hands away from her neck during the next round, because every time she touched them, Margie gave her side-eye. Probably due to the fact that she'd accidentally revealed that her ex-husband had given them to her. And she knew she should take them off, but whenever she tried, it made her feel exposed and nervous. It was the same sort of distress she felt when her hair was uncovered. She hated how short it was and how it had gotten that way.

"I think we're done for, but you gotta play your last card, girlie." Bridgette laughed and finished her drink. Marilyn indeed took the last trick after all the cards were played. "I think after that defeat we can call it a day."

Margie kissed Bridgette's cheek. "Don't be such a sore loser, Doll. Aster's trying her best, and we've been playing for longer than she's been alive."

"Sorry." Aster apologized.

Marilyn patted Aster's arm. "We'll switch teams around next time. You're learning fine."

She looked up at the clock and stretched. She needed to make lunch for the boys. Russ often made them lunch while he made his breakfast before going to work, but she didn't want to assume.

"Any luck with the job hunt?" Margie asked, gathering up the cards.

Aster sighed. "No. I'm not sure what I'm going to do. I worked at a daycare before I was a stay-at-home mom. My skills are limited, and I have to worry about Liam if I'm gone during the day."

"If you need help watching Liam, you let me know. He's a delight." Marilyn offered as they both pushed back from the table. "I should go see him before I head home. I'll see you ladies next week."

Aster and Marilyn drove her car over to Russ's trailer, which was odd. Marilyn had walked every other time so could get in her steps in for the day.

Liam bailed out of the tree house the second he saw Marilyn's car. "Grandma Marilyn!" He hugged her as soon as they got out of the car and waved at Aster. "Hi, Mom! Is it lunchtime already? We're not hungry."

"I am *so* hungry!" Seagar poked his head out through one of the tree house's windows. "I might die if we don't get lunch."

Aster snickered, that kid had the metabolism of a runner. Seagar was always hungry.

"Alright, I'll get lunch for you boys," Aster offered.

A chorus of yays and thank yous rang out from the four boys.

"I have a treat for you boys. Gather 'round." Marilyn motioned for them to come to the trunk of her car.

"Is it ice cream?"

"Cherry Coke?"

"Root beer?"

The boys chorused out their guesses as Liam huffed that they better be grateful, whatever it was.

"You are too serious sometimes." Marilyn ruffled Liam's hair, something he fussed about except when it was his new grandmother. She opened the trunk. "I hear you all are being pirates this summer."

"We are! I'm gonna be the greatest ever!" Seagar was hopping up and down. Amos grabbed the back of his shirt to try to get his cousin to settle down.

Cosmo was more than a head taller than the rest of them, and he was grinning ear to ear. "This is the best summer ever."

"Glad you think so. I've got you all some pirate gear and squirt guns." Marilyn started passing out hats, eye patches, bandannas, foam swords, and brightly colored water guns.

They all thanked her and started swashbuckling each other immediately, laughing and carrying on about their adventures ahead.

Aster couldn't keep the smile off her face. They were having the time of their lives. The solemn, scared child Liam had been seemed like a bad dream.

"She really is the best." Russ's voice came from behind her, making Aster jump. "Sorry. Leaving for work." He stepped down the plastic steps. "Corndogs are in the microwave, and I cut up the apples and pears for 'em too."

"Thank you."

He waved her off. "Just wash the dishes. I hate dishes." Russ hugged his grandmother before getting in his car.

"I hope you have a good day," Aster whispered to the man who waved as he pulled out of the driveway.

Aster poked the wine bottle with her finger, moving it further away from her. She rested her chin on the table, re-reading the label and sighing to the empty trailer. *Why had she even bought this?* She had only drank alcohol a handful of times in her life. What was she going to do with an entire bottle? She'd wasted money on something she didn't need.

She had gone to the store with Marilyn to pick up some groceries, while Erving had volunteered to watch the boys. She hadn't needed this bottle of wine, but she still bought it. There had been a tasting event at the store and when Marilyn encouraged her to try the samples, she just went along with it. The man running the event asked her which one she liked better, and when she told him, he put a bottle in the cart whispering, "she deserved some fun on the holiday."

Aster nearly had a panic attack, if Marilyn hadn't patted her arm, she might have broken down in the store. Aster didn't like strangers touching her or getting in her space, all too often she felt raw and exposed. It was as if everyone was looking at her and seeing something she couldn't. Aster knew she had responsibilities, but wasn't she allowed to have a little of herself for herself? A scowl crossed her features and she pushed at the bottle again. At any point during the shopping trip she could have set the bottle down or even told the cashier she'd changed her mind, but instead she bought it. She bought it because someone put it in her cart and she didn't know how to say no. Had she ever really told anyone no in her whole life? Had she always just done as she was told?

Tears filled her eyes and she put her head down, her forehead *thunking* against the fake wood grain. She stopped herself short of actually crying; too silly of a reason to cry. Aster wondered if Sariyah would like the flavor. If she gave the bottle as a gift, it wouldn't be a waste of money. It had only been two dollars, but it was two dollars spent not on food, finding a job, or things for Liam.

Raspberry Hard Lemonade. Aster had always liked lemonade, or really anything that was lemon flavored. Raspberries were good too. The man said it was wine. She was allowed to drink wine; a lot of mothers drank wine. Maybe she should put it in the refrigerator?

The lock of the door clicked and the door opened as Russ entered. "Oh, you're up. Hi." His dark blonde hair was wet and so was the rest of him. He was soaked.

Aster glanced through the window, and suddenly heard the pings on the roof. "Is it raining?"

"Just started." Russ nodded water droplets flinging everywhere. "We should open up the windows, get some cooler air in here."

"I can do the ones in here. You should go change out of your wet clothes." She shooed him towards the bedroom, trying not to notice how the material of his work shirt clung to him like a second skin. He was more muscular than she'd previously thought.

Desperate to get her hands busy, Aster got to work opening the window closest to her.

Russ disappeared down the hall and she slipped into Liam's room to open his window. The fan was loud enough in here that it was hard to hear anything outside of the room which was good. Liam could rest without Russ having to be silent when he got home from work. Her son was sprawled out on his back, one hand gripping the whale stuffed toy. She kissed his forehead before sneaking back out.

Russ was standing by the doorway, adjusting the screendoor so more air could get through it. A genuinely cool breeze ran through the trailer and she sighed. It felt amazing. She didn't think living a few hours north could make such a difference in the weather, but it did. The temperature dropped twenty to thirty degrees once the sun went down, it was because of all the lakes Margie had explained to her.

"Official drink of high school parties." Russ was holding the bottle of wine, and smirked as she felt herself blush.

Her hands went to the pearls around her neck. "The grocery store had them on sale. Wait can teenagers drink in this state?"

"Only if you count crossing the blue bridge when your nineteen." Russ laughed, setting the bottle on the table. "You never snuck a drink at a party when you were underage?"

Aster shook her head.

He scratched his goatee. "Yeah, you don't seem like you'd be the kinda kid who'd run wild. Didn't drink in college?"

"I got married young." She dropped her eyes to the floor, "I didn't go to college."

"Did you want to?"

"I never really gave it any thought." Aster glanced at Russ as he leaned against the door frame.

Allen told her when both of the kids were in school, she'd be allowed to study accounting, but that was before Liam was born. At Liam's gender reveal party, when they found out he was gonna be a boy, Allen had given her a card with a handwritten note promising two years of classes. He'd torn it up in front of her after Liam had to stay in the NICU. When they were finally able to take Liam home, Allen had apologized for losing his temper and told her he'd still let her go, but he never let her enroll—there always a reason to wait. Now she didn't even know if she could handle college courses. She'd been out of school so long.

"I'm gonna go back outside for a bit." Russ pulled his outside shoes back on.

She cocked her head to the side questioning, "in the rain?"

"Already wet." He shrugged. "And it feels great out there." He stepped outside and Aster walked up to the door, watching him find a spot to lean against the trailer under the awning.

She kicked off her house shoes and hurried outside through the downpour and under the cover with him. "I thought you meant you were gonna go stand in the rain."

"Never said that was the plan." He pulled out his lighter and cigarettes. "Switch with me." He patted her side and she shifted by him.

Aster arched her eyebrow at him despite her compliance.

A flame ignited from the lighter, bathing Russ in a yellow light for a moment as he lit his cigarette. "Didn't want you down wind of me," he explained.

"You only smoke at night." She realized out loud.

"Yeah." He took a drag from it, the smoke curling around him. "I cooked at a bar and grill when I was twenty. All the closers would smoke in the parking lot at the end of our shifts. Nothing to do in this town that late."

The rain intensified enough that she was getting a little damp, even under cover. Aster held her arm out into the rain. "I was twenty when Liam was born."

"When's your birthday?"

"March second and Liam was born on the twenty-second." She flexed her toes against the grass. "What about you?"

"May fourth."

Aster smiled. "Taurus. Stubborn."

"Been accused." Russ conceded, pinching off his cigarette and putting it back in the pack. "Gonna be muggy tomorrow, but it's nice to have a break from the heat tonight."

"It does feel really nice."

Russ's monitor started beeping the low battery warning. "Damn it. Guess I'm heading back inside."

She chewed on her lip. "I should go to bed anyway."

"Your call." He shook his head. "I'll put your bottle in the fridge, you'll want it to be cold when you drink it."

"Thank you."

"No trouble." Russ disappeared into the trailer.

Aster sat down on the chair under the awning and watched the rain for nearly an hour before heading inside.

CHAPTER 23

Sariyah secured the swim cap over Noni's short rowed-braids, while Aster applied a second round of sunscreen to Liam.

"Mom, I'm fine." He fussed watching the other kids already in the pool.

Aster kept hold of his arm. "You won't be if you get burned. Hold still one more second." She finished applying the lotion to his back. "Alright, all set. Go be free."

He let out a whoop of excitement, but still waited for Noni, who grabbed his hand and they raced to the pool together.

"They're thick as thieves." Sariyah observed. "Have you figured out which school you're enrolling Liam into? I know the third grade teacher at Noni's school from when Imani had her and she's amazing. Plus that school's not too far from the park."

Aster rubbed sunscreen into her neck and arms. It had been far too hot not to wear a sundress, but she had to ignore the paranoia that everyone was looking at her. She was being silly. "Which school was that? I know I have to register him soon."

"Seven's Creek. They updated last year, so it's still nice despite the state budget." She pushed her silken black hair away from her face.

So many things to think about, to plan, and so many unknowns. She hadn't realized how much she'd just done as Allen instructed instead of working things out for herself. She went from depending on her parents instructions and money to her husband with no pause. How was she going to afford everything? Public school was free, but Liam would need clothes, supplies, and if he wanted to play sports more expenses would be added. Aster pulled at her pearls. She had to make this work. She had to make this work for Liam. She couldn't fail him again.

Sariyah seemed to sense Aster's panic and redirected their conversation. "If you're still looking for work, my friend's a tailor and she says if you can sew, she can give you spillover work. It'd be per job payments and not necessarily regular pay, but it's something."

Aster smiled. "That would be amazing. I used to sew all the time. I'm sure it wouldn't be too difficult to get back into it."

"Fantastic. I can get you her number on Monday." She checked to make sure baby Joi was still in the shade of the umbrella.

"Thank you so much."

"No trouble at all. She's always complaining about having too much work all at the same time, but not enough overall to hire someone." Sariyah motioned for Zuri to come over to her and adjusted her swimsuit. "Your bottoms are ridin' up."

"It's 'cause a the slide." Zuri insisted.

"Just be careful with it." Sariyah kissed her daughter's forehead. "Stay close with one of your sisters."

"Yes, ma'am." The girl skipped off to join the other kids.

Liam and Amos were splashing water at each other while Cosmo and Seagar were dunking each other under the surface. Noni was yelling that they should all play Marco Polo instead of crazy boy stuff.

"She's so independent," Aster observed.

"You mean stubborn and bossy," Sariyah laughed. "She's got big opinions all the time."

"It's good she does. Girls are told to be smaller and I don't think it's good." She gripped her fingers together.

Her new friend looked at her, dark eyes searching Aster's lighter ones. "He made you small didn't he? Your ex?"

She couldn't bring herself to say it out loud, but she nodded as her fingers rubbed over her pearls.

"Aster, that's not *your* fault. You left. You got out."

"But I waited so long." Aster breathed out, a tear rolling down her face. "What if Liam never recovers from how his father treated him?"

Sariyah clicked her tongue and pointed towards where the kids were playing. "I see a kindhearted little boy. He may have a bit of a temper, but you can be kind and have a temper. Two things can be true at the same time."

Aster wiped off her face. Sariyah was right. Her mind drifted from how her neighbors viewed her ex-husband versus how she knew him. How everyone thought he was perfect and he hadn't been. They saw a man who always maintained himself, his house, and kept calm, but that was in public. At home, he didn't have to yell to be cruel, it was most often in the quietest tones he hurt her the most. The things he said about Liam and the things Liam heard him say. The nights at the kitchen table where Liam had to redo his homework over and over until it met Allen's standards. The frustration in his voice when Liam didn't get it right the first time. It was never raised fists or raging screams—it was always calm, cutting words and expressions of disgust. Aster was viewed as a monster for leaving with his son, but Allen didn't want Liam. He didn't care when Aster left with him. Liam's father didn't have the patience for him.

In contrast, Russ had nothing but patience for him. Aster lost count of how many times she'd woken up to them making breakfast together or Russ explaining a cooking technique three or four times before Liam got it. Russ would growl and fuss, sure, but he always praised Liam's attempts and successes. Seeing Russ beat up Kevin had been scary. The fact that it freaked Liam out was worse, but she wasn't afraid of Russ. She'd been so afraid of Allen, she'd walked on eggshells all the time. Focused on perfection and not being in the way. Russ told her to make the space hers and not to worry about the messes. Mess was a part of life.

"Are you staying for the fireworks?" Sariyah interrupted her spiraling thoughts.

Aster shook her head. "No." She pulled at the pearls around her neck. She hated loud noises. Allen took her to the gun range on some of their first dates and taught her to shoot. In retrospect it seemed like he enjoyed everyone seeing him teaching her to shoot more then her learning the skill. She'd hated every minute of it. The first time he mentioned stopping their weekly visit, she enthusiastically agreed. "I don't like them."

Joi fussed and Sariyah picked her up, giving her some crackers to chew on. "Hate to be the bearer of bad news, but half the county's gonna be lighting off their own fireworks. I think your trailer park is ground zero for the bootlegged ones."

Aster winced and took a long drink from her bottle of water.

"That bad, huh?" She let Joi pull on her bracelets. "I'll talk to Marc and you can come over with Liam. You guys can stay inside with me and Joi. We're in the city, so there's a little less raucous than out here in the sticks."

"Liam's really excited about the fireworks. I don't want him to miss them." She managed to smile at Sariyah. "Our neighbor is taking some of the boys out to the nearby lake. I guess they are going to light a bunch of them off over the water, then camp in the truck overnight."

"Country kid nonsense." Sariyah laughed and Aster echoed it.

"I guess it is. Liam's just thrilled he gets to be involved."

"Well, if you change your mind and want to come hang out, you let me know."

"I will."

CHAPTER 24

Bang. Bang. Bang.

She was safe. She was safe. Aster repeated the mantra to herself with measured breaths, trying to think of anything other than the fireworks outside.

Liam was with Erving and his grandsons having the time of their lives at the lake roasting hot dogs and s'mores over a fire. After the fireworks, they'd be sleeping in the bed of Erving's truck. A little boy's dream.

Pop. Pop. Crackle. BANG!

Aster yelped covering her ears. The sounds were so intense, they might as well have been in the trailer. Since dusk, they'd been going off nearly nonstop. She should have gotten earplugs at the store for herself when she got Liam's. It was just like her to not plan properly. To have the upcoming situation right in front of her and do nothing about it. *Careless. Immature. Childish. How had she not prepared?*

She made herself small, curling up as tightly as she could, letting out another pathetic sound as the raucous noise raged outside. There were dishes in the sink that needed to be washed. The floor hadn't been mopped yet this week. The clothes in the washer needed to be moved to dryer. She wasn't even dressed properly. Her hair wasn't pulled back and she was in sleep pants and a tank-top. Russ would be back soon, and she couldn't be a sniveling mess, hiding in the dark. She was a mother. She was required to look the part whether her child was present or not.

Four more loud bangs and she couldn't stop herself from screeching in terror. She was back at the shooting range with Allen. His arms around her, caging her in as he lined up the shot, forcing her finger on the trigger. A low whisper to squeeze the trigger and a 'that's my girl' when she hit the bullseye. Her eyes daring to meet his after trying to keep herself from shaking as he kissed her. They had been alone, he knew the range owner. It was just the two of them after hours. His hands under her t-shirt, seeking access to her untouched skin and a whisper of how long he'd waited for her.

Aster screamed as a particularly loud crack of sound seemed to shake the trailer. Rocking back and forth, she tried to calm herself down. She should have bought ear plugs, taken Sariyah up on her offer, or drank the bottle of wine so she would have passed out. She'd never been able to handle her liquor. Her mind kept turning back to Allen. His hands under her clothes, pushing, pulling, a wanting she wasn't ready for....

"Aster? Jesus! Are you okay? Aster?" Russ's voice broke through her scattered thoughts. He smelled like smoke and sweat. He'd opened the closet door and was kneeling next to her on the ground.

Her hands went to her bare neck, then to her uncovered head, letting out a strangled cry. She stared at him wildly, both grateful and horrified he was in front of her.

Russ closed his eyes, but didn't move away. "Is this like a modesty thing? Your head being covered? I can grab you something." He paused, explaining himself further, "You were screaming when I came into the trailer. Are you okay? Did something happen?"

Fireworks whistled overhead, so she covered her ears and clamped her eyes closed. She needed to answer him. Needed to explain herself. She was so pathetic, terrified over something that happened every fourth of July. This was uncalled for; she was being irrational. If she explained she was fine, he'd leave. Russ was exhausted from working, and she was making it worse. Her being here made his life worse. She'd taken his bed away, his peace and quiet. She'd ruined everything.

Something warm draped over her body and she was pulled off the ground into Russ' arms.

"Okay now." He pushed her covered head into his shoulder and pressed his hand to her other ear. "Whatever is scaring you. I promise you're safe. I won't let anything hurt you. If I'd realized you were this upset, I wouldn't have smoked before coming inside. I must reek of it. Sorry."

Her face wasn't covered and she gulped down fresh air despite the sob that escaped her.

"Aster. Hey Aster, listen to me, okay? You can cry. You're allowed to break down." His hand found hers, resting his palm under hers. "Just squeeze my hand so I know you're still breathing. I'm shit at CPR."

Aster gripped his hand with more force than she intended to, but instead of pulling away he gently flexed his hand back. His palm was calloused, but soft from the dishes he washed at work.

"There you go. Good job." Russ kept his hand over her ear as she wept. He spoke softly to her but with a gravel that never really left his tone. From smoking and him admitting to yelling constantly, there was always grit in his voice. "We can stay like this and we don't have to talk or you can say anything you want to. You're safe, Aster. I promise. I'm not leaving unless you ask me to. I'm right here."

Her lip quivered as a lock of her hair fell against her cheek. It wasn't fair that no one outside her household knew the truth about why it was short. It wasn't fair how Liam and Allison witnessed it happen or Allen's pathetic apologies that were too little too late. Her hair was a source of shame. Embarrassment kept her from getting it fixed, the pain of the betrayal too much to forgive. But more than anything it was fear. Fear of staying had finally overshadowed the fear of leaving. It had been the last straw. The scissors. The ponytail in his hand. Both children, horrified. Getting out because she knew what was coming next, cover-up and sunglasses. She wouldn't let herself be abused. She left. She'd had to for herself and for her son.

Pressure made perfect. But it hadn't perfected Aster or Liam—it had broken them. Liam was fixable. She wasn't as sure about herself. What grown adult hid from fireworks? She was in the closet being coddled like a child. She pulled at her hair with her free hand.

"Don't," Russ implored, calling her attention back. Her ear was against his chest, the vibration as comforting as the words themselves. "Scream, talk, whisper, or cry, but don't hurt yourself. Please don't do that."

She curled her fingers into his uniform shirt, middle finger finding one of the buttons. "He cut my hair." She managed to force the words past her lips.

Russ squeezed her hand again. "Who?"

"My ex-husband." Aster drew in an unsteady breath, "He cut off my ponytail."

"Well fuck him. I'll kick his ass, if he ever comes around." His tone was joking, but Aster didn't think he was kidding.

"No, don't do that."

"Shave a landing strip into his hair? Something to embarrass him."

She chuckled despite the tears that were still falling.

Russ shifted and leaned his head against the top of hers. "You got that bottle of wine for yourself when you got groceries. I can grab it and a glass for ya. Did you eat tonight? You should eat."

"In a minute." She rested against his chest, blanket between them. "I wanna stay like this for a bit. Can we?"

"Sure thing, Sunshine."

CHAPTER 25

Prison had made Russ more aware of his surroundings as a whole, which in reality translated to him being jumpy all the time. Few things were worse than waking up to someone staring you down. Liam had done it a few times when he was waiting for Russ to wake up so he could ask a question. The kid's expression was curious at best or annoyed at worst by how long he'd waited to talk to Russ. However when Russ felt the familiar, 'I'm being watched by a child' feeling this morning, it was accompanied by an unfamiliar weight against his chest.

Liam was sitting in Russ's chair, arms folded over his chest, eyes so full of rage if Russ could have died by a look, he'd be buried or in an urn already.

Russ glanced down and sure enough, Aster had fallen asleep leaning on him last night. Correction, they had drunk her bottle of wine, ate the leftovers she'd brought home from the picnic, and fallen asleep together on the couch. He held a finger to his lips, which didn't sit well with Liam either. Russ shifted Aster slightly, managing to get her laying down on the couch without waking her. She was still dead to the world. She mentioned she'd never been a drinker. Her face was flushed after one glass and her giggling was nonstop halfway through the second.

He stood up and motioned for Liam to go outside. The kid still looked ready to murder him, but complied. Russ grabbed two apples, the jar of peanut butter, and a knife, then stepped outside himself.

"Why were you sleeping with my mom!" Liam snarled the moment the door closed behind Russ.

He dragged his chair to the edge of his safe-zone and sat down.

Liam followed grumbling, "you didn't answer me."

"Sit." Russ pointed to the ground and cut two slices of apple offering Liam the peanut butter jar first.

"This is gross. Our spit will get in the jar." He unscrewed the lid and swiped his slice into it.

He held his hand out for the jar. "Don't double dip it. We're gonna talk and not wake up your mom. She needs the sleep."

"Her last tests were good." Liam would interrogate his mother post her appointments if he wasn't allowed to attend. Scratching notes in his spiral notebook so he could understand what was happening to her. "Did you hurt her?"

"No." Russ hesitated to say too much. Didn't want to scare Liam or upset Aster, but he also didn't want to sleep with one eye open. "She didn't like the fireworks. We stayed up pretty late trying to ignore them." He glanced around, seeing it was barely dawn. "What time is it?"

"6:30." Liam held his hands out for the jar again, and yawned.

"Aren't you tired?"

"Yeah," he nodded. "But Cosmo's dad wants to take us out fishing on a boat with Mr. Erving. I wanted to ask my mom if I could go, but then I found you sleeping with her." Liam bit into his apple slice.

Two things ran through Russ' head first, he really needed Liam to stop phrasing it that way; the whole park was gonna get the wrong idea. And second, he didn't realize an eight-year-old could chew in such a threatening manner. "You're for sure gonna have to ask her if you want to do that. Do you have a life vest?"

"Cosmo said I can borrow his old one, and I can swim. I got taught the correct way." Liam leaned back on his hands and looked behind him at his tree house. "I wasn't allowed to get out of the pool until I had it right."

Well, that sounded all sorts of horrifying. Every time Russ learned something about Aster's ex-husband, it made him want to break house arrest and pay him a visit. No one should terrorize their wife or child the way this asshole had.

Russ cleared his throat, unsure of where to start, but knowing he needed to clear the air with the kid. "Liam, I wanted to apologize about that fight I got into last month. I know it scared you." He should have talked to Liam about this sooner, but he never found the right time. Better to tackle it now instead of leaving it hanging longer.

"I wasn't scared of that." He scrambled up and started towards the trailer.

"You looked pretty scared."

"I saw the cop car." He explained with a shrug.

That didn't make any sense, why the hell would this kid be afraid of the cops? Kids thought cops were good guys, not something to run from. Well not all kids, but most kids at Liam's age. Before he could ask, Aster poked her head outside the trailer door with a strained smile.

"Are we eating breakfast outside?" she asked, pushing her loose hair away from her face. Even from where he was sitting, Russ could tell her eyes looked dull. *Shit.* She was hungover.

Liam wrapped his arms around her waist, leaning his chin against her t-shirt, and looked up with pleading eyes. "Mr. Sam wants to take us out on his boat to fish. Can I go? Cosmo said I can use his old life vest. Please, Mom, please! I'll listen to whatever he and Mr. Erving says. Please!"

She kissed the top of his head. "Go brush your teeth and change your clothes. Your swim trunks are in the dryer."

"Awesome! Thanks, Mom!" He threw the door open.

"Sunscreen. Get it from the bathroom. I have to put sunscreen on you before you go."

"Okay!"

The door slammed and Aster walked up to Russ, skirt swishing around her bare feet and wincing as the sun hit her face. "Is it bad if I let him go so I can go back to sleep?"

Russ offered her an apple slice with peanut butter on it. "Naw. Not even a little bit." She accepted the food and he assured her, "I'll make you a hangover cure when he leaves. It'll make it easier to sleep."

"If I go back to sleep, I won't get anything done today."

"So?"

Aster sighed. "I can't waste a whole day doing nothing. I've spent the last month...."

"Recovering. You've spent the last month recovering." Russ stopped her before she went into one of her 'I don't do enough' rants. He wished he could get her to just *be* for a bit.

"Do you work today?" she asked.

"No. Why? Are you gonna put me to work?" He smirked, unable to help it, and she blushed. *Was he being flirtatious? Oh no, he could not be flirting with her.*

She fidgeted with her necklace. "I was going to ask to borrow the car later. Sariyah has a friend who needs help with sewing. I was going to go see if I could find a machine at a second hand store."

Russ yawned. God he was ready to go back inside and take a nap. "Most of 'em will be closed; it's Sunday and a holiday." He smoothed out his goatee, "My grandma might have an extra one though."

"I couldn't ask her for one of hers."

He chuckled, "She's only got two hands, and if she's got more than one that works, she can't use them at the same time. If she really wants them both, she'll say no."

Aster arched her eyebrow, clearly skeptical. "Would she though?"

"Aster, when she wants her way, she gets it. She used to ask my grandfather three times to do things, then after the third time, she'd do it herself whether she knew what she was doing or not." Russ barked out a laugh as a memory came back to him. "I'm not kidding, she started putting holes in the support wall of our house, because she wanted it more open. Thought Grandpa was gonna have a heart attack when he got home. The roof was bowing in."

She giggled and covered her mouth. "Oh my goodness."

"Trust me. If she has a strong opinion, she'll make it known."

The trailer door burst back open and Liam rushed out. He was soaking wet, holding a towel, a t-shirt, and sunscreen.

"Did you take a shower?" Aster asked as Liam handed her the sunscreen and dumped the other items on the ground.

He nodded wet hair flinging droplets all over Aster. She laughed as he further explained. "I thought it would be faster if I showered and I brushed my teeth at the same time."

Russ stifled a laugh guessing the answer the kid gave meant he was simply wet and not actually clean. He stood up and stretched. "I'll make you a lunch to take with ya."

"Okay."

"Liam." Aster's voice was sharp with disapproval.

He sighed dramatically. "Thank you, Russ. But don't do the thing that you did this morning again."

Russ chose to ignore the threat, hoping Aster wouldn't ask to avoid the awkwardness. "No trouble. Can't let you guys starve." He reached the door when he heard Liam further question his mother.

"Why were you and Russ sleeping together, Mom?"

Like any man with any good sense, he knew when it was best to retreat and fled into the trailer, not waiting to hear her answer.

CHAPTER 26

Summers were never the longest season, but this one in particular was flying by faster than Russ cared for. When he and Jerry pulled up to the curb by the trailer, Liam was playing with Amos and Seagar, which was good. The kid found out the cousins were heading back home the first week of August and he'd cried half the night. The nightmare trio—okay, maybe nightmare was a little harsh—the trouble-making trio were enjoying their last two weeks together. Erving told them that the plan was to come back next summer, and the three all but demanded a contract to be signed with blood. Cosmo was only in the park every other week, but Liam would make friends at school. He'd be fine.

"Your lady friend got her car back, huh?"

It took nearly a month, but Russ finally got Jerry to stop calling Aster his girlfriend. "Yeah, she's sewing to make money. James finished up with it two days ago."

"Front bumper looks like hell."

"Liam's not a great driver." Russ got out of the car.

Jerry choked on his drink of coffee, "What the hell does that mean?"

"Nothing man. Have a good vacation next week." Russ waved him off and whistled to the boys holding up a bag. "I got donuts."

Those three could move at the speed of light when properly motivated. The three held out their dirt smeared hands. Russ arched his eyebrow. "Hose first."

They rushed to the end of the hose, which was hooked up to the sprinkler, and Seagar started to twist it off.

"Oh, careful!" Russ couldn't see her, but heard Aster plead. "I don't want to be splashed, guys, and please don't get the clothes wet."

Russ rounded the corner of the trailer to find drying bed sheets, jeans, and towels hanging by neon clothes pins blocking his view of the garden. He handed the bag to Liam and the kid immediately sprinted to the treehouse, demanding they sit down to eat. Seagar crying mutiny over donut theft and Amos threatening a lifetime feud with the blonde.

On one hand, Russ understood it. He'd do some questionable things for an apple fritter, but Amos's favorite was a plain, unfrosted donut. What kid wanted a plain, unfrosted donut? Amos. Seagar loved maple bacon, but Russ was convinced the kid just wanted the only one that offered meat on it. Liam wanted frosted croissants, but probably because he was trying to figure out how to make them.

He moved past the laundry to find Aster knelt down in the garden wearing a black t-shirt over her skirt. That was odd, he couldn't remember her ever wearing black.

"We got anything yet?" he asked. All the plants were bright green, despite the lack of rain this summer. Aster diligently cared for the little plot, the leaves and vines tangled together, fighting for space and sunlight, but they still looked healthy.

She held up a small cucumber with a grin. "I wanna try to pickle these. I couldn't go back to sleep this morning, so I weeded the bed."

"Is the school thing tonight?" The open house was the new cause of Aster's anxiety. They'd talked about it a couple of days ago.

"No, next week. I know Liam will be happy when we meet his classmates, but," she itched at her cheek, leaving dirt streaked across it. "He's so upset at the moment, I can't get him to think about it in a positive light."

Russ smirked, "Careful, you're getting dirty."

She rubbed at her cheek vigorously. "Better?"

"No, you just moved it around. Think you're gonna have to wash your face to get it." He turned to face the sun, letting his eyes drift close. Dr. Collins had told him that people were complicated plants and he'd buy that theory. "I don't think a little dirt will hurt ya."

"I'm glad you feel that way. This is one of your shirts turned inside out."

Russ turned to her with a wry smile, "Excuse me?"

Her giggle, the mischievous one he loved to hear so much, rang out from Aster. "I knew it was muddy and everything I own is pastel. I promise I'll wash it."

She held out her pinkie and, without thinking, he linked them together and they shook on it. She pulled her hand back, but he leaned forward and caught one of her blonde locks with his fingers. "Getting longer."

She didn't pull it back or cover it up all the time now, but he could tell she wasn't confident about it. He wished he was in the position to tell her how pretty she looked with it down. How it complimented her features and framed the healthy glow in her cheeks.

Aster blushed. "I feel like everyone can see me. I don't think I'm a short-hair person."

"Bridgette cuts hair. Ask her to clean it up." Russ still hadn't moved away. He was still playing with the lock, finally tucking it behind her ear. "Not dismissing how you feel about it, but the length of your hair doesn't define you. And looks good despite what you think."

"I guess it's a better length for t-shirts instead of dresses."

"You're pretty either way. Keep the shirt for gardening, looks better on you anyway." When her blush ran down to her neck, he realized how close they were and what he'd said. He scrambled to get up. "I'm gonna crash for a couple of hours."

Russ kicked his shoes off when he got into the trailer and switched his monitor's battery. He mentally thanked Jerry for the millionth time for the new monitor. The simplest change, but it made a world of difference. He checked his phone battery and flopped down on his back on his bed. Before he could talk himself out of it, he dialed one of his saved numbers.

"Tats and Trims." The voice on the other line was a friendly growl.

He stared at the ceiling for a second before sighing loudly.

"If you're not the pervert who called last week, you better say so, cause I'm getting my whistle."

"Bridgette." Russ yipped her name to keep from getting his eardrum blown out.

Now she sighed. "Russ, if something's broken, call Margie. You know I can't do anything when I'm at the shop."

"It's hair related."

"Your hair looks good. I don't know how you went from that lawnmower job you did in the spring to your current one, but repeat whatever you did." She chuckled and bid a customer welcome in. "I don't have time to jaw about—"

He interrupted her. Not letting himself overthink it and blurted out what he'd been on edge of asking her since the fourth of July. "Can you offer to cut Aster's hair? She won't ask. There's this open house thing at Liam's school and she's a ball of nerves." He didn't want to give out Aster's business, but also wanted to help her. "She hates how her hair looks now. I think her ex had something to do with it."

Bridgette clicked her tongue and the music from the shop got louder.

He cleared his throat, than tried to further explain, "Just give her a haircut experience. Something nice for herself."

"Russ, I see where your hearts at...."

"Heart's got nothing to do with it." He insisted. Liam's 6 AM question of 'why are you sleeping with my mom' had hit the trailer park rumor mill like a five-minute mile. Russ was sure there was a betting pool open as anyone he talked to in the park asked about how Aster was doing. No doubt Aster got the same questions, but they were both feigning ignorance around each other. Him playing with her hair wouldn't calm that fire if anyone had seen him.

He wanted to help. It had nothing to do with him being interested in her, which he wasn't, she needed a confidence boost. "I'll pay for it."

She snickered.

"What's so funny?"

"Oh nothing, just you thinking it's got nothing to do with your heart is funny to me."

"Bridgette, she's my roommate and that's all."

"Sure. Margie's just my roommate too." He attempted to argue, but she talked over him. "I've got time tomorrow with Raven, one of my trainees. I'll call Aster and ask. Talk to you later, *Rusty*."

CHAPTER 27

The bell chimed over Aster's head as she stepped into the gothic themed combination salon and tattoo parlor. Of all the business combinations she could have imagined, this one wouldn't have made her list of possibilities, but here it was. She opened her mouth to call out, but thought better of it. Bridgette was no doubt busy.

Aster looked around the waiting area there were pictures of couples, articles about LGBTQ rights' victories, and images of the Stonewall riots were framed on the walls and hung asymmetrically. She didn't really know much about this community, though her parents were vocal about it all being a sin and Allen had nothing but disdain for anyone in it. She rubbed her arms, eyes focusing on a picture of a younger Margie and Bridgette kissing in front of the Washington Monument. They looked so carefree and in love. *How could that kind of affection be wrong?*

This was such a welcoming space, even with the dominant colors of black, white, and deep red. There were splashes of purple paint on the walls behind the frames and various rainbow flags hung below the crown moulding. She wondered what this building had been used for before, the exposed piping made her think of dance clubs she'd seen in movies. There was a sort of magic here.

A yowl drew Aster's attention to the milk-white cat perched on a vintage, high-back purple velvet chair. All the chairs in the waiting area were similar in style. There was even a lounging chaise under the window.

"Hi, Hun! Welcome in. Ignore Jasper, he's been fed." Bridgette wiped her hands off on a towel and scratched behind the cat's ear. "Did you find the place alright?"

Aster nodded, "The landmarks helped." She pointed over her shoulder, "I've never seen a two story Taco Bell before."

"When more of the factories were open five years ago, it was the only 24-hour restaurant in town. So they took advantage. Now it's just a staple part of the community." She smirked and motioned for her to follow.

A dark-haired young man was sweeping by an empty chair. Brightly colored tattoos decorated his arms, and Aster noticed they were a different style than Bridgette's. *Did tattoo styles change with fashion?* Aster hadn't really ever given it much thought, and until recently, she wasn't close to anyone with tattoos. She wondered about Russ's as he had so many, but it felt too rude to ask.

Bridgette patted her shoulder, explaining, "this is Raven. He's the stylist who needs the practice hours."

"Hey." He bobbed his head, but his shaggy bangs, kept Aster from seeing his eyes. "I appreciate you coming in. Can you please sit in the chair for me?"

Raven sounded like he was reciting from a script, not in a rude way, but like he was nervous.

Aster sat in the chair and pulled the scarf away from her head.

"I'm going touch your hair to look at it. Is that okay?"

Why would he ask permission? She was here for a haircut. You couldn't give someone a haircut without touching them. Was he that nervous? A little worry in the back of her head popped up, perhaps he was too new at this? But Bridgette was here to supervise. Everything would be alright.

Aster offered an encouraging smile to the mirror, hoping Raven would see it. "That's fine. I trust you."

"Sick." He ran his fingers through her hair from the back to the front pushing it all forward. "I wanted to check cause, Bridgette said...."

The aforementioned woman cleared her throat loudly.

Aster kept her expression as neutral as she could, but now it made sense. Bridgette calling out of the blue asking her if she'd be willing to have a junior stylist practice on her hair. Russ had told her about Allen cutting off her ponytail. They were trying to make sure she wasn't going to panic.

"Uh, right." He paused, then rushed out a plausible excuse. "She said your last haircut was hella sketchy. Wanted to make sure you were chill with me."

She realized without the script, Raven used a lot of slang. This was what he really sounded like. With this place catering to an alternative crowd, it likely put folks at ease. She kept her hands in her lap, before continueing, "I'm um... totally chill with you." It sounded so foreign to her even as she said it, but Raven grinned.

Bridgette looked through her hair with Raven as the two muttered between themselves coming up with a game plan. The older woman sat in the chair next to Aster. "So we have gold, silver, and shit news."

She blinked, more positive than negative, that was something. "I'd like to hear the worst news first."

"It's crazy uneven." Raven pushed his bangs away from his face and clipped them back. Whatever color his eyes were, they were disguised by vibrant purple contact lenses. He was wearing earrings, one ear dotted up from the lobe to the arch. "We need to cut a bunch off to even it."

Aster winced. Shorter. The last thing she wanted, but a little discomfort to move forward. Her hair would grow and she would continue to get stronger.

"The silver news is we can use some of the uneven chunks to cut some sick layers into it," Raven continued, bobbing his head as spoke.

Layers. More hair gone. She drew in a deep breath. It was only hair, it didn't define her. She wasn't Samson from the Bible. If she had been, Allen cutting her hair would have ended her, not put her on the path to freedom.

She straightened her shoulders. "What's the gold news?"

Bridgette caught Aster's chin with her thumb and index finger. "You're gonna absolutely knock 'em dead with the cut we've planned."

Whatever Aster had pictured in her head was nowhere near what her hair looked like at the end. It was longer in the front, but the back was short, short. The layers gave it a lot of body without being too much. The woman in the mirror looked confident, like she could handle things thrown at her without grabbing at a set of old pearls. Tears misted her vision, and her voice cracked slighted as she complimented Raven's work. "It looks great. Thank you so much." She grinned at her own reflection and wiped the tears away from her cheeks.

Raven styled it with a messy look to show her how to do it fast, but explained she could straighten it too. Bridgette watched and critiqued the entire time, but never in a cruel or mean way. She really cared about teaching Raven to do a good job.

Aster had her head down, digging in her purse when the door chimed despite it being after hours.

"Almost done babe. Gimme five." Raven took the clip out of his hair, tipping his head down to ruffle it.

"How much do I owe you?"

Bridgette shook her head. "You were practice. No charge."

Aster bit her lip. "Can I tip him?"

Bridgette shrugged, "If you think he did a good enough job, sure."

She fished out a twenty and handed it to Raven.

When he reached for it, Aster noticed that he'd put on a slew of rings. "How much change you need?"

Aster shook her head. "Keep it. I was expecting to pay. So your blessing."

"Sweet! Thanks." He pocketed the bill. "Hey Tricky, you want Taco Bell for dinner?"

"Hells ya." Tricky's grin could be heard in his voice. "Starvin' I didn't work today, so no grub."

"There's food in the fridge." Raven swept up Aster's hair from the ground and offered her a hand.

Tricky countered. "I didn't wanna do dishes."

She looked at the lanky, black-haired man leaning on the door frame. There was no chance she'd met him before, and yet he seemed familiar. She couldn't put her finger on it.

"You can get going, Raven, walk Aster out." Bridgette shooed them towards the door. "Aster, tell Russ I said hi and that he didn't give me that potato recipe yet."

Tricky looked down at Aster, "You know Russ Hulston?" When Aster nodded he grinned. "Oh sweet, I work with him at the hospital."

She was equally surprised. "Um, yeah. I live with him." That's why Tricky seemed familiar. Russ had talked about working with a Tricky. Her assumption was that Russ was using a placekeeper name, not that he actually went by that name. How odd.

"No shit?" Raven held the door for them and lit a cigarette once they were outside. "Small fucking world."

Tricky flicked his lip ring with his tongue and looked up at Raven nervously. "No one knows at work."

Aster was lost again, but quickly realized the pair were holding hands. "Oh, I won't say anything. I can't imagine Russ would mind though. He's known Margie and Bridgette most of his life."

"Cool. Doesn't explain why he lied about you though." Tricky cocked his head to the side. "He said you two didn't know each other. He only caught you when you fell and you were only in hospital a couple of days. I remember, 'cause he kept doubling your meals."

"We didn't know each other at first." She fidgeted with her purse. "But we're friends now and we live together with my son."

Raven pushed his hair back revealing his confused expression. "Straight people make no sense."

"Word." Tricky barked out a laugh.

They followed Aster until she got to her car, then turned back to go inside the Taco Bell on the corner.

Aster drove home, sneaking glances at herself in the rear-view mirror. Her hair had always been long, but the more she looked at it, the more she liked her new cut. She got out of the car and looked up to the treehouse.

"Hi, Miss Aster." Cosmo waved to her from one of the windows, before looking down at Amos and demanding, "Put the can in the bucket."

Amos complied and the bucket ascended up on a rope.

"It worked!" Seagar's voice was unmistakable, as he rattled on, "Cosmo, you made an elevator! Amos, you gotta see this."

"I did see it." Amos rolled his eyes, then scaled up the ladder to join the others.

Where was Liam? Aster glanced around the yard, she could smell food cooking on the grill, but no one was there.

The trailer door opened, Liam bounding out with Cosmo's dad right behind him. "Buddy, Russ said it would be fine for another minute."

"I'm not your buddy, sir." Liam argued, "Russ is wrong, it's gonna burn. I'm not allowed to pull it myself off. I might burn my arm, so I need help."

Sam nodded to Aster when they made eye contact. "Oh hey, Aster. Nice hair cut, is it new?" He used the tongs to pull the foil packets off the grill and set them on the plate resting on the stack of empty milk crates.

She grinned. "It is. Thank you."

"Looks really good on ya." He took a drink from his beer, his hazel eyes focused on her.

Aster blushed at the compliment, not sure how to respond. It had been a long time since she'd gotten a compliment. Expect for Russ telling her she looked good in his shirt the other day. Her blush deepened.

Liam ran up and hugged her, "Mom, you look like a movie star."

She cupped his face in her hands, happy for the distraction. "Thank you, my little prince. What are you making for dinner?"

"We grilled chicken with spices and sauce in the foils. It's gonna taste better that way." He dashed up to the tree and hollered to his friends, "Time to eat!"

Seagar opened the trap door, shouting, "Cosmo made us an elevator! Let's put it in the bucket and eat up here."

Liam put his hands on his hips. "I don't wanna get sauce all over the place."

"We're not that messy." Amos challenged hanging from the climbing rope.

Liam huffed. "Are so."

"Aye," Sam called out, "out of the treehouse to eat dinner. Let's go." He gave her a wink, "now, they can have me as the common enemy."

Aster glanced back to the trailer. Russ's car was still in the driveway, he hadn't left for work yet. She wondered where....

"Thanks for coming over and helping with boys, Sam." Russ thumped down the trailer steps, but stopped on the final one, staring unblinking at Aster.

"No worries man. Happy to help out for a free meal. You and Liam cook way better than I do, the best I got is canned O-noodles with garlic powder or microwaved meals." Sam laughed and motioned to Aster. "Although I kinda feel bad, since she made it home before you had to leave."

"We're ready for food!" Seagar held out his hands.

Liam shoved his friends towards the house. "Wash your hands first."

"Grab plates to eat on," Aster called after them as they barreled by Russ, who was still on the last step.

"Yes, Ma'am." The chorus retreated as the door slammed behind them.

"They're gonna break that door." Sam shook his head, then arched an eyebrow at Russ, "You alright, man?"

Russ nodded, blue eyes still on Aster. "Looks good," he coughed, "I...I'm good. Just tired. Heading to work. Glad Bridgette could help you with your hair, Aster."

She nodded and fidgeted with her fingers. She couldn't remember the last time she'd made someone speechless.

CHAPTER 28

Aster smoothed her skirt for the third time, waiting to speak with Liam's new teacher. Her new hair had been a hit. She tucked the memory away to ward off future insecurities. Most of the other parents seemed to know one another, but hadn't been unfriendly. She could handle this.

Her car not starting earlier today had nearly thrown her into a panic. Thankfully it only needed a new battery, so it wouldn't be expensive to fix, but she still had to borrow Russ's car to get here. Which meant she had dropped him off for work and would have to pick him up tonight.

The school's open house party was full of kids exploring, parents catching up, and the teachers spending time with both students and parents. It was more laid back than the private school open houses Aster had attended before, which helped her anxiety.

Mrs. Wren Sol, the third grade teacher for Liam's class invited her students to sit in her room for a story while their parents took a tour of the campus. She took one-on-one time with each of the children who opted to listen to the story. After the kids exited the classroom, Mrs. Sol put up the schedule for her chats with the parents. Aster was the last name on the list, which made perfect sense. She had enrolled Liam fairly late.

The woman was tall, with ink-black hair that framed her delicate features. Behind silver glasses her keen eyes assessed Aster as she offered her hand. "You must be Mrs. Reign, Liam's mother."

"I am, but please call me Aster."

"Then I'm Wren. It's nice to meet you."

Wren held the door for them and Aster stepped into the brightly colored classroom. Desks were in clusters with pathways between and the chalkboard was covered in children's writings. Bookshelves, games, and posters created a calming but stimulating atmosphere.

"You moved to the area recently?"

Aster sat in the full sized chair across from Wren at her desk. "Beginning of June. I think Liam's adjusting well."

"He had some interesting answers to the questions I gave him." The teacher pulled out her notebook. "Very interesting indeed."

"If he's behind," she offered, "I can help him during August."

"He doesn't seem behind at all education wise. Liam's reactions to people is what caught my attention."

Aster felt her heart sink, her son must have lost his temper or made a fuss about something. What if he was doomed to forever be angry at the drop of a hat? She was really hoping his temper outbursts would get better as their situation became more stable. She rubbed her pearls. She needed to spend more time with him and make sure she was actively listening.

"He's got such a kind heart."

Aster felt her own shocked expression. She knew how kind and sweet her boy could be, but recently....

Wren inclined her head to the side. "Does that surprise you? He talked about you and how much he loves you and his new home."

A tear ran down her cheek and she quickly brushed it away. "We've just...we've had a rough year. I was worried he might be getting wrapped up in the negativity."

"A fair fear." Wren rested her elbows on her desk and her chin on her folded hands. "A few years ago there was a study concluding how 96% of men in prison for violent crimes against women were raised by single women."

Aster's jaw dropped open.

"It was a ridiculously inaccurate study. Once I gathered enough evidence to prove that, I sent it to the peer reviewer of the original article and the journal that published it." A sly smile crossed her lips. "The reviewer was so furious, he's made it his mission to discredit everything I've ever published."

Aster covered her mouth with her hand. "That's awful. It must be so stressful."

"Not at all. He's quite stupid and I enjoy proving it to the academic world. Don't worry about your prior situation affecting your son. He's doing fine." Wren glanced at her watch. "But there was one thing I wanted to cover with you before we go over any of your questions."

"Of course." She wondered at the way Wren switched gears so fast. Seemingly unbothered by someone trying to hurt her credibility and immediately addressing Aster's fears about her son without a sentence between.

"I told all the children they could ask me any question they wanted and I would likely answer it. I have to be careful—one year a child asked me where babies came from and her parents were unhappy when I gave the scientific answer." Wren took a sip from her water bottle. "Liam asked me what my favorite food was and he wrote it down."

Aster smiled. "He's learning to cook. Always loved anything food related, but my roommate is an incredible cook, and Liam's been his shadow for the last two months."

Wren chuckled quietly. "Would he be 'the grouchy guy' that lives in the trailer with you both?"

"Yes, that would be Russ." She laughed.

They had a lovely chat about the upcoming year and Aster helped Wren clean up the classroom before they walked out to the parking lot together. Liam had poked his head in and told her he'd be on the swings with the other kids and the chaperon from the school.

When they stepped out of the building, Liam was talking to a brown haired man in a flannel shirt. They were both looking down at something on the ground.

"Liam." Aster called to him. That wasn't the school chaperon.

"Mom, there's a turtle over here. It's so cool!" He waved for her to come over.

Wren walked over with Aster and knelt down next to Liam, "Chrysemys picta, or the painted turtle. They are common in North America, and are the official state reptile."

"He's so cool." Liam fidgeted with this fingers. "Mr. Sol says I should let him go on his way, cause he's looking for water."

"He is correct. Turtles are very stubborn, they will go where they know water is. You should never turn a turtle around." She smiled at Liam. "Perhaps we should see if our class can take a field trip to the nature center near the capital."

"That would be awesome." He grinned, but yawned.

Aster looked at her watch, it was already 8:30. "We should go, sweetie. Mrs. Sol and her husband need to get home."

"Oh, okay. I'll see you in class." Liam grabbed Aster's hand and waved to the couple.

In two steps, however, they realized they were headed in the same direction. Aster unlocked the car, but felt like she was being watched as she opened the door for

Liam to get into the back. She noticed that Mr. Sol was looking at her car, or Russ's car to be more accurate.

"Something wrong?" she questioned.

Mr. Sol didn't answer but he did walk around to the back of the car and let out a bark of a laugh. "Did you buy this car from Russ or Marilyn Hulston?"

Aster shook her head. "I borrowed it from Russ. You know him?"

"Yeah, went to high school together." He put his hands on his hips and shook his head. "You tell Hulston that DB says hi, and he still owes me a beer."

"Alright." She nodded.

DB helped Wren climb into a big red truck, and if Aster's eyes weren't playing tricks on her, Wren was taller than DB.

She started the car and waved to the pair.

"Hey mom."

"Yes, sweetie?"

"I think this school is better than my old one," Liam announced before launching into all the things he already liked, including his very pretty teacher.

He talked until they were half way back to the park when Aster noticed he was slowing down, then snoring in the backseat. It was already nine, and Russ was getting out at ten. *At this point, maybe she should drive to the hospital and pick him up?* Aster idled at the crossroads, fingers drumming against the steering wheel.

If they went back to the trailer, Aster would have to struggle with a half-asleep Liam twice, getting him out of and then back into the car. She couldn't leave him alone in the trailer, even for the forty-ish minutes the round trip would be.

Decision made, she turned left. Hospital here they come. She went through a drive thru and grabbed a drink for herself and Russ, because it would be rude not to, and parked in the side lot of the hospital.

Ten minutes after the hour, Russ came out of the hospital and Aster flashed the bright lights to get his attention. She switched to the passenger seat and they started back to the park.

He glanced back at Liam and asked, "He have a good time?"

"He did. His teacher is lovely and very smart—she mentioned she speaks five languages. I couldn't imagine being that smart." She reached for her drink at the same time Russ did and they both jumped as their fingers touched and muttered apologies. Aster cleared her throat. "She's a touch strange though. The way she brought things up and then breezed to the next topic. A little morbid maybe? But Liam adores her already."

Russ chuckled. "Aster, your kid adores anyone that's of the female persuasion. What's her name, the teacher?"

She pursed her lips not able to argue Russ's point. "Wren Sol, we met her husband DB. He said to tell you hi and that you owed him a beer."

"Rat bastard." Russ choked down his laughter as to not wake up Liam. "Yeah, I know him and I do owe him a beer. We were both flirting with Wren in a bar a couple of years ago."

"Oh." She toyed with her hair. "I think since they're married, he won that one."

"He really did. Good for him." He hit the turning signal and stopped at the light. "How did he know I knew you?"

"He saw the trunk of the car and asked if I knew you or Marilyn."

"Ha, I almost forgot about that. We stole the bumper for this car."

Aster gasped, "Why would you do that?"

"Young, dumb, and drunk."

CHAPTER 29

"Do we add it now?" Liam leaned towards the melting chocolate and Russ caught his collar to keep him from getting too close.

"Use the thermometer, not your face."

He stuck out his tongue. "It's on your side, I can't reach it."

Russ narrowed his eyes and retrieved the tool, keeping it in his hand. "You know how to ask."

"Can I have the thermometer, *please*." The sarcasm this kid had was beyond his years.

Russ would be more annoyed by the attitude if the kid didn't do everything with care and without hesitation. He was all bark. Liam didn't know how to express himself. The kid was scared of getting hurt, but the longer he and Aster were here, the better Liam seemed to get about it. Russ could relate. It had taken a lifetime and a prison sentence to rough up Russ' attitude, but Liam was eight. For the hundredth time, he wanted to ask the kid about his dad, but didn't want any of the answers.

"It's not ready yet." Liam huffed, his eyes focused on the reading as chocolate dripped on the counter. The tool *pinked* on the plate by Liam's cookies and the kid turned his attention to Russ. "Why do you have barbed wire on your arm?"

It had gotten hot in the trailer, so he'd rolled up the sleeves of his t-shirt to his shoulders, exposing the myriad of tattoos on his upper arms. "It was a popular tattoo to get when I was younger."

"Weird. What about that one?"

"Favorite hockey team."

"I've never watched hockey." Liam got himself a bottle of water from the fridge and handed Russ one as well.

"Your loss." Russ took a long drink. "We'll have to watch some games in the fall if the season doesn't lock out and see if it's your cup of tea."

"I thought hockey was a sport. Is it tea? And what's lock out mean?"

"Lock out means a strike, so they might not play if something doesn't get fixed." Russ wiped crumbs from the counter. "And 'cup of tea' is an expression. It means it's something you like."

"Seems dumb to call it tea."

"It's just a thing people say." It blew Russ's mind sometimes to think that Liam was learning things he was going to hang onto for the rest of his life. He wasn't concerned with the cooking stuff he was teaching Liam, but he worried about how much influence he might have otherwise. He wasn't a wholesome example of a life well-lived.

"What about this one? It's hard to see what it is. It is just letters?"

Russ turned his arm over, so Liam could see it better. "North, South, East, West and those are arrows separating the letters, it's the inside of a compass."

"It's messier than the hockey one."

"The skin on the under side of my arm is more sensitive it hurt like a..." He trailed off to keep from swearing. "It hurt more than the ones on the other side."

"What's on your other arm?"

Russ turned his back to the stove so Liam could see his other arm. "What do they look like?"

"I've seen your lines with the numbers in the middle, it's under your elbow. Why 69?"

Russ was glad he had a different answer for this one instead of the real reason he'd gotten it at eighteen. "I was born in 1969."

Liam scrunched up his nose, pointing out, "You're really old. Like my dad's age old."

"Thanks." Russ took a drink from his coffee cup.

"I kinda like your pirate ship. It's cool that there's red flowers in the water." He inclined his had to the side. "You have a pirate flag on your hand too. You must really like pirates."

"I do. I read the book Treasure Island when I was about your age. I have a copy of the Muppet movie. We'll have to watch it."

"Muppets are for little kids."

Russ rolled his eyes, "First of all, the Muppets are for everyone and secondly, you *are* a kid."

Liam tapped his foot on the metal step he was on. "What about your other hand?"

"I used to run in high school. I was very fast and six minutes flat was my best time. I was gonna go to college because of it."

"You don't seem very fast now."

He grimaced, "I got hurt. I can't really run anymore."

"Oh." Liam picked at his shirt for a moment then returned back to his observations of Russ's body art. "You don't have a lot of colors in your tattoos. Miss Bridgette has a lot of colors in her tattoos. I didn't think old people had tattoos. But she does and so do you."

"All right. That's enough of that." Russ grumbled and by a miracle the timer for the oven went off. "Get your mitts."

Liam hopped off the stool and put on his oven mitts. "Ready."

"Are you?" He tapped the counter. "Are your cooling racks on the counter?"

"I knew that." The kid raced to put the cooling racks down while Russ grabbed a towel for his own hand. "I want to pull them out myself."

"I'm only here to help." Russ reminded him. "You found the recipe and wanted to make these s'more cookies for you guys tonight. I'm just makin' sure you don't burn the place down."

He opened the oven for Liam and winced as the kid nearly burned his arm on the top of the oven. Thankfully he didn't and carried the baking sheet over to the other counter with Russ right behind.

"I'll hold the tray. Get the spatula so you can get the cookies down."

Liam carefully shuffled the tool under each cookie and got them on the cooling rack. "I got them all down without dropping any." His voice was mystified. "I did it right on the first try."

"Yeah, you're getting pretty good at this stuff." He ruffled the kid's hair, trying to get that stubborn section away from his eye. "Come up, Pup. Gotta check on your chocolate."

"Right." Liam rushed to the stove and checked the temperature. "Almost. Getting close. Should we get the marshmallows ready?"

"Your dish, your rules."

"Get 'em on a plate. It'll be easier." He handed Russ the bag to open.

"Nice bag." Russ smirked.

Liam sighed dramatically. "Can you *please* open it for me?"

"Yup. Works better when you ask." He opened the package and watched Liam pull out marshmallows one by one and set them on the clean plate until it was full. "Hey you might not wanna mention that whole old people thing around your mom. Mom's don't like to hear they're old."

"My mom's not old. She's a 70's baby. That's what my dad's mother called her." Liam examined his notebook where he'd written down his plan for this treat.

"You mean your grandma?" He was confused now. Aster hadn't mentioned any family, but then again, if it was her ex's family, it wouldn't be her family. Technically, his father's mother would still be Liam's family. Right?

"Mrs. Reign didn't want me to call her grandma. She said I was my mom's kid. That I wasn't like my dad or Allison." His tone was glum. "I was a failure."

Fuck. Now he'd depressed the poor kid. "That's a load of horseshit. You're ornery, but you're not a failure. Your mom loves you and thinks you're special. She's who you listen to."

Liam bit down on his lip. "Mrs. Reign said my mom was too young to know how to raise me right, and she'd messed up everything up, even me. I think my mom does a good job."

"She does a great job. Your grandma's a b..." Once again stopping himself from swearing. "Was a brat and she never should have said that to or about your mom. Moms have a hard job." Russ tapped the top of Liam's head. "And you aren't messed up."

He shrugged off Russ's hand and asked, "What's your mom like?"

Russ swallowed, "I don't have one. She died when I was younger than you are now. My grandpa and grandma raised me."

"You don't have a mom?" Liam was horrified. "How can you not have a mom? I would be so sad without my mom."

"You've met my grandma Marilyn. Doesn't she seem great? She raised me just fine."

"But you don't have a mom."

Russ was sitting outside having a cigarette when the trailer door opened. Aster stepped out and he tamped it out before she got close.

"You didn't have to do that."

He shrugged. "Almost done with it anyway. They unconscious?"

"Yup. Noni and Zuri are tucked into Liam's bed for the night and the boys are camped out in the living room." She sat down in her lawn chair. "The movie was a great idea. Liam loved it. Be prepared for it on repeat."

"I'll normally be at work when he's watching it. So that's more of a you problem than a me problem. How was the tournament thing? A lot of sewing emergencies?"

Marc's oldest daughter, whose name Russ couldn't remember at the moment, was a junior cheerleader and had a tournament this weekend. At the prior one, one of the girls had torn her skirt and the judges were harsh about it. Sariyah asked Aster if she wanted to be the on-site seamstress for a little cash. Her car wasn't working again and Russ couldn't go anywhere, so he told her to go for it and he'd watch Liam.

Aster tucked her legs under herself. "Only one. I felt bad taking the thirty dollars. I didn't do much and they fed me."

"But you were there all day, and you need the money for your car." He countered, as the fireflies blinked in the air.

"Those s'more cookies were good. How'd you think of them?"

He shook his head. "It was mostly Liam's idea. All I did was help make it work. He's a sharp kid. You're doing a good job with him."

She let out a bone weary sigh. "What did he say?"

Russ glanced at her out of the corner of his eye and chose his words carefully. "Nothing much. It sounded like you didn't get a lot of encouragement from your in-laws."

"Joyce had very high standards."

"So she's a bitch." Russ let himself laugh after seeing Aster's attempt to hide her grin.

She traced the arm of the chair with her finger. "That's not inaccurate."

"Your ex was a prick if he didn't stand up to her on your behalf." He kept his tone light, but he still thought knocking that asshole's teeth out might be worth another year or two. No, no. Rash thinking like that was what got him put away in the first place. Think first, weigh options, decide, and then act. He never was very good at planning then acting.

"He's very close to his mother, like Liam is with me." Aster's fingers went to her necklace. "What if Liam turns out the same way? Coming to me for everything, even after he finds someone."

"Impossible. You'd never make anyone feel powerless."

He meant it too. Aster was always encouraging the people she met. She made people feel good about themselves. Russ knew that no one made it through life unscathed, but Aster had gotten more scuffs than she deserved. Every time she pulled on that damn string of pearls, he wanted to chuck it in into the trash. It was the only piece of jewelry she'd kept when she ran. *What kept her tethered to it?*

When Russ looked back over to her, the phrase 'bathed in moonlight' came to mind. Aster's light blond hair and freshly tanned skin glowed in the light of the nearly full moon. She shifted in her chair, pulling her legs up to her torso and resting her chin on her knees.

She was wearing jeans. He'd barely registered her leaving this morning and, with four boys hollering and carrying on during dinner and setting up the 'inside camping,' he'd been oblivious to the fact until this moment. She had come home with two of Marc's girls in tow, adding to the chaos of movie night. Aster was wearing a fitted t-shirt with the cheer group's name and blue jeans and he finally clocked it. To be honest he was relieved he hadn't noticed before, it meant he hadn't checked out her ass at any point. Now he just had to remain outside until she went to bed.

"We should probably go to bed. With Seagar and Amos leaving tomorrow, it's going to be a long day." She blushed. "I mean, I'm going to go to bed. I'm exhausted."

"Yeah. I probably should too. I don't know how Erving doesn't lose his mind with Seagar in a confined space." Russ laughed. "He's a tougher man than me."

He held the door as they reentered the trailer. The TV was lit by the DVD menu screen, but the sound bar had already turned itself off, so it was silent. Russ nabbed the remote and hit the power button.

"Russ." Aster whispered to get his attention. She pointed to the couch he normally slept on and he groaned.

Seagar was on the ground, but he was on top of all of the sleeping bags spread eagle, taking up an inhuman amount of space and snoring away. Amos had abandoned the floor and was unconscious sitting cross-crossed in Russ's chair, leaning against the back. *That could not be comfortable.* Liam was curled up at one end of the couch and Cosmo was at the other.

"I can sleep on the floor in Liam's room with the girls." She offered, shooing him. "Go sleep in the bedroom."

He shook his head. "No, it's fine. I can switch my monitor's battery and sleep in my car."

"You are not sleeping in your car." She folded her arms over her chest. "Take the bed, I can handle sleeping on the floor for a one night."

"What if Liam wakes up in the middle of the night and freaks out 'cause you're not where he thinks you should be? Or scares the girls coming in to find you?" Russ countered. It wouldn't bother him to sleep in his car. He'd slept in worse places than a car. Prison. Sleeping in prison was a far worse place to sleep in than a car. Then there was that other issue. "If he scares the girls, Marc will kill me."

Aster bit her lip, trying not to laugh despite everything. She shifted on her feet formulating an argument to their solution; he could see the gears turning in her head.

Although unlikely, if Liam woke up in the middle of the night and Aster wasn't where he thought she was, he would panic. The kid hadn't had a nightmare in a couple of weeks, but when he had them, he *only* wanted his mother and he wanted her immediately.

"We can just share the bed," she informed him with a decisive nod of her head.

There was no way she was comfortable with this. *Bad idea.* He opened his mouth to argue, but she grabbed his wrist and tugged him forward. "We are both adults, and if it's too uncomfortable, then one of us can sleep on the floor."

Russ pulled his hand away and shoved them both in his pockets. "Fine. I guess." He breathed out, "but don't let Liam see us leaving the room together or the 'why are you sleeping together' question is gonna pop back up."

Even in the darkened room her blush was clear. "The whole park's heard that rumor."

"Grace lives on the other side of Erica's trailer and nothing escapes the Grace-vine. She is a one-woman gossip column."

"Noted." She nodded. "I'll make sure to wake up a bit earlier to avoid that."

"Appreciate it. I don't want Liam to stab me either. He's getting pretty skilled with those knives" Russ was mostly kidding when he said that. He didn't think Liam would literally stab him, but best to err on the side of caution.

She covered her mouth as she giggled. "I'll get cleaned up in the bathroom first."

Aster paced to the bathroom and Russ confirmed his lack of self-control. Her ass looked fucking amazing in those jeans. He was gonna sleep on the floor. He wouldn't stand a chance sharing a bed with her.

Chapter 30

Aster showered quickly and came into the room wearing a hoodie and sleep-pants. If the temperature hadn't done the sharp drop it had, she would have sweat to death. The reverse to this was he had to be grateful she'd nixed his 'sleep in the car' plan. He would have been miserable.

However all that being said, he was currently showering in water colder than the outside air. He was a man and Aster was fucking beautiful. The floor. He had to get to the floor to sleep without it seeming weird. If they shared a bed, his reaction to her would be obvious. Five years in prison and it wasn't like he'd had anyone between his release and the pretty woman crashing into his life. Dry spell was an understatement.

Russ shivered as he finished rinsing out his hair. It wasn't simply a dry spell though. In the most honest way, it was Aster. She was sweet and thoughtful and damn impressive, getting braver by the day. Her whole soul went into making this place a home for her and her son—he was the bastard lucky enough to go along for the ride.

He turned the water off and dried himself, dressing in the t-shirt and gray sweat-pants he'd brought in here with him. After ruffling the towel through his hair, he brushed his teeth and steeled himself to go into the room. Shoulda grabbed a hoodie, or he could still sneak out and sleep in the car. Aster was probably unconscious and wouldn't even notice.

A quick glance in the living room to see if a miracle happened and the boys had vacated the couch proved disappointing. One would think that he was scared of Aster, but no, he was afraid of himself. He and Aster were roommates. Friends. He didn't need to get any ideas to the contrary.

The pretty woman who shared his bed, just not at the same time he was in it, was awake. Her pearls were on the nightstand. His fingers twitched in his pockets, the urge again to throw them out the window was hard to resist. What stopped him was the fact that it would have freaked Aster out, and it wasn't his call to help her be rid of them.

"Was there enough hot water? I tried to be quick."

He nodded through his half-lie. "No complaints."

"Oh good." She smiled awkwardly and pulled the covers up to her chest. "I've been sleeping on this side of the bed. Is that alright?"

Russ was very aware she slept on the right side of the bed. The scent of flowers was always on her pillow. Guilt clawed at him for how many times, he'd woken up hugging that pillow and inhaling the scent. Her invisible presence had helped him fall asleep on more than one occasion.

"It's fine. I normally sleep on the left." The truth was he started on the left side, but rarely work up on it.

He side-stepped the corner of the dresser and double checked to make sure the skin near his monitor was completely dry. Once he confirmed that he reached for the hem of his shirt, but stopped. *Do not take off your shirt when you are sleeping with your roommate.*

"Good. Then this'll be easier. We're both on the side we normally sleep on." She fidgeted with her hands for a minute and jumped as the bed depressed with his weight "You aren't under the covers," she observed.

She was clearly trying to kill him. Russ tapped the space between them. "Didn't want you to be uncomfortable."

"I'm more uncomfortable with the thought of you being miserable and cold." She touched his arm and it was his turn to jump. "You're freezing. You're always so warm. Are you sick?" She pressed the back of her hand to his forehead.

Russ put his palm to hers and moved her hand away. "I am fine. I was warm and took a cold shower. You don't need to worry."

Her eyebrows were knitted together. "Alright." She bit her lower lip then blurted out, "Good night then." She rolled over to face the wall and clicked off the light.

"Good night." He echoed and mirrored her actions attempting to get comfortable on top of the covers.

The window was open, providing both plenty of cool air and noise from their neighbors. He listened to the cars pull by and recognized most of the music being played. After Sam's noisy Chevy rolled by playing some country tune Russ didn't know, it was silent.

He strained to hear anything other than his own breathing. Russ wasn't even sure if he snored anymore. His nose had been broken a few times, so logically he probably snored. But his cellmate never complained, so maybe not? When was the last time he shared a bed with another human? Oh god, it was her. He'd fallen asleep with her on the couch back on the fourth. *No, that did not count.* Furthermore, this didn't count. Sharing a bed was not sleeping together; those were two different things.

There were some critter noises, but it wasn't loud enough to be concerning. Normally he had the fan on since he slept in here when the day was warming up.

"It's fine if you're under the covers with me. I trust you." Aster's voice broke the uncomfortable silence.

On one hand, he could pretend to be asleep and avoid the awkward interaction on the other, he could have a conversation with the pretty lady he was in bed with. Russ knew the smartest thing to do was to admit defeat and sleep on the floor, but Russ never was labeled the smart one in class.

"I normally sleep with the fan on, but it's kinda loud. Might make it hard to hear if Liam needs you." He flopped over on his back.

Aster shifted on the bed and out of corner of his eye. She'd rolled on her side to face him, he kept his eyes on the ceiling.

"If we turn the fan on, it will be too cold for you to be uncovered."

He conceded to her point on temperature. "I can grab a sweatshirt."

"Do I make you uncomfortable? Would you tell me if I did?" Her voice was determined.

In spite of every warning bell going off in his head, he rolled over to face her. Only about a foot between them. Aster was biting the hell out of her lip.

"I think the important question is do I make you uncomfortable?" He leaned on one of his arms, keeping the other atop his hip. He had to keep space between them.

"Not really." Her eyes broadcast something to the contrary. Her fingers brushed the skin under her hoodie's collar, fussing nervously. "I've just only shared a bed with my ex-husband."

"I'll just sleep on the floor." He sighed. "You're tense as hell."

"I should be fine with this. I'm an adult. We're both adults. This should be fine."

Russ rolled invisible dice in his head. He tried to think of the best way to start this conversation in a way that would convince her, in a non-angry manner, to be okay with him moving to the floor.

"Can I ask you a question, and feel free not to answer, but how old were you when you and your ex got together? I got the impression from Liam you're younger than him."

"I was eighteen when we started dating." Her answer came so snipped and quick both of them jumped.

"How old was he?" Russ knew better than to ask, because odds were the answer was going to piss him off, but his mouth moved faster than his brain.

"Twenty-six." Aster closed her eyes. "I was an adult." Her hands clasped together near her throat and she pulled her knees closer to her middle. Half in a little ball, she drew in a slow uneven breath.

"Yeah." He fought the urge to touch her to give some kind of comfort. It wasn't the right time, she was vulnerable, and he wouldn't risk taking advantage. "I'm gonna—"

"No. We're just sleeping next to each other and for the love of all that's holy, that is something I don't need to feel guilty about." Her trembling hand rested on his cheek, her eyes brimming with tears. "Just because someone else touched me doesn't make me gross or less than. I'm not his anymore."

He blinked then blinked again. The urge to kick the ever-loving shit out of this piece of trash had returned in full force.

A tear ran down her cheek. "He hurt me. He didn't break me."

Russ couldn't stop himself from brushing the tear away from her cheek. He wanted to be soothing and comforting, but what came out was a growl. "He sure the fuck didn't break you. Sounds like that was his plan, but he's the fucking failure. Aster, you are here. You and Liam are doing great. You're doing this. I'm proud of you."

"Please stay. I don't wanna be alone tonight." She caught his hand in hers as she averted her eyes to the space between them.

"Sure. I can do that."

It was a terrible idea, and in the morning when Liam knocked on the door to find his mom, Russ threw himself off the bed. Landing in the space between the wall and the bed to avoid being seen. He nearly broke his own neck doing it, but when the benefit was being with Aster all night? It was worth it.

CHAPTER 31

Fall 2004

Aster looked down at the school list and compared it to the plethora of back-to-school ads on the table in front of her. She shouldn't have waited this long, but she'd had to save and scrounge to have enough to afford everything. Liam had grown two inches seemingly overnight, which meant nothing fit.

"We might have to get your jeans from the second hand store." She admitted to her son as he cut out a coupon from the flyer in his hand.

He cocked his head to the side. "We can wash 'em a bunch of times, right?"

"Of course." Aster tapped the table to get his attention. "Liam, I know your father told you only dirty people got their clothes at second hand stores, but that's not true."

"He said the clothes in those stores came from the garbage."

"Well, we used to donate our clothes when they didn't fit anymore. They weren't from the garbage." The school Liam was going to surely would have kids who wore hand-me-downs. She didn't want him being judgmental. "Second hand is just a way to let things have one more chance to be someone's favorite thing."

"I guess it's okay then. But I don't want used underwear. That's gross."

She kept herself from laughing, because Liam was quite serious about his request. "We will buy you new underwear, I promise." He held out his pinkie and she linked hers with his, and they shook on it. "Did you find the one for pencils?"

"In the pile already. Do you think I can get a cookbook? A used one would be alright." He set the scissors down. "Cosmo is only here every other weekend, and I get kinda bored now that my other friends are gone."

Aster squeezed his hand. "I know it's hard, sweetie. I'm really proud of all the library books you've read this month. Maybe we look at the library for cookbooks?"

It was difficult to balance everything. She didn't want to disappoint Liam, but there was only so much money. Once Liam started school, Aster could get a day job to make more money. Marilyn had offered to watch Liam, but Aster felt too guilty to ask. She'd accepted so much help from her and her grandson already.

Aster bit down on her thumb thinking about Russ. They hadn't mentioned the co-sleeping night since it happened, but Aster couldn't ever get it far from her mind. Russ had slept like a rock, but she had woken up a few minutes shy of 3 AM. It took a moment for her to get orientated, but she realized that Russ had pulled her close, spooning his body to hers while they were sleeping. His hand resting under her hoodie, fingers twitching over her stomach as she held her breath. She came to the shocking conclusion that she wasn't nervous, but turned-on.

"Mom? Are you okay?" Liam interrupted her train of thought.

Focus. Her child was right in font of her, she couldn't let her thoughts wander that way. "Sorry, sweetie. What was that?"

"I wanted to look for a cookbook to own, so I can make notes in it."

She pushed back from the table. "We will check every thrift store and garage sale we stop at. Is our game plan written out?"

Liam held up his notebook. "Yup!"

"Alright go to the bathroom, I'm gonna put our lunch and waters in the cooler." Aster pulled the cooler out from under the sink. "We should put the coupons in an envelope, so we don't lose any."

"'K. How come Russ made us a lunch when he knew we weren't going out until later?" Liam questioned getting the waters from the package on the floor. "He didn't need to do that."

"Because Russ shows people he l...." She stopped short and pulled the ice packs out of the freezer. "He shows people how much he cares about them by providing them with food."

"Huh." Liam got a bag of chips out of the storage box. "He must care about us a lot. That's a cool way to do it I guess, even if he is weird."

"Be nice." Aster kissed the top of his head. "Go get ready to go."

The door opened at almost 11 PM and Aster stirred on the couch, but Liam didn't move a muscle. Russ looked confused, but gave her a nod.

"Everything okay?"

She pushed the hair away from Liam's face. "He made dinner for you, wanted to stay up so you could try it. But he passed out about twenty minutes ago."

Russ smirked, "Well, shit. Are me and the pup moving out of mortal enemy territory?"

"Not exactly." She giggled, unable to help it, "I think his exact words were, 'I'll show him I make this dish better.'"

"You know I'm not gonna fight an eight-year-old but," He scratched at his goatee, "when is his birthday?"

"March 22nd."

"See, I'm not above fighting a nine year old. He better watch his back."

"Noted." She yawned, worn out from the day herself. "I'll make a fight poster for his birthday." She posed like a boxer with her fist up. "It'll be a match for the ages."

Russ stifled his laugh so he wouldn't wake Liam. "You are sneakily funny."

"Laughter jumpscares." She tucked her hair behind her ears.

"You want me to carry him to bed?" he offered.

"Could you? He's too big for me. I'm trying not to be a wreck about that fact."

"Kids grow up, kinda the point." He lifted Liam up from the couch and after Aster pulled the covers back laid him down.

Aster kissed her son's forehead and closed the door as they left.

"I'm gonna change quick, then we'll take a look at this dinner." Russ headed to the opposite side of the trailer. "Hey, did he plan on you eating some too?"

"I had some, yes." She couldn't hide the pride in her voice, "It turned out wonderfully."

"Okay, good, he didn't poison it."

They both laughed. In spite of all the back and forth between Russ and her son, she had a sneaking suspicion they actually enjoyed each other's company.

Aster went to the kitchen and prepped the dish for Russ the way Liam had done for her. Her son was a bit too serious for his age, but he'd had to grow up fast. He took so much pride in the dish, following every direction in the cookbook to the letter. They had found a cookbook in the third thrift store they'd visited and all the books there were a dollar. It was added to the clothes they both found and Liam had been beyond thrilled.

She'd found a second pair of jeans for herself. A black pair of jeans nearly identical to a pair she used to wear in high school and a couple of band t-shirts in her size. Currently, she was wearing a sundress with her pink hoodie over it as the air had gotten chilly after the sun went down. Before she married Allen, dresses and skirts were only church and special occasion outfits. But after they got married, he insisted she look more like the adult she was. She changed her wardrobe completely to make him happy, she'd thought that was the least she could do for the man who provided for her.

Aster shook her head to clear the thought and switched the clothes from the washer to the dryer. One thing she missed about her house with Allen was the giant washer and dryer, which could be run at the same time. During the summer she'd been able to dry things on a line, but it wouldn't be an option in a couple of months. Russ warned her it could snow on Halloween or even before.

This summer hadn't been very hot, but it had been dry. Their garden wouldn't have made it if she and Russ hadn't watered it nearly every day.

The bedroom door opened and Russ came out in his gray sweat pants and black sleeveless shirt. "Alright let's see this grand dish."

Aster had to turn her head. Every time he wore those pants all she could think about was the night he held her while they slept. She bit her lip and motioned at the table.

"Looks like broccoli cheddar soup." Russ stirred it then looked up at Aster. "I still can't believe that kid eats broccoli without a fuss. I was in my twenties before it became a staple in my diet."

She got a glass of water and sat at the table with him. "Someone told him eating his vegetables would make him grow up strong. So…"

"So he ate them to get better to impress his dad." Russ shook his head. "Have I mentioned that your ex is an absolute prick?"

She covered her mouth. "A few times."

"Good, don't want you to forget." He stirred the soup again, but ate a spoonful of it this time. His expression was thoughtful as he took another bite. "What did he do to it?"

"Hmm?" Aster was confused at Russ's reaction. "I thought it tasted great. Is something wrong?"

"What's wrong is I just got out cooked by an uppity eight-year-old." He blew air through his lips, making a raspberry-ish sound. "Seriously, what did he do to this?"

"We found a recipe book at a thrift store. He picked out the ingredients and cooked it himself." She beamed. It had been worth dipping into her money reserves for the extra ingredients.

Russ looked nothing short of distressed. "Where's the book?"

"Under Liam's pillow."

"Little shit." Russ winced, "Sorry, I...."

Aster laughed, "No, it's alright. He was pretty smug about it when he tried it. He put his book there on purpose so you wouldn't get it. Attitude withstanding, I'm proud of him."

"His attitude's not all bad." He took another bite of soup. "Damn that is good. He's lucky to have you for a mom."

She wondered about Russ's mother, especially knowing that his grandparents raised him. She kept meaning to ask, but had chickened out every time.

A thunk and a thud against the far wall, caused both of them to stand up. Liam, half-awake, was standing in the hallway rocking on his feet.

"Are you alright, Liam?" Aster questioned. She got to him and his eyes were only half-opened.

He blinked as it was brighter in here than his bedroom, then focused on Russ, pointing a finger at him. "It's better than yours, isn't it?"

Russ's lip curled up. "Pup, did you wake up just to interrogate me?"

Liam yawned twice in a row. "I need to know if it's better."

"I can admit defeat this once." He conceded. "Your mom said you did it by yourself. I'm impressed. You did a great job, Liam."

Her son grinned despite his very sleepy eyes. He wrapped his arms around Aster. "He said I did great, Mom."

Aster brushed his bangs away from his face. "He did. Maybe you can teach Russ the recipe like he's taught you things?"

"Maybe." He was half-asleep and leaned his face into her chest. "Mom?"

"Yes, my little prince?"

Liam yawned again. "Russ said he didn't really have a mom. You need to be his mom too, okay?"

If Aster could have had the earth swallow her whole she would have been grateful for it. Her face burned red as she ushered Liam back to his room. "Let's go back to bed now."

"Okay." He stumbled with her to his room.

The front door opened and closed, no doubt Russ going outside for some air. Aster made sure to go to bed as quickly as possible to avoid seeing him the rest of the night. In her embarrassment, she missed the alert on her phone that she had a voicemail from an unknown number.

CHAPTER 32

Margie and Bridgette's trailer was full of love and light. Pictures all over the walls, crystals hanging in the windows to make dancing rainbows on the floor, mismatched furniture, and the overwhelming scent of fresh flowers gave Aster a sense of comfort in spite of her unrest.

She tugged incessantly at the strand of pearls around her neck. She tightened them to the point that Bridgette had bopped the back of her hand bidding her to 'settle the hell down.'

Margie was searching through the pile of the mail in a little basket on her desk. "You wouldn't believe how much mail the postal service just drops off with me. Anything that's addressed to the park with the wrong or missing lot number becomes my problem." She pulled a handful of letters out and flipped through them.

Bridgette handed her a cup of tea. Aster didn't like tea, but it would be rude to refuse. She sipped from the black speckled mug, deciding she still didn't enjoy tea.

"So how did he get your phone number in the first place?" Bridgette lowered herself to the couch, lifting Jasper into her lap. The white cat purred loudly, flexing his claws into her jeans.

The pit settled in Aster's stomach. "The police. My number was in the report about the fight Russ got into. Allen has friends in the department. He knew roughly where I was headed, so I imagined he just kept asking around."

Margie grumbled about the amount of mail in her basket and continued her search. "What did he say he wanted?"

"To talk about the letter he wrote me about Liam." She forced herself not to cry and kept her hands on the cup. "I never got a letter, so that's why I thought it might have ended up here at the office."

The trailer's windows rattled as a vehicle rolled by, blasting music with heavy bass.

"I'm gonna blast an air horn outside that kid's trailer one of these days." Bridgette complained, glancing at the clock. "It's eight o'clock in the morning for fuck's sake."

"I just," Aster swallowed down her panic, "I don't know what he could want with Liam. When we signed the divorce papers he agreed to give me full custody and let me move out of the state if I signed the affidavit to waive child and spousal support."

"Not a good deal for you." Margie pointed out, holding one of the letters closer to her face.

"I just wanted out." Tears blurred her vision, but she wiped them away. She needed to be strong. She didn't even know if she needed to be as worried as she was. But she couldn't think of any reason Allen would want to talk to her about Liam. He'd never wanted anything to do with their, or rather her, son.

The trailer door opened, wind chimes were singing outside in the breeze. Marilyn swept into the trailer with a rope-woven shopping bag hanging from her arm and a box of donuts in hand. Her hair was covered with a plastic shower cap and there was an odd smell, Aster couldn't place. "I've got QD donuts and apple cider."

Margie paused her sorting and put her hands on her hips. "It's not even September yet."

"It'll be September in less than a week." Marilyn waved her off and set down the box and bag in the kitchen. "Now, Aster, have you ever had QD cider before?"

Bridgette got up from the couch and lifted Marilyn's shower cap examining the hair beneath it. She made a gagging sound. "I have told you a hundred times not to do these perms at home. Your hair's gonna fall out. Let's rinse that out."

"If my hair falls out, I'll wear wigs like Margie." Marilyn laughed and allowed Bridgette to bully her to the bathroom. "Help yourself to some cider and donuts, ladies."

Aster didn't know if she could eat or drink anything at the moment. Her eyes stayed fixed on Margie, who was wearing a blue and pink wig with a bandanna over top to secure it.

The second time the four of them played Euchre together, Margie had accidentally pulled off her wig when celebrating a victory. She'd suffered from alopecia since she was a young woman and rather than battle back and forth with patchy hair, she chose to regularly shave her head. She met Bridgette in college and it was love at first buzz cut. While society might not recognize their connection as anything other than roommates, Aster knew love when she saw it. It was so easy for her to see it now. It made her wonder, in hindsight, had Allen ever truly loved her?

"Here we are. Addressed to you with just the park's address. Got it about two weeks ago." Margie sighed and handed the letter to Aster. "I didn't give it a second thought, we don't have that internet company in this area figured it was an ad. Still should have gotten it to you. Sorry."

"It's alright." Aster managed. Allen always reused envelopes that came with the bills. She might have dismissed it as an advertisement too if she didn't recognize Allen's typewriter neat handwriting.

Lists. He always left lists for her before he went to work. What he wanted for dinner. What housework he expected to be done. What he wanted the children to learn or the sports he expected them to participate in. Any appointment he'd made for her or the children with needed money in an envelope underneath the list.

January 10, 2004 - take Allison for her haircut 1:30 PM. Make sure she gets a proper haircut for a girl. Don't let it be above her shoulders. Stay with her to make sure.

She could still feel the tug on her ponytail, hear the snip of the scissors and sense Allen's rage... She pulled on her pearls and lowered her head to keep from passing out. *How was he still affecting her this much? She had left months ago. She wasn't a victim of abuse. She didn't deserve to be this upset. Allen hadn't hurt her enough for her to react this way.*

An arm wrapped around her shoulders and Margie hugged her, patting her back. "Now, now. Let's read the letter before we start to panic. We're here for you, sweetie."

The idea of seeing him was terrifying, but if she had to do it, it needed to be on her terms. Allen agreed to a Friday meeting in public at the two-story Taco Bell across the road from Tats and Trims. He wanted to meet her at the local police station, but Aster refused. He had friends there, and she wasn't risking it. Bridgette and her business partner Felix, who ran the tattoo side of the shop, would be keeping an eye out for her. If she needed it, she had a place to run to.

His letter had been so simple, just a request to call him about Liam's future with no additional details.

She'd changed three times before settling on jeans and a hoodie despite the oppressively muggy 80 degree day. Aster couldn't bring herself to take off the pearls, but she didn't want Allen to know she was wearing them. The air-conditioned building was a godsend and she picked a table in view of the counter. She needed witnesses in case something went horribly wrong.

What if he changed his mind about custody? Was he here to try and convince her to come back to Mapleville? He had been so short on the phone. He was furious she refused to drive to meet him at the police station. Marilyn had held her hand when she stuck to her guns and insisted they meet here. After a nauseating back and forth, Allen agreed to her terms.

That was the biggest surprise. He had agreed to her terms. Allen had allowed her to make the decision about where their meeting would be. It was confusing to say the least. He must need something from her.

The fear was unrelenting. *What if he wanted Liam?* She clenched her hands, nails biting into her palms. She didn't have a real job and she lived with someone, so her name wasn't on the rental agreement. Allen would have the advantage in court. She wouldn't be able to afford a lawyer.

"Your hair's still short. I figured it would be longer by now, it's been almost a year." Allen's voice was firm behind her.

Aster steeled herself and turned to face him. She couldn't muster up any malice in her voice, but she was proud her tone stayed even. "It's been seven months, and it was extremely uneven because of how it was cut." No shaking or bowing her head in fear; however, her hands were clenched in the front pocket of her hoodie.

He was wearing his uniform, which she knew was uncomfortable in this heat. It was a constant complaint during the summers they were together. "I apologized, even admitted I was out of line. But you made me lose my temper because of that awful haircut you didn't stop Allison from getting." He narrowed his eyes, sounding exasperated. "If you would have just stayed with her, it wouldn't have happened."

"Liam wanted to go to that cooking fair and Allison was sixteen. She was old enough to make decisions about her own hair." She flexed her hands.

Allen put his hand down on the table hard enough to make her soda jump, but not so loud it would attract attention. "She is *my* daughter and I would have thought that *my* wife would have understood that *my* expectations mattered. How Allison conducts herself is a reflection of *me* and *my* family."

Aster struggled to keep her calm and took a long drink to center herself. "Why did you want to meet with me?"

He tapped his foot, a staccato rhythm showcasing his impatience and displeasure. A few months ago, she would have flown into tizzy attempting to fix whatever it was, but not this time. She held herself still and waited.

Bridgette had tapped her nose and repeated over and over. "Abusive men want you to act. Don't give him the satisfaction."

Allen sighed. "Do you want to eat lunch together?"

"I'm good with my drink." She met his eyes, but shifted her shoulders. "I would like to know why you insisted on meeting with me."

He had a packet in his hand. If it was a demand for shared custody, she'd need an empty stomach to keep from throwing up.

"You never acted like you should have. Always needed correction." He flopped in the plastic bench seat across from her and dropped the packet on the table. "I need to change the beneficiaries of my life insurance policy."

Aster was truly confused. She was certain she'd been removed from everything directly following the divorce. She reached for the papers, but Allen put his hand down on top of it.

"What does that have to do with Liam? You said this was about Liam."

Allen rolled his eyes and drummed his finger on the packet. "We took you off as a beneficiary, but not Liam. In order to remove him I either have to prove I revoked my parental rights to him completely or his guardian has to sign the form for the removal."

She blinked. "You want to revoke your rights to Liam completely?" She knew how disappointed Allen had been with Liam. The fact that he insisted that Liam go by his middle name instead of his first name of Adam to put distance between him and family showed that. But to legally disown him? That was farther than she thought Allen would go.

"No." Allen barked and Aster flinched away from the table. "Regardless of his failings he's still my son by blood. I just need you to sign off on these papers. It needs to be notarized and witnessed, which we could have accomplished at the police station. That's why I wanted to meet there." He sighed, "You make everything impossible."

"There's a bank across the street. We can take care of it there." Aster bowed her head. She was shaking again, she'd tried so hard to be strong, but she couldn't stop her hands from moving to her neck.

Allen smiled as her fingers touched her necklace. "I thought you pawned all your jewelry. I guess there are too many good memories linked to that piece."

She pulled the strand tight, but got on her feet. When Allen followed suit he left the papers on the table. She swallowed hard before questioning it, "I think, I think we need those to accomplish what you want."

He took the brown packet and held it out to Aster. "*My* papers are in my car."

She gripped the papers instinctively and gasped as he got closer to her. "What...what are these then?"

Allen chuckled and brushed his fingers under her chin tracing down her throat to her pearls. A tremor ran through her whole body and it took everything in her not to pass out as he slipped his finger under the strand and tugged on them. "Pressure makes perfect, Aster. I know you *tried*. Did the best you were capable of."

Aster took one step back and he let go. There were people in the restaurant. He was always more gentle in public. "What are these papers then?" she asked again. If she could focus on the paperwork then maybe she could get through this. She had always been good at paperwork.

Allen checked his watch. "Your grandfather, Charles, died last month. He left you something in his will. Your parents asked me to drop it off to you."

She pulled the packet to her chest. Her parents hadn't tried to reach out and tell her. Surely even with the lack of contact they'd had in the past, it was fair to expect them to tell her that. Her whole family knew how much she loved her Grandpa Charles.

"I guess I should see Liam before I leave." Allen rolled his shoulders. "Where is he?"

If she let Allen see Liam, it would be awful for him. Allen would interrogate Liam and belittle everything he loved about his new home. Nothing was ever good enough for Allen when it came to Liam's accomplishments and dreams. Her ex-husband would say that Liam was acting like a girl, learning to cook and playing pretend all summer was a waste of time. Her son would try to be tough, but he would fall apart as soon as Allen was out of sight.

Aster would not let Allen crush Liam again. She was frightened, but she was a mother and her baby needed her to stand up for him.

She lifted her chin and made eye contact with her ex-husband. "No."

"What do you mean no?" He snarled, "Do you not know where he is? How could you...?"

She cut him off, "I know where he is. We can handle matters between us, but you will not set one foot near my son."

"So you think your brave now?" His patronizing tone turned her stomach.

Her fear was very much present and she wanted to cry, but she didn't. Stronger than her fear was anger. She could cry later, but not in front of him. "For my son, I am brave."

CHAPTER 33

Dr. Collins tapped his pen atop his ever present notebook. "So they've been gone since Saturday morning? How are you feeling about that?"

Russ stared past the shrink to the motivational 'hang in there' poster on the wall. Dr. Collins's office was being repainted so they were using a room reserved for supervised visitation. The mix of all-age appropriate wall art, toys, and stress reducing white noise machine was world's different from his oak book shelves, mahogany desk, and framed accolades.

He shrugged, not sure how to answer. "It's quieter than I remember it being before they moved in."

"Do you not like the quiet? Last week you complained that you felt cramped in the space."

He ran his tongue over his teeth under his lip. "It wasn't...I felt cramped, but it wasn't because they were there. A situation happened at the beginning of August, and it was ultimately nothing, but I had to get it through my head that it was nothing."

The doctor raised a bushy eyebrow, "Do you want to talk about this situation?"

"Do I have to?"

"I can't force you to talk about anything. This is your therapy. It is court ordered, but it's up to you what you get out of it." Dr. Collins leaned back in his chair. "If you want to sit here quiet for the whole hour, I can read. But, I don't think you want that."

Russ rolled his shoulders and shifted in his seat.

"You keep trying to figure out why you get angry so fast and so often."

"Yeah. I don't want to be that guy anymore."

"Here's the thing." The knocker on the desk clinked back and forth in a rhythm that was supposed to be calming; it wasn't. "The last month you've talked about being annoyed and frustrated with challenges in your day-to-day life. The rage you used to display is tempered now. You used to describe everyday situations as if they were a precursor to a brawl. Now you want help to keep from snapping at your co-worker if they leave napkins on the plates you're washing."

"I'm trying to be better. I thought that was the point of all this."

"Russ, that's what I'm trying to get through to you. You *are* improving. You've been improving since our first session."

"Still have a lot of punchy thoughts."

"That's not unusual. You solved things with your fists for a long time, now you have to build new habits."

Russ sat back in his chair, rubbing his thumb over his 'run6' tattoo, his other knuckles were covered in scabs. "Does it make sense if I say, I thought I had my life all figured out at eighteen when I ran a six minute mile and when I tore my ACL, it derailed my whole life? I've been lost since then, aimless, and just surviving. I'm not living, I'm simply here."

The Doctor stood up and pulled a book from the bookshelf, he flipped through it as he answered. "Absolutely. We often make plans in our youth that seem like the only path for us. When those plans don't work out, it can take a lifetime for us to discover a new plan to move towards."

"I think most people figure it out before prison."

"And some don't ever figure it out. They leave this world without realizing their new path is before them." He scribbled down a few more notes. "Don't you think it should count for something that you've been working on yourself since your parole? Don't you think it matters that you took someone in, just to help them?"

Russ opened his mouth, but Dr. Collins held his hand up. "Don't give me the 'you were tired of eating eggs' excuse. No one hates eggs so much that they let a single mother and her son live with them."

He sighed. "I like having them live with me. Feels more like a home instead of just a place to sleep."

"I appreciate your candor. I know it isn't always easy to be honest about those things." The Doctor pulled a packet of papers out of his desk drawer. "So, Jerry and I have to have a meeting about this first, but I think I can recommend reducing our sessions to every other week. It'll let you get some more sleep."

Russ was shocked; he didn't think he was improving this fast or at all really. This would be a big step and having fewer miserable Fridays would be a bonus. But having Dr. Collins part of his week felt like a needed part of his routine. *What if he failed without it?*

Russ cleared his throat and looked anywhere but at the doctor. "What if I wanted to keep meeting every week? Can we do that?"

"I'll make you a deal..." He scratched his chin, "Give me a reason why, and we will."

He clenched and unclenched his fists ignoring the pain radiating through one of them. "Astor's ex-husband came to see her last week and she was so freaked out... I wanted to beat the shit out of him. *Actually* beat the shit out of him, not in the rhetorical sense, and I thought about breaking my parole to follow her there and do it."

"But you didn't." The doctor pointed out.

Russ hung his head and stared at his hands, "Yeah. But I punched a pallet at work until I had to go up to the ER to get the splinters pulled out."

Dr. Collins nodded and put the forms away. "Every week it is then."

"Thanks, doc."

"Russet, you look like hell." Marc waved him over to the back of the kitchen. "In fact you look worse than when Yesenia found you punching the hell out of that pallet. Talk to me. I know you aren't gonna talk to Ian."

"Why do you think I wouldn't talk to Ian? He's the nicest guy here." Russ shoved his hands in his pockets. He knew working with Marc was going to be rough tonight. He had managed to avoid the man since Aster left, but he knew his luck had run out.

"Because Ian is the nicest guy here." Marc shook his head. "Hard to talk to the nicest guy about not nice things. He probably won't get it."

"Yeah," Russ let out a deep sigh, "Aster's ex showed up to tell her grandfather died last month. She was crushed."

"Her family didn't reach out to her?"

"Marc, I don't think I've ever heard her mention *any* of her family. I was thinking maybe she was an orphan or something."

The larger man folded his arms over his chest. "Why was that your first thought?"

He tapped his heel up and down as he explained. "Aster and I were talking in bed and she mentioned that she was eighteen when they started dating, but was like it was rehearsed. And her ex was twenty-six then, that sits with me wrong, ya know? She was an adult, but he was older and...."

"You think he took advantage of her?" The muscles on Marc's forearm tightened.

Russ was glad that Marc was on his side on this. "I can't say without her confirming, but it sounds that way. I want to beat the shit out of him."

"Well, if you want to stay out in the world, probably shouldn't act on it."

"That's the goal." Russ itched at the hairnet that covered his goatee. "All I know is that Aster's been gone since Saturday, and I miss her and Liam."

Marc arched his eyebrow. "She not have a phone?"

"She does, but every time I think about calling, I talk myself out of it." Russ grabbed the dishes out of the washer and moved them down the belt to the dryer. "She just lost someone and what would I even say? The last funeral I should have gone to happened when I was locked up. My grandma had to bury her best friend, and I wasn't there to help. What use am I?"

"You want a forklift for all that guilt your lugging around?" Marc shook his head. "You sound like your qualified to drive one."

Tricky clocked back in and started spraying down the dishes. "Why does Russet look like a truck hit him? Is it cause someone stole his not-girlfriend?"

"Excuse the fuck out of you?" Russ growled and Marc cleared his throat. He corrected himself and rephrased. "Sorry. What did you say about Aster and someone stealing her?"

Tricky shrugged. "My...my friend, Raven, saw her walking to the bank with a security guard. She doesn't seem like she'd get into trouble, so we figured she was on a date."

Jose called out to Marc that he had a call incoming from one of the charge nurses and the manager excused himself.

"Who goes on a date to a bank?" Russ could never figure out what was going on in this kid's head.

"Old, straight people?" Tricky laughed then froze, water from the sprayer still going, but it was pointed at the empty sink and not the dishes. "Fuck." He muttered under his breath.

What Russ wanted to do was interrogate Tricky for anything he knew about this man with Aster. Just in case it was her ex, not for any other reason. But the kid looked like he was gonna bolt for the door. He cleared his throat. "Raven works for Bridgette, right? I've *known* her and Margie for my whole life. My grandma played cards with them the whole time I was growing up."

The relief was evident on his face, when he clarified, "Aster didn't say anything to you?"

Russ shook his head. "No, she's good at keeping secrets. *And* so am I. You're good, man."

"Thanks. We're real careful about who knows. Raven and I both got kicked out when our folks found out about us." He flicked his lip ring with this tongue. "We were livin' on the streets for a bit. Like we only found a place to stay a couple of days before you started."

He nodded, that would explain how quiet Tricky had been when they first met, kid was going through it. "You guys okay now?"

Tricky shrugged again. "We get by. Who was the dude with Aster?"

"Honestly, I'm thinking it was her ex-husband." Russ moved the dishes down the line, "Security guard uniform, huh?"

That would make sense with Liam being afraid of cops. To a kid, those uniforms would look identical. Uniform and a gun would mean cop to an eight-year-old. Russ had so many questions. Starting with why they had gone to the bank together—child support maybe? Aster never mentioned getting anything from her ex, and she was always picking up sewing jobs from the tailors in town. Money wasn't everything, but it didn't hurt.

"Raven say anything else about the guy?" He hoped his inquiry sounded casual.

"Just that he was short. Taller than Aster, but not by a lot." Tricky smirked, "Why? You jealous about your not-girlfriend?"

"I'm gonna check the yogurt." Russ plodded away from his annoying co-worker.

"Awe, Russet's got a crush on his roommate!" He called out loud enough to start the rest of the night shift laughing about it.

Russ threw open the walk-in, but when he reached down to grab the crate the door opened and closed again. "Just grabbing the yogurt. What do you need?"

Marc was standing at the door, arms folded over his chest.

He had a flashback to his first day and managed a nervous chuckle. "What can I grab for ya?"

"Just a quick thing." Marc smiled, one of those this-is-a-warning smiles, and clarified. "You said when Aster told you about her ex, you two were in bed together."

Russ adjusted his grip on the yogurt crate. "Just sleeping together, very casual."

"Aster doesn't strike me as a casual woman."

"Oh, no!" Russ yelped, "I meant we were sharing the bed. Not sex. No, no. Aster is not... She...." He trailed off, nothing he said was going to make this better. "I am not sleeping with Aster. That is not what she needs in her life right now."

Marc nodded and opened the walk-in for them. "Just so you know. If you take advantage of someone like Aster, someone who's been hurt—you end up in a very special section of hell."

Russ nodded and kept focused on task at hand. He needed all of these idiots he worked with to stay out of his non-existent love life. "Noted."

CHAPTER 34

Russ switched out his monitor battery, but before he could think about anything else, there was a loud knock on the door. It was just past 7 AM, hopefully it was just Erica with eggs or wanting a jar of tomatoes. His grandmother had come over the beginning of August and taught him and Liam all of her canning secrets. Grace had gotten the word out that Russ and Aster's trailer had canned vegetables, so that had been a thing. Better that spreading around than the rumor he and Aster were sleeping together and Russ winding up in the 'very special section' of hell for taking advantage. Which was not the case, they were only roommates. He was very careful to not look at Aster too long, but he couldn't always stop his subconscious. Cold showers were more habit than hot ones for now.

He opened the door to find Sam, Cosmo's dad. "What's up, man?"

Sam held up a note with Liam's name on it. "Cosmo's half-sister has a birthday this weekend, so he's not gonna be with me." Sam handed the note to Russ. "He wanted to make sure Liam knew what was going on."

Russ nodded, "Thanks. I'll make sure he gets it."

"Appreciate it." Sam rocked on his heels. "Say, and um, if I'm overstepping, feel free to tell me to fuck off. But are you and Aster together or just roommates?"

There was a superstition that things happened in threes, so he should be done explaining his living situation after this. "We're roommates. Her and Liam are staying here until they get on their feet. Soon as another trailer opens, I'm sure one of us will be moving."

"Huh. Okay." Sam spun his keys on his finger. "I thought you guys looked chummy and there was that rumor you were sleeping together—"

"A misunderstanding." He interrupted.

"Right, which makes sense since Liam says you're just-Russ."

A car backfired and they both turned toward the sound, before looking back at each other. Sam continued, "I know she's gone right now, but when she gets back. I'm gonna see if she wants to get a drink with me sometime. Could you maybe watch Liam if she agrees?"

What could Russ say? Up until this moment he'd liked Sam, now he wanted to lay him out on the lawn. But that wasn't fair. Sam wasn't doing anything wrong, he was just a guy wanting to ask a pretty girl out for a drink. The problem was that the pretty girl in question was Aster. A woman who, despite all of his protests, Russ had started to think of as his. His? No, someone he was interested in. The last thing Aster needed was anyone trying to put ownership on her again.

She wasn't his. Russ smiled back at Sam and agreed, "Yeah, if she wants to go out, I'll watch Liam."

"Thanks." Sam offered his hand and Russ shook it a little harder than he needed to. "Catch ya 'round."

Russ walked back into the trailer and resisted the urge to hit the wall. If he put a hole in it, he'd have to patch it. There were better ways to deal with inappropriate anger. Aster was only his roommate and Sam was allowed to ask her on a date. Russ shouldn't be angry about a potential date with a woman who he had no claim over.

He stomped to Liam's room and put the note on the kid's desk. Russ paused before leaving, with Liam gone he could look at that cookbook the kid kept under his pillow. He lifted Liam's pillow and laughed so hard he doubled over. Under Liam's pillow was a note that said "Nice Try OLD MAN."

Fuck, he missed that kid. Of all the changes that had happened in Russ's life this past year, getting close to that Liam had been the most shocking one. He never considered having kids of his own. He wasn't a kid person and yet, with Liam, it was different. Teaching the kid to cook was fun and he enjoyed seeing him improve and come out of his shell.

He should make dinner for himself and take a shower. Take a shower and not think about Aster like he did the first night she was gone. He was so glad she hadn't come back on Monday like she'd originally planned. He wouldn't have been able to look at her. For fuck's sake he didn't know if he'd be able to look at her when she came back whenever she did.

If she comes back. The voice in the back of his mind poked him. Aster didn't need to come back, everything here was replaceable. She didn't need to make the drive back to Everygreens. Those two could survive wherever they ended up settling. But Russ Hulston was beginning to doubt his ability to survive without them. What a sobering thought, alone in this trailer with the day too sunny to sleep and work not far enough away.

As long as Aster wasn't back with her ex. The idea made his blood boil. Why had he shown up in town anyway? Surely he could have called her. But they went to the bank together. Why? Then again, what if it was just someone Aster was walking with? It wasn't her ex at all and he was overthinking the whole fucking situation

Food sounded disgusting so he skipped it, opting to shower and crash in bed, away from Aster's side. If he fell asleep with her scent in his nostrils, he'd wake up depressed or turned-on. He needed neither of those issues before his sleep-deprivation day. Night shift to afternoon was the stupid schedule he chose to stick with weekly to keep himself out of trouble.

His dreams were haunted, both the good and the bad ones. It left him feeling gross with a pit in his stomach. The alarm going off at 11:30 AM was a blessing. Russ took a long hot shower trying to clear his head, but the thought repeated over and over: *what if they don't come back?*

He fought back against the dread, knowing that Aster and Liam had only gone back to Aster's hometown to pay respects. *Hell, what was wrong with him?* She was grieving her grandfather and he was moping around here like she vanished in the night with no explanation.

Russ settled for ramen noodles with an egg on top; he needed to eat before work. After getting dressed and switching his monitor's battery, he opened his door to leave. There was note taped to the outside, it was addressed to both him and Aster.

He recognized Margie's handwriting. The lawn was mowed, they'd paid rent already, and he'd snagged the mail after therapy. Rent increase? A jerk way to do it, but her park, her rules. Russ tore the envelope open and read the message three times before tossing it into the trailer without caring where it landed.

This was one of those times he was too upset to cry or swear. He pulled out his cellphone and powered it on. Aster's cell was listed as a contact for emergencies. Russ dialed the number, not at all surprised when it went to voicemail. She was home handling things, of course her phone was in her bag or turned off.

"Hello, this is Aster. If you're looking for me or Liam, leave us a message and we'll call you back. Have a wonderful day."

He swallowed as the beeps signaled time to record. "Hey, it's Russ. Margie left us a note. There's a trailer open on the other side of the park after the seventeenth. I'll get the paperwork from Jerry and figure out how we get me out of your hair. Hope everything's fine at home." He attempted a joke to hide the crack in his voice. "Per state mandate, I'll be back to the trailer by eleven."

CHAPTER 35

Aster hadn't been home in almost a decade and this homecoming came with a broken heart. She and Liam had gotten ready first thing this morning and left to drive the five plus hours to Mapleville. Back to the hometown Aster had grown up in, twenty minutes from where she lived with Allen, and a stone's throw from two people who should have been willing to help her, but hadn't.

Her car didn't have working air conditioning, so they stopped at a rest area ten minutes outside of town to clean up and change. She shimmied her simple black dress over her tank-top and spandex shorts and exchanged her flip-flops for her ballet flats. After fixing her hair and dabbing a bit of gloss on her lips, she exited the bathroom to find Liam struggling with his tie.

"Why do I need to wear a tie anyway?" he grumbled as Aster finished the knot of his crimson tie.

She cupped his face in her hands. "Because we get dressed up when we honor someone who's passed away. We've been to funerals before."

He nodded. "That's why we're wearing all black."

"It is." She held out her hand. "We're going to get flowers for my Grandpa Charles, and then we are going to see your grandparents."

"Mrs. Reign doesn't want me to call her grandma," Liam countered. "She doesn't like me."

"I'm not talking about Joyce. I'm talking about my parents." They both got into the car and Aster looked both ways before backing out of the space.

"I don't remember them." Liam pulled out his notebook. "What are their names?"

"Oscar and Gwen." Aster forced herself to stay calm. She'd have to take her pearls off before she got to her parent's home. They would have a fit if they saw her wearing them. One of the last things her mother had said to her was a comment about how Aster was always wearing them.

When she started dating Allen, her parents had been fine with it; they had paid for their wedding without complaint, but once Liam was born, everything seemed to change. After his first birthday, they mailed Aster a letter saying they couldn't be part of her life anymore. They were disappointed in her and never wanted to see her again.

When she finally left Allen, she had shown up on their doorstep, Liam sleeping in the car. She'd begged for them to sleep in the guestroom for a night. She promised they would be gone first thing in the morning, and they wouldn't take any food. Aster only wanted a safe place to sleep with her son.

Her father told her she should have planned ahead since she abandoned her home and responsibilities. Her mother cried, but Gwen hadn't stopped Oscar from closing the door in Aster's face. She'd found a well-lit parking lot and cried herself to sleep; waking up to a police baton knocking on the window. The officer told her to move on and from that point until this trip, that's what Aster had done: move on.

The last stop she'd made in this town was to see her Grandpa Charles at the retirement home. He signed the title of this car over and told her to sell it for money. It had been the only reason she had enough to leave the area. He'd also given her Margie's name and contact number. He'd helped her escape to a better place. She'd be forever grateful.

The cemetery was next to the church she'd attended her entire childhood. The winding pathway was steep and Aster worried about her car. It had held up for the trip, but she was worried about getting back home.

Her family had a set of plots near the back, by a group of oak trees. She stopped the car at the top of the hill and locked the emergency break. Aster took a deep breath and let it out slowly.

"I got the flowers, Mom!" Liam held the bouquet of multi-colored asters to her. "These flowers have your name."

"They do." She took them and pointed towards the giant oak trees. "We're heading up that way if you want to run up the path."

He grabbed her hand and stuck out his chin. "I need to be strong for you."

Tears filled her eyes instantly and she kissed the top of her son's head. "You really are my little prince."

They made their way to the group of graves, most bearing the surname, "Chapel." Liam read them out one by one until they found the one they were looking for: Charles Adam Chapel.

"My first name is Adam, like his middle one." Liam cocked his head to the side and noticed the one next to her grandfather's. "Her first name is Lillian, just like you."

Aster hugged Liam to her trying to keep from breaking down completely. "I was named after my grandma Lillian, and you were named after your great-grandpa Charles."

He looked up at her. "How come I don't remember them?"

"Grandma Lillian died when I was a little kid. That's why everyone calls me Aster. And..." She trailed off, how could she explain the complicated nature of her non-relationship with her family. "And when I was still married to your dad, I got in a big fight with my father, so we couldn't talk to him anymore."

"You look sad. Maybe we should try and fix the fight? Use our words, like Russ says." He swayed back and forth in her arms. "Mom?"

"Liam?" Aster smiled despite her tears.

"I'm hungry. Can we get into the cooler?" His stomach growled as if on cue.

"Of course." She laid the flowers on the grave and whispered a small prayer that her next move wasn't a mistake. When she put things into perspective though, she'd seen Allen yesterday and gotten through it. Not as calm or collected as she would have liked, but she didn't run. If she could face the man who'd kept her under his thumb, the man who'd mentally and emotionally abused her, then she could face her parents.

Liam made sure his tie was straight before they got out of the car. "Is my hair okay?"

"It looks great." Aster brushed it back away from his eye, but it flopped right back down. Liam was determined to make a good impression, she was hoping to get through this without a panic attack.

She took her pearls off and put them in her purse before they walked up to the front door. The daycare yard was empty and the sign was gone; they must have closed the business. Aster knocked on the door and counted in her head to ten. No one answered.

"Maybe they're at work?"

She knocked again and counted to ten, but this time she heard steps coming to the door. Reflexively, she put Liam partially behind her as the door opened. A young woman with blond curls opened the door and she and Aster stared at each other.

"Aster?"

"Helen?"

They both froze, neither knew what to say to the other.

"Hi, I'm Liam."

Bless that boy of hers. He waved as he introduced himself.

"Oh my god he's so big. I haven't seen since he was one." Helen gushed, then whispered, "What are you doing here? Mom and Dad will freak out."

Aster squared her shoulders. "I found out Grandpa Charles passed away. I wanted to see them since I'm in town. I won't be staying long."

"You won't be staying at all." Oscar Chapel appeared behind Helen, his steely blue narrowing at Aster. "Helen, go to your room."

She countered, "Dad. I'm an adult."

"Now!" Oscar barked.

Liam yelped, hiding fully behind Aster who hoped her son hadn't noticed she flinched.

"Dad." Aster put her foot in the door to keep it from being slammed in her face. "I just stopped to say hello. Please, talk to me."

"You lost the right to speak to us, when you embarrassed our family." He started to close the door, but paused when it hit her foot. "No one in this house has anything to say to you."

"Even with everything that's happened. How could you not tell me about Grandpa Charles?" Fresh tears filled her eyes. "I loved him so much. He was the only one who helped me."

"And you stole from him." Oscar accused.

"My mom's not a thief!" Liam stomped his feet and moved to Aster's side. "You take that back!"

"I would never steal from him," Aster insisted. "Do you mean the car? He wanted me to have a chance to get on my feet. He couldn't drive anymore. He gave me that car after my accident."

She was speaking, but her father's eyes hadn't left Liam. "Well, I'll give you this, he looks like Allen. You must have picked the right one."

Aster blinked confused by what her father said. "What are you talking about? Of course he looks like Allen. *Allen* is his father."

"We shouldn't do this in front of him." Oscar shook his head. "Leave. I won't have the neighbors listening to you wailing your lies."

"She's not a liar either. You're a jerk!"

"You need to control your child better! I will not be spoken to...!"

Aster put her hand up, seething at the man she once called father. "You will not talk to *my* child like that! Liam, go to the car."

"Yes, Mom." He rushed down the driveway and hopped into the passenger seat. Waving at her so he was sure she could see him.

"Now that he's out of earshot. What do you mean I picked the right one?" She surprised herself with her own bravery. "What exactly do you think I did?"

"Allen told us what you did." Her mother, Gwen, appeared behind her father. "How he forgave you for Allison and your son's sake. But how could you do that to him? He gave you everything. A house, a car, a family, and he loved you so much." She wiped the tears off her cheeks. "You cheated on him, he forgave you, and then years later you left him just because of a silly fight!"

"Silly fight?" Aster could feel herself crying, but refused to acknowledge it. Her voice was nearly void of emotion. "You think I cheated on Allen and Liam isn't his?"

"He told us." Oscar folded his arms over his chest.

"The whole town knows it," Gwen doubled down, voice cracking, "Do you have any idea how embarrassing that is for a parent? To have a loose woman for a daughter."

Aster couldn't believe what she was hearing, "You never asked me. We never spoke about this. Why wouldn't you ask me?"

"You would have lied! You lie about everything." Gwen was hysterical. "He told us how you really were. The world got a hold of you, it poisoned you."

"You believed him without even asking me? I am your daughter!" She screeched right back. "The world didn't poison me. Allen poisoned me!"

Her father opened his mouth to speak, but Aster didn't let him.

"During that *silly fight* Allen cut off my ponytail in a fit of rage. I came to you terrified and you turned me away. How could you?" Tears poured down her cheeks. "You didn't tell me my own grandfather died. You gave the information from his will to my ex-husband. Why would you do that?"

"We were hoping to get some of our money back." Her father's voice was so quiet she barely heard him above the train that rolled by behind their house.

Aster felt her body shake as she questioned, "What money?"

"We gave Allen ten-thousand dollars to invest as an apology for your infidelity. But the market suffered a loss." He drew in a deep breath, before continuing, "We were hoping to get it back from the inheritance from your grandfather."

"So you were going to steal from me? Well, at least I don't have to feel bad about you cutting me out of your life. You made your bed, lie it in." Aster removed her foot from the door and stomped to the car, ignoring her parent's calling her name.

Liam scrambled into the backseat, kicking the headrest of the passenger seat as he flipped himself over. Feet flashing in the rearview mirror until he righted himself. "Hey mom?"

"Yes, sweetie." She furiously wiped the tears off her cheeks.

He handed her his notebook. "That Helen lady wrote in my book, said to show you."

HC - Perkins on West 5th St - 6pm - my treat.

CHAPTER 36

Aster looked up at the ceiling of the restaurant as she waited for the clock to roll past 6 so she could leave with a clear conscience. There was no way that Helen would show up, not after the things her father said.

Liam cupped his hands on the glass case adjacent to the host's stand. "Mom, we should get a piece of pie. The peanut butter one looks good. Do you think they'd tell me how to make it?" He patted his backpack. "I brought my cookbook; it's got blank pages."

"That pie is a town favorite, I don't think they'd give up the recipe to just anyone." Helen came from inside the restaurant and motioned for Aster and her son to follow. "I got us a table already. I was early for once in my life."

"I didn't think you were serious," Aster admitted, gripping Liam's shoulder.

"Of course I was." Helen bit her lip, "I wanted to hear your side of the story. Do you not want to talk to me?"

She did. Helen was the baby of the family, ten years younger than Aster, and she'd missed her younger sister. Aster didn't even know who Helen was anymore; she was an adult now. "I think we can stay for a bit."

"Cool. 'Cause Brent is here too." Helen grabbed her hand tugging her forward.

"Who's that?" Liam questioned as he tagged along behind.

"He's your uncle..." Aster trailed off as she spotted her brother who was three years younger than her and the spitting image of their father. "And Helen's your aunt."

"I have an aunt and uncle?" Liam's jaw dropped open. "That is so cool!"

Aster hoped it was cool and not some kind of trap. She glanced around to make sure her parents weren't here. "Hi, Brent." She kept her free hand on Liam, Helen was still holding the other one.

"Hey, Aster." He nodded, before addressing Liam, "You must be Liam, nice to meet you again, Buddy."

Her son retracted behind her. "I don't know you yet, so I'm not your buddy."

Brent's eyebrow arched, "Kinda rude. Oof." He grunted as Helen elbowed him. "But perfectly understandable given the circumstances. Nice shirt, Liam. Who are the Red Wings?"

"A hockey team, but they might lock out this year and not play." Liam tugged on the sleeves of his red t-shirt.

"Okay, everybody sit, we're having dinner." Helen clapped her hands. "Aster, I'm dying to hear all about you and Liam here." Her little sister grinned. Helen's smile had always lit up every room she walked into, even as a child.

"Liam, go to the bathroom, wash your hands, then come straight back." Aster patted his back and pointed to the washroom.

Her siblings sat down, but Aster stayed on her feet. "I did *not* cheat on Allen, Liam *is* his son, and I did *not* steal from Grandpa Charles. I left Allen because..." She swallowed, "because he was abusive."

"He hit you? I'll kick his ass!" Brent banged his knees on the table attempting to get up, but Helen drug him back down.

She rolled her eyes at her brother, "You don't have to hit someone to abuse them. My psychology 101 class had a whole chapter on emotional abuse."

"You believe me?" Aster was mystified.

"Of course we believe you. Allen's a fucking creep." Helen took a drink from her water cup. "He's been over at mom and dad's once a month trying to figure out where you went."

"They would have told him too. It's good you aren't talking to them." Brent grunted. "I'm almost there myself."

"Ooo." Helen winced, and gave their brother a mournful look.

"What's with the face?" he questioned.

Helen patted his arm. "I'm gonna need you to take one for the team."

"Meaning?"

"Meaning, I need you to ask them to go camping tomorrow and keep them there until Friday."

Brent grimaced, "No, not a whole week in the woods with them. Why do you even need them gone that long?"

Helen caught Aster's hand. "Because Aster needs a place to stay. And Grandpa Charles's lawyer isn't back in town until Wednesday."

Aster shook her head. "I can't ask you to do that."

"You didn't." Brent gestured to Helen, "I'm being volun-told by the princess here."

Aster glanced around for Liam, realizing he wasn't back yet. She should have walked him to the restroom. Before she could panic, a red-haired waitress appeared marching, her son back to the table with his notebook in hand.

"This little charmer almost got my mom's pie recipe out of our cook." The waitress shook her head. "Keep him out of the kitchen, please."

"I am so sorry." Aster bobbed her head. "Liam?"

"I already apologized for going back there. Can we get dinner, please?" His hair flopped over his blue eye and he pushed it back away from his face. "She said they make az-para-gust pasta."

"You eat asparagus?" Brent was shocked.

"Yeah, if I don't eat it, I'll be short like you."

Helen burst out laughing and Aster covered her face in embarrassment.

Aster pulled up into the driveway of her childhood home for the second time this week and let out a long breath.

"It's okay, Mom." Liam assured her from the backseat. "Aunt Helen said that your mom and dad are gone fishing. We're okay."

She smiled back at him. "You're right we are. Let's go inside and see your aunt."

The garage door rolled up and Helen was standing in the middle of the open space motioning for her to pull the car inside. They exchanged hugs and Helen closed the door, leaving them in the dark, except for the sliver of light coming from door to the house.

"Well, that was terrible planning on my part." Helen's spirited laugh filled the space and she scuffed her feet until a thunk sounded as she kicked the steps. "Dang-it. Ouch."

The door from the garage opened into to the family kitchen filling the garage with warm yellow light. "Come on you two. I'm making potato waffles for dinner."

"You can make waffles with potatoes?" Liam gasped and scrambled to follow his aunt to investigate the new dish.

Aster paused at the threshold, gripping the pearls around her neck. So many memories in this house; she had lived here her entire life before Allen. Until recently, she thought all of her growing up had been done in this house. But the last few months had taught her, she had more growing to do.

This house was where she'd had a job at twelve, helping her mother with the daycare after school. The kitchen counter was where she'd done taxes for her family's business.

"You coming inside?" Helen asked.

Aster nodded. "Sorry, just a little tired from everything." She closed the door behind her and hung her keys on the hook by the door. When she was sixteen, her parents would let her drive to pick up pizzas on Friday nights. Her mother's voice was practically in her ear, questioning if she had put the keys back where they belonged.

"Mom, your shoes." Liam pointed to the neatly lined shoes by the door, his shoes were already off. His neon blue socks clashed against the muted burgundy rug he was standing on.

"Hey, Liam. Do you want to help me with dinner? This way your mom can rest for a bit." Helen smiled at Aster, as she clearly picked up on Aster's overly emotional state.

"Can I trade the recipes for doing the dishes?" Liam rocked back and forth on his heels.

"You'll do all the dishes?"

He nodded seriously. "Dishes are my job at home."

Helen smirked, "Game on, kiddo, you got a deal." She shooed Aster towards the stairs. "The two guestrooms are the first two doors on the right side. Yours and Brent's old rooms."

Aster hurried up the stairs, so Liam wouldn't see the tears in her eyes. He thought of Everygreens as home; she had provided her son a place to be safe. She forced herself to take long deep breaths in an attempt to ground herself, but there were so many memories here. And not all of them were good.

From the wall she was leaning against, she could see the front door of the house. She remembered being fourteen and meeting, Carla, Allen's first wife, and being handed a two-year-old Allison, who loved to cuddle. On the porch just outside that door, Allen had given her a pair of birthstone earrings for her fifteenth birthday.

Aster pushed away from the wall and fled to her old bedroom, which was now simply a guestroom. The echoes were still here though. When Carla died, Allison had been understandably inconsolable. Aster had comforted the little girl up here in her room, while they waited for Allen to come pick her up.

So many memories of Allison needing to stay past the normal daycare hours and Aster always being willing to care for her. There were nights when Allen would lift a sleeping Allison out of Aster's bed. Her parents never batted an eye at him going into their teenager's bedroom while she was sleeping.

She sank down to the floor and pulled her knees up to her chest, trying to breathe. Allen had asked her father's permission to take her on a date while they were sitting on the patio and Aster pushed Allison's on the swings. Four days after her eighteenth birthday Allen took her on their first official date. For their one-month anniversary he'd bought her the set of pearls which were still around her neck. Her fingers curled around them pulling them tight to her throat.

Less then a year later she and Allen were married in the backyard by the lilac bushes. She could almost smell them and her stomach turned. Aster was nineteen, because they were married in May and her birthday was in March; Allen had been twenty-six.

Frantically she pinched the skin between her thumb and index finger to keep herself from vomiting. She had been so young. Why had Allen picked her? She was a child when they had met. Why had he pursued her? She could feel his hands under shirt, fumbling to unclasp her bra at the shooting range. His hand on her knee, sliding up her thigh under her flower-print skirt when they took Allison to the movies.

She managed to make it to the bathroom before vomiting her breakfast into the toilet. Aster rocked back and forth, heaving for air as she braced her hands at her collarbones.

Suddenly tension against her neck evaporated and Aster stared at the pearl necklace in her hands. Had it broken? She examined it, her breathing evening out as she was distracted. It looked as if it had somehow come unclasped. How long had this been a symbol of Allen's control over her?

Maybe after she got home, she would be strong enough to take it off. She imagined Russ would love to throw them into the trash. She didn't miss him looking at them from time to time.

Aster got back to her feet and cleaned herself up, before putting the stupid pearls back on. She wasn't sure how to be without them, yet. But she would learn how to be. She wasn't going to let her past control her anymore. The memories of this place, weren't welcome in her new life. She would leave them here.

A knock sounded against the door and Helen called out, "You ready for dinner? I think your kid, out garnished me. What eight-year-old knows how to garnish?"

Aster opened the door. "Mine." She linked her arm with her sister's. "Let's go eat. I'm starving."

"Do you really have to leave right after we go to the bank?" Helen pouted, sitting on the bed as Aster packed her bag.

"Liam missed his first week of school. And, as much as I've loved catching up, I really want to go home." She paused midway through folding the shirt in her hands. "Is it weird in only a handful of months Everygreens feels like my home?"

The nineteen-year-old flopped on her back and smiled up at her. "Naw, it sounds good there. Plus Russ sounds hot."

Aster felt her cheeks burn. She knew she shouldn't have talked about him so much. "I'm not ready to think about anything like that yet."

"Fair. But...."

"But?" She folded her socks and attempted to get her sister to finish her thought. "But what, Helen?"

The younger woman hopped off the bed and checked the hallway first. "You need to lose the pearls."

Aster's hand went to them immediately, breath quickening.

"No, no." Helen threw her arms around Aster. "No. Allen doesn't get to hold those over you anymore. Mail them to him. Let him know you're free. You're tougher than he is and you've proved it. You are thriving with your son."

She closed her eyes. "I'm not sure I am tougher."

"Well, I *am* sure." she said, squeezing Aster tighter, "If you can't believe in you, believe in me, believing in you. I *know* you're stronger than you think you are."

Aster pulled away. "I'm not sure I'm ready to not have them on my neck."

"What if I got you new pearls? I have a set that were Grandma Lillian's. Mom gave them to me for graduation." She raced out of the room and came back with them. "Let's compare them."

The sisters laid the two strands side by side. The ones Allen gave her were perfectly round and devoid of color, while the other had two misshaped ones and two that had an iridescent shine to them. All four of the imperfect ones were by the clasp, so it wouldn't be obvious they were different.

"I can't take them." Aster shook her head. "They're yours."

"I don't want them." Helen lifted the newer strand and held them out. "And if you put them on, then you are deciding to keep a wall up to keep yourself safe. But it's *your* wall of safety, not one of fear." She popped out her hip. "And when you decided it's safe enough to trust the hot man, you're living with. You can take them, *and maybe some other things*, off and take down that wall."

She took the strand from Helen and picked up the other off the bed. Allen had bought her the necklace after they got engaged, so she would look more adult. Then her clothes changed, the way she did her make-up, her hair, and even how she interacted with the world. Scared and broken.

When she arrived in Evergreen Park she had been beaten down to a shell of a person. She and Liam had been lost, but that wasn't the case anymore. Life wasn't perfect because no amount of pressure could make it perfect. However she didn't need to be perfect to be happy. Happy was watching Liam and Russ glare at each other when they thought she wasn't paying attention, but secretly loving each other. While she hadn't heard from Russ during the trip, Liam had wondered aloud about Russ over a dozen times. Russ cared about her son, taught him without losing patience or insulting him. Russ was gentle with her, always aware of her boundaries.

She'd found a way to work and made friends. Marilyn, Margie, and Bridgette let her play cards with them and included her in all the gossip. Aster had grown a garden this summer. She had enrolled her son in school. She had faced her parents and didn't regret how she spoke to them. Dealing with Allen had been the hardest thing she'd faced since leaving. When she got home, she'd curled up in a ball and cried, but she had gotten through the meeting. She had survived telling Allen he wasn't allowed to see Liam, and she'd held her ground when he pushed. Aster had found strength she didn't know she had, and maybe a change on the outside was what she needed.

Aster took a deep breath and let the pearls that had lived around her neck drop to the bed.

Helen clapped her hand. "Yes, you keep your pearls and no more fear of the dickbag."

"What if I'm still afraid of myself?"

"That's what therapy is for." Helen rolled her eyes.

"MOM!" Liam called out from the hallway.

Aster put her new pearls around her neck and realized this set was lighter. They were a little longer too, they didn't feel tight on her neck, and they were cool to the touch. She left them on, not missing her sister's grin. "We're in here, Liam."

He raced into the room already dressed in his t-shirt and shorts. He held out her phone. "Russ called and left a message. When we get home, can I make the honey grilled chicken for him?"

"Have you decided to be friends with Russ?" She was genuinely shocked by his request.

"No." Laim shook his head. "I want to show him I can cook chicken better than him too."

"Nephew, are you in a food war with a grown adult?"

"Naw, I'm winning the war against Russ. He's just a weirdo."

Aster dialed her voicemail. "Please stop calling him that."

CHAPTER 37

Friday shifts were longer than most, not by number of hours, but lack of sleep made them exhausting. This particular Friday, there had been some kind of major accident on the highway, so the hospital was full of people. Feeding people in the hospital was its own thing. Comfort food was a must, but so was healthy food. The trick was to balance them. Give the kid with cancer chocolate cake and chicken nuggets, but have a salad for the woman forcing herself to eat while a loved one is in a coma.

He weaved his way through the tables and set the baked cinnamon apple in front of the dark haired woman, who'd asked he could make her one earlier in the evening. Russ refused her attempt to pay, he'd already taken care of it. She'd been in here every night for a month and it was the first time she'd even attempted to eat. Normally she sat alone for over an hour, glancing at the clock as she nursed a cup of water or coffee.

Jose was right—the coffee down here was shit and Russ relented to pick himself up a 'fancy coffee' from the shop near the gift shop on the ground floor. Yesenia got his attention, clicking her nails on the wall by the time clock.

"Captain American or Thor?" She inclined her head to the side, as if trying to decide for herself.

"Well both of those are better than Russet. So either's good." He finished stocking the fruit and rested the empty plastic crate over his shoulder against his back.

She laughed, "Not a new nickname. Russet is gonna stick. I meant for Halloween."

"I don't really do Halloween." He moved to put away the crate, but Yesenia let out a sharp whistle drawing everyone's attention.

"Halloween is a big deal." She tapped her finger on her chin, looking him over. "I'm leaning Captain America, but your goatee says Thor. How do you feel about shaving?"

"Yesenia," Russ patted himself on the back for pronouncing it correctly, "I wear a hairnet on my face, to keep my facial hair. I am not shaving."

"Thor is it." She grinned.

"Am I missing something?"

"Bragging rights," Jose explained, clocking in. "Won last year. She likes the wins."

Yesenia filled in the blanks, "The hospital does a costume contest every year to cheer up the kids. Our department did super heroes last year and we won. And Jose, is right, I do like to win."

Russ swept the floor and kept his head down. "I guess I'll think about it."

"Think good thoughts," she ordered. "I want a solid ensemble cast. I am an amazing Wonder Woman."

"I have no doubt." He dumped the dirt from the floor into the trash and tied off the bag. "Shouldn't we stick with DC or Marvel?

"I'm sorry," she said, pressing her hand against her chest, "I was unaware you knew comics. Where has this geek knowledge been hiding?"

"In my backpack in middle school." Russ shook out the new liner for the trash can. "I can look into some ideas, I guess, if it's for the kids."

"Are you bullying him about Halloween already?" Marc clocked in and turned to Yesenia. "It's barely September."

"Russet will need time to make a costume." Yesenia paused and grinned. "Unless your lady friend will make you one."

"Damn-it, Tricky." Russ cursed the kid, who wasn't working tonight. The rumor was a day old and just as hot as it was yesterday. "Marc, do you mind if I clock out ten early? I'm exhausted."

"Toss the trash and you're good."

Russ took care of his last task and clocked out. The first breath of fresh air made him wonder why he bothered clocking out early. To go home to an empty trailer? Be reminded that Aster and Liam weren't coming back? If they were coming back, Aster would have reached out to him. Then again, he didn't call her until today.

He lit a cigarette and leaned against his car, closing his eyes as he inhaled and exhaled. Three packs in five months and almost an entire pack since last Friday. He couldn't afford his habit the way it was pre-prison. The nicotine soothed his nerves a bit, but he couldn't just stay here. Even when he was off the clock for work, he was still on the clock from his bad mistakes.

Russ turned into his section to see the best thing he'd ever seen, followed by the worst. Aster's gray Oldsmobile was parked in the drive, but Aster was talking to Sam. He stopped his car, glancing at the clock, he had thirty minutes until he had to be in range. They wouldn't be able to see him with a tree on the corner obscuring the view.

A pit formed in his stomach, threatening to swallow him whole. Both Aster and Sam were single parents, and Sam was a good guy. The kind of guy who hadn't been to prison and wasn't on parole. Russ turned on his cellphone, and waited for it to finish powering up, as he watched the pair talk. Aster's hands never left her sides, never went anywhere near her neck. Maybe he'd voluntarily fall into that ever-widening pit. She was comfortable around Sam.

Russ glanced at the small screen on the outside cover of his phone. One missed call. One new voicemail. Misery loved company, and it was for the best to rip off this band-aid. He called his voicemail and punched in the code.

Near the trailer, Aster waved goodnight to Sam, while her recorded voice played in his ear. "Hey. We can talk about it when you get home. Hope you're having a good day."

He sighed, deciding against another cigarette and pulled into the driveway so he could get it over with. Aster was perched on the trunk of her car. Her face lit up when they made eye contact.

Russ got out of the car ready to paint on a fake smile on for her, but he never got the chance as Aster crashed against him. He staggered back a step, caught off guard as he gripped her waist to keep them balanced. She threw her arms around his neck, her body pressing into his. The smell of flowers filled his nostrils, her damp hair tickled his face, she murmured something he couldn't make out.

He shifted and looked down at her face. "Huh?"

"My feet are off the ground." She giggled and hugged him again. "I missed you. Welcome home."

Russ was not above the temptation of enjoying this contact—he hadn't meant to pick her up, but now? He didn't ever want to let her down. Aster was soft, warm, and seemingly fucking happy. He wouldn't deny himself this moment, especially if it was just a moment.

"Missed you too, Sunshine."

"I got you a surprise." Aster patted his shoulder and he reluctantly put her down. She opened the trunk and the cooler that was still in it, grabbing two glass bottles. "I got you an Ale8. It's ginger ale, like Vernors."

He took the bottles from her, examining the labels.

"It's better, I think." She smirked, "You have a bottle opener?"

"I'm allowed to have those, yes." He smiled as he pulled out his keychain and flipped the caps off both drinks, handing one back to her.

She shut the trunk and hopped back up, taking a sip with a smile. "I used to drink them all the time." She was in jeans and a t-shirt, but the moonlight reflected off her pearls.

"So what was Sam up to?" Russ shouldn't have asked, but he needed to know if he was going to be watching Liam for their upcoming date. That was his mental reasoning, anyway, for being nosy. He took a drink and promptly spit it out. "What the hell?"

Aster covered her mouth. "Um... not a fan?"

"I'm not sure." He turned the bottle to examine the label before trying another sip. "On second drink, it isn't bad. It's just not Vernors. Don't tell people it tastes like Vernors."

"Noted." She took another drink and tipped her face up to the sky. "I wasn't sure how to describe it. It's ginger ale."

"Call it ginger ale. Vernors is its own thing." Russ leaned against her car, close, but not touching her. "Vernors will cure most anything. Damn-it." He cursed and took another drink.

"You want a Vernors now, don't you?"

"For more than one reason." He muttered.

"Huh?" She brushed her fingers over his forearm. "I didn't hear you."

Now he was trying to get his brain to restart. Surely it was better to know than not know if she was going out with Sam. But he didn't want to ask again.

"Did you know Sam was interested in getting a drink with me?" Aster broke the silence as she swung her feet back and forth listlessly. "Like a date."

"He mentioned it to me." Russ kept his tone nonchalant, he hoped anyway.

"Hmmm. When did he mention it?"

"This morning."

"Oh." She took another drink from her bottle. "I told him I wasn't interested. I'm not ready for anything right now."

Russ let out a sigh far too loud for it to be casual, then coughed trying to cover it up. "How'd the trip go? You okay?"

"You know? I think I am. It went both better than I could have hoped and was also truly awful." Her toes were painted, the glitter in the polish reflected the outside light.

"You a millionaire now? That packet looked thick." Russ had been curious about it before she left.

She laughed. "No, Grandpa Charles was just really specific about things. That was a copy of his entire will—all three hundred and twenty-five pages. He left me three thousand dollars, a box of pictures, and my grandma's cookbook."

"Liam already claim it?"

"Under his pillow with his other one."

He chuckled. "Pup's gonna have as many books in his bed as on his bookshelf."

Aster echoed his laughter. The scent of citronella was heavy in the air from the candles on the porch, keeping mosquitoes at bay. The citronella and rosemary they'd planted by the door, hadn't survived the dry spell they'd been having.

"My ex-husband told my parents I cheated on him, and they never talked to me about it. They believed him and cut me off because of his lies." She sighed. "They helped him isolate me. They were embarrassed of me, and I never did anything."

"Fuck 'em." Russ growled, trying to not fully lose his cool. "I guess you got the memories of your grandfather at least."

"Mhmmm," she agreed before pulling out her phone and showing him a grainy picture. "And my sister and brother want to be in my life again."

"Didn't know you had siblings"

"Until I went home, I didn't. I hadn't spoke to either of them since Liam was one. But they were really happy to see me." She wiped her eyes, "Sorry. You're tired from work and we need to talk about the trailer situation." Aster swung her legs over the side of the car and put them shoulder to shoulder.

Russ kept his eyes forward, he didn't want to look at her. She needed her own space, said she wasn't ready for anything. In the space of a week she'd gone from being terrorized by her ex and crying in a closet to sitting in the night air bringing up hard topics with confidence. Selfishly he wanted to keep her, but him staying wasn't what she wanted. He knew that for sure.

"I'll tell Jerry I need to move," and "I want to keep living with you," came out in a rush as they talked over each other.

Russ shook his head and walked away from the car, far enough that his monitor flashed a red warning and he retreated a couple of steps closer to her.

"Do you want to move out?" Aster looked confused and hurt.

He knew he looked equally confused. "You want me to stay?"

Crickets and frogs filled the silence between them until Aster bit down on her thumb and stared down at the ground. She said something, but it was so quiet Russ couldn't make it out.

He took decisive steps back her until they nearly touched. Before he could stop himself, he brushed the back of his finger against her thumb. "I didn't hear you. What do you want, Aster?"

"I want to keep living with you." Her eyes met his, and she tugged on the string of his hoodie. "If you still want our company."

Russ leaned his forehead against hers. "Yeah. I really do."

He couldn't contain the grin that spread across his face or handle the fucking beat his heart skipped when she grinned back. Her voice like joyful music as she giggled. "Good!" She ducked her head under his and wrapped her arms around him in a fierce hug.

It took every ounce of Russ's self-control to keep himself from kissing the top of her head. *Roommate. Aster was his roommate. His very pretty roommate, who wanted to keep living with him.*

Despite all his screw-ups, he must have done something right or he wouldn't be here. Russ squeezed Aster a little tighter, making sure not to look down at her as to tempt fate. They were here together, and it was enough to make life brighter, even in the dark.

CHAPTER 38

"Cut away from yourself, you're gonna filet your thumb at the rate you're going." Russ tapped the cutting board on the counter.

Liam glared up at him. "I am doing it like you showed me."

"I promise, that is not how I showed you. Try it like this."

Aster couldn't keep the smile off her face as she watched the two make dinner together. It was the end of September, but it was still warm enough to have the windows open.

Russ stirred the pot on the stove, giving Liam a sly look. "Your homework done?"

"I gotta finish my math still." Liam held his hand out and requested, "I need the oregano."

"I thought oregano was for savages." Russ pulled the spice down. "I can help with your math." He handed over the spice, "Wait what grade are you in?"

"Third." Her son scooped up the chopped peppers into the small pan. "And oregano is fine, you just use too much."

"I use the appropriate amount of oregano." He stirred the sauce on the burner, "And I can still help with your math. Third grade math isn't that hard."

"Whatever."

Aster laughed and Russ shook his spatula at her behind his head. "I don't hear any writing back there, Sunshine."

Aster looked at her pile of applications. "I've done six already. I think that's as many as I mentally handle in one sitting." She stood up and stretched. "How long until you two are done with dinner."

Liam looked at his cookbook, "It says thirty more minutes."

"Did you decide what you wanted to do for Halloween?" She gathered up her papers and found the cleaner to wipe down the table.

"Spiderman for sure." Liam turned his head and Russ clamped a hand down on his shoulder to keep him still. "What?"

"What is the rule when you have a knife in your hand?"

"Eyes on it." Her son set the knife on the cutting board and rushed up to hug her. "Can you make a Spiderman costume for me? It'll be so much better than the ones at the store."

She brushed back his hair, nodding. "We should be able to find a pattern. I'll run to the craft store tomorrow."

"Cool! You're the best mom."

"Let's see how it turns out first."

"It'll be good, you...." The house phone rang and Liam rushed to check the caller ID. "It's Seagar. Can I talk to him in my room? Please, please, please!"

It was hard watching him grow up sometimes, but Aster nodded. "Keep your door open and only until dinner."

Liam whooped and snatched up the cordless phone, already talking as he rushed down the hall. "Hi Seagar! I'm gonna be Spiderman for Halloween. Isn't that awesome?"

"I lost my sous chef." Russ observed as Aster moved Liam's step stool to the side.

She smiled up at him, "I can help. What's next."

"Nothing really. Just layer it and put it in the oven." He shook his head, then requested. "Can you get the casserole dish down for me?"

Aster climbed up onto the counter and stretched to reach the dish on the top shelf of the high cabinet. She bit her lip and pulled it towards herself with her fingertips.

"Ma'am, we have a step stool you can use for these situation." Warm breath by her ear nearly made her drop the dish. "I forgot it was that high up," his laugh was low but amused, "and you know the rule about being up on my counters."

He looped an arm around her waist and set her on the ground, taking the dish from her. Aster blinked, trying to settle her heart down from the contact. Russ still had her backed against the counter, his hand resting on her hip. He surely hadn't meant anything by it and she shouldn't flirt with him. They were roommates. But her mouth got ahead of her brain and she questioned with a flirtatious tone, "am I going to get punished for breaking the rules?"

She yelped and slapped her hands over her mouth. Russ started laughing as he stepped away from her.

He turned his back to her, assembling the dish. "You are full of surprises."

Aster had to clarify. *How would she eat dinner with him otherwise?* "I didn't mean anything weird by that. I promise."

Russ was still laughing. He laughed more often now. Aster noticed a shift in him when she told him that she wanted to stay in the trailer at least until his parole was completed. She liked being a team with him.

"I didn't figure." He put the dish in the oven and set the timer. "Hey, I have a favor to ask."

"Sure." She was always happy to help and anything to steer the conversation away from the awkwardness she'd just created. She sat down at the table.

"So the hospital has everyone dress up for Halloween to cheer the kids up. Do you think you could help with my costume?"

Aster nodded, "It shouldn't be a problem. Did you know what you wanted to dress up as?"

"Yesenia, she's one of the managers in my department, wanted to do a superhero group." He smoothed down his goatee, "I guess they won last year and she wants a repeat. I don't wanna be the one who messes it up."

"Which character did you have in mind? I know there are a lot of superheroes." She wasn't very familiar with comic books, but they had some at the library.

Russ ran his tongue over his teeth under his lips and rubbed the back of his neck. "She was thinking Captain America or Thor. I don't want to shave, so I'd prefer to go with Thor."

Aster held her hand up, trying to imagine Russ without his goatee. She imagined he'd look quite young without it. "I'll have to find a picture, but I can see what I can do." She got up and picked through the storage tote with her sewing things.

"You don't need to start on it right now."

"I have to get your measurements." She explained, grabbing a notebook and pen along with her measuring tape. "If I'm going to get fabric for Liam's costume, I should get yours too."

She paced up to him and held out her own arms. He copied her, but she realized that she wouldn't be able to hold both ends.

"Can you pinch this end?"

"Sure."

Aster paced behind him making sure the tape was as flat as it could be and scribbled down the length of his arms. "I'm gonna do your waist next."

"Yup." Russ was tensely still as she reached around him.

Thankfully, she knew how to take measurements quickly, so this shouldn't be too uncomfortable for him. He was so much taller than she was. "Wrap that around your chest, please."

"Guess this give new meaning to finding out if I measure up." He cleared his throat as Aster put her finger on the tape balancing up on her tiptoes.

"Perfect. Just need to check your legs." She pressed the tape against his waist and followed it down to his ankle. "Last one is your inseam..." She was so glad she was looking down, she could feel how red her cheeks were. "Can you move your legs a little more apart for me and give me your hand?"

She was not putting her hand that close to his crotch, she would die of embarrassment. Not after that measure up comment. She put his hand in the correct place to hold the tape in place and knelt down to see the number she needed. On her knees was better, it gave her more distance from parts of him she should not be thinking about. Except now she was on her knees in front of him, and that could be... no, Russ wouldn't be thinking about her like that.

Russ cleared his throat and shifted his foot side to side. "This the last one?"

"Mhmmm." Aster agreed, not daring to meet his eyes or get up. "All set."

"Thanks. I'm gonna take a shower before we eat." He spun on his heel. "Keep an eye on the timer. If I burn it, Liam'll never let me hear the end of it."

CHAPTER 39

"Trick or Treat!" Liam shouted as he and Aster walked into the decorated cafeteria. His face mask was pulled off so his face was visible. Aster had done a great job on their costumes, including the Sue Storm one she was wearing. When she tried it on last week, it spelled the end of Russ's sleep for three days straight. She hadn't even designed it skin tight, but it was fitted enough. Russ was a man and, while he was one-hundred percent was in charge of his actions, his eyes wandered and his subconscious was a bitch.

The boiling water for the potatoes he was making spilled over and he burned his hand, "Son of a bitch," he grunted under his breath.

"You alright, Russ?" Ian lumbered over, clipboard in hand to check on him. Ian's Kingpin costume was a suit from the thrift store, which Yesenia raised all kinds of hell about. "Go get the first aid kit if you need it."

Russ shook his head, "Not that serious." He turned the heat down on the potatoes. "Watch that for me? I'll run this under water for a sec, then go say hi."

The manager waved him away, "Go, go. We'll consider it your break."

"Thanks." He turned on the water and hissed as he put his hand under the stream. It wasn't that bad of a burn, just a little red.

Aster's little giggle of joy, made him look up. She was talking with Sariyah and handing out popcorn balls to Marc's girls. Sariyah twirled in a circle showing off the Storm costume that Aster had made her. Russ flexed his hand and shut off the water watching, Nate, who was on duty tonight, compliment both women and give high-fives to the kids.

"I might end up with a fifth kid." Marc coughed, pulling at the collar of his Black Panther costume. "No wonder she wouldn't let me see it before I left for work."

"In the most respectful way, you have a beautiful wife." Russ confirmed, before picking on him, "You aren't getting sick now, are you?"

Marc shook his head. "She's taking the kids out the church's trunk or treat. They're just here to see me before they go."

They both walked around the counter, to say hello. Marc's girls all squealing when they saw him.

A happy chorus of "Daddy!" echoed through the cafeteria as Marc lifted three of the girls off the ground and into a hug.

Russ didn't know who Imani was supposed to be in the puffy ice-blue dress, but recognized the yellow dress Zuri was wearing from Beauty and Beast, and baby Joi was in a mermaid costume.

"Hey, Noni, are you spidergirl?" Nate asked the little girl, who huffed as her father put her back on her feet.

"No, I'm Spiderman, but a girl. Girls can be heroes. I'm a hero like daddy." She puffed up her chest.

Liam nodded along. "And like me. We match, 'cause we're best friends. We're gonna make sure the princesses can get to the ball." He was out of serious mode and was acting like the kid he actually was.

"Was the cape a problem?" Aster made him jump as she sidled up next to him.

He managed to shake his head. "Too much fire. It was dangerous. We got it in the pictures earlier."

"Pictures!" Aster clapped her hands together. "Sariyah, where's your camera? I can get some pictures of all of you together."

"Bless you, girl, I woulda forgot." Sariyah handed Aster her bag, "Left pocket."

"Liam, come over here a second." Aster arranged Marc and his family in a few poses. "This is a really nice digital camera."

"Thank you, I told 'im that was the right one to buy." Sariyah smirked up at Marc, who seemed to have heard this before.

"Your costume turned out good, Pup. You like it?" Russ asked Liam to keep his attention.

Liam nodded, "Yeah. Mom always makes the best stuff. Even you look cool right now."

He ruffled the kid's hair and Liam swatted back at him, but he was grinning.

"Liam!" Noni yelled, drawing his attention. "I want us in a picture."

He raced over to his friend without hesitation and the pair showed off their superhero moves, while Aster took pictures.

"Daddy, hold me upside down for some, please!" Noni pleaded and Marc complied, making the girl squeal.

Marc nodded his head to Russ, beckoning, "Come on and grab yours."

Russ froze not sure what to do. He understood what Marc meant in the literal sense: go pick up Liam for the picture, but Liam wasn't his kid. Aster looked back at him and they both paused, waiting for Liam to fuss. He didn't. Instead, the kid motioned for Russ to hurry up. *That was new. Wasn't it?* Then he thought about all the time they cooked together. Liam might not be his kid, but Russ was the main male figure in his life. No pressure, just be a better role model then Aster's ex was. He was overthinking this, it was just a picture, nothing to get shook up over.

Russ walked over and hauled Liam off his feet, swinging him back and forth like a pendulum.

"Now we're both the coolest kind of Spiderheroes!" Liam gave Noni an upside down high-five.

Aster got a few more pictures before Sariyah announced she had to get going with the girls. "Wait, wait. We need a picture of you three together."

"Yeah, Russ, you gotta take one with me and mom," Liam insisted, pulling at Russ's hand.

Aster handed Sariyah her camera back and stood next to Russ and Liam. "Gimme smiles."

Russ always felt awkward in pictures, but he did his best to smile. He glanced over to Aster who was beaming as Liam shifted closer, Russ's hand landing on his shoulder. If he could see Aster this happy, dammit, it was worth feeling silly for a bit.

"Okay my lovelies, time to go. Hugs and kisses for your daddy," Sariyah directed the girls.

Russ tapped Aster on the opposite shoulder, making her turn the wrong way. She rolled her eyes as he asked, "are you going with Sariyah and the girls?"

"Mhmm." She nodded. "We're driving separate, but Liam's excited we're gonna get candy."

"Can we go, Mom? I want to get there with Noni." His blue eyes bright were as he bounced up and down on his feet.

"Okay, let's go." Aster agreed, but caught Russ' hand, giving it a quick squeeze. "I hope you have a good night."

"You too." He smiled then ruffled Liam's hair again.

"Stop." He growled this time, than a mischievous look crossed his features. "What's your favorite candy?"

"Reeses. Why?"

"None for you. I'm gonna eat 'em all." Liam raced out the door and Aster threw her hands up in the air.

"I'll hide one for you, promise." She waved and they disappeared around the corner. "Liam, slow down."

Russ hustled back into the kitchen to save his potatoes from Ian.

The dark-haired manager was regarding the pot. "I think they're ready."

"I'll check on 'em. Thanks." Russ poked one with a fork, it was very much not ready. Ian had nearly turned the heat off. Russ turned it back up.

Marc instructed Tricky on the next trays to run upstairs and the kid, dressed as Robin from Batman, took it into the elevator.

"You're gonna have to hustle," Marc called out to Russ. "We've had two call-ins, and I don't want Tricky stuck with double clean up."

Russ flashed a thumbs up. "Do what I can."

They worked in silence, prepping and cleaning as they went. After the song changed on the overhead speakers for the third time, Marc cleared his throat.

"Last time we talked about Aster. I gave you some advice...."

Russ was scrubbing one of the pans. *What the hell had gotten burned on here?* He sprayed it down again as he assured Marc he remembered. "Special section of hell. You were very clear."

"Yeah." The dark-skinned man leaned against the counter, his brown eyes fixed on Russ. Something was clearly on his mind.

"What?" Russ turned the water off and asked. "Did I miss something?"

"I'm starting to think you two might be good for each other."

Russ blinked and then turned back to the dishes. "She needed a safe place while she got on her feet. And that's all it is. End of story, no special section of hell required."

CHAPTER 40

"Liam, you've got twenty more minutes, then we're going home." Aster called out to her son. "You've got school tomorrow."

He grumbled but flashed her a thumb's up and raced back across the parking lot with Noni.

Sariyah laughed. "She's gonna be asleep before we leave the street."

"I'll be lucky if I get Liam in bed before 11." Aster glanced at her watch. "He's gonna be wired from the candy I know he's been sneaking."

Her friend brushed the locks of her white wig behind her shoulder, "Well, since he got the candy here, you know it's safe at least."

"I appreciate you inviting us." She shook her head as Liam traded away another one of his Reese candies for something else. "Hopefully next year, I'll have enough to afford a camera of my own so you won't need to print pictures for me. Did you need more than five dollars for that?"

Sariyah dismissed Aster's concern, "Five's plenty, and I don't mind. I see you at the kid's school all the time; it's not out of my way."

Music played in the distance and a couple of the older kids started dancing and teaching the younger ones the steps.

"Thank you for recommending the school. Liam loves his teacher, Mrs. Sol is delightful."

"She's the best." Sariyah confirmed. "Imani was heartbroken when she changed grades."

"Does she strike you as too intelligent to be teaching elementary school?" Aster wondered out loud, because that was the impression Aster got from even their limited interaction.

"Who's too smart for what now?" One of the older women from the church chimed in.

"Oh, her son's in Mrs. Sol's class with Noni this year." Sariyah interjected, before whispering a warning in Aster's ear, "Diane, knows all the town's secrets and she'll collect yours, if you let her."

"Wren Sol?"

Aster nodded.

"That girl has brains on top of her brains." Diane blew her nose, "I remember when she was little; she got locked in the library overnight, and she wasn't even bothered. Had her first degree at sixteen and there's been no stopping her."

"It just seems like teaching third grade would be awfully boring for her." Aster checked her watch again.

"Oh, Wren took in a fellow prodigy. A teenage boy working on being a doctor, a real life Doogie Howser in training," Diane explained. "Otherwise, she'd probably be working on another Masters degree. You have any ambitions like that? Or your son? He seems smart." She looked Aster up and down.

"Diane, I think Brother James is looking for you." Sariyah pointed toward the church steps and the older woman wandered away. "That woman's head nearly exploded when I started dating Marc. It was all she could talk about for weeks. What a scandal." She faked a gasp. "The preacher's daughter marrying a man, who'd been to prison. Honestly, just ignore—"

Liam interrupted, rushing up to Aster and holding out his bag. "I'm gonna swing on the swings, then I'll be ready."

She tugged the mask off his face. "Eyes clear, there's littler kids around."

"Okay!" He wiggled in place, like he had a secret.

"Wait." She held onto his collar. "What's going on in that busy noggin of yours?"

He flashed a toothy grin. "I traded away all my Reeses. I win! Be right back."

Aster rested her hand on her forehead and sighed.

"Did I miss something?" Sariyah pointed to Liam. "Why was he trading away some of his candy?"

"Because Reeses are Russ's favorite and Liam wants to make sure he doesn't get any." Aster bit her lip attempting to hide her own smile. "It's revenge for Russ ruffling his hair."

"That boy holds a grudge."

"He does. Russ is so patient with him, though." She rubbed her arms in an attempt to warm up. Russ told her any Halloween that there wasn't snow on the ground was a win, but it was too cold for Aster's liking.

"I keep meaning to ask you about him." Sariyah switched Joi to her opposite shoulder. "How are things there?"

Aster's cheeks flushed. "We're living together at least until his parole is up. We both like the company."

"Mhmm."

"No, no." Aster motioned with her hands, "it's nothing like that. I'm not sure after my ex-husband if I'd ever want another relationship like that again."

Sariyah pulled her camera out of her bag and powered it on. She thumbed through the pictures on the screen, stopping on one and turning it to Aster. "Don't have a relationship like you had with your ex ever again. Have one where your man looks at you like this."

A picture from the hospital glowed on the digital screen. She and Russ stood side-by-side, each of them with a hand on Liam. Aster and her son were both smiling at the camera. But Russ? He was smiling at her, gaze soft and eyes crinkled at the corner. She'd never noticed his dimple before, but she had never seen him smile so brightly either. So happy.

"I'm printing two copies of this one for sure." Sariyah smirked, powering the camera off as Aster gasped. "What? Russ needs a picture of his roommates for his locker."

Aster's ears were hot and she shoved her hands in her pockets, "Liam! Time to go."

"Hey Aster, I'm only picking on ya," Sariyah said softly as she touched her shoulder. "But don't throw out Russ because of your ex. Allen doesn't have power over you anymore. I can see it."

Aster's heart clenched as she did her best not to cry. Choosing to hide her watery eyes by hugging her friend.

Baby Joi fussed at the jostling, but curled herself closer to her mother rather than cry.

Aster pulled away wiping off her cheeks, so much for not crying. "Thank you."

"Anytime." Sariyah promised. "You came back different. You faced the past, and now it's time for your future."

"I'm ready, mom." Liam announced, turning to waved goodbye to his friends. Liam's bag was bursting with treats and he chatted a million miles per hour as they neared the car, hopping foot to foot, needing to get his energy out.

"Race ya to the car, mom!" he shouted and ran off ahead. Fear struck her as she noticed the large, white van parked directly next to them.

"Liam, Wait!" Aster called out, picking up her pace. They were at a church, sure, but no place was entirely without danger. She shouted his name again, but Liam was already talking to the man loading the white van.

The giant of a man had his face painted green and wore a pair of Shrek ears. He looked familiar, but she'd met so many people tonight her head was spinning.

"How's the treehouse? You have fun with it this summer?"

"It was the best summer I ever had! My friends and I were pirates, it was awesome!" Liam swung an imaginary sword as Aster came to his side.

"Well, that sounds like a good summer indeed." The older man sat on the bumper of the van and it lurched forward. "My boys loved being pirates when they were about your age. Guess pirates are always cool."

"The coolest!" Liam tugged at Aster's hand. "Mom, this is Brother Thomas. He built the tree house for me! Do you remember him?"

It was only a handful of months ago, but it had been a crazy time for her. She smiled and bowed her head. "Thank you again for doing that for my son. It really was so kind of you and your friends."

"My pleasure to help someone. You should always help someone when they need it." Brother Thomas shook his finger at Liam, saying, "You'll do well to remember that now."

"I know that already. Russ helped us when we needed it. He's grouchy, but he does good things." Liam looked up at Aster. "Mom? Are you sad?"

Aster wasn't sad, she was happy. If she were being honest, she didn't think she would have survived here, if it hadn't been for Russ's kindness. He was a positive force in Liam's life. Russ was good role model for her son. She'd needed help and Russ had offered it. No strings attached, other than washing dishes and grocery shopping. He treated her with respect, even when it was only the two of them. He didn't need an audience to be kind. Russ cared about them, wanted them in his life.

"Mom?" Liam tugged on her belt to get her attention. "Are you okay?"

She brushed away her tears. "Just thinking about happy things, nothing to worry about. Now into the car it's late."

When Liam slammed the door, Aster reached out her hand to Brother Thomas, his hands dwarfing hers as they shared a handshake. "Thank you again."

He held Aster's hand for a moment, "It was a good day. And *you*, you look like a new person. Glad to see you doing so well." He patted the back of her hand. "You keep taking care of your son and the Lord will surely bless you."

Chapter 41

Winter 2004

Liam and Russ were sitting on opposite ends of the table, glaring at each other. This staring contest was entering its third solid minute.

The eight-year-old tapped his grandmother's cookbook. "The recipe says we need a big turkey for Thanksgiving."

"We are only four people, us three and my grandma's coming over. That's too much bird. It'll go to waste." Russ folded his arms over his chest.

"We can make sandwiches," Liam countered. "Sandwiches are Mrs. Sol's favorite food, along with coffee. I haven't made her a fancy sandwich yet."

"We are *not* getting a 30-pound turkey so you can make sandwiches for your teacher." He tapped his foot, attempting to reason his way out of this. "Pup, we will be eating turkey for a month and a half. You'll get sick of it."

Liam rocked back and forth in his chair. "What if we fed more than just us?"

"Huh?"

"Like we could make plates for Erica, Holly, and Saul, plus Margie and Bridgette probably would like ones too." He pulled his notebook out and flipped through the pages. "I have their favorite foods all here. Well, Saul's a dog and he'll even eat chicken poop, he's not picky."

Russ got up and poured himself a cup of coffee and leaned against the counter. "What about Sam?"

"Cosmo said they were going to his grandma's cause of the football game."

Ah yes, the yearly tradition of watching the state's NFL team lose while in a food coma. Russ had memories of his grandfather waking up to yell at the refs, then falling immediately back to sleep in his recliner. There was always company in and out of the house on Maple. His grandmother loved the little apartment she lived in now, but damn, Russ missed the house he grew up in.

"Big turkey." Liam flattened his hands on the table, "and I'll do all the dishes for the whole day."

"Tempting." Russ arched his eyebrow. "Counter offer. Medium turkey, you wash all the prep dishes, and I teach you how to make a pie crust from scratch."

"A fancy crust, like the leaf ones?" He rebutted.

Russ blew air through his lips. "Ribbon crust, and you let me peel the potatoes."

"But I need to get better at it."

"I can do it faster. You can do the rest of the prep and mash them."

The two fell back into silence, regarding the other. Liam drinking from his water cup and Russ from his coffee cup.

Finally, Liam let out an exasperated sigh, "Fine. But I want to make the stuffing too."

Russ held out his hand, "Deal."

"Deal." Liam turned a few pages in his notebook. "We need to make a shopping list."

Russ looked up at the clock, it had gotten later than he realized. "We'll start on it tomorrow. You need to get ready for bed."

He fidgeted with his fingers. "Mom's not home yet."

Aster had found a part-time job at a coffee shop. On Monday's she worked the late shift, leaving Russ was in charge of getting Liam to bed, which wasn't the hardest thing in the world. But the kid hated to go to sleep without Aster being home. Separation anxiety or something, Dr. Collins had called it. With what Liam had gone through, it wasn't a surprise. The doc suggested they do their best to make Liam feel safe and secure in his environment.

"You know the rules. You've got school tomorrow, and it's almost nine."

Liam slumped out of the chair and dragged his feet down the hallway. "Okay." This kid somehow tugged at his heartstrings at the weirdest times.

Russ cleared his throat, "Get ready in ten minutes and we can watch an episode of whatever's on Food Network."

Liam whirled around, his hair flopping in front of his face. "Really?"

"Nine minutes." Russ tapped his wrist, and Liam bolted to the bathroom. He hollered after him, "brush your teeth and rinse with your cavity stuff!"

"I know!" Liam yelled back.

Russ flopped down on the couch and flipped through the channels until he got to the one he was looking for, praying it was a thirty-minute show and not an hour one. When Aster got her job two weeks ago, she decided she would pay for them to have cable. One thing Liam missed about his old house was watching cooking shows, so it was an expense she didn't mind shouldering. Russ paid for part of it, so he could catch more hockey games. Unfortunately, he didn't get to watch hockey this year because of the stupid lock-out.

Back to the issue at hand, Aster would ring his neck, if he let Liam stay up late again. His track record for Liam being in bed when Aster got home was sitting at zero. It wasn't like he was trying to let the kid up stay, but Liam distracted him. To his annoyance, the show currently airing was Kitchen Nightmares which was an hour. Did Liam even like this show?

The kid had already changed into his pajamas when he jumped up onto the couch. He kicked off his slippers and sat criss-crossed. "This is the British guy who curses a bunch. He's not my favorite."

"Do you want to watch something else?" Russ offered. "Cut off is 9:30."

Liam yawned. "Naw. This'll be okay."

He was sure they'd watched the episode before; it seemed familiar. Russ propped his feet up on the coffee table and set the remote on the arm of the couch.

"How come my stomach hurts when my mom's not here at night?" Liam curled up against the couch's opposite arm.

Russ was not qualified to answer this, but saying nothing would be worse. He cleared his throat. "I think it's 'cause you and your mom are a really close team. Your mom's always taking care of you all on her own, so it feels strange to not have her around all the time."

"Does that mean I'm weak?" Liam pulled his knees up to his chest. "I'm a boy, I should be tougher."

"Whoever told you feeling upset makes you weak, is a dumbass." Russ growled, "You're a tough kid. Don't believe anything else."

"Thanks, Russ."

"Don't mention it." He yawned, letting his eyes close.

Liam's voice was sleepy, "Hey, Russ?"

"Yeah, Liam." Russ didn't even bother opening his eyes.

"Is it okay if I like you more than my dad?"

Russ took a deep breath in and let it out, trying to ignore the sting in his eyes. "Well, your dad's a jerk, so sure; I guess it's okay if you like me more than him."

"You're still a creepy weirdo." He pulled the blanket over himself.

Russ shook his head and chuckled. "You've got until you're nine, then we're gonna fight."

"Okay." Liam murmured, "I'm still a better cook."

Russ wasn't sure when he fell asleep, but a loud commercial startled him awake. He shut the TV off and put Liam in his bed. He was tired enough that he could probably fall asleep on the couch again. It was just past ten and Aster wouldn't be home til after 10:30.

There were leftovers in the microwave, so she'd have dinner if she wanted some. He went to the kitchen to make sure the dishes were done and that sneaky little brat had distracted him with the Thanksgiving talk. There were still dishes in the sink.

He turned on the hot water and let it run for a minute, then added soap. There were only a couple of plates, the baking pan, and his coffee cup. He gulped down the last swallow of cold coffee and scrubbed that first. Russ turned on the radio to the local rock station and sang along to the quiet music. The last plate slipped through his fingers and hit the sink splashing him with water.

Now he was wet. No good deed went unpunished. He finished washing the plate, put it on the drying rack and drained the sink. He sighed and pulled off his shirt, bad enough his shirt was wet, but the waistband of his sweatpants were just as wet. Now he needed to change.

Russ walked to the hall as the door of the trailer opened. Aster was home.

She jumped back, but recovered. "You startled me. You…." she trailed off, her eyes clearly running up and down his torso.

Somehow in the many months living together she had not seen him without a shirt. The summer hadn't been that hot, and he hadn't wanted to make her uncomfortable. However, she was absolutely staring at his body.

"You have so many tattoos." She blushed and covered her eyes. "Sorry, that was rude."

"Nope, my bad. 'scuse me." He retreated towards the bedroom, "I'm gonna change and crash on the couch. Dinner's in the mic."

She had been staring at him in concern over the tattoos, which Russ conceded was more than fair. Not all of them were great, some of them were downright stupid. The tribal pattern by his hip was a perfect example of a dumb tattoo, not his dumbest, but it was in the top five.

He was going to lay down on the couch and pretend to fall asleep immediately. For once take advantage of her, 'don't want to be a bother' mindset. An awkwardness between them would pop up from time to time. They were clearly friends by this point, and he didn't want to make any assumptions about her looking at him. They were both adults in a confined space and a glance here and there wasn't unusual.

He truly did try his best to keep his hands to himself, but occasionally when she needed help, he'd get too close. The next couple of days he'd spend more time outside and berating himself over the mistake. Hard to be good with the pretty woman who lived in the trailer with him was always giggling and smiling now. The more she shined and came into her own, the more he wanted her. That was not on the table. Roommates until his parole was up, then go from there.

A quiet knock on the door made him wince and he pulled on the first shirt in his drawer. He opened the door and Aster pointed behind him, "I wanted to grab a change of clothes."

"Sure." He let her pass by him to get into the closet.

"Russ, can I ask you a question?"

Russ turned back to her, "Yeah."

She toyed with the hem of her button-up shirt. "If this is too personal, then you don't need to answer, but...."

The list of his tattoos ran through his head as he waited for her question. Praying she wouldn't ask about the date over his heart. He was in a good mood, despite everything, and it would sober the mood.

"I saw you have an angel and a devil wing on your shoulders. But I'm not sure the words were in between them." She blushed, "I was just curious."

He bit the inside of his cheek and shook his head as he explained the faded words. "It's a lyric from Unforgiven."

Aster inclined her head, "The Metallica song? I don't remember that line. I know I've heard that song."

"It's not from the Metallica song." Russ smoothed out his goatee, "it's from a Creed song with the same title."

"I'm not familiar with Creed."

He sighed, "No one should be," and closed the door behind him.

Most embarrassing tattoo explained. Check.

CHAPTER 42

"I'm gonna throw up."

Liam immediately looked up from the potatoes he was stirring. "No Mom, you can't in here! The food will be contaminated! Go to the bathroom!"

"Pup, it's an expression, your mom's just nervous." Russ ruffled Liam's hair on his way into the kitchen. "She doesn't need to be."

Liam stuck out his tongue. "Are you *finally* going to work?"

Russ motioned him to come over to the oven, but closed it before Liam could check the turkey.

"Hey!"

"Hay's for horses." Russ tapped the oven door, "You wanna learn or not?"

Aster took a long drink from her water glass and smoothed out her skirt. Her hands were shaking; this was a horrible idea. Why had she thought this would be a good idea? She couldn't handle this on her own. To be fair, when they made the plan, they had forgotten that Russ would be going in early today so everyone on shift could see their families. Russ was the newest hire, so he got the long swing shift. He'd be home earlier, so he'd have more sleep for Friday, but he would be gone sooner today. Aster watched the hands of the clock move closer and closer until it was time for him to leave.

Russ gripped her free hand, "Come 'ere with me for a second. Liam, the potatoes are good. Start arranging the vegetables on the tray."

She followed Russ outside, it was so cold she could see her breath. He draped his coat over her shoulders, before jogging to start his car and warm it up before he headed to work.

He jogged back up to her and rubbed her arms through his jacket.

"Aren't you cold?" she questioned looking square at his chest.

"I'll live, it's just five minutes." Russ tipped up her chin. "Take a breath. Breathe in and think of something that calms you down."

She complied, letting her eyes fall closed as she did so. Letting the warm male scent mixed with spices from whatever he cooked and a hint of smoke that lingered in his jacket fill her scenes.

He moved in closer to her. "Any better?"

Aster nodded and leaned her forehead against his chest. "I'm worried it'll all go wrong."

"Kick 'em out then." Russ laughed at her gasp. "And don't say, you can't do that—because you absolutely can. You were so excited to see your brother and sister. What changed?"

"I know they would never do it, but...." She pulled her arms to her chest, rubbing the collar of her sweater. "It's silly." She huffed, defeated.

Russ wrapped his arms around her, shivering from the cold. "If you're this upset, it isn't silly."

She craned her neck up to look at him. The kindness in his eyes always made her safe. He engulfed her in his sturdy embrace and it made her prior fear seem silly. Knowing it was a bad idea, she wrapped her arms around his waist and hugged him back, feeling him shiver again. "I thought you weren't cold."

"Macho male stuff, can't let you be cold." His words rumbled in his chest beneath her ear. "Now what is the not silly thing that is bothering you?"

She sighed. "I had a dream my parents followed my siblings here and wouldn't leave."

He chuckled, "Okay, that might be a little silly."

"You just said..." Aster poked her finger into his chest, but stopped short as a car pulled in the driveway. Brent and Helen were already here.

Russ had turned at the sound, showing off that jawline of his that her heart flutter. She really needed to stop thinking like this.

"Should I check the trunk for your folks before I take off?" He smirked down at her, wincing dramatically when she smacked his chest.

They disentangled and Aster waved at her siblings. "You made it."

Brent was staring at Russ, and Helen was already grinning ear to ear. *Oh no.*

"Sorry to say hi and take off, but I gotta get to work." Russ offered his hand to Brent first. "Russ."

"Brent, and this is Helen."

"Nice to meet ya." Russ affirmed and pointed to the trailer. "Liam's inside, finishing things up. Help yourself to anything."

Aster hugged Helen and her sister whispered far too loudly in her ear, "My god! He is a sexy giant."

She pushed Helen and Brent towards the door, "Go get inside and get warm."

The pair grabbed what they brought with them and disappeared into the trailer. Aster took off the jacket and handed it back to Russ.

"See no parent's in sight." He pulled it on, eyes never leaving hers.

It was an impulse, but she found herself acting on those more now and pushed herself up on the tips of her toes to kiss his cheek. "Thank you. I hope you have a good day."

Russ stepped back from her, nearly tripping over his own feet. "Yeah, you too. Make sure Liam saves me a slice of that pie."

She giggled and rubbed her arms. "I promise."

Thanksgiving was always a formal affair when she lived with Allen. Everything was a production, despite how much Aster struggled putting it together and making it perfect. It was her job as the wife and mother. They took pictures every year by the hearth, wearing coordinated outfits and smiling too brightly. None of that pageantry had been real. It had been the expectation of her mother-in-law and tradition for Allen to have a new perfect image for his desk at work. Looking back now, it was just one more way Allen painted her into a corner, one more handle of control.

This year was nothing like that. The trailer was filled with laughter and nonsense as the football game played out. Erica and her granddaughter, Holly, had stopped by for a plate. Erica had gone back to her trailer with treats for Saul, but Holly was on the floor with Helen, the girls both talking about their college classes. Marilyn and Margie were explaining euchre to Brent, no doubt to lure him into a round of cards after the game. Liam was passed out on the couch, he'd been up early and helped with every dish that they'd served.

"Have you ever thought about putting some copper color in your hair?" Bridgette asked, startling Aster out of her daze.

She shook her head. "I've never dyed it any color. My parents were strict, then my ex...."

"Was a douche." The older woman finished, touching a lock of Aster's hair. "I think copper would be cute. It would give you some warmth, your base color is a little cool"

"Maybe." Aster bit her lip, "Would you have time before Christmas to try it?"

"Hun, I'm offering to do it now. I cannot watch that slaughter of a game for another minute." She grumbled, "they lose every year, but this is ridiculous."

Aster grinned. "You know what? Yeah, let's do it."

"Fantastic." Bridgette squeezed Margie's shoulder, "I'm gonna go home, get some stuff, and be right back."

Margie looked confused, "What stuff?"

"I'm gonna put some color in Aster's hair." Bridgette answered and kissed the top of Margie's head. "I'll be right back."

Brent stood up, "I'll walk with ya."

"Do I look like I need an escort?" She put her hands on her hips.

"No ma'am, but if I don't get some fresh air, I might fall asleep." He sheepishly admitted.

"Alright, but don't you ma'am me again." Bridgette huffed, but stopped just short of opening the door. "Are either of you girls interested in getting your hair colored? We can make it a party."

Holly and Helen both squealed and started asking about colors, opting to tag along with Brent and Bridgette.

Aster washed a couple of dishes to keep her hands busy. Margie settled into Russ's chair with her kindle, thick glasses balanced on her nose.

"I think this was the best Thanksgiving I've had in a long time." Marilyn bumped Aster with her hip. "Too bad that turd grandson of mine had to go to work."

"Liam made him two plates." She smiled, "He wanted to make sure Russ could try everything."

"How's he likin' school?"

Aster used the back of her hand to brush away the tears forming in her eyes. "Marilyn, he loves it here, and I can never thank you enough for everything you've done for us."

Marilyn hugged her from the side. "Girlie, that's what family's for."

It was nine at night and Aster was trying to stay awake on the couch, flipping through channels. Maybe the Christmas movies were starting already? She loved Christmas. Even when things got rough, Christmas was always a bright spot in the year. She settled on a rerun of CSI, only half-awake as the opening credits played.

Their company had already gone home and Liam was in bed, sleeping. He'd played catch with Brent in the yard and showed off his tree house to his uncle. Aster, Helen, and Holly rotated into the Euchre game as the dye set in their hair or needed to be rinsed.

Aster made sure color didn't stain anything in the bathroom. Helen had just tipped the edges of her hair hot pink, and all three of them had helped dye a rainbow into Holly's hair. Brent had brought his xbox and played Madden with Liam. Allen hadn't allowed video games in the house. Allison even had to beg for a computer to do her school work because Allen felt it would be a distraction.

The entire afternoon and evening had been chaos, but Aster didn't have a chance to get anxious. In fact, more than once her stomach hurt from laughing. Marilyn had the most unbelievable stories from her and Margie's younger years. The day truly couldn't have been better.

Her eyes drifted closed. It had been such a good day. She won a round of Euchre, spent time with her siblings, hadn't been insulted once the whole day, and had even gotten highlights in her hair. Aster's hand went to the pearls around her neck. Her Grandma Lillian's set, not the ones Allen put around her neck. These were a strand she put on herself. The set Allen gave her sat in the back of the closet, hidden. She hadn't found the courage to get rid of them yet. *But what was holding her back? What was she still afraid of?*

Aster got off the couch and went to the bedroom, pulling out the black padded envelope with Allen's address printed on it. She tapped it against the palm of her hand as she paced, pausing at the dresser. There were framed photographs atop it now. The frames were simple plastic brown frames from the dollar store, but the pictures in them were priceless. She and Liam would paint on smiles for their annual Thanksgiving portraits, but these photos from Halloween showcased their real smiles. She bit her lip, finger tracing the image of her, Liam, and Russ. They looked like a family. Not a traditional family, but people that loved each other.

The pearls from her grandmother represented love, but not the ones she'd received from Allen. His pearls were a noose, a collar…and she didn't need it anymore. *No.* Aster puffed up her own chest. She didn't want them anymore and she refused to keep them.

She eyed the envelope critically, it wasn't that wide. It would fit in the mailbox at the front of the park. She could be rid of them tonight. Allen already knew she lived at Everygreens, there was no reason not to send it. She needed to do this, needed to get rid of this last piece of his control.

She scribbled a note on the whiteboard, just in case Liam woke up before she got back, and locked the trailer door behind her. She wandered up to the front of the park. Even bundled up in layers, it was still freezing. The cold nipped at her ears and she regretted leaving her hat in the trailer.

Her breath hung in the air as she jogged to get her blood moving. A walk was good for her, but she wished it wasn't so dark. There was a nagging thought that nothing she was wearing was reflective. She would have been so upset at Liam for doing this, but here she was risking her life. She shook her head, clearing the thought. She was paying attention, she was an adult, and she was perfectly safe. A quiet had settled over the park and any incoming cars would be easy to hear.

Reaching the mailboxes, she expected her hands to shake or to feel fear pull her back, but it didn't. Instead her hands were steady as she unlocked the box and put the package into it. She slammed it closed and did a little dance to celebrate, cutting it short as headlights pulled into the park. That could have been embarrassing.

"What are you doing out here in the dark?" Russ's voice sounded amused, not angry. She pointed to the mailbox and he laughed, leaning over to open the passenger door for her. "Get in, I'll give you a ride back."

Aster climbed into the passenger seat and sighed at the warmth. "I did not," she breathed in sharply, "realize how cold it was until I got all the way here. Thank you." She could feel her own smile.

"It's snowing." He pointed out as he accelerated.

She looked out the window and sure enough there were light flakes in the air. "It's pretty."

"If ya say so." He turned the corner for their side of the park. "Everyone have a good time?"

"The best time. I think Liam's gonna sleep until noon tomorrow." She shifted on the seat as they pulled into the driveway and her hood slipped back off her head.

"Good. Liam, save me a slice of that peanut butter pie your sister was bringing?" Russ questioned, turning to face her, his speech slowing down. "I will tussle with him over pie."

Aster moved to cover her mouth to muffle her giggle, but Russ caught her hand, holding it in his. Her heart pounded in her chest as he held on. His eyes solely focused on her face.

"You changed your hair."

Aster wasn't sure how to describe his voice other than awestruck, but surely she was imagining things. She wasn't that kind of attractive. She knew she wasn't ugly, but she wasn't 'stop a man across the room' beautiful. But the way Russ was looking at her...maybe in this moment she was.

She licked her lower lip, Russ's eyes followed her tongue. "Bridgette thought some copper in it would warm up the look. I think it's pretty."

"It's fucking gorgeous." He cleared his throat and opened his glove compartment, pulling out his cigarettes and lighter. "I mean, looks great on you. Bridgette knows her shit."

Russ bailed out of the car and Aster got out on her side. The core of her being tingling as she watched him light a cigarette and take a drag from it. He looked up to the sky, then over his shoulder at her. "I'll be in, in a bit. Go get warm."

Aster nodded and hurried inside. She fanned herself, knowing Russ couldn't see her and attempted to calm down. He was attracted to her. The way his eyes dilated, the stiffness in his posture, the gravel of his voice. He was interested in her. She rushed to the bedroom to muffle her scream into her pillow.

She looked at herself in the mirror, breathing fast, heart fluttering, copper and blond locks framing her face, eyes just as dilated as Russ's were. Now she knew he was interested in her and she was attracted to him. It was more than close quarters, it was the moments where Russ was there for her. He encouraged her, cared about her child, helped her find a new life. Aster had done the work to grow, but Russ had given her a place to *be*. She wasn't entirely sure what she wanted in the long-term, but for now, she wanted more than a roommate. The question was, how to show him?

CHAPTER 43

"You want another blanket? It's wicked cold in here." Russ didn't want to get up from the couch, but Aster had pulled the throw closer to her chin for the third time.

"How much warmer would it be if I'd bought the right window plastic?" she questioned as the flimsy covering they'd applied sucked itself to the window and breathed out in tandem with the strong wind outside.

"Warmer than it is now." Russ shrugged. "If you grab it tomorrow morning, I can put it up before I go to work."

"Are they really going to make you go with all the snow we're supposed to get tomorrow afternoon?"

"You really are from the south adjacent." He chuckled. "Up here, we don't close unless it's feet in hours and hospitals don't close at all." He turned his attention back to the movie for a moment as the music picked up.

Aster folded her legs under herself. "What if you get snowed in at the hospital?"

"Unlikely as that is, I'd just call Jerry." Russ wasn't worried about getting that much snow. The weather was calling for the craziest storm in years, which meant it was going to blow by them. "Sorry we can't bring the tree in yet. Gotta wait until it's dry."

She smiled, looking over at the empty space where the Christmas tree was going to be put. They had shoved the table against the wall, so there would be walking space between the table and the tree when it was up.

"I can't believe your friend delivered you a tree." Aster shook her head. "And you knowing Liam's teacher's husband makes the world seem so small."

"DB's a stand up guy, and he's a sucker for Christmas, so he didn't mind. Getting one the Saturday after Thanksgiving is a family tradition." Russ cracked his knuckles. "Have you thought about how you want to handle things for Liam?"

"He knows there won't be a lot of presents."

He bit the inside of cheek, he hated the idea of the kid going without. Liam had a rough year, a good Christmas might be a way to make the next year seem brighter. "Santa Clause could always figure something out."

Her fingers went to the collar of her shirt as she lowered her eyes. "My ex told him Santa isn't real. Liam wanted to believe in the magic of the season, but his father told him to grow up and live in the real world."

Russ clenched his fist, "He's fucking eight. He was seven last Christmas!" He took a breath trying to calm himself down, he was having a good night and he didn't want to lose his temper. "Full offense, your ex is a douchebag."

"He really is."

Russ arched an eyebrow as he leaned closer to her. "I'm sorry, did you just agree to a direct insult?"

Aster picked at the blanket. "Him being a bad person, isn't a reflection on me. Me figuring that out isn't some world-shattering progress in my healing."

"I think you realizing his shit isn't your fault *is* progress." Russ tapped her chin, coaxing her to look up at him. "Whatever you want to do for Christmas for Liam, we'll make work. I can even act confused about the gifts."

"Honestly, I think he's most excited about making candy with Marilyn." She hadn't moved away from him. Her impossibly blue eyes meeting his. "Being here has been so good for him; good for both of us."

Russ could smell the mulled cider on her breath and see flecks of glitter on her cheeks from the holiday cards they finished up this afternoon. On the TV across from the couch, the character's were sharing the infamous 'get-together' kiss. The holiday magic was in full force.

Her honest but enigmatic eyes were fixed on his. It was too much. The music swelled, but all he could hear was his heart in his ears. Her hair had grown out since the summer and the copper Bridgette added suited her. Russ tucked a longer lock behind her ear.

"I can't thank you enough." Aster looked up at him through her lashes.

"For insulting your ex?" He tried to make light of the moment, anything to break to spell. Keep himself from making a mistake. "No trouble."

"No. For the Christmas tree outside, the tree house you built for my son, for a space to live," She touched his cheek and holding him parallel to her. "For letting me *be*. I can't ever put into words..."

"Aster." He leaned forward, but a crash made both of them jump apart.

"Mom." Liam, half-awake, had stumbled into the living room from his bedroom.

Aster got up to check on him and Russ could take a hint from the universe when it fell into his lap. The kid had good timing, stopping Russ from doing something so incredibly stupid there was no taking it back. This was the second time too. Thanksgiving had only been two days ago, and he'd almost crossed the line in his car then.

He muttered he was gonna get changed and hurried out of the room. Anything to get some distance to calm down and make sure Aster didn't notice how turned on he was by their almost kiss.

Russ sat on the bed and ran his hands over his face. How many nights had he laid there catching her scent in the pillows and reminding himself that she wasn't for him? How could he be such an idiot? She didn't need his drama. Healing was important and she certainly wasn't ready for anything yet. He misread her gratitude for affection.

Three quiet knocks forced him to get up and open the bedroom door. Aster was standing in the doorway, with a determined look on her face.

"Everything alright?" Russ barely got the phrase out when Aster pushed herself up into his space and pressed her lips against his. It was barely a peck, he felt a puff of her breath as she backed away from him.

His eyes drifted from her five-alarm blush across her cheeks to her neck where her hands were clenched together at her bare neck. Her pearls were gone. *Fuck.*

Russ pushed her hands apart and framed her throat, his thumbs keeping her looking up while they moved together back against the door frame. He swallowed, trying to gather the words of why this was a bad idea so he could express them. He needed to be moving away, not leaning closer. How had he never noticed how short she was?

Aster bit down hard on her lower lip, but he pushed his thumb against it. He hated seeing it, she did it when she was nervous. This might be a bad idea, but if it happened, he didn't want fear to be a factor.

"It's a bad idea." He managed through a dry throat, but instead of moving away he slanted his head and captured her lips. One of his hands stayed at her throat, her pulse thundering under his thumb as the other tangled in her hair. If the little surprised sound she made hadn't shot straight to his dick, her hands pulling him closer by his shirt would have.

He knew it was too much and knew he shouldn't, but he couldn't stop himself. His tongue ran along her lips and when she granted him access, it became a frenzy. Russ knew nothing in that moment but the taste of mulled cider as their tongues explored and Aster's enthusiastic reciprocation driving him to continue.

She anchored herself to him, throwing her arms over his shoulders as she balanced on tiptoe. Her body shook as her knee bumped his thigh.

With one swift motion he hauled her up by her thighs, his mouth never leaving hers. She clung to him, legs wrapping around his waist, panting between kisses as she whimpered his name. He abandoned her lips and stared at her. Both of them were out of breath as the realization of where they were dawned on them.

Aster cupped his face in her hands. "Don't apologize. I came to your room because I wanted to kiss you."

One of his hands stayed at her hip, while he leaned his other arm against the frame. He rested his forehead against hers. "Mission accomplished."

She giggled and traced a finger over his eyebrow. "I think you're better kisser than I am."

"I think I might have hit your head. 'Cause you have that backwards." He smiled at her, before sighing. Knowing he needed to be better than he felt like being. "I should take a shower. Give you some space to get your feet under you."

"You'll need to put me down first." She hugged herself tight to him and kissed his neck.

"Hey, hey." He paced away from the wall and deposited her on the bed. "We shouldn't do this."

"What?" Tears misted over her eyes and her confused voice softened as she caught her hand in his. "Are you not interested in me?"

Fuck. He had opened his mouth too quick. She confused his 'not yet' for 'no' and that was on him.

"Let me try that again. We shouldn't do this *tonight.*" Russ knelt in front of her. "We need to go slow. You're worth going through the steps right, enjoying each one as we come to them."

"But...." She swallowed. "If...."

"Aster, I want to take this slow so we're both sure." He leaned up ignoring the crack from his knees and brushed his lips over her cheek, "*I* need to take my time. Let me, please."

Aster nodded. "But maybe we share the bed tonight?" She blushed again, eyes averted. "Just being close, not anything else since you want to go slow."

"You're gonna be the death of me. I'm sure of it." Russ kissed her other cheek. "I'll clean up and be back."

They slept side by side exchanging soft kisses as they fell asleep, but he was careful to keep his hands to himself for the most part. He hadn't been able to resist playing with her hair and pulling her against him. The scent of her and the warmth of her body had kept him asleep all night.

In the morning, Russ got that unsettling feeling he was being watched.

Oh fuck.

Russ lifted his head over Aster and sure enough Liam was standing in the doorway. The kid's arms were folded over his chest, eyes were narrowed in what Russ imagined was rage. He disentangled himself from Aster, not waking her by some miracle and motioned for Liam to let him out of the room.

He closed the bedroom door and turned to see Liam sitting at the kitchen table. Russ sat down across from him. "Okay Liam," he paused. What the hell was he going to say to this kid? How was he going to reassure him without overstepping?

"Don't hurt her." Liam interrupted his thoughts.

Russ arched his eyebrow.

The eight-year-old flipped open his notebook and doodled in it as he continued, not looking at Russ anymore. "My dad hurt her. Made her cry a lot. If you make her cry, I won't forgive you." Liam put down his pen, "So, if you don't hurt her, I guess it's okay if you like each other."

He looked Liam in the eye. This kid who was called a failure by his father and honestly only had his mother parenting him his entire life, was willing to give Russ a chance. Not how he was expecting this to go, but Liam was nothing if not a child who constantly surprised him.

Russ offered his hand to Liam. "I will do my best to never hurt your mom."

They shook on it and Liam went back to his notebook. "Her favorite breakfast is french toast."

He chuckled and ruffled the kid's hair. "Come on, get up and help me make it."

"I'll make it better than you." Liam grabbed his stool from the corner.

Russ rolled his eyes, "We'll see about that, Pup."

Russ watched Liam and Cosmo throw snowballs at each other in the yard. "Don't hit each other in the head." The last thing he needed was one of them getting bloodied because they mixed gravel into the snow.

"We should build a snow fort!" Cosmo flattened the ball in his hand into a brick. "This is good packing snow."

"Do it over by the tree." Russ pointed.

Liam somersaulted into the snow, laughing as he blew the snow off his face. "We can eat lunch in it."

"You both got forty minutes." Russ grunted and tossed the last shovelful of snow into the space between his and Erica's driveways. "It's too cold to be here out for hours. I'll holler for you when lunch is ready."

"We can take it outside, right?" Liam yelled over a gust of wind.

"We'll see how cold you both are in twenty minutes and go from there."

Russ stomped off his boots on the trailer steps and sprinkled a fresh layer of salt over to keep ice from forming. These were a death trap. He'd build wooden steps next summer to replace the hard plastic ones; they turned into a sheet of glass whenever it was cold. After resting the shovel against the side of the trailer, he banged the toes of his shoes one at a time against the threshold and hurried inside.

He blinked as his eyes adjusted to the muted light. If there was one thing he hated about the snow, it was the snow blindness from too much white. In the trailer it smelled like soup, felt like comfort, sounded like Aster singing Christmas pop songs, and looked like his girlfriend was climbing up on his counters again.

Russ kicked off his boots and hung his coat and winter gear out to dry. He crossed the trailer with a couple of strides and wrapped his arm around her waist pulling her down. "Now Sunshine, we've talked about you climbing on my counters." His lips brushed over her ear. "There is a step stool next to the washer and dryer. Your son is excellent at using it. Why are *you* breaking the rules?"

Aster leaned back against him. "I needed the extra bowls." Her fingers danced over his forearm. "You are freezing."

He hugged himself to her rocking them back and forth, trying to get his blood going. "It is very, very cold outside."

"Are the boys okay?" She glanced up at him, biting down on her lip.

"They are fine. We'll call them inside in thirty minutes or so." Russ slipped his hand under one layer of her clothes.

"No!" She yelped and squirmed to get away from him. "No, no! Your hands are freezing don't you dare."

He laughed against her neck. "What about my nose? If that cold too?"

"Yes." She giggled and struggled against his hold. "Russ, you are cold all over. You wouldn't let me go outside to help because of the cold. Now you're trying to be *handsy*."

"Yeah, but using you to warm up is more fun." He managed to get his hand under her shirt, but she stiffened and he immediately backed away. "Too much?"

Aster spun around to face him flattened her hands on the counter behind herself. She didn't look like she was going to cry, which was a good sign. But she wasn't smiling anymore.

"Sorry, I…"

"It isn't anything you did." Her eyes darted down, then back up to meet his. "I have a scar from when Liam was born. My ex-husband thought it was ugly and I...."

Russ caught the back of her head and crashed his lips over hers, silencing whatever else she was gonna say. He took his time exploring her mouth until she relaxed enough to rest her hands on his hips. He kissed both of her cheeks. "You gotta quit telling me things like that." His lips brushed over her forehead. "It makes me want to either drag you into the bedroom, which I do not have time for before work, or drive to your ex's and beat him bloody, which will send me back to prison. And I'm not entirely opposed to doing more time if...."

Aster pressed her finger to his lips. "Don't. Please, don't even think of hurting him and risking your freedom. Me living happily with someone so caring is good enough revenge."

He felt his cheeks get warm, which he was sure was him thawing from being outside and had nothing to do with what Aster had just said. "Okay. Since you asked so nicely." He hugged her to him and kissed the top of her head. "You are beautiful. I hope you believe me when I tell you that."

She nuzzled against his chest. "I do, it's just hard sometimes. Can I ask you a favor?"

Russ looked down at her, nodding. "Sure."

Aster tugged at his belt loops. "Can you..." she paused, cheeks staining pink, "can you stop sleeping on the couch when you get home from work? I'd like you to sleep with me in the bed, please."

He blinked and drew in a deep breath, but before he could say anything she fidgeted and continued.

"I don't mean," she lowered her voice despite the fact they were alone, "sex. Like just sleeping. But I'm not opposed to *things*. However, you said you wanted to take your time and I...."

Russ laughed, unable to help it as Aster attempted a scowl. He caught her hand, "Sunshine, if that's really what you want, I can do that. But if we're in bed together, I'm gonna be very..." he cleared his throat, "*aware* of your presence and my hands might wander while I'm sleeping."

Her blush deepened, "I don't think that would be a bad thing."

"Gonna be the death of me." Russ hauled her up and sat her on the edge of the sink. "Talkin' like this less than two hours before I go to work and now you want me to try and sleep next to you."

"Yeah." Aster giggled and smoothed his goatee. "You said you wanna take your time. Maybe I wanna be temptation. If you're really worried about it. We can leave the door opened."

"So Liam can shank me? No thanks." He put his hand in the dishwater and snaked it under her shirt.

"Russell! You brat!" Aster squealed, splashing him with water. Both of them laughing until the front door crashed open. They froze as the boys scrambled inside.

"It's too cold out there. Is lunch ready?" Liam questioned stomping off his boots. "Can Cosmo have lunch with us?"

"Of course he can. It's almost ready." Aster slipped down from the counter and out of Russ's arms, so he grabbed the bowls down for her. She admonished the boys, "everything with snow on it needs to be set down right by the door. I'll put them in the dryer."

Russ got out the bread and cheese to start on sandwiches.

"Miss Aster, why is your back all wet?" Cosmo asked.

"Russ and I were doing dishes."

"Russ," Liam said, folding his arms over his chest. "Dishes are my job. Don't make my mom do them."

He chuckled and agreed, "alright, Pup. They are all yours after lunch." Aster came up beside him to help butter the bread. He kissed her cheek. "And I'm all yours after I get home from work."

"Good." Aster shimmed her shoulders as she giggled again.

How the hell had he gotten so fucking lucky?

CHAPTER 44

Aster opened her eyes and smiled at the man sleeping next to her. Russ was on his back, mouth slightly parted as he breathed deeply. Her fingers itched to touch him, but she held herself back. It had been a little over a week since their first kiss, and it was hard not to feel like she was floating. They shared the bed now, even with Russ insisting on going slow.

Watching him sleep in the morning was one of her new favorite things. When she was married to Allen, she would bail out of bed as soon as she was awake to try and make things perfect in the house. With Russ, she could stay in bed and relax, but this morning she needed to get up. She had work today.

"Are you memorizing my nose?" Russ grumbled rolling over and hauling her close to him. His lips brushed the top of her head, fingers slipping under her shirt to rest on her hip.

They were chest to chest and Aster cuddled against him. He was so warm, and it was freezing in the trailer.

"When do you need to get up for work?" His finger's trailed up her spine, making gooseflesh run all over her body. He chuckled and planted more kisses on her head.

She pouted. "The alarm's going to go off soon."

"I should start breakfast." Russ yawned.

"What if I want to cuddle?" She kissed along his jawline. "You are so warm and perfect to curl up to."

He lifted her chin with a single finger. "Are you using me for heat?" Aster wrapped her arms around his neck, pulling herself up to kiss his lips, nipping at them playfully. Russ rolled her under him, parting her lips in a heated kiss, their tongues tangling together.

Her alarm beeped and he pulled away from their explorations, growling into her neck. "I'm gonna toss that thing into the yard."

She arched her back from the feeling of his heated breath and he held her hip down. His large hands searing her even with clothes between them. "You should have started here last night." She kissed the side of his head.

"Forgive me for wanting to woo you a little." He flopped over on his back.

"Woo? What an old fashion—" Aster giggled as Russ covered her mouth playfully. He glared at her, as he removed his hand. "Sorry, what I mean was, what a different way to say that."

He muttered something under his breath and rolled up and out of bed. "Go shower. I'll fix breakfast."

"Russ?" she called after him.

He paused in the doorway, "Yeah, Sunshine?"

Aster couldn't keep the grin off her face at the use of her nickname. She told him that she liked it and he'd been using it more often now. "Thank you for being willing to *woo* me. But," she said, biting her lower lip, "I promise, I'm ready for more than wooing."

Russ paced back to her and sat on the bed, tucking her hair behind her ear. "Yeah? You sure?"

"Yeah." She pulled him down for another kiss, the bed bowing beneath his weight as he put his hand down. Between kisses she whispered, "I'm ready. Let me, please."

On Sundays the coffee shop closed at 5-sharp, and Aster was grateful for it. She hated driving in the snow in the dark. They were far enough north that Russ warned her snow was common well into April. She made a face as a truck roared past her. She was going to drive slow and make it home safe. It wasn't worth dying in a car crash, trying to make better time. No place was worth her life.

Aster's brows scrunched as she pulled in the driveway. The lights were off.

"That's odd," she muttered, glancing at her watch. It wasn't even six yet; neither of those two would be ready to go to bed. She slipped out of the car and waved at Holly, who was on the phone outside Erica's trailer. Aster reached for the handle and noticed there was a sign taped to the door.

Please knock

She cocked her head to the side, confused, but still knocked. The door flew open and Liam stood in the doorway dressed in his button down shirt, tie, and slacks. The trailer was dark, the only light was from the hood over the stove, the Christmas tree, and the strings of white lights hanging both over the kitchen cabinets and on the opposite wall.

"Welcome to our restaurant." Liam ushered her in and closed the door. "Let me take your coat, please."

Aster gave her son her coat with a giggle, perfectly happy to play along. She looked to the kitchen and found Russ leaning against the counter, a lopsided smile on his face. The fitted smoke-gray long-sleeved henley and dark washed jeans compliment- ed each other and the man who was wearing them. Most of Russ's clothes were bulky and hid his build, but this outfit showcased the broadness of his chest and his muscular arms.

She blushed and smoothed her hands down her work jeans. "I don't think I'm dressed nice enough for this place."

"This way, Mom." Liam took her hand and walked her to her bedroom.

A dress was laid out on the bed with a note on top of it.

"I'll let you change. Knock when you're ready." He winked at her and rushed out of the room.

Aster turned on the bedroom light and picked up the note first.

Keep your socks on; too cold in here without 'em.

Aster picked up the dress laying out on the on the bed. It was a floral print, new, and in her size. She ran her fingers along with the soft fabric, forcing herself not to cry as she hugged the dress. Allen never bought her clothes without her. They'd spend hours in the stores, while she modeled progressively smaller sizes until Allen picked one to be a 'goal outfit.' Russ had somehow gotten her a dress just for tonight when no one else would see them. It wasn't a gift so Russ could show her off, it was a gift *for* her. It was even pink, her favorite color. She couldn't remember the last time anyone had put so much thought into a gift for her.

Drawing in a couple of breaths to center herself—because nothing was going to ruin this night—she put her work clothes in the hamper, pausing by her top drawer and switching into her nicer bra with matching panties. Just in case. She looked at herself, minus the scar on her stomach, she didn't look so bad.

There was a knock on the door, "Mom, are you ready?"

"Just another second." She answered quickly and pulled the dress over her head, letting it fall over her body. She kept her socks on and knocked on the door.

The door opened and Russ was standing in the hallway. "Hey."

"Hello." She blushed as he looked her up and down. "I love the dress, it's beauti- ful. How'd you get it?" Aster swished side to side letting the skirt move. "Oo! It has pockets!"

"Sariyah really liked the potatoes I made for the fourth. Cost me the recipe." He took her hand and kissed it.

Liam cleared his throat loudly.

"We're gonna miss our reservation." Russ winked at her before turning to Liam. "Apologies, sir, is our table ready?"

"It is." Liam pointed to the dining table, which was covered with a black sheet, and the three wick candle in the center made the room smell like raspberries and lemon. He pulled out a chair for her and gave a little bow, before marching around the tree to the couch.

"What is he doing?" Aster mouthed as Russ sat down across from her.

Russ tugged at his collar and mouthed back, "You'll see."

Liam returned with two papers and handed one to each of them. "Here are your menus. I will go get your water, would you like lemon?"

"That would be lovely, thank you." Aster bit down on her lip to keep from giggling. This was so cute.

The menus were written by Liam and were front and back with small doodles in the margins. There were three appetizer options, three main course options and on the back side of the paper three desserts and three drink options.

Had they cooked this much together in just the few hours she'd been gone? If they had, they wouldn't have to worry about cooking for a few days. Plenty of leftovers.

She motioned to Russ to give her some kind of clue what was happening, but he shrugged. "Liam's show."

Speaking of, Liam came over with two glasses of water, one with a large chunk of lemon floating in it. "Your drinks." He pulled a small notepad from his pocket, "Have you had a chance to look over the menu? Can I give you a recon-man-da-tion?"

Russ took a long drink of his water and Aster waved her finger at him as a silent warning not to make her laugh. She turned to her son. "I would love to have your recommendation, please."

He straightened himself up, "For the main course, I would suggest our shrimp and lemon pasta it goes with…." He paused, thinking for a second, "It goes well with our spinach salad appetizer."

Liam glanced at Russ, who gave him a thumbs up.

"That sounds amazing. I would love to try the shrimp pasta and the salad." Aster watched Liam scribble down her order.

He turned to Russ, "And for you, sir?"

"That salad sounds good, but I think I'd rather have the garlic knots." Russ itched his goatee, "And the lasagna for the main course."

Liam scribbled again in the notebook, then took the menus from them. "Very good. I will start the music for you and get those orders in."

Aster could tell it was killing him not to run, but her son marched to the kitchen, taping their orders to the wall near the stove. He turned on the TV and it was already on the Christmas music channel.

"This is so amazing." She whispered to Russ, who pointed behind her. Liam was pulling on a chef's hat and gloves. She turned back to Russ, asking, "How did you two pull this off so fast?"

Russ caught her hand and gave it a squeeze. "He asked me how I was going to take you out on a date since I'm stuck at home. When I said I couldn't, he said we should turn the trailer into a restaurant."

"You guys planned this in one day?" She was flabbergasted.

"No. We've been planning this all week." Russ took another drink of water. "Cooked everything today. I did get a bottle of wine for later, if you want."

It never ceased to surprise her, how creative Liam could be when he put his mind to something. He plated their dinners and served each course with intention. Aster invited him to eat, but he insisted he had eaten before his shift. The only concerning thing was Liam excusing himself to go have a 'smoke break' retreating to his room with a rolled up piece of paper between his lips. Russ winced and promised her to be more careful about smoking around him.

They shared a piece of cheesecake for dessert, but as Liam went to get their drinks. He yelled out 'pause' allowing Russ to help him pour and serve the coffees, then he restarted the game. After they were done eating, Liam took a bow before looking up with a wild grin and bright eyes. "Ta-da! Did you like everything, Mom? Russ needed help, so I helped him. I made a bunch of it myself!"

Aster hugged her son, "It was all delicious. I think you might end up being a chef one day if you keep this up."

"Mom," Liam regarded her seriously, "I'm going to *own* my restaurant one day. I might even let Russ work there, if you still like him."

Russ snorted. "You think I'd work for you? Your attitude needs work."

"I'm like the chefs on TV, but without the swears," he argued.

"No more Kitchen Nightmares." She put her foot down.

Liam sighed dramatically. "Okay, I'll be nicer *and* do the dishes."

Russ stood up and held out his hand, helping her out of her chair. "Go sit, put a movie on. I'll help him with the clean-up, then we'll relax."

Aster flattened her hands against his chest, "This is..." she trailed off, eyes misting over, leaning into his palm when he wiped the tears away. "Thank you."

He kissed her forehead. "Movie. Liam and I will keep you company in a bit."

"Russ, you're supposed to be on a date with my mom." Liam hollered over the running water. "That means you stay with her."

Russ rolled his eyes and paced into the kitchen, "Pup, when you're an adult, you'll realize that clean-up is everyone's job and families are package deals."

"Whatever." Liam huffed. "I'm sitting in the chair, you have to share the couch with her."

Aster pulled the blanket over her legs and found White Christmas on TV. Letting herself get lost in the film, but not missing the creak of Russ's chair as Liam flipped into it. Russ's arm settled over her shoulders and she leaned against him.

"Liam, you're allowed to sit with us." She offered.

He put his finger up to his lips, "Shh. Mom, it's the movies now. You're still on the date."

Russ's laughter was silent, but Aster felt the shaking of his chest. "Yeah, shh," he teased. "We're here to watch a movie together."

Liam fell asleep halfway through the film and Russ carried him to bed, leaving them alone in the living room. For all her expectations of Russ whisking her off to bed, for the few uninterrupted hours they'd have while her son slept, he seemed content to simply hold her on the couch.

Allen stopped romantic things like this once Liam was born. She pushed the thought away. She wanted to be in this moment. Here with someone who truly cared about her and her son. Aster snuggled against Russ's wide chest, her hand wandered down his stomach, but he caught it in his own, holding it.

"I love this movie." She whispered as the final number started on screen.

Russ kissed the top of her hand, keeping a hold of her hand as he brought them to their feet. "Come 'ere."

"I'm here." She forced herself not to be bashful or nervous meeting his gaze as she balanced on the balls of her feet.

"So you are." He looped his arms around her waist and she settled her arms on his shoulders. As "Dreaming of a White Christmas" played in the background, Russ started swaying ever so slightly side to side with her.

Aster leaned her head against him, keeping her voice low as she asked, "Are you dancing with me?"

"Badly, but yes." He sighed. "Been a minute since I held a girl in my arms under soft lights. Doin' my best."

She let her eyes drift shut as they moved in time. "You're doing wonderfully. More than I could ever...." Aster caught herself, she almost said the word *deserved*, but that wasn't right. She deserved nice things. She deserved love and kindness and romance. She was worthy of those things and more. These past months living with Russ had taught her that. "More than I could have ever expected. But you didn't have to go through all of this."

Russ leaned down and captured her in a dizzying kiss, her hands gripped his shirt to stay steady. His hands left her waist and moved up her body, burying themselves in her hair. More intense than their previously stolen moments, his tongue explored her mouth with what felt like a single-minded goal to steal her breath.

Mission accomplished. A moan escaped, her and she felt him shiver. "Russ."

He pulled away slightly, but his lips brushed over her cheek and down the column of her neck as he spoke.

"I *want* to do things like this. I *want* to make you smile, make you laugh, and make you feel special." One of his hands found her hipbone, pulling her flush to him. "I also want *you* in every way you'll allow me to have you. A night, a week, or just until we decide this ends, I want you. You can't imagine how much."

Aster felt a tear slip from her eye, and he caught it with his thumb, brushing it away.

His breath mingled with her own as he whispered his overwhelming words over his lips. "Sunshine, let me show you. Let me, please."

"Yes."

CHAPTER 45

Russ was not a player. He'd never had been inept at picking up women, but he didn't hook up with anything in a skirt that passed him by. Picky wasn't the right word. It was more like he knew he wanted more than a night, and if he thought a night was all he was in for, he wasn't interested. Strangers that fell into bed could become more, but he never started anything there and had it stick. But Aster wasn't a stranger. He knew who she was, had learned her so intimately since she'd stumbled into his life. She was a smile, a kind word. A stronger person than he could ever be. The brightest sunshine warming his entire world.

He wanted more than a roll in the sheets and prayed her 'yes' meant she understood that.

She slipped out of his arms and tugged him to the bedroom behind her. He closed the door behind them and let her push herself up on tiptoe.

"You are so tall," she murmured, her lips moving slowly against his as she untucked his shirt, hands seeking skin. "I've thought so many times about touching the pattern of the tattoo on your hip."

"How long?" He smirked.

"Since the first time I saw you without a shirt," she admitted, sounding a little embarrassed. "Thought about you shirtless more times than I should have."

He found her lips again. "You have no idea how long I've been thinking about you like this."

"Since my haircut." Aster teased, "You were speechl—"

"When you hugged me outside the jail and called this stupid trailer home." Russ cut her off and held her face in his hands, "I didn't even know what it was yet, but I knew I wanted a home with you."

Her heart skipped a beat as she looked into his eyes. "Russell, you're gonna make me think you're a romantic."

Russ cheeks heated up and he cleared his throat. "You said you wanted see the pattern on my hip." He gripped the back of his shirt and yanked it off, tossing it towards the closet. "Go for it."

Aster gave him a wry smile and swirled a single finger through the tribal themed ink. It disappeared beneath the waistband and he shifted against the door.

"How many tattoos do you have?" Her voice was innocent as she looked up at him from beneath her lashes, but her finger running across his waistband was anything but.

"I stopped counting after twelve," He breathed slowly through his nose, trying to keep his wits about him. "But I'm pretty sure there's about double that now."

"Do you have any I haven't seen?" She bit down on her lip, her palm pressing into his skin as her thumb hooked his belt loop and began a slow tug downward.

She squealed as Russ hauled her up and deposited her on the bed. He leaned into her space forcing them nearly horizontal. "Aster, are you trying to get my pants off?"

She rubbed her foot against his leg, "Yes. I thought you wanted me in every way." Aster captured his face in her hands. "Can't you see how I want you the same way?"

"Christ, woman." He pressed his forehead to hers. "How am I supposed to focus when you say shit like that?" Russ palmed up her thigh, but her skirt was stuck beneath his leg. "We should get this dress off you. I don't want to tear it."

Aster bit down on her lip but nodded as he shifted away from her.

Russ knelt down, kissing the outside of her knee, then the top, and nudging her legs apart to press his lips to the inside of her knee. He rolled up the hem of her skirt, just enough to expose a bit of her thighs, exploring her legs with his mouth as he bunched up the fabric.

His finger flexed on the fabric, rolling it up to her hips giving him a view of the light purple lace she was wearing beneath. "Sit up."

Gooseflesh danced across her skin as she did he requested, allowing him to slip the dress over her head. She started to fold her arms over her body, but he stopped her.

"You still good?" he questioned, his voice low.

She nodded and rested back on her hands, pushing her chest out. The matching purple lace bra was partially see through.

He rested his chin on her thigh, staring unabashed at her uncovered skin, the pale light pouring through the window. "Fuck, you are gorgeous."

Aster combed her nails through his hair and he couldn't stop the shudder that ran through his whole body.

Russ dropped his head and kissed her hip bones, lace scratchy on his lips. His hands trailed up and down her thighs, spreading them farther apart. He was hard enough to make it distracting and he bit the inside of his cheek. He needed to stay in control.

His tongue found her soft flesh by the edge of her panties. The weight she'd put on in the last months, made every curve of her body more pronounced and breathtaking. She was the picture of feminine beauty. Her body served her, kept her going, and now he was more than happy to serve that body and push it over the edge.

A soft whimper passed through her lips as she dragged her nails back through his hair.

"You can make noise. You're allowed." He growled, laving his tongue up her belly, over a scar.

Her blue eyes met his and she shook her head. "He used to make me make noise, say things. I just wanted to feel it."

"Got it." He pressed one knee into the bed, now parallel to her and teasing with feather light touches. Tracing the shell of her ear with his tongue, his voice husky in her ear. "Lose the bra."

She jerked in surprise, turning to face him and catching him in a wild kiss. Her hand twisted behind her back undoing the clasp and flinging the item behind her. They never broke that wicked kiss, melting into each other in a way Russ didn't know existed. This moment was all there was. Her mouth on his and their bodies clicking together like the pull of a magnet.

His fingers teased her covered flesh, while his mouth found her tits, sucking on her nipples and swirling his tongue over her stimulated flesh. Her body trembled as her breathing quickened.

Her reactions only urged him on, he coaxed her to lay down, pressing open mouth kisses to her shoulders and up her neck. Nipping her earlobe, before changing his mind. There were other places he wanted his mouth.

Retreating back to the kneeling position, he pulled her panties down as he went. Kissing his way back up her legs until he was between them, further tormenting her by kissing everywhere but where he imagined she wanted him to.

Russ trailed a single finger up and down her slit, testing how wet she was. A quiver ran through her frame as he teased her opening with that one finger until he slipped it inside. She was so wet and eager.

"Oh my God...." Her breathless whisper made him chuckle low.

"Getting you some old fashion religion is the plan." He added another finger, slow and controlled as he brushed the tip of his tongue to her clit.

Aster's back arched and, while she didn't make a sound, the grip she had on his hair told him all he needed to know.

He growled over her heated pink folds. "Been a while, huh?"

His fingers kept their pace as he sucked on her swollen bud. The pull and push he was creating was purposeful, driving her arousal, to get her to lose herself in the moment. He savored her taste, licking and sucking incrementally until her whole body quivered, driving him to increase the speed of his fingers and pressure from his mouth.

A desperate soft cry escaped her as she came on his fingers, pussy pulsing with aftershocks. He kept stroking her through it, his eyes focused on her body heaving for air. Russ wiped off his chin and goatee before pressing one knee into the bed, between her legs.

One shift of his knee made her body jerk from the stimulation. Aster's face was flushed, her eyes glassy, lips parted and drinking in precious air and Russ robbed her of it. Plundering her mouth with his, dragging his, he dragged his tongue against hers. His hands found his button and zipper and he started the desperate game of getting out of his pants.

"Damnit." He grunted against her mouth. Finally surrendering and backing away from her so he could rid himself of these stupid pants. It was just as well, he needed to get into his nightstand, before this got any further along.

He shucked his remaining clothes to the ground and grabbed a condom from the two pack he'd bought at the gas station. Did he think this would be happening so soon? No, not at all. Did he buy this pack last week just, in case? Yes, because he was not missing the opportunity due to lack of protection. The package tore easy and he rolled it over his cock.

Russ climbed back onto the bed and pulled Aster up onto his lap brushing her sex over his. His back near the wall in case she needed the leverage. He wanted to watch her when they fucked. Needed to see her every response and drink in her abandonment.

She reached between them, stroking him as she pressed her forehead to his. "I want you."

His eyes drifted shut as she continued to work him. "Keep that up and we're gonna have to wait for round two." It had been so long since someone else touched him.

Aster shifted on his lap, one hand bracing on his shoulder, the other guiding him inside.

"Fuck. Fuck. Fuck." He growled into her shoulder.

His cock throbbed as she lowered herself over him slowly taking him into her molten heat. Her body was searing. Blood pounded in his ears as he groaned, shaking with the effort it took not to move. Aster rolled her hips, building a slow rhythm. Her voice hoarse against his ear, whispering, "So good."

"Aster." Russ couldn't vocalize more than her name as plea. She was a vision in his arms. Sweat dotted along her hairline as the friction built between them. His palms mapped her back as he delved his tongue back into her mouth. She fed back on his fire, matching the frantic pace of his kiss.

He was going to drown in her. Her hands buried in his hair, her kiss fierce and unguarded. Russ drank in every twitch, shiver, and cry. He pressed his mouth to her neck and clamped a hand on her hip, driving deeper into her. "My beautiful girl."

She set the pace riding him, chasing that high just out of her reach. Both hands braced on his shoulders, her nails bit into his flesh as she impaled herself over and over. Her pussy flexing on his dick, making it harder not to fall over the edge.

"Russ." She whimpered in his ear. "You make me feel so good."

Russ ran his hands up and down her back, massaging her flesh as she panted in the heat of the moment. He gripped her hips driving her heady movements. Holding her in his arms he marveled at how fucking sexy she was.

A carnal moan escaped her and he thrust up into her unable to hold back. Their bodies crashed together, her tits against his chest, and it was too much for him as he bucked up into her, releasing into the condom.

His fingers slipped between them, working her clit. "Sorry." He heaved out a drugged breath, "Let's get you there, Sunshine."

She writhed on top of him, as he played with her bud. Russ watched her breathlessly, until she found her second release, pussy gripping his softening cock.

Aster's legs encircled his waist and they gazed at each other. Completely spent but running on his remaining few brain cells, he pushed her tousled hair away from her face. He caught her chin and pulled her in for a slow sensual kiss, sipping at her lips, as his finger followed the path of her spine.

She hugged herself to him. "Thank you."

He chuckled and hugged her right back. "I'm supposed to be thanking you. You look fucking incredible."

"You aren't looking at me." Her shoulders shook.

"Yeah, but you're naked and on my lap, that does make you more attractive by law." He kissed her cheek, nuzzling affectionately. "I don't want to, but we both need to get cleaned up."

Her tongue ran up his ear. "I still need a shower."

"Mhmmmmm."

"You're invited."

"Fuck. You are amazing."

Chapter 46

"And this one." She traced the eagle on his ribs. "Didn't it hurt? I would think ribs would hurt."

"Just thought it looked cool." Russ kissed the side of her head. "And it hurt like a bitch."

She was snuggled in bed with him, wearing his shirt and a pair of underwear and him just in his boxers. He complained of being cold for a half a minute, but she told him she wanted to look at his tattoos. All of them, because she kept finding them.

"Roll over." She nudged him.

He groaned, "I have a nearly naked woman pressed against me and you want me to lay on my stomach?"

Aster poked his side. "I wanna see the ones on your back."

"Fine." He grumbled, but rolled over on his stomach, yelping as Aster sat on his butt. "Ma'am?"

"Don't ma'am me, we're in bed." She snickered and ran her hands up and down his back, his skin was so warm. She kneaded his shoulders massaging his flesh, biting her lip to keep from laughing as he moaned in pleasure. Leaning down she whispered in his ear, "I've been told I give amazing back rubs."

Russ shivered under her and his voice dropped low as he warned, "Keep that up and we're not sleeping tonight."

Aster rolled her body and sat back up, "Oh, I see. Sensitive back."

"Old back, sensitive everything." He shifted his shoulders. "And there's a pretty girl touching me."

He couldn't see it, but she blushed at the compliment as she continued to trace over his body art. There was a cross that didn't look as crisp as some of the other, she outlined it.

"Got that one in prison. Crosses were popular." He grunted. "What I do is between me and God or something like that."

"Rose and dagger by the small of your back? It's got color."

Russ pulled his arms under his head. "Tattoo artist wanted to try color and an ex-girlfriend picked the design."

She felt this odd prick of jealousy. "Did you date her long?"

"Not really," he sighed, "found out she'd been lying to me about her past. Didn't need that in my life."

"Honesty is important," Aster agreed. Far too many times secrets had ruined her life. She wouldn't have lies in her life either. *Not anymore.* She smirked and tapped the skull and crossbones on his thigh. "You really have a thing for pirates."

Russ twisted beneath her and flipped her under him, bracing his weight on his forearms. His smile teasing, dimple showing. "Pirates steal all the best things."

"Like pretty girls?" She touched the side of his face, pulling him in for a slow kiss.

He brushed his nose over hers, "Naw, we ask them to join the crew. No ship is complete without a woman who knows the way."

Aster patted his side and he flipped back over, resting on his back beside her, pulling her close again. His breathing softened as her hand skated across his stomach, until she reached the roman numerals over his heart. "What about this one? I don't remember all of these from school. The first one is ten, I know that."

"October 15th, 1974." Russ lifted her hand away from his chest and brought it to his lips. "The day my grandparents adopted me." He kept a hold of her hand as he cleared his throat. "They were in their forties and my mother was a wild child. Bailey, her name was Bailey. She met my father in college and ran off with him. They ended up in Blue, California, which is where I was born. There was a car accident, both of them died. I was alone."

"How old were you?" Her heart broke. This poor man. But how lucky to have his grandparents take him in in the midst of that tragedy. He'd never said much about his grandfather.

"I was five. Don't remember much, just being scared, and then I wasn't." One of his hands held fast to hers, while the other traced back down her spine. "They didn't need to take me in, and I'm forever grateful they did. I had a chance to be something and show them I was worth all of it. I ran a six minute mile in high school, got a full college ride, and everything...." He closed his eyes.

She hated the idea that he thought he had to accomplish something to be worthy of love. It was something she understood far too well.

"Just went downhill from there."

"What happened?" Aster had been tempted to ask more details about how he ended up in prison. She always stopped herself out of respect. She wasn't worried about Russ getting angry, but it seemed like such a personal thing to ask.

"I tore my ACL and that was it." Russ kissed her hand again and shifted his hips. "Dropped out of college and bounced around doing a helluva a lot of nothing. If my grandparents were disappointed in me, they never said." He turned his head and cleared his throat. "Then my grandfather died when I was 29, it was one of the worst days of my life. I didn't do anything for him to be proud of when he was alive."

She looked up at him. His face was wet and she wiped off his cheeks. "You don't have to...."

"S'okay. Kinda part of the tattoo story." He rested their entwined hands over his heart. "I got the tattoo a few days after he passed from a heart attack. For the first year, it was all about handling things ya know? Life insurance, documents, accounts, funerals, and making sure my grandma was alright. All this stuff you don't know you have to do when somebody... dies."

She watched the pain on his face as forced himself to continue. Aster's heart broke for him. His grandfather must have been so important to him.

"But then the year anniversary came up. I know you're not supposed to dwell on the day someone dies. You're supposed to celebrate their birthday or some shit. But I couldn't get it out of my head that he'd been gone exactly a year." He swallowed, "So I went to this bar and started drinking. *And* kept drinking."

Russ shifted, his ankle monitor brushing against Aster's leg and she forced herself not to react to the scratchy device. She needed to be still and listen.

"I get mad and punchy when I get really drunk. What I didn't know at the time was that I picked the wrong bar."

"How so?"

"You know how I said I beat up a cop?" He met her eyes for a moment, then looked up at the ceiling. "There was a conference in town for cops. Teaching about truck driving and human trafficking."

His hand that had been resting on her back clenched into a fist, before he let out a long slow breath and started rubbing her back again.

"One of the cops was running his mouth about how all truckers were scumbags."

The pieces of Russ's past fell into place for Aster. "Your grandfather was a truck driver."

"Bingo." Russ breathed out. "I didn't know he was a cop, just knew he was talking shit. I sucker punched him. Then he said something to me and I remember his mouth moving, but not what he said. I broke a bottle over his head and then...."

He shifted in bed again. "There's a report about everything I did, but I don't remember much. He's not the only person I hit, but I focused on him. Broke his arm, six of his ribs, his head needed stitches. I know he was mouthy, but he was smaller than me, and I shouldn't have done that."

Aster could barely breath as he described the fight. "When...When was this?"

"January 15, 1999." He answered, rubbing her back, "I didn't even bother with a trial once I learned he was a cop. I took the deal for five years in with two years probation after. They had him read his victim statement over the phone, so it was on the record, he was still in the hospital. Fuck, it was hard to listen, knowing I hurt him that bad."

She hugged herself to him, not able to stop herself from shaking.

"Hey, hey." Russ kissed the top of her head. "It's okay. I messed up and paid for it. That's in the past, I'll never let myself be that guy again." He noticed the tears in her eyes, "Oh hey, Aster...."

She found his lips and she kissed him with a desperation she knew he didn't understand. "I'm sorry. I'm so sorry." Her voice broke between kisses.

"No, no. I shouldn't have spilled my guts like that." He held her face in his hands. "Look, if you're scared of me, if you want to go—"

"NO." Aster yelped and hugged him tightly. "I could never be scared of you, and I don't want to go. I never want to go."

"Okay. Okay." Russ held her in his arms, whispering softly that everything was alright and that she could stay as long as she wanted to...

...but she couldn't.

CHAPTER 47

Russ reached out his arm for Aster, surprised when he found the space beside him empty. He rolled over and listened for noise in the bathroom, but it was eerily silent. Maybe Liam woke up? He yawned and glanced at the alarm clock it was almost one. What woke him up? Snow crunched beneath tires as a car passed by the trailer. Someone was leaving the park late. Not that someone wasn't always coming or going around here. Still, something felt off.

The hair on the back of his neck stood up and he stilled in the too-quiet trailer. Something wasn't right. Russ stumbled out of bed, pulling a dirty shirt from the floor over his head. Aster had been wearing this when they fell asleep. He felt guilty about scaring her last night. He shouldn't have dumped it all on her at once. *Fuck. He messed up.*

When Aster would get restless she would turn on one of the music channels and doze on the couch. She would let him have the bed earlier when that happened. He stepped into the living room finding it empty. *No, no. This wasn't happening. She wouldn't have just left... She couldn't...*

Liam's door was open and his bed was unmade. Russ's breath caught in his throat. *No. There had to be another explanation.*

He took a step forward and cursed, his bare feet now wet from a freezing puddle of water on the floor. *What the hell?* The other bathroom door was open, they weren't there either. They weren't in the trailer. *No. No. No!*

The blood pounded in his ears and he raced back to the living area, throwing open the door. Aster's car was gone. *Why...why...what had he...*

He stood in the doorway absolutely dumbfounded. Had Liam gotten sick? It was the only thing he could think of that would have sent them out this late without saying anything. Russ closed the door to keep the cold out and paced back to Liam's room to see if there was any evidence the kid had fallen ill. He turned the blankets over and felt something hard near the pillows. Liam's cookbooks. They were still here. The kid wouldn't have left those, something was very wrong.

Russ stomped back to the kitchen, breathing in through his nose and out through his mouth trying to stay calm.

Deep breath in. One. Two. Three. Hold it. One. Two. Three. Deep breath out. One. Two. Three. Repeat.

His phone was charged and he dialed Aster's number, which went straight to voicemail. "Hey. Let me know what's going on. Kinda freaking out here." He snapped the phone closed and bit the inside of his cheek.

The pantry was opened. He moved a few things around and took mental stock of what was here. There was food missing and bottles of water gone from the pack. She wasn't not here, she was gone. She left. Why?

Him. He was why she left. Of course he was why she left.

His stomach turned. She *had* been afraid of him last night. She'd said what she thought he wanted to hear. He was just like her ex-husband. *What the fuck had he done?* She realized she didn't need another asshole in her life and she'd made a break for it.

But why? If she asked, he would have moved out, and she knew that. She didn't need to interrupt Liam's life over them not working. *What had happened while he was sleeping?* Thirty minutes, he'd only been asleep for thirty minutes.

Russ growled his eyes scanning the room for anything out of place. Something indicating that she hadn't left of her own free will. Wait, what if it was her ex? He showed up in the middle of the night and forced them to leave. No, Liam would have thrown a fit. Unless the asshole threatened Aster, then the kid would have done what he was told. But there still would have been some noise and Russ would have heard it. How would her ex have gotten into the trailer in the first place?

His eyes fell on the whiteboard by the door where they left notes about the grocery store. There were four words in her handwriting: ***I'm so sorry - AR***

His mind was blank for about a minute before he dialed another number. It rang twice.

"Are you dead?"

"Jerry."

"Have you been shot?"

"Jerry."

The older man grumbled, annoyed by the wake up, which was fair. "Did you shoot, harm, or maim someone? Attempt to run? Because it had better be one of those to call me this time of night."

Russ admitted. "No, it's Aster. Her and Liam are gone. I think her ex might have forced her to leave with him."

A yawn on the other end of the line, "Is her car gone?'

"Yes, but..."

"More than just her tire tracks in the driveway?"

"Not that I noticed."

Jerry sighed, "It sounds like she ran away."

"Why would she do that?" Russ tapped his foot up and down incessantly. "Jerry, she just told me she wanted to stay. Why would she leave right after telling me that without talking to me first?

"Russ," Jerry growled into the phone, "I'm not calling you a dumb ass, but how exactly did you expect this to end?"

"What the hell is that supposed to mean?" Russ was beyond agitated. Why did it seem like Jerry knew something about Aster that he didn't.

"You hooked up with the ex-wife of the cop you beat the brakes off of. How did you think it was gonna go?"

Russ felt his legs give out beneath him, he crashed to the floor. Mouth dry, palms sweating as he forced himself to breath and not go into a full blown panic attack. Her ex-husband was the guy he beat and went to prison over? Aster's shaking hadn't been about the story, it was her realizing who he was. *Why hadn't she just told him?*

"Russ? Hey, Russ! You still there?"

If Russ didn't know any better, he'd think the old bastard cared about him. "Yeah..."

"You didn't know?" Jerry questioned, the disbelief clear in his voice. "How did you not know? She still has his last name."

"I didn't know." Russ leaned the back of his head against the back of the couch. "I don't think she knew either." He jumped to his feet. He had to find her. "I need to go find her."

"No, you don't." Jerry grumbled. "You aren't becoming more paperwork for me."

"Then help me. Jerry, I'm begging you. I can't let her run because she's worried about me getting hurt by that prick."

"Biggest pain in my ass." The old man muttered, and the sound of Jerry cursing filled the other side of the phone. "You better be ready when I get there."

Russ set his phone down and pulled on warmer clothes. He had no idea where Aster would go. Hide with one of her friends up here? Back to her sister and brother? Where did they live? Where would he even start? A loud knock rang against the trailer door. It couldn't be Jerry. It would be at least another five minutes before he got there.

He pulled open the door to see Holly, Erica's granddaughter. One in the morning was not the time for social calls. "Everything alright?"

She shook her head, rainbow hair peeking out from beneath her stocking cap. "Grandma's fine. But I was passing by the highway and there a was big accident by the highway entrance ramp. I think I saw Aster's car."

His vision swam and he braced his hand against the trailer. *No.*

CHAPTER 48

Beep. Beep. Beep.

"No. Mom, I like it here. I have school today and Grandma Marilyn is gonna let me make candy with her on Saturday, and Russ and I are learning a new thing to cook on Thursday."

Beep. Beep. Beep.

"I'm not failing here. I wanna stay."

Beep. Beep. Beep.

"Mom, I lied alot before I like Russ. I don't wanna go."

"Liam." Her son's name passed through her lips. The tempo of the beeping increased as Aster regained consciousness, but everything was fuzzy. *Where was she? What had happened?*

She had been with Russ, in his arms, happy, but then he told her that story... it was Russ who'd beaten up Allen all those years ago, and she had tricked him by her very presence. Russ would never forgive her and Allen... Allen would want revenge.

All the strength she'd built up over the past few months was gone. She was back in Allen's net, acting on the influence of his power over her. But she couldn't stay. She couldn't. She had panicked. She had gathered up herself and Liam and gotten into the car. It had been dark and snowy, the roads slick, Liam had been crying, and she had been crying.

Red taillights in front of her in the swirling snow had caused her to slam on the brakes. The back end of the car had swung out violently, then she couldn't get the brakes to work. There were bright lights and then the ditch.

Aster drew in a sharp breath, the pain searing her chest. She blinked and looked around at the white, sterile walls. She was back in the hospital. "Liam," she moaned as she fumbled for the call button.

A pair of soft hands gripped hers as Marilyn assured her. "He's being checked out in the children's ward, but don't you worry, he seemed just fine." She clicked her tongue and shook her head. "You gave us quite the scare."

"Why are you here?" Aster choked out the question, not brave enough to meet the other woman's eyes.

"Rusty called me when you guys got here. He was so worried about you." She hugged Aster carefully, "you rest. I'll send him in and go check on Liam."

"Wait, Russ is here? How can he be here?" Her heart clenched, he couldn't be here. He wasn't allowed to be here unless he was working. What if they sent him back to prison? It would be all her fault.

Marilyn paused at the doorway, "oh, Jerry's gonna be give him hell for a month or two. Rusty woke him up then demanded to go out lookin' for you in the middle of the night, missy."

Her chest ached even more. *What had she done?*

"I'll be back in a bit. You two need a chance to talk." The older woman disappeared out into the hallway.

Aster looked at her arms covered in small cuts and her head throbbed, it was bandaged. She hadn't even made it to the highway, the snow had been more slippery than she accounted for. Her car was likely totaled. Tears rolled down her cheeks and she covered her face with her hands. Nowhere to go and no way to run.

Russ mentioned that he couldn't be with someone who kept secrets. This secret was too much for him to bare and the truth was so dangerous for him.

Her past was going to destroy her future. Allen would never let it go. The idea of the man who hurt him living with his son would be the breaking point. They would end up in court fighting for custody and she would lose. Allen would take Liam, not because he wanted him, but to spite Aster.

A sob ripped from her throat. She could feel the phantom pearls around her neck and Allen pulling them tight. Her hands scratched at her neck until two large hands pulled them away. Warm arms pulled her into an embrace as Russ's low, calm voice rumbled in her ear. "Don't hurt yourself. It's gonna be okay."

Aster bawled and held tightly to him incoherently attempting to apologize. He rocked with her and kept telling her it was okay, over and over.

He patted her back, and kissed the side of her head, "At least I know I beat the piss out of your asshole ex."

Despite everything she choked out a laugh. "He...he..."

"Is a douchebag who deserved the beating. More than I knew." Russ didn't loosen his hold on her. "My anger management session is gonna be wild this week. I feel vindicated now. Think the doc will agree?"

"Legally, I don't think he's allowed to." Her voice was muffled in Russ's shirt. "Allen won't be okay with us living together. He'll try to take Liam."

"Hmmm. I guess I'll have to beat him twice as bad as last time. Then by the time I get out Liam will be an adult, and I won't have to suffer through his teenage years." Russ shifted back, and touched her chin. "Pup, already read me the riot act about potentially reading his cookbooks."

"How...how are you not mad at me?" Aster heard her own mystified tone.

He gripped her hands, Aster noticing the bloody bandages wrapped around them. "I'm not mad, I get it. You freaked out and ran. But Aster, all you needed to do was talk to me. I'm not scared of your ex and we will figure it out. I—"

"Russ, for Gods' sake, I told you I would treat you on the down low in the children's ward and had to chase you all the way up here." Nathan shook his head and came in with a handful of supplies. "Hey Aster, how are you feeling?"

The nurse that had treated her months ago was motioning for Russ to sit in the chair next to her bed.

"Hold 'em out you crazy animal." Russ held out his hands and hissed as Nathan unwrapped them. "Oh quiet. Oop, no that was stuck on there. Sorry man."

"What happened to your hands?" Aster sat up straighter in bed to get a better view. Russ's hands were covered in blood with dark cuts all around his knuckles.

"Macho man here decided waiting until the fire department got there wasn't an option and punched out the back window of your car to get your son out." Nathan shook his head and pulled a sizable shard of glass out of Russ's hand.

Russ hissed in pain, but looked at Aster. "Liam was awake and complaining when I left 'im. More worried about you, than anything." He winced again, but continued, "they had to scan his head to be safe. As soon as he's clear, my grandma will bring him up here so you can see him."

"You saved my son?" A tear ran down her face, but she wiped it away. He'd hurt himself to save her son. She wished she could get up and hug him. Aster didn't have any words for her gratitude.

"Just glad you're both safe," Russ growled at Nathan through clenched teeth. "Fuck, man, bedside manner."

"Bedside manners are for patients." He chuckled. "I don't think any of these are deep enough to be concerned about. They've stopped bleeding, so they probably don't need stitches. Keep 'em clean and dry." He rolled up the supplies in the blue paper he'd set them on. "If Heather asks, I was never here."

"Sure." Russ thanked Nathan and the nurse left the room, leaving them alone again.

Aster tried to find her courage. "Russ."

He sat down on her bed and cupped her face with his hand. "Why did you run without talking to me?"

"In what world would you not hate me?" Her lip quivered as she asked.

"This one." He pressed his lips to hers and touched his forehead to hers. "This one right here. Where I am more glad you're alive than upset you took off. Where I love you and your stubborn kid living with me." He kissed her forehead, and whispered into her skin. "I wanna fight for you, Aster. Let me, please."

All she could manage was a nod.

CHAPTER 49

Russ yawned as he wiped down the last table in the section he'd been cleaning. He only had an hour and half to go before he could clock out and go home to catch a nap for his afternoon shift later today. Doing this overnight Thursday shift then a Friday afternoon one was killing him. He was too old for sleep deprivation.

But soon this might not be a thing anymore. On Jerry's recommendation to the judge after the first of the year, he might be allowed off the monitor. It was more than Russ dared to hope for. Two days 'til Christmas, and there might be a miracle in the making.

Aster had all the presents wrapped in their shared closet and Russ was looking forward to Saturday with a giddiness he didn't know he still had.

Liam was already having a good holiday week, he had a little scar through his eyebrow from the crash that all the kids thought made him look super cool. One eye that his hair constantly covered and the opposite eyebrow with a scar. His teenage years were gonna be a nightmare. Liam had made glass candy with Grandma Marilyn, flavoring some of them with coffee for his teacher. He was so proud of how they turned out and Russ was impressed the kid kept at it despite it, not working the first time.

Aster loved Christmas and she was remarkably unashamed about it. Singing to the holiday songs and sitting them all down for holiday movies. Thankfully, all of her injuries from the crash were superficial, but just in case, she was on a blood thinner for a few months. The doctor didn't want to risk another clot forming, like in her prior car crash. The only issue with it was how damn easily she bruised. Liam asked if they were rough housing at night and told them to settle down. Both of them had turned red and found somewhere different to be.

Things were good. Even with the happenings of today. Allen was coming up to see Aster and neither of them were happy about it. She was scared but determined. They couldn't worry about things until they happened.

"Excuse me."

Russ stopped in his tracks, pocketing the rag in his hands. "Yes, ma'am." The dark-haired woman looked familiar, but Russ didn't think he actually knew her.

Her eyes went to his name badge. "Russ. I didn't catch your name before. Do you remember me?" She was sad, her body language was unmistakable. "You helped me back in September."

He felt awful, because he had no clue what she was talking about or how he could have helped her. "I'm sorry, I don't remember."

"You made me a cinnamon baked apple and wouldn't let me pay," she explained.

"Oh, yeah, it wasn't any trouble." Russ recalled her sitting in the corner with a cup in hand for hours every night for a month. He was worried she wasn't eating anything at all, her clothes had been noticeably baggy. He also couldn't figure out how to proceed. "Are things any better than they were in September?"

"No." Her smile was thin and she drew in a slow breath. "My son was dying, brain dead to be more accurate, and I couldn't let him go. I couldn't make myself eat or leave the chair in his room."

He shifted on his feet, not sure what to say.

"The night you baked me that apple was the first time I ate something of substance." She pulled an envelope from her purse and hugged it to her chest. "I was able to let him go that night. This is a Christmas card from one of the people that received one of his organs." She put it back away and touched Russ's arm. "You feeding me that night, gave me the strength I needed. And changed the lives of six people. Thank you, Russ."

Russ attempted to speak, but there weren't any words.

The woman patted his arm, before turning to leave. "Merry Christmas."

"Yeah. You too. Merry Christmas."

The Christmas music seemed too cheery for a moment, and Russ couldn't get a clear thought in his head. He opted to bag the trash and go toss it outside, the biting cold and snow clearing his head a bit. Too much gratitude over an apple. Feeding people was just a part of life. This would be good story to tell Aster. She'd see the good in it and help him sort it out his head.

He wiped down the counters and glanced at the clock, only forty-five minutes left. What else could he finish up?

"Russet!" Tricky called out to get his attention.

Russ was sweeping by the walk-in, "Whatcha need, Tricky? I'm almost done back here."

"Some guy's here to see you."

Russ arched his eyebrow, not sure who would wanna see him at six in the morning.

He passed by Tricky and the kid muttered under his breath so only Russ would hear him, "Bacon dish only has 13 or 12 minutes 'til it's done, just so ya know."

Bacon. Shit. The warning was loud and clear with touch of anarchy. Not a surprise that Tricky wasn't a fan of cops. But Tricky had met Jerry and wouldn't be warning Russ about him.

He rounded the corner and...*What the fuck!* Allen Reign was standing in the hospital cafeteria all five feet, six inches of chicken-shit he was.

Russ pulled his hands out of his pockets and made sure they were in full view of the area's cameras. He should have kept a neutral face or looked angry, but he couldn't help the smirk that crossed his own features. Allen had an ugly red scar by his left ear, his buzz cut made it easy see.

"You remember me?" Allen asked.

"I do." His smirk turned into a lopsided smile.

He folded his arms over his chest, "Do you find something amusing?"

Russ chuckled, "Yeah, I was just thinking about how I beat the shit out of you and how you deserved it."

He kept his palms in view of that camera. He was not being smart right now. Allen was an asshole and Russ was pushing his buttons. He was meeting with Aster later, and the last thing Russ should be doing is winding him up. He needed to chill out.

"Still a criminal." Allen dismissed him.

"On my record for life," he agreed. "How can I help you, officer?"

"Sergeant," Allen corrected and took a step closer to Russ.

Russ took a slow calming breath. "How can I help, Sergeant Reign?"

"I just wanted to see the piece of shit who tricked my stupid ex-wife into a relationship." The shorter man looked Russ up and down. "You're about the level of trash she deserves."

He balled his fists, and clenched his jaw. "Don't talk about her."

"I'll talk about that whore however I want." Allen snorted. "I broke her in, and she'll always be mine deep down. Nothing *you* can...." He shoved his finger into Russ's chest.

Russ was going to lose it. He was gonna hit this motherfucker and not regret it until way later down the line. He had to start tuning this asshole out.

Suddenly Allen stumbled back a few steps and Russ would have panicked that he'd unconsciously shoved the man, but Marc was standing next to him with one massive hand on Allen's shoulder and the other on Russ's.

"Sorry, sir. We don't allow patrons to touch our staff." He leaned down until he was nose to nose with Allen. "And *I* don't allow anyone to speak about my friends like you just did. Now get the *fuck* out of my cafeteria."

"He said what?" Aster crossed her legs at the ankle in the waiting room of the lawyer's office.

"Get the fuck out of my cafeteria." Russ laughed. "I swear, Aster, if Marc said that to me leaning that close? I'd of shit myself."

She giggled and covered her mouth. "I'm so sorry he showed up at your work."

"Don't sweat it."

"Make sure you tell Liam to be quiet so you can get some sleep this morning."

Russ clicked his tongue. "I called my Grandma, they went out to do some last minute shopping."

"Shopping for what?" Aster questioned, heart freezing as Allen stepped into the lobby, "What could we possibly still need?"

"He got there huh?" Of course Russ recognized the change in her tone.

"Yeah. I gotta go."

"Love ya, Sunshine. You got this."

Aster drew in a deep breath. Russ had never said it like that before. She would so much rather be with him right now, but she wasn't going to not say it back. "Love you too."

The law clerk came to get them, and she and Allen went into the small conference room, sitting on opposite ends of the table, with a lawyer between them. The lawyer cleared his throat and set out the papers. "To clarify, I am acting as the filer of these petitions and only in that capacity. No changes can be made. Is that clear to both parties present."

"Yes."

"Yes."

"Good." The lawyer handed the packet to Allen, "Mr. Reign, by signing the documents you agree to give up all parental rights to Adam Liam Reign, your biological son. Once these rights are revoked your position cannot be changed. You will have no legal right to your child in any capacity. Understanding this, do you wish to proceed?"

"I do." Allen scratched through all the papers signing and dating them with a carelessness that broke Aster's heart.

The lawyer reviewed the documents, stamped them and retrieved copies for both Allen and Aster.

They walked into the lobby together. She cleared her throat. "You could have done this in Mapleville."

"I wanted to see you." Allen reached for her and she sidestepped his touch. "Brave girl now, huh?"

She crossed her arms over her chest. "The agreement stands. You *never* tell Liam about this. He might not want you in his life, but knowing you are willing to walk away from him will hurt him. You will not hurt him ever again."

He rolled his eyes. "Don't act all high and mighty, you abandoned Allison and never looked back."

"I miss her terribly, but one of your conditions of the divorce was no contact with her." Aster strained to keep her cool.

"As if the law is something you're worried about." He snorted.

"I have to go." She started for the door, but Allen grabbed her arm. "Don't touch me." She hissed and pulled away sharply.

"Why did you mail me the pearls back? I have to know."

Aster looked him in the eye. "I never have to explain anything to you ever again."

Russ felt a weight on top of him and pulled the flower-scented person closer to him. "The point of Liam leaving with my grandmother was so I could sleep."

Her giggle sounded in his ear, making him smile.

"What's so funny, huh?" He slipped his hands under her shirt, fidgeting with her bra clasp.

"I won. He asked me something and I didn't answer." Aster squirmed in his arms. "What are you up to? I came in here to give you a quick kiss."

"There's a toll in this bed. If your name is Aster and you wake me up, then you have to let me play with your boobs. It's the rules. We have no choice." He undid the clasp and grasped the back of her head, drawing her down for a kiss.

"I picked up breakfast," she murmured between breathless kisses.

Russ snorted. "My breakfast is right here."

She squealed as he rolled them over, but moaned as he mouthed his way down her neck. "You're supposed to be sleeping. You'll be so tired."

Russ paused his path down and nudged her nose with his. "Aster."

"Russ." She smiled up at him, pinching his goatee. "What?"

"Any lost sleep is worth it for extra time with you."

She trailed her hands up his bare chest, resting them on his shoulders. "I love you."

"Good." He kissed her again. "Because I love you, too."

The End

Epilogue

Spring 2005

In a subdivision far too perfect for belief where all the homes were two-stories, had covered porches, and manicured lawns with thirty thousand cars in the driveways, Aster sat in her rusty sedan. Across the street from a home with no flowering plants, she watched a blond teenager leave the house. She drew in a deep breath and climbed out of her car.

"Allison," she called out.

The girl blinked, seemingly frozen in place. "Momma Aster?"

Astor's heart broke. Allison stopped calling her that when she turned thirteen. She had been referred to as 'her stupid stepmom' until Aster left last year. The little girl, who Aster had known since the age of two and parented from the age of seven was only a memory. They had been so close before Liam was born. But anytime Aster tried to rekindle that closeness, it fell on deaf ears.

Allison shifted on her feet. "Dad's—"

"He's at work," Aster interrupted. "He always worked early on your birthday, so we could go out to dinner together. I remember the restaurants you picked, styling your hair to match your dress, because you were always so fashionable. Even when you were super little, you wanted to look your best."

She pulled at her fingers. "I'm sorry." Tears ran down her cheeks.

"Sweetie, don't cry." Aster touched Allison's elbow and the teenager threw her arms over Aster's shoulders hugging her tightly.

"It's all my fault! I was awful to you, and Liam, and then daddy cut your hair, but...but...." she clung on tighter. "It was all my fault. You left because of me. Daddy said—"

"No." Aster pulled back and caught Allison's face in her hands. "No. I left because of your father. Not because of you. There are so many things that happened that you didn't see or know about. Don't ever let yourself think it was your fault, ever."

"I miss you," Allison admitted, wiping off her cheeks as she stepped back. "Can you stay? Daddy's got this awful new girlfriend. She's still in college and she's mean to me. If you come back to town, maybe you guys could work things out?"

The hopefulness in Allison's eyes cut into Aster's heart, but she shook her head. "I can't. I have to go home."

"Then why are you even here?" Allison's lip curled up. An expression she inherited from her mother. Carla would sneer like that when she picked up Allison on Allen's late-night shifts. Allison was trying to throw up walls to protect herself. *Anger was easier than sadness.*

Aster handed Allison a brightly colored bag. "I wanted to give you a birthday present. Eighteen is a big milestone. Should be celebrated."

Allison peaked in the bag. "Is this a blanket?"

"Yup, pink and yellow. Your favorite colors." She nodded. "My number's written on the card and you can call anytime you need to."

Aster gave Allison one last hug to comfort her, but she knew she shouldn't stay much longer, it was risky. She needed to get back on the road, even if, she was tired from driving. There was a rest area twenty minutes outside of town; she could stop there and catch a nap before heading home.

Allison's voice was muffled in her shoulder. "You put me first again."

"Huh?" She pulled away and regarded the girl. "What did you say, sweetie?"

"You're here and not with Liam on our birthday. You put me first again." She motioned to herself.

"We're celebrating his birthday on Sunday. His friends are on spring break next week and they're coming to visit." Aster paused and caught Allison's hand. "Liam wanted to make sure I saw you today. He made cookies for you. They're in a butter container at the bottom of the gift bag. Coconut crisps."

Allison's eyes lit with surprise. "How...?"

"He remembered you always took the Almond Joys out of his Halloween candy."

Allison laughed, "He's a good little brother." She couldn't look Aster in the eye as she admitted, "he deserves a better big sister than me."

Aster shook her head. "You two were pitted against each other and it wasn't fair. I should have tried to stop it instead of working around it." She checked her watch, "Do you want me to give you a ride to school? I don't want you to be late."

"Dad bought me a car." Allison pulled her keys out of her pocket. "But if I so much as scratch it I have to pay for college myself. Plus, I'm pretty sure he low-jacked it."

"That sounds about right." She chuckled, before she heard a door slam and glanced across the street to see a neighbor peeking through the window. "I need to get going before someone calls your father."

"Yeah." They shared one more hug and Allison squeezed her tighter. "I'll text you later. Maybe you can call me when you get home and I can talk to Liam? Wish him a happy birthday too."

"That would be great."

Aster opened the door to the converted double-wide trailer that acted at the meeting house for the park. Two buckets of ice cream hung from her arms as she escaped the rain outside to be welcomed by the party in full swing inside. "Sorry I had to go across town to find Superman flavor. Where's my little prince?"

Liam raced around the corner holding a pirate hat for her. "Mom, I saved you a hat."

"Thank you so much." She put the hat on her head. Hearing a thud, she looked across the room to see Russ hobbling on a fake peg-leg. "Did you *really* need to make him wear a peg-leg?"

He laughed, "I wasn't gonna, but Mr. Jerry said he'd pay me five dollars, if I asked him to."

Aster glanced over to see Jerry Gristol, Russ's parole officer, sitting in the corner with Erving and Marilyn. He'd offered to hang out at the party so Russ could be here. But in two weeks, it might not be a concern. If the judge reviewing his case approved it, Russ would still be on parole, but not house arrest anymore. He'd be able to move about the state without restriction. She had her fingers and toes crossed for him.

"Liam, when's cake? I'm gonna starve without it," Seagar lamented.

Amos paused his foam sword fight with Cosmo, reminding his cousin, "We just ate sloppy joes."

"Those aren't cake," he insisted.

Aster tapped her son's nose. "Are you having fun?"

Liam grinned. "This is the best birthday ever."

The door opened and Liam rushed to welcome Noni and her family inside. "You're just in time for the cake. I helped make it."

"That's so cool!" Noni grabbed his hand and they raced over to the other kids. Sariyah hugged Aster. "Girl, you've got a full house."

"In the best way, it's not my house. Less clean up." Aster returned the hug as they shared laughed. She excused herself and rushed to set the ice cream on the table next to the cake. She gave Russ a quick kiss. "You are amazing for getting the party started without me. Thank you."

"My pleasure." He held onto her for another moment, then nodded to Marc. "Welcome in man. Help yourself to some food and drinks are in the cooler."

"Mamma, can I have a shark tattoo? They're pretend." Noni asked Sariyah, who shook her head.

"Not a shark. If you can find a flower, we can do that one on your arm." She shifted Joi to her other hip. Cosmo, whose arms were covered in temporary star tattoos, handed a rose application to Noni and she grinned at her mother. "Alright. Let's get it on real quick," she relented.

"I wanna be a pirate with the boys." Noni grabbed her sister's hand, "Zuri too. She's a mini pirate. Is there a bunny one?"

Aster watched them all run around, glad they'd opened the windows earlier, it would be too hot on top of all the noise. "I think it's time for the cake. The pirates are getting restless." She commented to Russ, who set his peg-leg to the side. "Too hard to balance on it?"

"Yes." He conceded and called to Liam, "Okay birthday boy, let's get these candles on." Russ used his lighter for the candles. "Nine's an important birthday. You ready?"

Liam questioned, "How old are you gonna be this year?"

"Thirty-six."

"Whoa that's old!" Liam exclaimed, then looked up at him concerned. "Wait, didn't you say you were gonna fight me when I turned nine?"

"Yup. So you better enjoy this party." Russ ruffled Liam's hair.

Everyone finished singing happy birthday to her nine-year-old and Aster couldn't be happier. She slipped in her hand into his. "Russ?"

"Yeah, Sunshine?"

"Please, don't fight my child."

"No promises, he's nine and that's fair game." He kissed her hand.

ADDITIONAL
HANKS

This book would not be possible without the following amazing people. First to my husband, who has mostly come to peace with me disappearing for endless hours to write, edit, format, market, and generally lose my mind as I chase my dream. My parents, who helped support my writing in every way they can. My brother for helping write this one, again this wouldn't be the book it is without you. Mary for helping me with authenticity - I know you don't think it's a big deal, but I promise it is to me. Nikki and Angela for their Alpha-reading both helped me improve it so much - you both do love to push me to be a better writer. Tasha, who helped me with early edits and all her amazing feedback. Watch out girl, I'm gonna get you more involved in the indie-author world <3 Lyssa my cover artist, everyone I have shown this cover to gasps at it - it's just so damn pretty. To Julie who edited this in rapid speed, seriously... how? You are incredible.

To all of my friend, who encourage me to keep writing. I live in my corner of the internet where everyone is writing books and I forget that not everyone does that. I forget what an accomplishment completing a book really is. Thank you for all of your kind words and cheers; they mean the fucking world to me.

ALSO BY AUTHOR

The Goodroe Brothers Duet:

- Love Is...

- Love Stories Are...

To stay in the loop about future projects check out Sweettaleswithspice.com or on Katharine's social media accounts (TikTok, Instagram, Facebook, and Pinterest) "Sweettaleswithspice"

About Author

Katharine Sweet is a Michigan girlie through and through. Give her all the crisp nights, bonfires, apple cider with donuts, hockey games, and general fall vibes whenever possible. She's got a penchant for dark humor, but always offers a smile to anyone who needs it. She gets through life with the help of coffee, kindness to others, and a splash of spite.

She's had a wild imagination from day one creating characters of her own to pretend to be in her favorite cartoons with her brother and devouring most any book she could get her hands on. It's no surprise to anyone who's known her for any stretch of time that she's publishing books.

Writing is her passion, but especially creating characters that her readers can relate to in meaningful ways. She writes with intent and empathy that any reader can recognize. Although, she may confuse other creatives with her constant use of spreadsheets to keep track of story information.

Katharine loves her family and her husband who is no doubt her rock. When she isn't in her writing cave she is with him hanging out on the couch or they are with their friends. She also loves dogs, rest in peace to her two fur-babies, Novel and Athena.